Divinity

The Kingdom of Heaven is within you.

A Novel by James Harrington
ISBN: 978-0692336410
Copyright © 2014, James Harrington
First Printing: November 2014
Editing by Kathy Hearns
Cover art by Brett Warniers
Printed and Bound in the USA

Divinity

This book is dedicated to my son, Gabriel, whose birth and naming compelled me to alter one of the main characters.
Love ya buddy!

𝕬 note from the author:

Hello and welcome! I hope that you will enjoy your journey with Giovanni and Adalyn as they embark upon their adventure. Before you begin, I just wanted to clarify a few things.

You will encounter many characters, both fictional and historical. The fictional characters are just that; fictional. Any resemblance they bear to real people is purely coincidental.

As for the historical figures that appear in the pages ahead, I have done the best that I can to portray them as accurately as possible, based on the information available on each. However, please understand that I am exposing them to fictional situations. It is impossible to predict definitively how one might have actually reacted in these events, so again, this is based on what information is available.

Lastly, I would just like to note that this story in no way should be taken as a criticism of the beliefs of any denomination of Christianity. As a catholic, I acknowledge that the leaders of several denominations weren't always the most upstanding of people and that is what is reflected upon in my writing, but that does not invalidate anyone's belief in God or the teachings they follow.

I hope that you will enjoy this work of fiction for what it is; a work of fiction. Thank you and God bless!

Jim H.

And Jesus said to them, "If your leaders tell you, 'look, to the sky, for the kingdom is there,' then the birds of the sky will be ahead of you. If your leaders say to you, 'Look to the sea,' then the fish will be ahead of you. Rather, the Kingdom of Heaven is within you."

- The Gospel of Thomas

BOOK I
Before the Fall

I

A cool breezed passed through Azrael's hair as he and his apprentice, Adalyn, touched down on the steps of the Most High's temple. It was a beautiful morning in the Celestial World. There was not a cloud in the sky to impede their flight.

Azrael landed first, his silver armor still showing tarnish from the days of war long passed. His wings were in no better shape; many of their feathers had been stained black or red from the fighting. He was a worn, but proud warrior angel.

Despite his less than glamorous appearance, he still tried to make himself presentable for his audience with the Most High. His brown hair had been cut short and he wore a new white tunic with red seems under his armor. He sucked in a deep breath and turned in time to see his apprentice hovering at his side, "Adalyn, you land this instant. Don't forget that even now you're in the presence of the Most High!"

Adalyn hovered for a moment before folding her wings behind her and dropping to the balls of her feet, "Forgive me, Master. I guess I'm just more used to flying than I am walking. I never understood why the Most High would forbid us from flying in his presence."

"Ours is not to wonder why." Azrael replied. "Just do as you have been commanded as is our mandate."

Adalyn nodded, "I understand master, I am doing my best."

"How is it you fought through as much of the war as you did without having to use your legs?" Azrael asked in a simultaneously amused and annoyed tone.

Adalyn shrugged, "I guess I just got lucky. There was always enough space to fly. What little time I actually spent on my feet, I was usually hiding."

"Luck is a fickle thing. It can run out very easily. You'd best get used to using your legs. They are far sturdier than your wings and can help supplement your speed. Someday your wings could get injured and you'd be forced to use your legs to walk. Where would you be then?"

Divinity

Adalyn nodded, though his words seemed cryptic, "Master… I understand. I will endeavor to do so."

Azrael nodded, "Good."

"I wonder why the Most High would summon us at such a late hour when he plans to take rest." Adalyn said as she brushed a strand of blonde hair away from her face and tucked it behind her right ear.

"Such is the way of the Most High." Azrael responded. "We're angels; our job is to be at his beckoned call. Be patient, we will soon discover his motives behind this meeting."

Her bright blue eyes shined with wonder as she looked up the long staircase of ivory and gold to the massive cathedral at the top. The stairs were long and winding, and seemed to go on forever. It would not be a quick stroll for them.

Adalyn stretched her clean white wings and then folded them behind her back with a single thrust. She didn't want to anger the Most High or her master as they made their way to his chambers. She wasn't used to walking, but she had good enough balance to manage.

Adalyn had only been called before the Most High once or twice previously and those times were during the war. At that point, the no-fly restriction had not been imposed around the Most High's home. Just looking at the stairs, she could tell that her legs were going to be sore.

Azrael beckoned to her forward, allowing her thoughts to escape, as he moved, "Keep up Adalyn, he's waiting for us."

Adalyn nodded as she adjusted her beige maiden's dress and tightened her sash. The soft cotton tightened around her hips as her hands moved to her hair. She parted it in the middle and made sure that the few loose strands were brushed back behind her ear once again. The blonde strands flowed to her neck and shimmered in the sunlight.

Once she felt presentable, Adalyn followed close behind Azrael. Finding balance wasn't easy for her, but she did the best she could. She found it hard to believe that the Most High's beloved children had to walk like that every day of their lives.

Divinity

It took some time for the two angels to reach the top. The stairs seemed to stretch onward forever. They were beautifully carved and perfectly smooth, but the ivory still began to hurt her feet as they were not used to continuous walking.

Once at the top, Adalyn saw two large gold statues standing with their spears crossed, blocking the entrance. Neither statue reacted to their presence as the angels approached. They looked like nothing more than large, lifeless pieces of metal.

Adalyn took a close look at one of them, examining its face. The sun gleamed from the statue's shiny surface. Its eyes were glossed over, making it difficult to tell if they were opened or closed. She turned to Azrael with a surprised look on her face, "I wasn't aware that the Most High employed titans."

For a moment, it appeared as though Azrael didn't hear her. He simply closed his eyes and nodded at the two guards. Adalyn's eyes narrowed as she reached out to her mentor, "Master?"

As though responding to some silent command, the statues immediately came to life. What looked like nothing more than shiny metal, now looked organic as the statues pulled their spears back and cleared a pathway for the two angels. Their movement was sudden and unexpected, causing Adalyn to jump back with a slight yelp.

Azrael smirked at her reaction, knowing that this was not her first encounter with these creatures, "Why were you startled? You saw titans on the battlefield, you know?"

Adalyn nodded, "Yeah I remember, but they weren't so... mechanical at that point. I never saw them as statues."

Azrael shook his head as the two angels proceeded inside. Adalyn's eyes remained on the guards as she passed under their spears. Part of her expected to see them come crashing down on her as she walked.

Once the angels were through, the massive guards closed the doorway and resumed their silent vigil. There was no further movement from them as the angels continued forward. Adalyn looked back at them for a moment, studying their stance.

Divinity

After a few seconds, she turned back and followed closely behind her master. The stone tunnel was dark, but there was a bright light at the end. It was the only illumination that the tunnel had.

The next room was unlike anything a mere mortal could imagine. The cathedral ceilings surpassed the beauty of those in the mortal city of Rome. Murals of all creation covered every inch of the ceiling above them.

The tall, lead plated, windows stretched up to the top of the walls. The dome at the top had windows with multiple beautiful colors carefully laid into the panes, while the glass lower to the ground was crystal clear and looked out on a star field. Whole galaxies could be viewed from any one of the windows.

The ground was an unusual combination of stone and grass with cool mist slightly obscuring it. Adalyn's bare feet tickled as she slowly stepped out on to the small field. It was a sensation that she was unfamiliar with, having relied mostly on her wings for travel.

The top of the cathedral was an ornate dome with several murals depicting the deeds of the Most High's children. Hovering near the ceiling was a bright star-like orb that pulsed slowly. The silhouette of a human was in the center of the orb.

Azrael walked out onto the field and stopped directly under the orb with Adalyn to his left. There was a brief silence when Azrael closed his eyes. His chin rose slightly as though he were listening to someone above him.

Azrael opened his eyes, "Yes Master, I understand. The final pockets of resistance from those loyal to Lucifer have either been banished from the immortal realm or eradicated. Our work here is finished, the war is over, and the restoration of our world has begun."

Again, Azrael closed his eyes briefly and then reopened them, "The mortal world has gone awry? How?"

There was a long hum before Azrael responded, "A recent increase in the wars amongst your children? So you believe that the recent increase has been engineered somehow... No, I don't believe that the continuous fighting is coincidence either."

Adalyn rolled her eyes, "The mortal world is continuously at war with itself. I should know. I'm the one ferrying their souls to Hell. They find new ways of killing each other all the time, what makes you think that this is any different?"

Azrael turned and glared at his apprentice, "Adalyn!"

The chamber shook with a mighty roar as a nervous Azrael turned back, "Forgive her, master. She is still ignorant of the proper decorum when in your presence. I accept responsibility for that."

Another low hum emanated from the ceiling. Azrael smiled and nodded, "I will, don't worry about her…"

Then his face quickly turned serious as he spoke, "Master do you believe that Lucifer is behind these events?"

The room began to tremble as though something massive had slammed into the wall. Azrael twisted his lips thoughtfully and shook his head, "No, I don't believe so either. His powers outside the underworld are severely limited. I agree that he is most likely no longer a threat."

There was another brief silence before he continued, "Master, is it not possible that the ones you love the most have begun warring on their own? Our prophets and our messengers ceased so long ago. Given how easily corrupted their minds can be, is it not possible that your children are warring because of their own lust for power?"

Azrael could feel an angry vibration under his feet as Adalyn defended his position, "The Church you guided and helped to create has taken over most of the known world, but they have become corrupt and decadent. Their power is beginning to dwindle. The uprisings of these new revolutionaries, who are now waging a religious war, must truly be a burden on you."

The room trembled harder this time. Tiny cracks appeared in the wall, causing Adalyn to step back. She clenched her jaw as she looked up, "Master, with the utmost respect, they're a savage race, not worthy of this much compassion…"

"Adalyn, be silent!" Azrael yelled out as he stepped in front of his apprentice. "You've said enough."

Divinity

Adalyn lowered her eyes and stepped away, "Forgive me."

With his apprentice finally subdued, Azrael turned back to the star, "Master, do you believe it may be time for another cleansing, as it was in the time of Noah?"

The floor rumbled for a moment, causing Azrael to frown, "Perhaps not…"

At that moment, the echoes turned their attention away from Azrael. The Most High's attention turned to the younger angel. Azrael turned nervously to his apprentice to see what she was going to do.

Adalyn closed her eyes as the floor began to tremble under her, "Yes, I do understand Master, but I do not share your faith in human kind anymore. They fight and tear one another to pieces. Would it not be better to start over and…?"

The room shook harder as an angry moan resonated around the room. Adalyn stepped back, "Forgive me, Master, it was not my intention to speak out of turn. You are right; perhaps such actions are no longer appropriate. Humanity is not so quick to believe that you are responsible for such natural events any longer."

Azrael shook his head as the voice turned back to him. Once it quieted down, he spoke, "Very well, Master, we will investigate your suspicions to the best of our ability and report them to Michael if we see anything suspicious. Until then, we are to continue to repair the damage done to our world."

He then bowed and turned to Adalyn, "Come, the Most High needs his rest. The battle with Lucifer and the situation in the Mortal Realm have left him weary."

Adalyn curtseyed before following Azrael, "Rest well, my lord."

The two angels turned and exited the massive cathedral hall. The bright aura levitating near the ceiling slowly dimmed as they exited. Adalyn looked back to see the room slowly going dark.

Neither one of the angels spoke as they made their way outside and back down the ivory staircase. The silence lingered until they reached the misty ground. It was an

uncomfortable walk for Adalyn. She could feel tension in the air as she followed her master. It didn't help that her feet were also aching as she walked.

Neither angel wanted to face the grim reality that everything they had known was changing. Adalyn knew in her heart that their world may never be the same. Its beauty that was at one time unequaled was now healing from a war that had been over for eons.

Large fields where angels had once frolicked were now scorched from a massive flame and peppered with massive craters from demon attacks. The angels had begun restoration work, but it was mired by the remaining pockets of resistance from the war, as well as the work in the mortal world. It seemed like the restoration would never get done.

Once they had reached the misty ground, Adalyn stretched her wings and turned to Azrael, "The humans may be warring, but at least there is finally peace in the Celestial Realm. With Lucifer and his top followers finally gone, things should settle down."

"Peace..." Azrael responded as his battle hardened features began to soften. "It's hard to believe that something so beautiful could be so fickle. Do not trust it and never count on it lasting. There will always be darkness in the distance. It is the reason we must remain vigilant at all times."

Adalyn nodded, "Your words are true and wise, Master. I spoke without thinking, forgive me."

Azrael smiled, "You are still new to the way of the orders, your duties and the wars have stalled your training. The innocence you possess is not a failing. You will learn quickly. There is nothing to forgive. Do not be afraid to speak your mind around me."

"Thank you, Master." Adalyn responded appreciatively. "Your patience is most kind. As it was when you trained me during the war."

"You have become a fine warrior for the Most High and I am very proud of everything you've accomplished." Azrael replied, "Remember everything that I have taught you... Remember the swordsmanship, remember the techniques and the power, but more important than anything, remember to keep your heart true."

"Yes Master," Adalyn said obediently, "always."

"Good, just remember everything that I have taught you..." Azrael said darkly, "and you should be safe."

His words sent a chill down Adalyn's spine, causing her wings to flutter. She looked at her mentor with an air of concern as she spoke, "Safe from what? Is everything okay, Master?"

Azrael blinked as though he were coming out of a trance, "Oh, um, yes, everything's fine. Don't mind me, I'm just feeling a little ominous right now."

Adalyn smiled, "You're always feeling ominous, Master. It's like the war has made you paranoid."

"Maybe it has." Azrael admitted. "Would you excuse me, Adalyn? I have some work to do."

"Work?" Adalyn asked. "I thought we were going to make for the training grounds?"

Azrael nodded, "I know, you go on ahead. I'll meet you there later... once I'm done."

"If you're sure. Finding someone to spar with shouldn't be a problem while you're gone." Adalyn replied.

"Good." Azrael said. "I'll leave you to it."

Azrael gave Adalyn a smile before spreading his wings and launching himself into the clouds. At that moment, his form disappeared into a bright light. It almost seemed like the sun had momentarily expanded as Azrael disappeared.

Adalyn covered her eyes to protect herself from being blinded. The light lasted only a moment, but when it disappeared and she was finally able to lower her hands, Azrael was gone. There was no sign of him anywhere near by.

Adalyn could make no sense of her master's cryptic words. Her heart was filled with wonder as she contemplated what he had said. Did he know something that could threaten the fragile peace that they had fought so hard for? He had been acting unusual recently, but Azrael was known for being eccentric.

Throughout the war, Azrael had been more than a mentor to her; he had been a close friend and confidant. No matter how much work it was, or how stubborn she could be, he never gave up on her. Part of her always suspected that he did not entirely trust her, and tried to keep her at arms length. She resented it, but he may have been trying to protect her.

After a few minutes of tossing her thoughts back and forth in her mind, she decided that it was best to just let it go for now. He had never led her awry before, so there was no reason to believe he would now. She trusted him, but made it a point to ask him to explain his words later.

II

Adalyn stood watching the clouds go by until her legs ached. She looked down at her scrawny knees and frowned. She had focused so much of her time strengthening her arms and wings, but her neglected taking the time to work on walking. *Azrael is right... I have no lower body strength. Perhaps that's what I should start working on today.*

Adalyn spread her wings as far as they would go. A gentle breeze caressed her feathers as she pushed off of the ground. The muscles in her wings tensed and relaxed over and over as she became airborne. She pushed herself higher into the clouds with almost no effort. Her wings were in perfect shape and could hold her in the air indefinitely as she soared.

Adalyn made her way over to the choir chambers. She passed over a fluffy white cloud that blocked her view of the realm. She instantly grinned, folded her wings behind her, and dove into it. She free fell through the cloud, getting soaked by the cloud's moisture.

A second later, Adalyn burst through the other side, leaving a gaping hole in the white fluff. The cool mist was refreshing and made her skin gleam in the sunlight. She quickly spread her wings again to stop her descent and looked down at the realm with her view no longer obstructed.

Small droplets of water flew from her feathers as her wing caught the air. The sunlight reflected off of the droplets, making them twinkle like newborn stars in the blue sky. She brushed the wet hair out of her face to reveal a content smile.

Another flap of Adalyn's wings sent her flying on her original course. A new building quickly came into view in front of her as the Most High's resting place disappeared into the clouds. She immediately recognized her home. This was where she had taken up residence following the war.

The choir chamber was an unmistakably beautiful building. Like all other buildings, it was constructed from white ivory, gold, and marble. A large dome, adorned with intricate carvings of angels, protruded from the top of the

Divinity

complex where the choirs met. Below that were several smaller buildings that made up a cityscape. Each building was connected either by bridge or foundation to the main meeting area.

Adalyn set down in front of one building that had two statues of fit-looking angels armed to the teeth with as many weapons as they could carry. She gazed at the angelic sword of fire in the hand of the statue on the left and wondered when she would get her own sword. She had proved herself during the war, but it would only be hers when she ended her apprenticeship and joined an order.

She smiled as she walked by, "Some day."

Her concentration was broken by a voice that appeared behind her, "Adalyn, good to see you, I'm glad you're here!"

Adalyn turned around to see a familiar face behind her. A tall angel with beautiful long curly brown hair stood behind her. The warm smile shown on her face revealed a level of compassion and happiness that few, even in the Celestial World, could match.

Adalyn's face lit up as she approached, "Roselyn, how are you?"

"I'm well, sister." She replied. "I'm heading over to the training grounds for a little exercise."

"I was heading there too." Adalyn said, looking at her legs. "I need to work on lower body strength, care to spar with me?"

Roselyn smiled as she stood next to her sister, "I was going to ask you the same question."

Adalyn placed her hand on Roselyn's shoulder as the two angels entered the training facility and looked for an open sparring room. At the end of the long hallway, the last room on the right was available.

Roselyn walked out to the middle of the room and turned to face Adalyn with her hands in a defensive posture, "So what shall it be today; martial arts, swords, staves, or something else?"

Adalyn glanced over at the dull training weapons for a moment, deciding what would be best for her training, "No weapons, only martial arts, and no use of our wings either. I need to strengthen my legs."

"No wings?" Roselyn asked in a surprised tone. "Interesting... very well."

Adalyn stepped out to the center of the room and began the match. Roselyn folded her wings back and stepped sideways. She had a lot more fighting experience than Adalyn, so her legs were well toned and ready for this.

Adalyn was not so lucky. While her legs had some muscle, her lower body strength left much to be desired. She had to mind her footwork carefully as she stepped in the opposite direction. She watched Roselyn's movements, deciding what technique to deploy first.

Adalyn waited until Roselyn's left arm moved to the side. The moment it did, her left shoulder was exposed and Adalyn took advantage. She struck first, putting only a mild amount of power into the fist. Roselyn countered, pushing her arm away and spin-kicking her legs.

In real combat, Adalyn would have taken flight and dodged the low kick, but she knew that she couldn't use her wings and instead attempted to jump using her knees. Her reflexes proved too slow and Roselyn's foot impacted against her knee.

Adalyn lost her balance and fell backwards. Her back hit the ground with a loud thud. She winced as she rolled over her wings, on to her side, and struggled back to her feet.

As Adalyn hit the floor, Roselyn laughed, "Come now, I would have expected better from the great hero of the Celestial War! How could you have made it this far with so little foot training?"

Adalyn sighed, "Will you please stop calling me that? We just did what we had to. Azrael said the same thing."

"Never." Roselyn replied with a mischievous grin.

She extended her hand to help Adalyn up, when she noticed her friend's skin going pale. Her eyes widened with worry, "Adalyn, are you all right?"

Adalyn's eyes closed and her breathing increased as she stopped moving. In her mind, she was suddenly ripped from the training chamber and taken far across the land to

an unknown location. There, she saw Azrael lying on the ground in a pool of his own blood. He had been captured, chained, and was being tortured to death by unseen entities.

Roselyn saw beads of sweat forming on Adalyn's brow as she knelt next to her sister and shook her arm, "Adalyn, girl, come out of it! What's going on? Please say something!"

Adalyn gasped as her eyes opened. She was breathing even more heavily now and tears began to fall from her eyes, "Azrael... no…"

Roselyn's eyes narrowed as she wiped the tears from Adalyn's face, "Azrael, what about him?"

Adalyn struggled to respond, "I... I saw..."

She gave up trying and closed her eyes. *If Azrael is in danger, I have to help him.*

Roselyn nodded, "Okay, take your time. Breathe and tell me what happened."

Adalyn's mind focused on one of Azrael's teachings that involved using one's mind to find answers that were beyond normal sight. Remembering his instructions about reaching out and picturing a tunnel through space and time, she closed her eyes and focused. Her head ached as she pushed hard to find him.

A sudden gust of wind struck Adalyn's face and she felt herself propelled forward as though flying through the air at speeds no angel had ever achieved. Her mind scanned the entire kingdom, but found no sign of Azrael. She began to expand her search to the outlying realms.

Roselyn was getting extremely worried as Adalyn refused to respond, "Adalyn what's..."

"Shh!" Adalyn replied harshly as she concentrated.

This time, within a few moments, she heard a high-pitched scream and a cold feeling came over her. Roselyn watched as Adalyn's skin broke out in goose bumps and her body shivered as though a cool breeze had touched her. A moment later, a sense of death came over Adalyn as though a life was about to end.

"No!" Adalyn gasped as she opened her eyes.

Her mind couldn't reconcile what she had sensed. *The Asphodel fields... why Azrael? Why go there?*

Divinity

The Asphodel fields were beyond the borders of the Kingdom of Heaven and no place for an angel. Going there was expressly forbidden by the choirs and the price of disobeying that mandate was severe. She knew the risks, but could not let her friend die. *It would be better to let the choirs know first... but he could be dead by then. I... I have to do this alone.*

"What," Roselyn asked in a panic, "what happened?"

Adalyn knew what she had to do. At first, she turned to Roselyn with the intention of telling her everything. Adalyn wanted to tell her, but then Roselyn would want to go with her. Adalyn was unwilling to risk getting her friend in trouble, "I'm sorry sister, I can't say. I have to go..."

Roselyn watched suspiciously, "Adalyn, I don't get what's going on. What just happened? You can't just take off on me like this!"

"I don't have a choice. Believe me; I don't get it either, sister." Adalyn replied. "I wish understood what was going on, but I don't. I have to go find some answers before it's too late."

Roselyn nodded, "All right, we'll both go."

"No." Adalyn replied adamantly. "For now, I can't let you get involved. If I need your help, I'll come back for you."

"Adalyn..." Roselyn was almost hurt by her refusal.

Adalyn looked into her eyes. Roselyn's brown eyes connected with Adalyn's blue. She was happy that Roselyn was willing to help her with so little information, but she was not about to put her sister at risk, "Please trust me sister, I won't leave you in the dark for long, just trust that I know what I'm doing for now."

Roselyn sighed, "Very well... but you better come find me if you get into any trouble!"

Adalyn kissed her on the cheek, "I will sister and I'll tell you everything as soon as I know. I promise."

Adalyn left Roselyn behind as she walked through the chamber doors. Roselyn shook her head and began trying to scan the area with her own mind to try to figure out what Adalyn had seen. She pressed on for a few moments, but could not find anything.

Concerned that Adalyn was getting herself into trouble, Roselyn quickly turned to chase after Adalyn, but she was already outside of the training compound. There was nothing Roselyn could do.

As soon as Adalyn was outside, she leaned forward and began to flap her wings. She then took off running and used all the strength in her legs to push herself off the ground. In less than a second, she was in the air. As the wind blew past her, she spread her wings and began to push herself higher. She could feel the wind blowing over her body even harder as she picked up speed and altitude.

Beneath her, Adalyn could see a small building that was intricately carved out of the purest ivory with another long staircase. It was designed to be an informal meeting and recreation center for the angels and was a popular meeting place when they were off duty. She spent a lot of time there when not training.

The Seraph angel Ariel, who was friend of Adalyn's and a treasured comrade since the war, was sitting at the entrance. She had just received orders to lend aid to the restoration work on the Celestial Temple. She sighed, knowing her job would be nothing more than ordering around a bunch of duty angels.

What I would give for something else today. Ariel thought to herself. *Anything else.*

At that moment, what looked like a massive white comet shot through the sky. Ariel's eyes narrowed as she detected intense concern. She reached out to try to get a better picture. The image of the comet in her mind quick took the form of an angel.

Ariel's eyes widened when she realized who it was. "Adalyn!"

Ariel quickly took flight and tried to catch up. Unlike Adalyn, Ariel was a seraph angel with four wings that glowed red, so she was able to quickly match Adalyn's speed. After a few hard thrusts through the air, she finally got to within ear shot of Adalyn and called out, "Sister, where are you off to in such a hurry?"

Divinity

Adalyn smiled at hearing the sound of her closest friend, "Hello Ariel, I can't talk right now. I fear Azrael might be in trouble!"

"Really?" Ariel asked in alarm. "I always thought Azrael was someone who could take care of himself! If he's in trouble, all hell must be breaking loose! I am…"

"I'm sorry sister, I have to keep moving." Adalyn insisted, too preoccupied to hear anymore.

Ariel flapped her wings harder to keep up, "Adalyn, what makes you think he's in danger?"

Adalyn looked back and frowned with apologetic eyes, "I just know... I felt it."

"Do you want me to come with you?" Ariel offered. "I have an assignment to complete, but if you need my help..."

Adalyn shook her head, "It may turn out to be nothing... I hope it does. There is no point in you getting in trouble for not following your orders if that's the case."

Ariel looked at her earnestly, "Are you sure, sister?"

"Yes," Adalyn replied, "please don't worry, I can handle myself, and we'll talk more as soon as I get back, I promise."

"You better, this will drive me crazy otherwise." Ariel shouted back with a smile, "I'll see you later on at the meeting of the choirs."

Adalyn nodded, "Agreed, see you then!"

Ariel veered off and headed back to her own chamber while Adalyn continued on alone. Both of them were now extremely worried. Ariel feared for her friend while Adalyn's thoughts dwelled on her mentor.

Azrael... Adalyn thought to herself, *please have a good reason for this!*

Adalyn's mind was overflowing with unanswered questions as she flew. What could he possibly be doing? What could have compelled him to go to the Asphodel fields? Was it an order, or something more sinister? She had to find out.

Asphodel was considered a border zone between the Celestial World and the Nether World. Penetrating into that area without permission could result in her being brought up on charges by the Choirs if she was wrong, but she didn't care. Azrael had looked after her for years. No matter how headstrong or defiant she was, he never gave up. She swore that she would do no less.

Adalyn quickly blew past the Celestial lands where angels and other divine creatures dwelled. She could no longer make out what she was flying by as the world around her had become a blur. The further she went, the darker the land became. White mist was replaced with dark, damp, smog that beat on her wings and soaked her dress. Her flying became more and more labored, but she pressed on.

III

Adalyn finally touched down in the misty swamp that she had seen in her vision. It was all exactly as her mind had shown her. The land reeked of the smell of rotting flesh and waist from a battle long ago. There were shattered skeletons littering the fields, covering the black grounds with filthy white bone.

In the distance, she could see mountains of dust, no doubt the remains of her fallen comrades. Broken and dead trees could be seen for miles in this once lush land. Adalyn remembered how close the celestial plains came to looking exactly like this.

The feelings of sorrow and pain were potent and almost visible to someone who, like Adalyn, was sensitive to such things. They echoed in her mind like a loud horn being blown right next to her ears. She fell to her knees in agony as the sound of battle overwhelmed her senses. Her head throbbed in pain as her vision became blurred and the loud noises in her head continued to get worse. Pain slowly began to overtake her senses, making it impossible for her to go forward.

If I have to endure much more of this, I won't survive, she thought to herself. With her last flicker of sanity, she remembered Azrael's teachings on how to quiet her mind. At that moment, Azrael's voice appeared in her head, "Adalyn, there may come a time when you need to confront the sorrow and death of a past battle. Angels are sensitive to the tormented pleas of lost souls. These will overwhelm you unless you learn to shut them out."

"How," Adalyn asked, trying to fight through the pain, "how does one shut out something so powerful? It hurts too much…"

Again, her mind flashed back to Azrael's words, "Clear the thoughts from your mind. Stay your emotions as best you can. Picture a barrier between you and them and the words of the souls just bouncing off of it. Picture it and then focus on it. If you are successful, the voices should have little effect on you."

Adalyn closed her eyes and pictured the wall in her mind as Azrael had instructed. Slowly, the voices began to dissipate and become quiet. She let out a deep sigh as she stood up, brushed herself off, and got her bearings before proceeding on foot. The voices were now little more than a whisper on the wind.

Only the roar of unholy beasts in the distance could be heard. She made her way through the lifeless brush of the forest, walking forward no longer afraid. While the beasts in this unholy land were fearsome, none of them possessed the power to harm an angel. This was assuming that the demons of the Netherworld had not found a way to breach the borders again.

Adalyn continued cautiously until she came across a small grove with grass that was inexplicably still alive. The sun was bright in this land that reflected off of a large crystal in the center. She could not believe what she was seeing. This land looked like one of the celestial plains from the kingdom of the Most High.

A dark figure stood staring between Adalyn and the crystal as it stared into it. The sunlight's reflection made it impossible for her to make out the figure's face, but it appeared to be an angel. She narrowed her eyes, but the light was still blinding. She knew that the only way to solve this mystery was to get closer.

To avoid being seen, she knelt down and shrouded herself with her wing. Doing so slowly caused her to fade from view until she was completely invisible. Safely shrouded beneath her wing, she slowly crept closer to the figure.

An ancient language spoken in a raspy voice emanated from the crystal as it slowly spun in a circle. The figure nodded in response to its words, "Yes Master, your plan has worked perfectly. The wars on Earth are continuing to spread and will soon encompass the entirety of the known world. The Choirs of Angels barely suspect anything and will not realize what is going on until it is too late. By the time they draw up arms to fight, we will already be on top of them."

Divinity

Adalyn gasped, she recognized the voice almost immediately. There was no doubt about it. The voice was that of her mentor, Azrael. She covered her mouth as her eyes widened, *Azrael... no... no this can't be real!*

Hearing his voice speak of treason was like a knife to Adalyn's heart. She still had trouble believing that this man was her mentor, yet there he was. Could it be some kind of trick? Is it possible that he was under some type of control?

Adalyn shook her head as she watched him. *No... I would have detected something like that by now. There is nothing holding onto his mind.*

The almost beast-like voice responded, this time in a language she understood, "Then my ascension will come soon. The Most High was a fool to create a child race that could do him damage. The final truce and my banishment has only served to give me the time I needed to build up a new force to take on the Most High in another battle. I have lost much at the hands of your Most High, but will soon have my revenge. Until I signal again, lay in wait. This will be the last time we speak until I am ready."

Azrael nodded, "Then you plan to move soon?"

"Be patient, we will begin our move against those who still remain loyal to him soon enough." The crystal replied.

Adalyn gasped, realizing that the Celestial Temple was now in danger. A faint sound escaped her lips as she quickly covered her mouth. Her eyes widened as Azrael reacted.

Azrael heard the noise and turned around. He drew his sword and scanned the area. Adalyn froze in place and remained perfectly still, hoping Azrael's sight would pass her by. Her mentor's eyes panned the surroundings before turning back to the crystal. The voice emanated again, "Something wrong?"

"Apologies... I thought I heard something," Azrael responded, "It appears I was mistaken."

He smiled maliciously before bowing, "Your will be done, Master. You needn't worry; soon the Celestial Realm will be yours for the taking."

Adalyn had heard enough, it pained her heart greatly to hear Azrael betray everything that they had fought so hard to protect. She clenched her teeth as her face heated up.

Her wings shuddered with anticipation as she was about to reveal herself.

Adalyn felt her face heat up as she reached for her knife. She felt horribly betrayed and was ready to attack Azrael. She tensed her muscles, ready to strike, but then she paused. *I can't take Azrael alone,* she thought to herself as she looked down at the dagger attached to her sash. *I'm going to need help. If he has the support of Lucifer, then the Choirs need to be made aware of this immediately.*

Adalyn resisted the urge to attack and slowly began sliding her feet quietly across the ground. She moved so slowly, it felt like she was walking for hours as she made her way back into the brush. Her eyes never left her master as he stared into the crystal. It was a tough fight to resist the urge to attack, but she knew she had to.

The moment Adalyn was far enough away, she began to run, this time faster than before. Using every ounce of strength she could summon, she pushed her legs and wings to speed up. She stumbled a few times as she ran but finally began to run fast enough to launch herself into the air. A final push sent her airborne. She quickly ascended into the clouds and fought to gain altitude. Her wings flapped mercilessly against the wind as she began picking up speed.

Back in the grove, Azrael watched an image of Adalyn on the crystal as she flew away. At that moment, he began to fade into mist and became nothing more than a blur. The remaining entity began to laugh, "And so it begins…"

IV

Adalyn pushed her wings harder than she had ever before. Her muscles ached as she tensed them with each flap. She had never put them under so much strain, not even during the war. Her speed became so great that the friction of the air began to singe her feathers. She knew that if she kept this up, she could do permanent damage and lose the ability to fly, but she did not care. All other concerns were secondary. She had to report what she had seen.

I must get back and warn the others, nothing else matters. Adalyn thought to herself.

Everything was at stake, but who could she tell? Would Michael believe her? Azrael was a close friend to the archangel. He'd most likely just brush her off and dismiss her words, but she had to try.

Adalyn continued on as the heavens passed before her eyes. It wasn't long before she came upon Michael's lair. The building was a large temple carved out of stone that sat on a cloud by itself. Unlike other buildings, Michael's lair seemed very plain.

Adalyn guessed that as a soldier, he had simply become accustomed to a spartan lifestyle. Her bare feet were caressed by the mist as she landed and rushed into Michael's dwelling. She was determined to convince him.

The first room was little more than a large hallway. It was decorated with colorful plants, many of which were the last of their species. The war had cost the angels much, but the land had paid the highest price for their victory. This room served as a reminder to her of the results of war, as if she could forget.

The next room was a large chamber with a domed ceiling. It was smaller than that of the Most High and, like the exterior, was very plain. Another big difference between the two rooms was that this one had two large white tapestries flowing from the ceiling instead of a glowing orb. The tapestries waved as though wind was blowing through them, despite being indoors with no breeze. They began to flow side to side even more in reaction to Adalyn's presence.

Divinity

After briefly looking around, she rolled her eyes and looked up at the tapestries, "Michael, I know you're up there. I've discovered something terrible… a betrayal of the Most High!"

A gentle wind blew past and a barely audible voice could be heard on the air, "Yes, I felt you approach. I sense that you are troubled. Speak your mind, sister."

Adalyn nodded, "Azrael has betrayed us!"

Before Adalyn could elaborate, the tapestries began to tremble until they fell from their hanging position. As the two pieces of white cloth floated to the ground, they folded into the shape of wings. Michael appeared between them and landed on one knee. He raised his eyes to look at Adalyn as he stood. The look on his face was a medium between anger and earnestness. His lips curled into sneer, "What charge do you bring against my friend?"

Adalyn took a small step back in fear, "Master, I followed him to the Asphodel field after I sensed that he was in pain. When I arrived, I heard him communicate with Lucifer. He is planning a coup!"

Michael shook his head, "Impossible, Azrael has been on a mission for me for the past two hours. It was a last-minute assignment that I needed him to take on."

A confused look appeared on Adalyn's face, "Michael… I know what I saw!"

"Do you?" Michael asked. "Do you really? You are aware that the Asphodel field is known for being able to trick the senses, yes?"

"This wasn't a hallucination, Master!" Adalyn shot back.

"Silence!" Michael replied. "Asphodel is forbidden territory. That you went there without orders is extremely troubling. I am willing to overlook your transgression this time, but I will not indulge any dilusions, especially not in regards to accusations of treason against a highly admired angel."

Adalyn shook her head, "Will you not hear me? Will you do nothing?"

Michael sighed as he looked at the earnest expression on her face, "I'll consider your words."

Divinity

"That's all?" Adalyn scoffed. "Michael, we can't afford…"

"Enough, I've given you my answer." Michael interrupted. "Now return to the compound and do not speak of this again unless I summon you."

Adalyn lowered her eyes, "As you say, Michael."

She didn't say another word to the archangel as she turned and made her way outside. *He's not going to do anything.* She thought to herself. *It's impossible for him to believe that an old friend is capable of treason… I guess I can understand that, but still… to risk all of existence on it…"*

Adalyn finally came to the grim conclusion that she had feared might be her only answer. There seemed to be no way to avoid it if she were to save the Celestial World. *Though I'll be damned for doing so…If Michael won't listen… then I must go before the Most High.*

Adalyn knew what the penalty was for violating the Most High's decree, but there was no other choice. She quickly took off and flapped her right wing to make herself turn. Her mind was made up; she was going to his temple. There was no other choice to be made in her mind. She'd have to convince him of the coming danger.

As she picked up speed, an intense burning sensation entered the skin of her wings as the feathers began to singe. She flew through a nearby cloud in an attempt to cool them down. The mist coated her wings for a brief moment before drying off and creating a second cloud of steam. Adalyn ignored it and pressed on as hard as she could.

At the entrance to the Most High's dwelling, the titans heard a loud boom in the distance as one of the clouds above them parted. What could only be described as a meteor fell from the sky and landed a few feet from them. There was a thick cloud of smoke obstructing their view of what had crashed.

A figure appeared from inside the cloud, waving her arms, trying to clear the smoke. As it faded, the titans saw Adalyn on her knees struggling to breathe. She was sore and exhausted as she attempted to stand. Her legs would not support her and her wings were badly singed with smoke still rolling off of them. It took a few minutes for them to cool.

After regaining her composure, Adalyn folded her wings on her back and nursed them for a moment to try to relieve the pain. Several of her feathers had been burned so badly that they were falling out while others were turning black and smoldering. It would be a while before she would be able to take to the air again. She got to her feet, brushed herself off, and straightened her remaining feathers. Once she felt presentable, she staggered towards the titans.

The taller of the two gigantic guards came to life and thrust out his hand, "Halt, the Most High has decreed that he is not to be disturbed during his time of rest."

Breathing heavily, Adalyn responded, "This is a critical matter, I must speak to him now. Believe me, it is enough to justify waking him."

The other life-like metal giant stepped forward with his spear, "The Most High's decree cannot be reversed for any reason. It is absolute and beyond questioning. You know the punishment for doing so. If this is as urgent as you say, inform the Choirs of Angels. You have already violated the Most High's no-fly order. This infraction will be reported to the Choirs."

Adalyn knew that the titans had been created for a single purpose and no matter what she said, they would not allow anyone to pass. The titans were strong warriors, but did not possess the ability to think on their own. When given an order, they carried it out with question and without hesitation. She looked at them for a few moments and sighed, "Noble titans, I hold no ill will towards you. You have performed your duties adequately, but I must pass."

Before either titan could respond, Adalyn raised her hands, touched both of their foreheads, and closed her eyes for a moment. When she reopened them, her pupils were glowing bright blue. She looked both Titans in the eyes, one after another and softly spoke without moving her lips, "Sleep…"

Both titans instantly fell to the ground unconscious with a loud crash. Adalyn felt a great deal of regret for what she had done, but once again, she had to justify it by saying that it was for the greater good. As she proceeded into the next chamber, she contemplated how many crimes had been committed for the greater good. It weighed heavily on her heart, but she knew that it was the right thing to do.

Adalyn cautiously made her way down the next corridor and found herself at the door to the Most High's temple. She pressed her hand against the door, ignoring the voice in the back of her mind screaming at her to stop. To her surprise, it slowly creaked opened with the slightest touch. Mist shot through the crack as the door opened enough for her to squeeze by it.

The chamber of the Most High was as dark as night. Stars could be seen twinkling through the windows, giving her some illumination. The room shook with the sound of heavy breathing.

Adalyn regretted having to disturb such a tranquil scene, but there was no time to waste. She quickly tiptoed to the center of the room and looked up. The large orb was very dim and flickered slightly with the sounds of breathing. The figure in the center of the orb was lying down, not moving.

Adalyn took a deep breath as she closed her eyes. All the while, the voice in her head got louder, "This is wrong, you are heading into trouble. Will any good truly come of this? Go back and talk to the Choirs! Force them to understand!"

Adalyn put the voice aside, out of her head, and moved slightly forward. She noticed that there was no grass on the floor anymore. The mist parted revealing a black marble floor with small crystal inlets, resembling stars.

Adalyn looked at it in amazement; this was a map of all of creation and most likely how the Most High viewed existence. At the center of this map was an ornate trumpet seated on a small pedestal in the middle of the room on the floor. It had been left there to alert the Most High should he be needed. She mustered up her courage and picked up the horn. Looking up into the temple, she blew into the horn, making a loud noise and signaling the Most High to awaken.

Divinity

The entire room began to shake and a loud hum echoed through the walls. Adalyn began to shudder as the room trembled so violently that it looked as though it were about to come apart. She could hear the stones around her begin to grind.

Adalyn closed her eyes and spoke, "My lord, I implore you, please forgive me. I am aware of what I have done and will gladly accept whatever punishment you have in store for me, but please listen."

The voice roared again. Adalyn nodded, "Yes, I am fully aware that the only ones who should be waking you are the Archangels, but this is a matter of urgency. I must speak with you, please! You must hear what I have to say!"

The voice quieted as Adalyn opened her eyes, "Master, there is a plot currently unfolding to begin a new war. Except this time, we would be caught off guard. More of our allies are turning on us and it appears that the plan is to attack you while you are weak. This is the missing piece of the puzzle!"

Adalyn's hands shook as she continued to speak, "If this is allowed to continue, we may not be able to prevent the onslaught. There are still too few of us and we are scattered throughout the celestial realm! I cannot even begin to fathom the ramifications of their success."

The voice began to roar again, shaking the temple at its foundation. Adalyn nodded, "Yes Master, I am aware that Lucifer has been driven out of the Celestial World. I fought in that battle and am aware of the details, but please believe me, I witnessed the treachery myself. Azrael is plotting against you. Master please, have the Asphodel fields searched, you will find his hideout in a small grove and know what I am saying is true."

Another loud roar emanated from the temple, "Yes Master, I violated our borders... I am aware of what I have done but..."

The voice cut her off before she could finish pleading her case. When it finally quieted down, Adalyn's mouth dropped open, "But Master..."

Three more angels, including Michael and Azrael suddenly appeared. Azrael stepped forward with a shocked look on his face, "Adalyn what have you done?"

Michael raised his hand to silence Azrael and turned to the Most High, "I am sorry, Master. We got here as soon as we could. I take full responsibility for Adalyn's actions. We did not believe this girl would be so brash. I will have her removed and I promise you that she will be dealt with according to your will."

He turned to the third angel in the room and beckoned to him forward. The angel, in full battle armor, grabbed Adalyn's arm, "You need to come with me right now."

Adalyn fell to her knees, "Most High, will you not hear me? Will you not even consider what I have said?"

"Silence!" Michael shouted. "Cease and desist immediately as you have been instructed. Things will only get worse for you if you don't."

He quickly turned to the guard angel holding Adalyn's arm, "Guard, remove her, now."

Adalyn lowered her eyes and stood up, it looked like she was about to comply, but instead darted forward and fell to her knees again on the other side of the room, "Most High, please hear me, Azrael is a..."

Before she could say anything more, her eyes blacked out as her body fell limp and settled on the floor. Azrael turned to see Michael's eyes glowing and his fist clenched, "Was that really necessary, my friend?"

Michael nodded as the guard flew over to her and picked her up, "She disobeyed orders and refused to stand down. Our laws are clear on this. I will not have our master disturbed any further by this!"

Michael and Azrael turned back to speak to the Most High and attempt to calm him as the guard carried Adalyn's body out of the chamber. Michael spoke in an obedient voice as he tried to quell the Most High's anger, "Forgive me, my master, she will be dealt with. You need not worry. I will attend to everything, I promise."

The Most High responded with a low hum. Michael nodded, "Yes Master, she told me the same tale, but I can vouch for Azrael. I know where he's been. Still, I will look

into Adalyn's claims about the Asphodel Fields… with your permission of course?"

There was a brief hum, which made Michael nod, "Very well, I'll send my best scouts to investigate."

When he turned away from the Most High, Azrael spoke up, "Michael, she is my student. I know her well enough to tell you the she would never do anything so brash if she did not truly believe something was amiss."

"The scouts will investigate Asphodel." Michael responded sympathetically. He had a twisted expression on his face. "If they find anything out of place, you have my word, it will be dealt with."

Azrael could feel Michael's unease and decided to confront him, "Is there something else you want to say to me?"

"Your apprentice accused you of plotting against our master." Michael responded in a hesitant voice.

"What?" Azrael gasped, unable to grasp what he'd just heard.

Michael told him what Adalyn had said about the grove she'd discovered deep in the Asphodel fields. Azrael couldn't believe it, "But that's not possible. You knew where I was the entire time. You sent me on a mission."

Michael nodded, "I know my friend, that's why I'm not taking you into custody. However I do have to investigate this. We have a serious problem here as angels don't go around accusing one another of misdoings. When one does, it must be looked into according our laws. Ridiculous as this may be, I have to have you investigated, but there are bigger issues."

Michael pointed to the door, "Your apprentice has some very serious charges against her now… violating our borders, reversal of the Most High's decree, assaulting the Most High's guards, and disobeying orders. Also, should her accusations not pan out, a charge of bearing false witness will be added to that. Not since the war have we had so many infractions. This is not looking good for her, old friend. The penalty for such crimes is absolute and severe."

Azrael didn't want to give up, "Surely there is room for mercy. Her services during the war have made her a hero amongst the people of our realm. She still has a lot to learn, but she has continuously proven herself to be a worthwhile apprentice and a skilled soldier."

"Then you should have kept a tighter leash on her." Michael responded sternly. "You are getting far too soft in your old age, my friend."

V

Adalyn was shackled and weighted down so that she could not fly. She looked at the guard who placed the cuffs on her arms and frowned, "These really are not necessary. I have no intention of attempting to escape."

The guard shook his head, "After everything you've done, it's the least you deserve."

Adalyn lowered her eyes, "If the Most High truly wishes to sacrifice me and place my head on a pike for all to see, then I would gladly give it."

Once her shackles were tightly secured, the guard grabbed her shoulder and took her into a dark chamber hidden behind the council chamber. She was then taken to a small cell with no light. It was little more than a closet with a single barred window.

The entire room was covered in dust and silvery cob webs. It looked as though it had not been used in many years. There was an old wooden chair that had long since rotted to the point of collapse and a stone slab that protruded from the wall to be used as a bed. There was no mattress and nothing comforting about it at all, not that anyone who utilized this cell deserved any better. The guards gave Adalyn a harsh shove and sent her stumbling into the cell, sealing the heavy metal door behind her.

Once the door was secured, the older guard looked in at her through the small barred window, "So foolish... what were you thinking? Disturbing the Most High in his sleep like that."

She looked back at him, "Please... regardless of what happens to me, someone must investigate Azrael. I know I will be condemned for what I've done and I accept that, but don't let the rest of the world suffer!"

The guard turned his back to her. He quietly muttered as he left the room, "Get some sleep, you are going to need it."

*

Adalyn spent the next two days in solitary confinement while the Choirs of Angels convened to deal with this incident. She spent the entire time on her knees,

Divinity

reciting the same prayer over and over again. It was pointless and she knew it, but at this time, it was her only comfort.

As Adalyn expected, her prayers went unanswered. The Most High was asleep and the Choirs would not listen to her pleas. She had all but surrendered to her fate as she knew what was to become of her.

Tears rolled down her cheeks and she continued to pray, "Lord, please, if you can hear me, I had everyone's best interest at heart. Please let this fate pass me by this day."

A response came in the form of a humming sound as the door to her cell was unsealed and the guard entered. She stood up with her eyes locked on him. He returned her look with a sneer.

Adalyn recognized him as one of the lower ranking angels. He had fought in the war, but had never really found his niche and took a quiet job where he could find some peace. Such was the tragedy for many of the angels that had seen those violent days. She couldn't blame him for choosing the life he had.

After pulling the door back, he spoke to her in a low voice, "It's time to go, the Choir has summoned you, traitor."

Adalyn stood, revealing the worn spots on her dress from all the time she spent on her knees. She stared at him without the slightest hint of emotion as he beckoned to her. At first, she didn't move at all.

The guard pulled a spear off of the wall outside the chamber and pointed it at her, "I'm not going to be very patient with you. You have been summoned by the Choirs, now move."

Adalyn fluttered her wings in defiance and took a step forward. She slowly made her way to the main council chamber where everyone was waiting for her. There was an air of doom about her. She understood all too well what awaited her in the next chamber. Terrible things were done to angels that had violated the Most High's decree.

The room was a massive ivory amphitheater with accommodations for literally thousands of spectators. Each section was organized and gated off for each of the choirs to be seated by rank. On the theater floor, off to the side closest to the entrance where everyone could see it, was a large podium with ornate golden chairs. These were to accommodate the Seven Archangels.

The chairs were incredibly luxurious. The gold had been carved into small cherubs sitting on leaves, forming the backs of the chairs. The padding was shiny red velvet that looked more comfortable than any material the angels had seen before.

Almost every seat was taken for this meeting. Adalyn was very well known throughout the realm and every angel that was not currently on assignment was present. Literally hundreds of discussions could be heard throughout the room. The sounds of their voices became more excited as Adalyn appeared on the floor. Pointed fingers and accusing looks were directed at her as she took her place in the center of the room.

Adalyn didn't look at anyone. She was either uninterested or completely unaware of the accusing looks that were being levied against her. She did the best she could to shut out the world as she awaited her fate.

Michael stood at the center of the stage behind the podium with the other archangels standing on either side. When the audience saw them, everyone instantly quieted down. Adalyn followed procedure and knelt before the Seven Archangels out of respect, though anyone watching her could clearly tell that it was insincere.

Each of the Archangels were dressed in a brown underlay and draped with silver armor. The armor also had gold lining on the neck and arm sleeves, giving it a luxurious look. The archangels were an imposing sight with such armor.

To Adalyn, this armor appeared to be little more the prestige and made the Archangels more attractive targets. These were dress uniforms to establish rank and nothing more. Their true armor was far less glamorous in appearance, but far more effective on the battlefield.

Michael raised his right hand for all to see. Everyone took their seats as he spoke, "Arise, Adalyn, and face the judgment of our lord Most High."

As Adalyn returned to her feet, Michael looked around the room before turning back to face her angry stare, "Do you know why you are here? Can you understand the severity of the charges that have been levied against you?"

Adalyn's gaze never left Michael's eyes. The level of crass in her voice was unmistakable, "Respectfully, Master, I am here because of your unwillingness to hear the truth. Your blindness will lead you to far larger tragedies than the wrongful prosecution of an angel who was just doing her job."

Uriel, the archangel seated to Michael's right stood up with an angry look on his face, "Such insolence from a young angel! This will not be tolerated. You will show the proper respect in the presence of your superiors!"

Michael raised his right hand to silence Uriel and then turned back to Adalyn, "You appear to have learned nothing from the war. It appears that you were not ready for the tasks given to you. Perhaps you should have spent more time as the guiding light for the damned before petitioning to join us here."

Michael shook his head and sighed as he continued, "A true pity… you represented hope for a future within the Choirs, but now you have reversed the Most High's decree, assaulted two of his servants, and falsely accused a high ranking and well respected angel of treason!"

Adalyn's eyes continued to focus on Michael as she spoke, "I did not falsely accuse anyone… if you would investigate what I told you, you'd see…"

"That's the problem," Michael interrupted, "I personally sent scouts out to check Asphodel. We found no trace of any oasis like what you described and I can say beyond any doubt that Azrael was innocent. Do you think that I didn't know where he was while you were off violating our borders? Do you think that I am so blind that I do not keep tabs on my friends? You should have had more faith then that. I do not know what you suddenly have against your former master, the one who trained you and called you friend, but it does not matter now."

Adalyn looked away, "I know what I saw. I will not recant."

Michael frowned as his eyes remained fixed on Adalyn, "No, I didn't think you would. Well... what are we supposed to do here? The Most High is quite upset, and demanding that the situation be dealt with. Perhaps we could have looked the other way on your transgressions had you not drawn his attention, but..."

"Master," A voice interrupted, "I must be allowed to speak. I request the floor."

Michael looked up to see who had spoken. To his surprise, it was none other than Azrael himself. Michael smiled nervously and raised his hand, beckoning his old friend to come forward, "The Choir Council recognizes the voice of the honorable warrior Azrael. You have the floor, you may speak."

Adalyn glared at her former mentor as he walked past her. Azrael did not return her gaze, but instead focused on the council and spoke directly to his old friend amongst the Archangels, "Master, I have come before you to plead for the life of the accused. She is still young and impetuous, and still has much to learn, but her actions during the war have made her a hero and should entitle her to some consideration."

Michael nodded, "As I said, had she not involved the Most High, I might have looked the other way. I'm sorry old friend, but she's had several millions of years to learn our ways."

Azrael disregarded Michael's words and continued, "Were we any different at that time? Do you not remember the adventures we undertook when we were new?"

Michael chuckled, "No we weren't... but as reckless as we were, we never violated the Most High's decree. You of all people know that."

"Yes I do," Azrael replied, "but her failings are my responsibility. I offer myself in her place. I failed her and I will accept the judgment of the Choirs."

Divinity

All this time, Adalyn was extremely confused. *What is going on here? Why is Azrael doing this? He could easily eliminate his accuser by keeping quiet, yet here he is trying to save me.*

The questions filling Adalyn's head suddenly vanished when an irritated look flashed through Michael's eyes, "My friend, stop. You know that you did not commit the crime. I will not prosecute you for failing a pupil. Your actions today, while honorable are completely futile. Cease this posturing and return to your place, now!"

Azrael's face hardened and he stepped up to the podium so that no one else could hear him. Michael leaned forward to listen to his friend. Azrael's eyes had a pleading look in them as he spoke, "Michael, please… I beg you to see reason here. We accomplish nothing by punishing the hero of the Celestial War."

Michael shook his head, "There is nothing I can do my friend. This has gone too far for me to stop it."

Azrael shook his head as he stepped back in front of Adalyn. He turned back one more time and glared at Michael, "I want my objections noted on the record."

"Of course," Michael nodded, "as always, it shall be done."

Azrael defiantly stepped back, but only far enough to be standing next to Adalyn. Whatever sentence would be passed upon her, he was adamant that he would face it with her. Michael ignored this and spoke directly to Adalyn, "For your crimes, young angel, you are hereby banished from the Kingdom of Heaven and the entire Celestial World forever. You are to be stripped of your immortality and sent to the Corporeal World. At this time, the Year of our Lord 1519 is upon the Most High's beloved. They are still primitive and paranoid. They find creative new ways of destroying one another. You will no doubt quickly meet your end at the hands of these primitive people."

"What?" Azrael's voice burst out next to Adalyn.

He stepped back out in front of her on the council floor and this time he was joined by Adalyn's friends Ariel and Roselyn. Ariel stepped forward, "Michael please, that is excessive! Even Lucifer was shown some mercy! You're not simply condemning her to death, we're talking about brutal torture!"

"Yes," Roselyn chimed in, "is there truly no room for leniency? Torture and death for such crimes is going too far!"

Uriel stepped forward, "Silence, clear the floor, all three of you!"

Ariel's eyes glowed as though an angry fire burned within them. She reached for her sword, but did not draw it, "No, I will not stand by and allow this brutality to take place! I will..."

"Enough!" Adalyn yelled, stepping in front of them, "Don't get yourselves into trouble. I won't have you suffer for me."

Roselyn looked at her desperately, "But Adalyn..."

"No," she said adamantly, "I love you for what you're trying to do, but you're putting yourself at risk. Stand down."

Ariel lowered her eyes in defeat as Adalyn turned back to the Seven, "If you will not listen to me, do as you must."

Adalyn looked over at her friends as she continued," I only hope my sacrifice will inspire others into action! All of existence may depend on someone taking up the reigns you refuse to!"

"Very well then," Michael replied in an unemotional tone, "your sentence shall be carried out immediately."

Michael twisted his wrist, "Farewell, young Adalyn, you will be missed here."

Adalyn began to tremble as the mist next to her parted to reveal a deep hole. She had a feeling that she knew what was coming through and it made her blood run cold. She closed her eyes, just waiting for it all to be over.

A large serpent emerged from the hole and slowly slithered over to Adalyn. Without warning, it clenched its fangs around her ankle, allowing them to cut into her skin. She screamed in pain as she could feel her entire body pulse and the life force drain from her.

A gold aura emanated from Adalyn's body and slowly began to pull away from her. The aura took the form of an orb. Her body began to feel hundreds of times heavier and

Divinity

her breathing became more labored. She was unable to move under the strain.

Azrael grimaced and turned his back while Ariel had to restrain Roselyn from running to Adalyn's side, knowing full well what would happen if she touched Adalyn now. Ariel's heart ached as she too wanted to run to Adalyn's side.

The serpent released Adalyn's leg and slithered back into the hole. The moment the snake was gone, the hole vanished from sight. The orb exploded into sparkles right in front of Adalyn and disappeared.

As her powers vanished, Adalyn felt naked in the presence of her former comrades. A chill came over her and she rubbed her arms to try to keep warm. She was more alone in that room full of prying eyes than she had ever felt before.

Michael stared at her in the pitiful state she was in for a moment as he raised his right hand. He held it in place for a moment with a sympathetic look on his face, but finally lowered it. The mist under her feet parted and she fell through.

Adalyn watched as she plunged through the puffy white clouds, past the stars, and into the blue skies of the Mortal Realm. More clouds passed by as she continued to plummet towards the earth. She tried to spread her wings to break her decent, but her wings were still too injured to hold her and just made her spin downward out of control.

Ariel closed her eyes and began to focus her mind. Roselyn saw it and stepped in front of Ariel so that the archangels couldn't see what she was doing. Ariel continued to focus as Roselyn whispered, "What are you doing?"

Ariel shook her head, "Interfering."

"You could lose your wings for this." Roselyn replied.

Ariel frowned, "I don't care, this is wrong. At the very least, I'm going to alter her descent enough so that she stands a chance of being discovered by someone who won't try to kill her."

Roselyn could see Ariel struggling. After a few more jolts with her mind, Ariel gasped and opened her eyes, "It's no good, I've directed her to the general vicinity, but I'm not powerful enough to do more."

Roselyn shook her head, "No more, sister, I won't risk you being discovered."

Ariel turned to leave the chambers as Azrael stood glaring at Michael, "Come, we have much to discuss."

Azrael nodded and followed the sisters out of the room.

**

The mortal realm quickly came into view and Adalyn saw that she was plunging towards water. She struggled repeatedly to slow her decent, but nothing she did made any difference. Her wings were too weak to hold her and when she tried to use them, she was hit by continuous waves of pain.

A second later, Adalyn struck the water face first with a massive splash. The water plumed and then closed around her. She disappeared beneath the waves as her world went black.

BOOK 2
Questioning Beliefs

I

On the shores of the Venetian coast, the Patrisi home was busy with activity. The small stone house which sat on the shoreline of the local harbor, just outside of the city of Venice, was completely deserted. The lights were out and the doors were closed, however there was evidence of considerably activity recently. Leftover food, wine, and sympathy presents had been left unattended.

The Patrisi home had been the site of much sadness recently as the second youngest son of Beanti Patrisi had recently been buried nearby. Everyone from the small fishing community nearby had come to pay their respects. The boy was the latest victim of the white plague outbreak. His funeral was overseen by his younger brother, Giovanni Patrisi, the last of the family. The lone child was now left alone to carry on his line.

The funeral had ended hours ago, but Giovanni had not noticed. He maintained a silent vigil over his brother, who was now buried in a row alongside the other members of his family. Giovanni's heart clenched with the realization that he would soon be joining them.

No one knew that Giovanni had contracted the White Plague during the time that he had cared for his brother. It was still in the early stages so he was able to keep it hidden, but that would only last him a little while longer. It had already begun to ravage his body and affect his breathing. He looked at his father's grave as tears entered his eyes, "Papa, your son is on his way to you. Don't worry, he passed away in his sleep, so he probably didn't feel any pain, and he didn't die alone."

Giovanni couldn't hold it back any longer. He had held back his sadness and fear during the funeral, but he couldn't do so anymore. Like water flowing through a broken dam, his sadness flooded his mind.

The tears flowed down Giovanni's cheeks from his brown eyes as he continued talking, "Don't worry about me. I've taken care of the family fishing boat… and the house. I'll do what I can for as long as I can, but I'm afraid that I may be joining you soon as well. I'm sorry Papa, I did the best I could to avoid getting infected, but I just wasn't careful enough."

Giovanni looked up to see the sun setting on the horizon. It would soon be dark. He turned back to the fresh grave where his brother now rested as he got to his feet, "Well... I better get going. I... I'll come back soon Alej, I promise. I hope you're finally at peace. I love you."

Giovanni looked back at the empty cottage at the bottom of the hill and then back at the grave. He dreaded going back to his home. To open the door and see a house that was once filled with life, now empty and filled with death, was more than he had the strength for.

After everything that had gone on, Giovanni desperately needed someone to talk to. Unfortunately the life of a fisherman was one of solitude unless one was a part of a larger crew. He really didn't have many friends except for his old mentor, Padre Benito Antonelli, the local pastor.

Giovanni decided that he wanted to speak to the old priest and made his way down the old dirt path, headed to the church on the outskirts of his village. He didn't know if going there would provide him any relief, but this was where he went when he needed spiritual answers. At the very least, talking may give him some comfort.

**

Padre Antonelli was closing up the church for the evening. The last of the sermons had already been given that night and although the doors to the church were never locked, he would be retiring to his residence once the candles were put out.

The church was small and only modestly decorated on the outside, but Antonelli wouldn't have had it any other way. It was a humble setting in a nice quiet town. After a lifetime of adventure, the priest had grown accustom to the quiet.

Antonelli looked out on the town with a content smile on his face. He let out a quiet sigh as his head turned in the other direction and looked towards the Patrisi house. *Poor boy,* he thought to himself. *I wish I could have spent more time with him, but my parishioners would have unleashed*

the devil himself had I not been present for the afternoon sermon.

Antonelli turned back and began put out the candles when he heard the sound of footsteps in the dirt and heavy breathing in the distance. He was surprised to see Giovanni coming and recognized the inquisitive look on his face. Antonelli welcomed him with open arms. "Young Giovanni, it is good to see that you have finally departed your brother's burial. I was concerned that you would be there all night."

Giovanni straightened his dark brown hair and bowed, "Padre, please let me thank you again for your words of kindness at my brother's funeral. I know he would have appreciated it."

Padre Antonelli nodded, "Your brother was a good man, and truly lived his faith in the Lord. Finding a kind word for him wasn't difficult and performing the ceremony was no effort. You and your family are good friends. Heaven shall be a better place once your brother arrives there."

"Yes…" Giovanni said hesitantly "Padre, it is my faith that I wanted to speak to you about."

Antonelli looked inquisitively at the young man. Giovanni took in as deep a breath as he could before continuing, "How was Job able to keep his faith about him after so much tragedy. Everything was taken from him for no reason, yet he still remained steadfast in his belief that God has a reason for everything he does."

The old priest smiled warmly, "Do you see yourself as Job, my son?"

"No Padre," Giovanni said remorsefully, "I fear that I have not been so steadfast in my own faith, but I feel as though his story does pertain to me in some way."

"The Lord giveth and the Lord taketh away." Padre Antonelli said as he remembered back to that story from the Old Testament. "We do not always understand his reasoning, and we are not meant to. That's not our job. As long as we are faithful to the Church and to the Lord our God, then we can be sure that our loved ones will live forever in paradise."

Divinity

Giovanni looked confused, "But sir, what of those who have not been so loyal to the Church, but still claim to be believers in the one true God? What of those fighting for their reformation, are they not…"

Antonelli cut Giovanni off quickly, "Hush my son, perhaps it is best not to speak of these things here. Perhaps another time when we are behind closed doors?"

Giovanni nodded, "Forgive me Padre… I misspoke. Thank you for your words of wisdom. I will be sure to reflect on them tonight when I am praying."

Giovanni bowed to the priest as he turned to head for home, "Goodnight Padre."

Padre Antonelli returned the gesture and bid Giovanni a good night, "Rest well, my son."

Giovanni left the priest to finish closing up the church and started for home as the sky got darker. He walked as quickly as he could down the old beaten dust road that he had walked thousands of times before. It was his hope that he would be able to get home before night took over, but that seemed like an unattainable goal.

Giovanni was forced to make several stops to catch his breath. His modest clothing allowed the warm summer breeze to caress his skin, but it did not feel the same as it used to. As the plague slowly claimed him, it began to affect his ability to feel anything. His senses had become indifferent to the world around him. Things he used to take for granted now seemed out of reach.

Giovanni's home quickly came into view from the road as he walked. The lamps he had left lit from earlier were still burning. They provided enough illumination for him to see out to the pier. His father's ship was tied up at the very end, awaiting his next voyage. It swayed back and forth peacefully as the waves passed over its hull.

The cottage where Giovanni lived was a fair sized home for a fisherman's family. The entire house was built out of stone on the outside with a wooden roof. Inside, it was divided into three rooms which included one master bed room, a kitchen/living room, and a makeshift bunk room where Giovanni once slept as a child. This room was also used as a storage room.

The fireplace in the kitchen heated the entire house, allowing him to stay warm even on the coldest winter nights. The walls were built in a way that would allow the heat to flow through the rooms. The floors were all wood planks that were beginning to wear from constant use.

Giovanni entered the cottage and slowly closed the door behind him. At last he was alone and could release his clenched insides. As the muscles keeping his lungs tight released, he began to cough uncontrollably.

It got worse as the moments passed and Giovanni found himself unable to remain standing. He dropped to one knee and pressed his hand against the wall to prevent his body from falling all the way to the floor. The coughing got so bad that his vision became blurred and he was unable to move. If this continued much longer, he knew that he would inevitably lose consciousness.

Giovanni forced air into his lungs over and over until the coughing finally subsided. He looked at his right hand, which he had covered his mouth with. The palm was stained crimson with blood. This was no surprise to the young man as the same thing had been happening for weeks since he discovered that he was infected.

Giovanni looked at the gold crucifix hanging on the wall which was the one item of value in the entire house. With tears in his eyes, he folded his hands and prayed as he straightened himself out, "Lord, watch over me as a shepherd watches over his flock. Cure me of this plague that sealed the fate of my family and do not forsake me… I beg of you heavenly father… Please give me another chance. Don't let me die this way. In Nomine Patris, Et Fili, Et Spiritus Sancti, amen."

Giovanni received no answer to his plea. He repeated the prayer again, but was left in silence. His lungs would still not accept as much air as they used to. He closed his eyes, embracing that he would receive no answer.

After praying, he lay down on the cot in the corner of his bedroom and fell asleep. Even with the tragic death of his last brother, he still had a big fishing trip that he could not miss tomorrow if he planned on being able to feed himself and try to bring in some money. Fear gripped him as he closed his eyes, alone in his house.

II

The next morning, Giovanni was awakened by the sound of activity outside his door. The fishermen were getting ready for the next trip out to the fishing grounds. Some were tending to worn sails while others worked on their fishing nets.

Seagoing songs and folktales could be heard on the air which set a happy mood as the day began. It was something that Giovanni had grown to love about this small village. As long as the sun was up, there was always something going on in town.

Giovanni got up, cleansed his face in the bowl of water he kept by the door, and made his way to out to begin the day. As he opened the door, wooden carts were passing by with supplies, and entire harbor was ripe with life. Other boats were already leaving the harbor on their own craft.

Giovanni's boat bobbed up and down, tugging at its mooring as though beckoning him to get aboard so that they could begin the fishing trip. He smiled and ran down the pier. He quickly stepped out onto the gangway and jumped onto the deck.

The wood creaked under Giovanni's feet as he went to work. The young fisherman untied the lines and pulled at the rigging. The moment his boat was free, he grabbed a plank that he'd kept on deck and used it to shove off from the dock.

This was difficult for Giovanni as usually there would be two or three people pushing the boat, but after a few good shoves, the boat slowly began to turn away from the pier. He could hear the hull creek as it slowly turned far enough that he could let the sail do the rest of the work.

Giovanni quickly pulled the plank on deck, ran to over to the tiller, and placed a brace on it so that is stayed hard over. He moved to the main mast and brought down the sail. It took him slightly longer as he had to stop every few minutes to catch his breath, but once everything had been attended to, Giovanni sat at the tiller and watched as his boat pulled away from the dock. He rested himself comfortably against the back railing.

Divinity

The sail flapped in the breeze for a moment before catching the wind and stretching around it. The initial tug caused the boat to suddenly jerk forward. It began to pick up speed as it headed out into open water. The wooden mast creaked as it adjusted to the sudden pressure.

On either side of Giovanni's ship, other boats both large and small were also making headway with the favorable wind. Giovanni looked on either side as the other boats made their way to the fishing grounds. Some were smaller rowboats only holding one or two people while others were massive ships with larger crews. Several of these boats were equipped to bring in hundreds of pounds of fish.

To some, Giovanni's boat would have seemed somewhat small, but to him it was a mighty ship of the sea. The ship resembled a small caravel like the ones that Giovanni had seen the Venetian government employ on trade missions. It was about 80 feet long with two masts that were rigged with lateen sails. The forward mast and sail was considerably larger than the aft one, so he only used that sail when he went out fishing.

There were times when Giovanni would have loved to get the boat going faster, but tending to both sails was a job for a small crew and he was only one man. If his brothers were still alive, it might be different, but he would have to make due. The aft deck was about 7 feet above the main deck, giving the ship's helm an unobstructed view of the ocean. It also allowed for the Patrisi boys to build a small cabin underneath the tiller.

After his father died, Giovanni carved a small window in the aft section so he could see outside when resting, but he did not have the money for glass. That meant that he would be colder during the night from the sea breeze, but it was better than the trapped feeling that he experienced when all he had to stare at was four walls.

Off the port bow, a much larger fishing vessel with a crew of no less than five passed. He could hear them singing a folk melody in the distance. He tried to memorize their tune, but the ship pulled away too quickly. He soon gave up on it in order to keep his ship going in the right direction.

Divinity

As Giovanni's boat cleared the two rock formations on either side of the harbor exit, he saw a rather large, lavishly painted ship bearing the Papal Cross. It passed by going in the other direction. *No doubt on its way to the Capital.* He thought to himself as it sailed into the distance.

Such a sight was not uncommon in waters so close to the city. The ship was large with three masts that each had a white lateen sail that were fully stretched in the wind. It was most likely crewed by at least 60 men and was unusually heavily armed for a ship of its size.

Giovanni could see soldiers standing along the deck with smoking fuses held above the cannons, poised and ready to fire at any poor soul who got too close. He knew enough to keep far away from ships like that in order to avoid attention. Most fishermen had seen firsthand what happened to the crews of ships that got too close to a vessel under the protection of the Church. That was considering they survived a barrage of cannon fire. *The bishop must be returning from another visit to Rome... I wonder why.*

Giovanni's stitched cloth lateen flapped in the wind as the small fishing vessel increased speed. Waves crashed over the bow of the boat, seagulls flew overhead and in the water Giovanni could see dolphins swimming alongside his boat as though they were guiding him to the fishing grounds.

This was the only time that Giovanni truly felt alive as his boat glided across the sea. Looking out on the waves, he appeared to be flying through the winds. *The Lord has truly blessed this voyage. Here's hoping that it's a good one.*

Giovanni tied a brace to the tiller in order to keep his course. Once the helm was secure, he stood and walked to the side. Spreading his arms and leaning over the railing, he felt the spray of the waves hitting him in the face. His clothes were getting soaked, but he could barely feel it. Regardless of that fact, he was thankful for what he could still experience.

Giovanni did not want to give this life up and die, there had to be another way. He intended to do whatever it took to fight the plague and live for as long as possible. He did not want to be a victim like his brother had been. It was unacceptable. He was the last of his family and he was not going to die lying in bed from illness.

After a few hours of sailing, Giovanni finally reached his father's fishing ground. He knew exactly where he was judging by the position of Venice on the horizon and the position of the sun in the sky. His father had taught him how to navigate there so that he would always be able to find that exact spot.

Giovanni dropped the anchor and began to chum the water with sliced fish entrails. The odor from the fish was rank as he threw it into the water. When he was younger, the smell came close to making him vomit, but after years of fishing, he had gotten used to it and barely noticed.

Once his buckets were empty, Giovanni lowered nets into the water to soak. He waited and watched as the nets began to jolt and tug at the ropes as they submerged and caught the current. There was a low creaking noise as the roped tightened and gently pulled against the hull.

When his net was fully released, Giovanni performed the sign of the cross in hopes that the lord would grant him a bountiful catch that day. Fishing had not been as good as it had been recently. Still, he held out hope that today would be different.

A short time passed before Giovanni brought the first net up. As he pulled on the rope and the net came into view, he could see that it was nowhere near full. Having only a few fish to put into his hold, he was able to get his catch stored away quickly. He packed them in salt and moved on to the next net, hoping for a better haul.

Net after net came to the surface and each was barely worth the bait he had used. He had to stop between nets as the plague reared its ugly head, making him cough, but he still managed to keep a steady pace. The last three nets did have a decent amount of fish, but he had yet to haul in a full one.

Perhaps that is for the best. Giovanni thought to himself, *I don't know that I have the strength for a full one anymore.*

The catch that day was not what he had hoped it would be, but he was satisfied that he would have enough to feed

Divinity

himself as well as bring in at least some profit. At the very least, he was doing better than breaking even on supplies and bait. As long as his family was able to feed themselves, they were always satisfied with their catch.

As the hours passed and night began to fall, Giovanni decided that it was time to stop working. He lit the old lamps on the bow and stern of the ship, and then lit the fire pit in front of the cabin door in order to keep warm. The small ship lit up as the fire pit took over while the sun went to sleep. Other ships on the horizon did the same to avoid collisions in the night.

Once the sun finally disappeared in a beautiful hue of purple and red, darkness took its place. He watched as the colors of the heavens faded to black and the lights of the city, as well as other ships on took over brightening the sky. All around him, small stars both from the sky and on the water illuminated his surroundings. In another time, he would have stopped to admire this, but the plague had worn him out.

Giovanni promised himself he would sail back in the morning to beat the other fishermen to the market. For now though, he relaxed on the deck of his ship and stared at Venice in the distance. Even at this late hour, the city still appeared alive with bright lights on the horizon and people were still finding things to do.

Giovanni remembered how he used to go to the festivals of light with his family when they were young. He could still taste the treats from the stands and see the beautiful colors that people wore as they danced in the streets when an occasional wedding would pass by. His thoughts finally helped him drift off to sleep on deck as the calm sea rocked him back and forth.

**

Giovanni would only get a few hours of sleep that night. When the sun began to rise, a loud boom broke through the clouds. It was followed by a loud splash indicating that something massive had hit the water nearby.

Giovanni was jolted awake by these noises and scanned the horizon for their source. *What was that, it sounded like a cannon!*

Divinity

He ran from port to starboard, carefully examining both sides. *It can't be corsairs... I would have seen them by now.*

He continued to search for the source of the loud boom. His eyes scanned the horizon for several minutes, but the only thing worthy of notation was a rather large wave that slightly rocked his boat as it struck the side. Normally a wave like that would only have been caused by the wake of a larger ship, but there was nothing that large in the vicinity.

Giovanni began to wonder if perhaps his mind had played tricks on him while he was asleep. He dismissed the mystery and decided to get an early start back to port. *Perhaps it was just a random boom of thunder and nothing more. It does happen now and then, I suppose.*

Once his nets were secured and the ship was ready, Giovanni pulled down the sail and raised the anchor. It took him an hour or so to get everything secured, but eventually his ship began moving through the waters back to town. The large lateen sail caught the wind, causing the ship to jerk forward.

As the ship quickly picked up speed, Giovanni was almost knocked over by the sudden jolt forward. He quickly regained his balance and braced the tiller so he could watch the city grow larger in the distance. He was then reminded of a song his father had taught him some years ago,

"Sing loud,
Let your soul run free,
Horizons calling,
Adventure lies ahead,
Danger in the distance,
It won't touch you,
Don't be afraid,
Release the fear in your eyes,
It will pass you by,
And all will be all right,

--

How could it be,
That our time has come,
As the winds change their course,
On invisible wings,

Divinity

My sails will fly
To take you away…"

Giovanni continued to hum the tune over and over again as the sun came up. The family fishing boat continued to draw closer to the harbor as Venice appeared in the distance. His ship soon slipped past the outer marker as he brought the boat around so that it would have a straight line to sail back to his dock.

As Giovanni's ship neared the old wooden pier, the sun went behind a patch of trees and something caught his eye in the distance. Out in the middle of the harbor was a small rock formation that stood out as a point of reference for the fishermen. It was a small protrusion that he had seen many times before during his previous fishing trips, but something about it was different today.

At first it looked like a large group of seagulls were huddling around something. The he realized that it was one solid mass. He could not tell for sure, but it looked like someone wearing white was draped over one of the larger rocks. *What could it be, perhaps a shipwrecked fisherman or some poor fool who got pulled out by the tide?* Either way, it was clearly someone in need of help.

Giovanni pulled on the tiller and brought his ship in as close as possible to the rocks. There was no way to get the boat close enough for him to safely swim to the rocks, but he got as close as he could. Looking at the formation, he could plainly see that if a single wave picked up, he could be smashed into the rocks and badly injured. He knew that he'd have to use the small emergency raft that he kept on deck to rescue whoever it was. Rocks like that could spell doom for the hull of a wooden ship and he didn't want to join this person on the rocks.

The young fisherman quickly threw the anchor over the side before turning to the rigging. He pulled on a rope that was attached to the sail, causing it to roll up tightly against the yardarm. He pulled hard until the sail was tight and could not come undone on its own.

As soon as Giovanni was convinced that his ship was safe, he quickly tossed the raft over the side. He then climbed over the railing and down to the waterline. The raft was small and not the most stable craft, but it would stay afloat better than Giovanni would on his own. He quickly grabbed the paddle that was tied to the raft and made his way over to the rock formation.

The tide caused the waves to crash hard against the rocks. Giovanni carefully paddled his raft around the first stone. He continued toward one of the larger rocks that he would be able to step on.

Once he was close, he called out to the figure on the rock, "Ahoy there… are you alright?"

No reply came and the figure was not moving. Whoever it was, they were either unconscious or dead. Giovanni performed the sign of the cross as he paddled as close as he could to the rocks and brought the raft right up against the formation. He then dropped the paddle and looked at the stranger lying in front of him.

Blood stained blonde hair blocked its face. Giovanni gently placed his hand on its forehead and pushed the hair back. A beautiful female face was revealed underneath. Giovanni's eyes narrowed as he inspected the woman lying unconscious on the rock. Her face was bruised, she had cuts and scrapes from head to toe and there was blood dripping from her nose and eyes. Her clothes were tattered and looked like they had been burned.

Giovanni's eyes narrowed as he looked her over. Even in her condition, there was an unmistakable look of peace on her face as she slept. Her hand was gently pressed against the rock almost as though she were touching a fragile piece of glass.

After seeing her injuries, Giovanni was certain she was dead. She would need a proper burial at the church in town, so he quickly grabbed her wrist and tried to raise her arm to pull her onto the raft. An odd sensation entered his left hand in the form of a pulse. His eyes lit up and he quickly looked at her chest. Her lungs were expanding and depressing at a steady rate, and she was somehow still breathing. *She's still alive,* he thought to himself. *I've got to help this poor soul!*

Her face was covered in blood and to Giovanni's horror, most of it seemed to be coming from her eyes. He quickly tore a piece of his shirt, wet it, and dabbed the blood from her face. His work was in vain as more blood dripped from her eyes to replace it. He dipped the rag back into the water to clean it. He then wrapped it around her head over her eyes in an attempt to stop the more serious bleeding.

Once her eyes were covered, Giovanni pulled the bandage tight and tied the ends together on the back of her head as he spoke to her, "You poor thing, what happened to you?"

Giovanni carefully began pulling her on to the raft so that he could get them back to the ship. He slowly tugged at her left arm and reached his right arm around her back. When he rested his hand on her back, he noticed something unusual. It almost felt like there were feathers attached to her. He moved to his knees to figure out what it was, expecting to see a dead gull of some kind behind her.

As Giovanni pushed against the unconscious woman, she rolled slightly on to her stomach, which revealed a pair of soaked wings folded behind her. Giovanni's eyes widened when he realized what he was looking at. His legs gave out from underneath him and he fell back on the raft, "Bless my soul... an angel, a real angel in the flesh. This... can't be..."

She was more beautiful than anyone Giovanni had ever seen before. Her straight blond hair came halfway down her neck, but did not touch her shoulders. On the right side, it had been brushed back behind her ear while on the left side her bangs touched the bottom of her cheek. Her skin was only slightly tanned in color, but was flawless where she wasn't injured. She had a slightly rounded face that even in distress had a peaceful aura.

Giovanni noticed that she wore no shoes, but her feet looked like they had never touched the ground. She had no calluses and the skin was soft. Her beige maid's dress was completely soaked and ripped beyond recognition. It still covered what it needed to, but even the most skilled tailor could not make it presentable.

Though the injuries on her body looked like they could heal up okay, Giovanni could not say the same about her wings. They were definitely in much worse shape. Some of

Divinity

her longer feathers were missing while others looked like they had been set on fire. Those that were still intact were drenched in blood and stained a crimson red.

Giovanni placed his hand on her back and hooked his other arm under her legs. He gently picked her up and tried his best to support her wings while he set her down on the raft. There was barely enough space, forcing Giovanni to stand over her as he rested her head on the wood. He balanced himself by laying her across the middle of the raft.

Once she was safely onboard, Giovanni rowed back to his ship as fast as he could. It took him some time to get her and the raft on board by himself, but he struggled through it as best he could. His arms ached as he quickly rested her head on deck before yanking up the anchor.

Not knowing how stable this angel was, Giovanni worked frantically to bring the sail down. He then ran to the tiller and quickly jerked it to the side to bring the ship around so that it was heading to his pier. *Come on, come on...* Giovanni thought to himself as the ship slowly came around.

**

Another twenty minutes went by as Giovanni brought his ship into dock at his pier. The moment the boat was secured, he covered the angel over with some of the spare sail cloth, and quickly brought her to his house. He moved carefully so that he did not rouse suspicion or do anything to further injure the angel's wings.

After looking around to make sure that no one had seen what he was doing, Giovanni carried her inside and barred the door. He then looked out the window as his eyes darted back and forth. There was no one, the area was completely deserted. It looked like he was in the clear.

Safe from watchful eyes of his neighbors, Giovanni quickly laid the angel on his cot. He made her as comfortable as possible before lighting the fireplace and hanging a small kettle full of water over it.

As Giovanni went to work tending to her wounds, he was relieved to see that a lot of the blood on her arms and legs was mostly from wounds that were already beginning to close. He grabbed the hot pot off of the fireplace and rested it on the floor next to the angel.

Giovanni wasn't a healer, but he had been taught how to treat injuries, both minor and serious, by his father. This was crucial learning as fishermen were prone to getting injuries when they couldn't get to the nearest healer. He thought back to his father's teachings as he carefully tended to her wounds.

Giovanni grabbed a clean cloth that he'd left on his table and dipped it into the warm water. Knowing that if he was not careful, her wounds could be reopened, he gently dabbed them. Even though most of the injuries were starting to heal, it was a miracle that she had survived long enough for her body to repair itself.

The real worry however, was the damage to her wings. Giovanni couldn't do much for the feathers that were falling out, but he tried to wrap the large wound on her right wing. It looked like the skin had been torn open under the feathers.

Rips and cuts healed differently and torn flesh might not heal at all, but Giovanni managed to wrap it up enough to prevent any more blood from escaping. He worked as gently as he could to part the feathers and tie the wounds closed with whatever cloth he could find.

Even with Giovanni's help, he didn't know if she would survive. He wasn't a healer, though as a fisherman he had dressed his fair share of injuries. Still, in all his years, he'd never dressed a wing. He did everything he could to keep it safe in hopes that it would heal on its own. Looking at the injury, he wondered if she would ever fly again, assuming that she even survived.

Once Giovanni had the more serious injuries dressed, he wanted to see how bad the damaged to her eyes were. Given how much they were bleeding, he needed to recheck them. Gently, he unwrapped the bandage that covered her eyes and cleaned off the dried blood. He then pinched her eyelid, and raised it in order to see what he was dealing with.

Her eyelid parted to reveal a black and crimson oval where there should have been a white one. Clearly her eyes would need a lot more time to heal. *She must have hit the water head first.* He thought to himself.

Giovanni quickly rewrapped her eyes with a clean cloth and then turned his attention to what she was wearing. He didn't like the idea of undressing her without her permission, but in her weakened condition, she could catch her death if she remained in that soaked dress. He slowly went to work, doing the best he could to pull it away without being indecent. *Gentle Giovanni, be careful...*

Using care, Giovanni covered her over with a warm blanket and slid her dress off over her head. After hanging the stained, raggedy, dress over his fireplace to dry off, he went through an old trunk, looking for something for her to wear. *I've got to have something here that would suit her.*

A few minutes of digging revealed one of his mother's old gowns. Giovanni stopped for a moment and tried to think of her, but after all these years, he could barely even remember what she looked like. He started to wonder how quickly he would be forgotten when the plague finally claimed him.

When Giovanni snapped out of his depressing thoughts, he took the gown and cut two slits in the back with his knife. He was about to try to put it on her, but he realized that there was pretty much no way to get her into it without being indecent. Such things were completely unacceptable, so he left the blanket where it was for now.

Seeing her resting comfortably now, Giovanni sat back on the floor and sighed. *Your father would be proud of you.* He thought to himself. *After he took a belt to you and demanded an explanation as to why a girl was in your bed, that is.*

Giovanni chuckled at the thought, convinced that he had done all he could. He quickly got up and sat in one of the chairs at the nearby table and began to think. What was he going to do now? He had done all he could to heal her, but what happened when she woke up?

She was clearly an angel, but Giovanni had been taught that they were immortal and thus could not be hurt. *Strange,* he thought. *Could the Church have been so wrong about such things? Perhaps in the end they really did not know*. However, the Church had been correct about one thing; the beauty of angels. At least this one verified their story. Even battered and bruised in ways no one should ever have to experience, her beauty showed through.

Giovanni quickly shook the sinful thoughts from his mind and decided that he needed answers before he helped her any further. *Get your head on straight Giovanni, this is serious. Either she's an angel or a demon; you have to find out before she wakes up. Go get Padre Antonelli, he will know for certain.*

Giovanni frowned as he looked at the door to his house and back at the angel. He couldn't decide if it was really a good idea to leave her alone in his home. If she was a demon, what evil could she inflict on the house if she woke up?

Then Giovanni stopped in his thoughts. *She could desecrate my home even if I'm here. Either way, I'm going to need to know what I'm up against.*

After making up his mind to go speak to his pastor, Giovanni made sure that the angel was as comfortable as possible. He replaced her pillow and placed another blanket over her before setting out. He locked the door behind him, determined to make sure that the creature could not escape and no one could get in. He then checked the windows and the back door, making sure that everything was locked up tight. Confident that the house was as secure as Giovanni could make it, he turned and made his way out the front door.

III

Giovanni paced himself as he made his way to the church, knowing that he had to keep his illness concealed. He wasn't able to run as fast as he wanted to, but he kept a steady pace. As the old steeple came into view, he stopped running and walked slowly towards the building while trying to catch his breath.

The doors to the church were shut, but Giovanni could see a light on inside. Instead of just barging in, he knocked politely on the old wooden door. The sound echoed as he waited for a reply.

Inside, Padre Antonelli was in the middle of his noon prayer when he heard the knocking. His eyes opened and he looked over at the door. *Now who could that be?* He thought to himself.

Antonelli pulled himself up off of his knees, signed the cross, and walked to the back of the church. Questions raced through the old pastor's mind as he wondered who would be bothering him at this point in the day. He reached for the handle and slowly pulled the door open.

As light began to pour through the growing crack between the door and the hinge, Giovanni appeared, standing in front of the old priest with an eager look on his face, "Giovanni, why are you here? There are no services today, if memory serves. What brings you to my doorstep this afternoon?"

Giovanni had an eager look on his face as he spoke, "Questions Padre, I have read more into the good book and I am in need of answers. Do you have time? They really can't wait."

The old priest sighed, "Always more questions. Well, very well then, come in and let us see if we can give light to the darkness within your mind."

Padre Antonelli guided Giovanni inside and sat him down in one of the front pews of the church. These seats were solid wood and were well polished and smooth. Antonelli sat next to him as he looked around.

Throughout the church, Giovanni could see statues of the Blessed Mother, the Holy Son, and the Father himself.

Divinity

He also saw several murals of angels along the walls which intrigued him the most. One mural in particular caught his eye. It depicted an angel guiding those lost at sea to the afterlife. Much to his amazement, that angel looked strikingly similar to the one resting in his home. It was a bit of a shock, but he maintained his composure.

The priest breathed in deeply, "Okay Giovanni, what knowledge can I provide to you this day?"

Giovanni opened his mouth about to tell Padre Antonelli the entire heroic tale about how he found an angel out in the harbor, but then he paused. Should he tell his friend everything? What would the priest think if he did?

Giovanni's father had told him many terrible stories about what happened to people who crossed the Church's path and it gave him pause. What would the Church do with news of the existence of an angel? Would they help him care for her or would they jump to conclusions and try to harm her? The young fisherman just wasn't sure.

Perhaps it might be best to keep that quiet for now. Giovanni thought to himself. *I trust the Padre... but this is an unusual situation, who knows, he could order me to undergo an exorcism or something like that. I think I'll wait for now.*

Padre Antonelli could see that Giovanni was in deep thought. He was about to ask the young fisherman what was on his mind, but Giovanni finally decided to speak, "Padre... are angels immortal? Is it not impossible to harm or kill one of them?"

The priest thought for a moment before responding, "Well, we have heard stories of a saint who dared to challenge an angel and lived to tell the tale. So I suppose it is possible. That being said, all we know about angels is that they are beings of perpetual innocence and beauty. They are perfect in every way, immortal, wise, omnipotent, and they live as servants to God himself."

"Perfect..." Giovanni let slip as he looked at the mural.

"What was that?" Padre Antonelli asked suspiciously.

Giovanni brought himself out of the thought and replied casually, "Nothing Padre, so what would be your

Divinity

assessment if someone were to find one, injured and near death?"

The old priest's brow ruffled for a moment. This was an unusual question from his young friend. Normally, his questions were limited to questions about inconsistencies in his faith. This was an entirely different subject matter altogether.

Antonelli thought carefully for a minute before responding, "Well admittedly our information on angels is somewhat limited, but the best advice I could offer someone in that position would be to stay away from it or kill it quickly."

Giovanni's eyes widened, "Why Padre?"

This line of questioning gave Padre Antonelli pause. Random questions were always the norm when he spoke to Giovanni, but where did this sudden interest in angels come from? He watched Giovanni's reactions carefully as he replied, "It is my understanding that if an angel were found that way, it would most likely be a fallen angel... a demon who was removed from God's grace, usually for treason or satanic acts."

Giovanni's face remained blank as Antonelli continued speaking, "An abomination like that should be killed immediately before it can run amuck. No good would ever come from keeping it alive. It is an unclean spirit, a demon, and nothing more. It will only cause pain and torment."

Giovanni looked at the priest in shock, "A demon... really?"

"Yes," he replied, "demons are, after all, nothing more than fallen angels that have either disobeyed God's decree. Or they were cast out for abuse of some of their power."

This sent chills down Giovanni's spine. "So she's evil then... but she looks so innocent."

"She?" The priest asked in a surprised tone, "My boy... is there something you need to tell me?"

Giovanni once again snapped out of it and looked at Antonelli, "Sorry Padre, no there is nothing. I was just thinking to myself about something."

Padre Antonelli looked into Giovanni's eyes, "Are you sure, my boy? I cannot help you if you are not honest with me."

Giovanni nodded with a reassuring look on his face, "I am quite sure, Padre. I was just thinking out loud. I do that a lot lately."

Padre Antonelli feigned a smile, even though he wasn't truly convinced of Giovanni's truthfulness, "You should have joined one of the holy orders. Such an inquisitive mind would have benefitted the Church and been welcomed."

Giovanni bowed, "You honor me Padre. Again, I thank you for your time."

The hair on the back of Giovanni's neck stand up as Antonelli stared at him. The young fisherman felt extremely uncomfortable as he bid farewell to his old mentor. He wanted to get out of the church as quickly as he could.

Antonelli continued to eye him with a suspicious expression, "A pleasure as always, Master Patrisi."

Wanting to get out of there, Giovanni quickly stood and walked out the door. He was quite shaken by what the priest had told him and his thoughts were divided on what he should do next. There was apparently a demonic presence in his home, though he had a hard time believing that she could be evil.

Giovanni knew that he needed to get back before the angel woke up, so he began to run as fast as he could. *Could it be true? She looked so innocent and beautiful. I must admit that for once, I am having a hard time believing what Padre Antonelli said. What am I supposed to do?*

IV

Giovanni burst through the front door of his house wheezing and spitting up blood. He had not given his body a chance to get enough air into his lungs and now he was paying the price. Blood trickled from his lip as he quickly looked around.

There was a time when running that distance would have been easy, but now it was just one more thing that Giovanni had to now bid farewell to. There were so many things that he had taken for granted in his short life. Most of them seemed so unimportant, but now that they were gone, he had to make adjustments to his new limits.

Giovanni took a moment to catch his breath and then tiptoed to his father's chest near the fireplace. The large wooden box contained many of his father's tools for when he would work on the boat. It was an old box that looked like it was ready to splinter as it sat in the corner. He opened it and sifted through everything.

There was an assortment of nails, hammers, and various knives inside. He quickly found the knife that he was looking for. It was a large sheering blade that his father had rarely used and thus was extremely shape. He removed it and stood up, dreading what he knew he had to do. He sucked in as deep a breath as he could with the knife in head.

Giovanni's feet treaded softly toward the next room. The floor softly creaked under him as his feet slowly and quietly made their way across the kitchen. With each step, he prayed that he had not awoken the demon. He slowly reached for the handle to the bedroom door with a shaking hand.

Fear filled Giovanni's heart, causing him to stop as the door creaked open slightly. He pressed his head against it to listen for any movement or any evidence of stirring. When no signs of life became apparent to the young fisherman's senses, his hands carefully pushed the door further open until it was enough for him to squeeze through.

The angel was still lying unconscious on Giovanni's bed, not moving at all as it slept. Giovanni tiptoed over to her bedside and raised the knife over her. There was no way to control his apprehension, but he knew that this might be his only chance to rid the world of this corruption.

For a moment, he stood ready to deliver the killing blow with the words of Padre Antonelli passing through his mind, but something inside of him stopped the knife from coming down. It was as though an unseen hand, perhaps from his own conscience, prevented him from lowering the blade. He found himself unable to kill her.

Giovanni watched the angel for a moment as her body quivered lightly. She began to stir as her face turned in Giovanni's direction. It was as though she were looking right at him. Giovanni's heart froze in his chest as a look of terror instantly came over the angel's features.

Giovanni's hand began to shake as the muscles in his arm tensed. Seeing the look on her face caused his heart to ache. He could feel his hand begin to sweat, which made holding the blade far more difficult. *Stay your senses Giovanni... keep it together.*

Giovanni held his breath for what seemed like an eternity. His heart beat rapidly as his lungs trapped the air for as long as they could. It was as though all of his strength came from the air he was holding on to and he was losing his grip.

After a few moments, Giovanni could not hold on anymore. He released his breath, expelling every ounce of the strength that would have brought the knife down. He rubbed his forehead with his right hand. *It's no good, I can't do it...* he thought to himself. *Though I'll be damned for it, I can't just kill her like this... I won't.*

Giovanni turned away, placed the knife on the table by the wall, and sighed as he leaned against it for support. All the tension that had built up inside of him evaporated as the air escaped his lungs. His conscience had won out over his beliefs and he would just have to wait and see if he'd made the right decision.

When Giovanni finally turned back to take another look, he saw the angel sitting up on the cot. Her face was looking down, emotionless. The blanket had fallen in a way that it was mercifully still covering her chest, but if she moved too much, that could change. Startled, he gasped quietly and froze in place. His muscles tensed and held his body perfectly still. The angel was blind, but he had to be careful that she did not hear him.

For a moment, neither one of them moved. Giovanni even quieted his heavy breathing so as not to be detected. He was petrified of what she would do if she discovered that he was in the room with her.

A second later, her body came to life. She turned one way and then another as though she were looking around. In a panic, she put her hands to her face, feeling the blindfold and discovering the damage that had been done to her eyes. She gasped, realizing that she was blind.

The creature quietly whimpered as her hands began to shake. She breathed rapidly and put her hand against the wall, trying to figure out where she was. Feeling the stone behind her, she planted her palm on it for support and reached out her other hand. It was as though she was trying to block an incoming attack.

Giovanni cautiously watched her struggle. The angel was obviously powerless and unable to defend herself. If anyone were to attack her at that point, she would not survive. Realizing that terrible fact, she curled up in a ball, bringing her knees to her face on the back edge of Giovanni's bed. Even more alarming to her was that the only thing covering her nakedness was a single blanket, which she began holding onto tightly. What had gone on while she was unconscious?

The angel gasped when she realized that she was partially exposed. She grabbed each side of the blanket, wrapped herself tightly in it, and then pulled it up to her shoulders. Her good wing wrapped around her figure for further protection as she did her best to hide her body.

Giovanni could clearly see that she was frightened. It caused his heart to ache, but he was still afraid of what he might be dealing with. This could all be an elaborate ruse, perpetuated by a demon that wanted to corrupt his soul. On the other hand, his fear could be forcing him to allow an innocent to suffer needlessly. His mind was extremely conflicted as he weighed his options. He found himself unable to decide as his heart began to race again.

More than anything in the world at that moment, Giovanni wanted to get out of the room. He slid his feet across the floor, quietly trying to back out the doorway he had entered. Chills ran down his spine every time the angel looked in his direction as it reached out.

Unfortunately for Giovanni, he was being so careful not to make a noise that he did not watch his footing. He accidentally nudged the chair next to the table that he had been leaning on. It barely made a noise, but the low scrape was audible enough for the angel to hear it.

The angel's body flinched in reaction to the sound. She turned quickly to face the direction it came from. Unsure what had made the sound, she reached out her right hand with her palm up. Though she was almost certain that she was in danger, she hoped that her hand would find someone kind to take it.

The angel was fluent in most human languages, but she had no idea where she was. She could have tried a hundred languages and still not have been able to communicate. Having no other choice, she decided to speak in the language of the Church. It was risky, but as the Church was everywhere in the known world, it was the best chance she had of being understood. She took a deep breath and cried out in Latin, "*Is someone there?*"

Giovanni didn't realize how heavily he was breathing. It was faint, but when combined with the pounding heart in his chest, the noise was enough for the angel to sense his presence. She was now positive that someone was in the room with her.

The angel's quivering increased and her beautiful voice became more panicked as she called out again in a frightened tone, "*Please, I know you're there, I heard you. Please answer me! There is no need to hide, I mean you no harm... won't you say something? Help me please, I'm scared and in pain.*"

At first, Giovanni didn't know what to do. Should he try to run away or continue trying to help her? The angel's head darted back and forth as she tucked herself even tighter

Divinity

into the corner, but kept her hand outstretched. The continuing silence made her even more afraid, "*I beg of you, don't hurt me... I have nothing of value! I need help... please?*"

Hearing the fear in her voice melted the apprehension in Giovanni's heart. He could no longer stand by and watch her suffer. No longer caring about the consequences of his actions, he carefully moved his chair close to her bedside and placed his hand into her outstretched palm as he sat down.

Giovanni used what little Latin that Padre Antonelli had taught him and attempted to communicate. He spoke in as comforting a tone as he could, "*Try calm down, you aren't in any danger.*"

It wasn't easy and he wasn't sure that she would understand him as he continued, "*I found you in the harbor. I beg your pardon, but I barely speak this language. Do you speak Vèneto?*"

Though Giovanni had been become somewhat proficient in Latin, he was not fluent. He could understand what she was saying, but wasn't sure that she could understand him. Was this demon trying to deceive him or had he been wrong about her? It was a question he was about to have answered.

The angel turned a little more in the direction of the voice and nodded as she wrapped her fingers tightly around his, "Yes, yes I do!"

Relieved that she could communicate, the angel's voice calmed down a little as she spoke Giovanni's language, "Where am I? Why are my eyes bandaged? What happened?"

The angel's Vèneto was almost perfect. She spoke with a golden voice, but a few of her words were slurred by an accent that was unlike anything that Giovanni had ever heard. The slurring only made her voice more attractive to the young fisherman.

Giovanni moved his chair closer to her, having a hard time believing that an angel was so fragile, "Take it easy, you are in my home in Venice. I found you on a rock in the harbor. You were injured and barely breathing. I don't know

Divinity

what happened, but your eyes took the blunt of it. They appear to have been drenched in blood. I am not a healer, so I can't tell you when or if your eyesight will return."

She lowered her head, hiding her face on her bent knees, "Venice... so close to Rome..."

Giovanni shrugged with a half-smile, "Well perhaps for you, I on the other hand would have to walk as I don't have wings."

"At the moment," she said as she flapped her wings weakly, "I am no more capable of flight then you are."

A cool breeze ran over the angel's skin causing goose bumps to appear. Realizing that her skin was exposed, she gasped and again struggled to hide herself in the blanket. She pulled her hand away from Giovanni and pressed it against herself, "Why have you removed my clothes? Please return them to me!"

"Your dress was soaked and ragged." Giovanni replied defensively. "You could have caught your death if I had left it on you. I'm sure I have something else around here that you can wear, but if you insist on having the dress back, I'll give it to you once it's dry."

The angel's face filled with humiliation as she pushed back tighter into the wall. Giovanni sighed and tried to reassure her, "Don't worry; I covered you over with the blanket before I removed the dress. Your honor has been maintained."

Her face turned to a scowl and she shook her head as she remembered the experiences of the evil souls that she had taken away from the world, "I do not believe you! I know how your kind treats female prisoners. The violation your kind subjects them to goes beyond savagery, what did you do to me?"

Giovanni was shocked by the audacity of this angel after what he had done for her. He had never before been accused of anything as despicable as what she was insinuating and he was not about to tolerate it in his own home. His brow furrowed in anger as he spoke, "Listen, I understand that you're frightened and hurt, but I saved your life and brought you into my home to heal! You could have

drowned, froze, or bled to death on those rocks without help. I would think you would be a little more grateful!"

The angel didn't move or even try to respond. Though her expression didn't show it, she was deep in thought, contemplating his words. She didn't want to trust this human, but she couldn't escape the fact that he was right.

Giovanni watched for a moment as it appeared his words didn't even faze her. Finally, he shook his head, "Very well then, you can just sit here alone and rot for all I care."

Realizing that she had gone too far, the scowl vanished from her face and she reached out her hand to Giovanni again, "Wait..."

Giovanni ignored it, got up, and turned to leave the room, "Good luck to you."

"Sir, please!" The angel cried out, swallowing her pride.

The desperation in her voice halted Giovanni in his tracks, "Yes?"

The angel bit her lower lip. She still wasn't convinced that she had falsely accused him, but she had no proof. He had dressed her wounds and kept her comfortable, so perhaps she was wrong. Either way, she wasn't going to survive on her own.

Defeated, the angel spoke to her rescuer in a nervous tone, "I… I… Will you swear to me that you have done nothing indecent? Will you swear it on your own soul?"

Giovanni was about ready to pick her up and throw her out the door onto the dirt road. He had no tolerance for what she'd said, but as he looked at her, his anger subsided. The scars on her arms and legs, and the bandages over her eyes convinced him that she'd been through enough. He was still upset, but he decided to try to be patient with her.

Giovanni sighed as he spoke, "If that is what it takes for you to at least be civil, then yes, I swear it on my soul and that of my deceased family. I have not harmed you in any way."

The angel lowered her head and bit her lip. She was slightly ashamed of her behavior, but was still not willing to fully trust this young man, "Then I have little choice but to take your word at this point."

"Thanks… I guess." Giovanni replied.

He was not pleased with the way that this creature was reacting to him, but he put his feelings aside as best he could, "May I at least know your name?"

The angel paused for a few moments. She didn't want to tell him more then she needed to, but in her heart she knew that if he was being honest, she at least owed him a name. She responded in a slightly annoyed tone as though he were asking her to do something difficult, "If you must. It's Adalyn… may I know yours… kind sir?"

Giovanni smiled at the sarcastic tone of her response as he replied more politely, "Giovanni Patrisi, pleased to meet you."

Adalyn nodded and breathed deeply as she sat back. Giovanni grabbed the robe that he had prepared for her and held it out, "Here, you can wear this until we can find something better for you."

Adalyn touched the robe with her hand. The cloth was very smooth. Whoever made it was very skilled. She wrapped her fingers around it and took it from him, "Thank you."

Giovanni nodded, "My pleasure. Do you need any help getting it on?"

Adalyn's face turned to Giovanni with an angry expression, "Stay away… please! I can do this on my own. Look away!"

Giovanni sighed and turned away, "All right, I'll be in the next room."

The young fisherman walked into the kitchen without another word and closed the door behind himself. He stood quietly on the other side listening to the sound of her struggling with the fabric. The cot Adalyn was sitting on creaked as she worked.

Finally, Giovanni received word from the next room, "Okay, you may come in now."

Giovanni opened the door to see that she had managed to successfully thread her injured wings through the slits in the back. The robe had been pulled tightly around her chest and tied with the sash. He entered the room as she was covering herself over with the blanket. The cotton fabric protected her skin from any further chill caused by the draft. She sat back and sighed as she relaxed with her skin now protected from prying eyes.

Giovanni could see that some of her bandages were stained red with blood that had escaped the healing wounds, "I'll need to change your dressings. I'm going to remove the bandages and put on new ones. I promise to be as gentle as possible, but it may still sting a little."

Adalyn nodded and held still as Giovanni went to work. He removed the wrapping and gently dabbed the blood away with a rag. His hands slowly rubbed over the healing cuts as he worked.

Adalyn clenched her muscles, expecting pain, but to her surprise, it barely hurt at all. She could feel Giovanni's hands on her, but he worked with a level of care that she had never seen in a member of his kind. She found herself being comforted by his gentle care. A deep sigh escaped her lips as he worked.

The moment Adalyn realized that she was getting too comfortable, she tensed herself up again. Giovanni saw the shift in her body's stiffness and smiled. He knew what had happened.

When Giovanni was done cleaning away the blood, he dressed her wounds with clean bandages. Adalyn quivered as he worked, "Why are you doing this, what do you intend to do with me?"

Giovanni shrugged, "Nothing, I'm just trying to tend to your wounds. You were in distress in the harbor and looked like you needed help. At the time, it seemed like the right thing to do."

"And what do you want in exchange for this care?" Adalyn asked.

Giovanni sighed, "Have I done something to make you believe that I expect payment or that my intentions are to hurt you? Has it ever crossed your mind that maybe I was just trying to help? Maybe I'm trying to play the part of the Good Samaritan?"

Adalyn shook her head, "No it did not."

Divinity

Giovanni could feel his annoyance building again, "Well can you tell me what I've done to make you so suspicious of me?"

"You personally haven't done anything." Adalyn admitted. "However... every experience I have ever had with your kind has been very telling of what you are capable of. You are a violent, primitive species, which seems to be bent on destroying itself."

"I'm not asking what other members of my species have done." Giovanni replied. "As you said, I have personally done nothing wrong, right?"

The angel shook her head, "That I know of."

"Well can't you trust me until I do?" Giovanni asked.

"No," Adalyn replied, "because I do not trust your species. Evil is within your nature."

"All right... well... I am not going to hurt you. I hope you come to realize that." Giovanni said through a sigh. "Either way, I have plenty of space and if you can find it within yourself to stop being so rude, you are welcome to stay here as long as you like. If not, then once you are on the mend, we will go see Padre Antonelli, figure out what to do next, and I will leave you in the care of the Church."

The mention of a priest made Adalyn's heart race. She began trembling, and grabbed his arm, "No, you mustn't let the Church find me! Please hide me! I apologize for being so rude. I will make it up to you in any way I can."

She squeezed his arm tightly with a pleading expression on her face, "You win... I... I will work on trusting you. Please, won't you show me mercy? If the Church learns of me, they will believe that I am an unclean spirit and they will kill me... I know it's a lot to ask, but I'm in real danger here... There is nowhere else for me to turn... I beg of you... please?"

Tears mixed with blood began to fall from under the blindfold on her eyes. Giovanni grabbed a rag and quickly wiped them away. He then took her hand and stroked it gently to calm her down. Her skin was as soft as silk as his fingers traced over her it, "Okay, okay, as you wish. I won't take you to the Church then. Please try to rest easy; there is no need to fear me. I don't wish to see you harmed. I do not

Divinity

know where you got such a negative view of humans, but we are not all the uncivilized, brutal, animals that you clearly believe us to be. Again I promise that I will not hurt you!"

The gentle caress of his hand as he spoke earnestly succeeded in calming her down a little more, causing her breathing to slow down, "Thank you…"

Giovanni smiled triumphantly, "Well… it's nice to see how quickly your attitude changes when you need something."

A shocked expression appeared on Adalyn's face as though she had just been slapped. She yanked her hand away from Giovanni a second time and sat back against the wall sulking. She was more ashamed then angry. She knew that she had been ungrateful and abusive, but she still didn't appreciate his snide comment.

Giovanni smirked as he turned back to the pot sitting on the floor next to him. He picked it up and went to the door to empty the water from it. He then turned to a jug he had in his pantry. He emptied the contents into the pot and put it on the fireplace to heat up.

Adalyn heard the clatter of the metal pot and turned to the direction the sound came from, "What are you doing?"

"Relax." Giovanni replied. "I'll be back in a moment."

As soon as the liquid was warm, Giovanni grabbed a wooden cup and submerged it in the pot. He then pulled the full cup out and brought it over to Adalyn, "Here, drink this."

Adalyn took the cup and held it under her nose. Unable to tell what the scentless liquid was, she turned and faced Giovanni with a suspicious expression, "What is it?"

"Warm milk." Giovanni replied. "It always helped me relax when I was younger."

Adalyn still wasn't sure that she trusted him, but she accepted the drink and slowly sipped it down. As Giovanni pulled his chair back over to the bed and sat down, Adalyn flinched and pushed herself further away. A defensive look came over her.

Giovanni sighed, "Please try to relax. I've already promised you that no harm will come to you in my home."

Divinity

Adalyn nodded and slowly pushed herself away from the wall, "I… believe you. Forgive me sir; I did not expect such kindness from anyone in this world."

Giovanni's eye's narrowed, "Why not?"

"Our experiences," she replied, "angels are the servants of the Most High, but we also passively do work in your world. I have seen how evil your people can be. It's easy to assume the worst when you've experienced what I have."

The blood stained tears had stopped flowing, but now the bandages on her eyes were stained dark red. Giovanni was beginning to worry that her bleeding was not going to stop. He had no idea how to heal eye injuries. All he could do was continue to redress them and hope for the best.

Giovanni spoke calmly as he reached for the bandages, "I'll need to replace the dressing on your eyes."

Adalyn nodded and lowered her head to make it easier for Giovanni to remove them. She was once again comforted by his care. This time, however, she did not tense up and just let him work. She kept her eyes clenched shut as he removed the bandage and replaced them with new ones.

Once he was done, Giovanni sat back, "Okay, hopefully I won't have to change them again. If the damage isn't too bad, the bleeding should stop."

He looked at her oddly as she sat back, "May I ask you a question?"

"I am sure you have many questions." She replied. "Go ahead, I will answer what I can."

He looked at her nervously for a moment, fearing the question he was about to ask, "Are you a demon?"

His question caused the features on her face twisted into a slight look of shock, "A demon?"

"Yes." Giovanni replied softly.

"Do you believe that I am?" She asked nervously.

"I don't know," Giovanni admitted in a low voice. "Padre Antonelli told me that an angel capable of being hurt is a fallen one, and all fallen angels are demons…"

"Well by that standard, I am a demon." She replied, not looking up. "Your people no doubt believe that."

Divinity

Giovanni rolled his eyes, "That's not an answer. I'm not interested in what people believe. I want the truth!"

Adalyn shrugged as she responded, "I may not be able to give it to you. Truth is often a point of view."

A hint of annoyance entered Giovanni's voice as he spoke, "You're dodging the question. I'd appreciate it if you gave me a clear answer."

Adalyn took in a deep breath, "Fine... the reality is that I am a fallen angel, but that certainly does not make me a demon. I have not been twisted by the ways of evil, nor do I reside in the underworld. You must be careful what you believe from the mouths of those who claim to be servants of the Most High. Too often they serve their own purposes first and then the Most High's if it suits them. Their stories are often just that, stories."

As she spoke, Giovanni noticed that her wounds had finally stopped bleeding. He reached behind her to check the dressing on her wing, but she turned and slapped his hand away the moment he touched it. She backed away, wincing in pain.

Giovanni shook his head, "Sorry, I was able to dress most of your injuries, but only time will tell if that one heals properly."

"Please don't do that again." She replied, "I'm suffering enough right now."

Giovanni frowned as he looked over the injuries, "How did all of this happen?"

Adalyn slowly teetered to the side like she was about to fall, "I am very tired... can we talk of this later? I need to rest."

Giovanni nodded, "Um... of course. Try to take it easy for now."

"Thank you." Adalyn replied as she lay down on the cot and immediately went to sleep.

Giovanni turned away and tended to his fireplace. He was unnerved by Adalyn's unwillingness to respond, but he'd give her another chance as soon as she was feeling better. He was convinced that she wasn't a demon, but there was a reason that she had fallen from Heaven and he was determined to figure out what it was before she regained too much of her strength.

V

Giovanni skipped the next day's fishing trip to tend to his guest. He woke up very early in hopes of getting out to and from the market before she woke up. He quickly threw on some trousers and a shirt before quietly heading out the door.

Giovanni quickly ran down the pier to his boat and loaded the fish that had been packed in salt onto a small cart that he used to transport them. The sun had not yet come up over the horizon as he wheeled his catch off of the boat and headed to the market to sell them.

By the time he got everything together and made his way to the market, the sun was already coming up over the horizon. The market vendor saw him coming and smiled, "Giovanni my boy, it's good to see you!"

Giovanni nodded as he brought the fish over to the stand, "And you as well, old friend. How's business?"

"As good as can be expected." The vendor replied. "How are you holding up? I admit I didn't expect to see you so soon."

Giovanni shrugged, "Work doesn't end just because of tragedy. I still need to be able to feed myself."

"True enough." The stand keeper replied. "These are hard enough times as it is."

He looked over the fish Giovanni had to sell and shook his head, "Looks like the fishing hasn't been too kind to you either."

Giovanni looked up, surprised, "The other fisherman haven't been doing well either?"

"Not over the last few weeks." The vendor admitted. "The fishing has been somewhat scarce for everyone."

As he counted the fish, the vendor smiled, "The good news is that I'll be able to give you a better price for your fish as a result."

The market began to get busy with activity as vendors made their way to the stands. Giovanni turned away after collecting his coins, "Good day to you, sir."

The stand keeper nodded, "Good day to you, Giovanni."

A few hours passed as the young fisherman made his way through the market buying food and materials for his ship. His purchases included new netting, food, and cloth for his sails. As the sun continued to rise in the sky, he collected a few more goods before deciding that it was time to head for home.

Giovanni let his body make the decisions for him. He could feel his lungs beginning to give him trouble. He didn't want to break down and start coughing out in view of the public. His family's closest friends had known about the disease, but that was it. If it became public knowledge, he could expect to be carted off to some leper community where he couldn't spread the infection. He knew that he had to be careful.

Giovanni placed the last bits of cloth on the cart and pushed it forward, heading for the outskirts. His eyes looked back and forth at everyone going about their business. He didn't get far before his eyes passed over the tailor's stand.

Giovanni had been a customer there before, but usually only for inexpensive clothing for himself or when his trousers needed mending. He had never thought about going there for more luxurious clothes.

At that moment, Giovanni remembered what the dress Adalyn had been wearing looked like and thought she'd appreciate something new. At the very least, it might make her relax and improve her disposition towards him.

Giovanni didn't have a lot of money left over, but there was enough for two or three dresses from the tailor. He made his way over to the stand. His cart was heavy with all of his supplies, but he was able to quickly pull it over to the side of the road.

The tailor was an older man who worked his craft with the help of his wife. His eyes lit up as Giovanni approached, "Young Master Patrisi, it is so good to see you up and about. Many of the townspeople thought you'd disappear for a few days at least."

The tailor's wife sighed, "Giorgio, the boy is probably trying to get by as best he can. Why not see what he needs instead of reminding him about his bad fortune?"

"Of course, Agnese…" Giorgio replied as he turned his attention back to Giovanni. "So what brings you to my establishment this fine morning? Have you worn out the knees on your trousers again?"

Agnese scoffed under her breath as she worked thread through a pink cloth behind him, "With the way you stitch things, it's a wonder he has anything that's still wearable."

Giorgio turned and glared at his wife, "What was that, old critical shrew that I'm married to?"

She shook her head, "Nothing, just help the boy you dumb lout!"

Giovanni smirked as he replied to Giorgio, "Actually, with respect sir, it's your wife I'm here to see. The stitching on my pants has held up just fine."

Giorgio rolled his eyes as his wife stood up, "Oh dear God, I'll never hear the end of this…"

Agnese pushed past her husband and smiled as she leaned on the stand, "You wish to utilize my services, my boy? Wise choice, but you know I don't work on men's clothing. That's my idiot husband's job."

"No, I know that, madam." Giovanni replied. "I'm in need of a few dresses."

Agnese's eyes lit up, "Well now you're speaking my language."

"But why would you need dresses?" Giorgio asked.

Agnese elbowed her husband in the gut as she looked at him, "Never mind that, you old fool! It's not our business to know who he's getting them for. What matters is that it seems he may not be as alone as we thought."

She winked at Giovanni as she placed her right hand on his shoulder, "Come inside and let's see if we can't find something to suit your lady friend."

Across the street, Father Antonelli was preparing for his daily sermon out amongst the people. He was standing at one of the wine stands, sampling the latest spirits, when he saw Giovanni being led into the dress shop. The old priest's eyes narrowed as he disappeared. *What could this be about?*

Giovanni smiled as Agnese led him into the workshop. Dresses lined the table all around them. They were clearly the work of Agnese. Though Giovanni was too polite to say

it out loud, even he had to admit that Agnese was the better clothes maker.

Agnese beamed as she showed off her work. There was an air of delight in the way she walked as and spoke, "So my boy, tell me about this lady friend of yours, how tall is she?"

Giovanni had to guess as she had yet to stand up next to him, but judging by how little of cot she took up, he guessed that she was up a little past his shoulder. He raised his hand to show her how tall, "She's not very tall, maybe a little lower than my neck."

Agnese nodded, "Tiny thing, isn't she?"

Giovanni's eyes narrowed as they looked at the elderly woman who was less than five feet tall, "Not that small."

Agnese chuckled as she moved on, "What color is her hair?"

"Blonde." Giovanni replied. It comes down to the bottom of her neck.

"Does it?" Agnese asked in an intrigued tone. "I've never met a woman who keeps her hair so short."

Giovanni nodded, "Yeah she's… well she's not really from around here."

"That so?" Agnese asked. "Where is she from then?"

Giovanni didn't like lying, especially not to someone who had been a family friend. In this case, however, it seemed almost inevitable. He struggled to find some way of keeping it to a minimum as he spoke, "Um… well… I'm not completely sure. She's from the far north, I know that."

Agnese turned back and looked at her dresses, "Well that would explain the blonde hair."

She examined the various dresses for a few moments before continuing to question her young friend, "What kind of build would you say she has?"

"She's small." Giovanni replied. "Not really petite, but she does seem somewhat skinny."

"Bust?" Agnese asked.

Giovanni felt a chill trickle down his spine. He didn't want to give the seamstress any indication that he had been gazing at Adalyn's chest. A nervous look came over his face, "Um… well… I don't know… average I guess?"

Divinity

Agnese burst out laughing as Giovanni's face turned bright red, "Oh you poor boy, trying to play the gentleman... okay, let's go with a medium size based on her build."

"Sounds good," replied a relieved Giovanni.

Agnese smiled, "How many dresses?"

"Three." Giovanni said, counting his remaining coins.

"Anything fancy or just every day wear?" Agnese asked.

Giovanni felt like he was being interrogated by the city guards. He had never had to answer so many questions when shopping for himself. How could shopping for a woman be so complicated?

Giovanni was beginning to get irritated. This was taking too long and the girl that the dresses were for wasn't worth the frustration with the way she'd been acting. He sucked down the annoyance and shrugged, "Just normal every day wear."

Agnese turned to her table, "You know, I can't explain it, but I had a feeling someone would be stopping by sooner or later with a request similar to yours."

She sifted through a few dresses until she found what she was looking for, "Ah, here we go, three maiden's dresses."

She picked up each dress, one at a time, and showed them to Giovanni. "The off-white color of these will blend nicely with her blonde hair while fitting her smaller form."

She then held up a third one that was considerably more luxurious looking and green in color, "This one was made out of a fine silk. It might be a nice change of pace from the other two every once in a while."

Giovanni's eyes widened and he shook his head, "I don't think I can afford that one. It looks extremely intricate."

Agnese shook her head, "I'll charge you the same for this as the other two. Your father was good to us over the years. It's the least we can do."

Giovanni nodded hesitantly, "Well... that is very kind of you, are you certain?"

"I am." Agnese replied as she handed him the dress.

Divinity

Giovanni quickly paid for the dresses and headed back out to his cart. Agnese followed closely behind him and stood by her husband's side, "Now you be sure to bring her by here at some point. I'd love to see how she looks in these."

Giovanni nodded, "I'll… do what I can."

"Goodbye Giovanni." Agnese replied.

Giovanni smiled, "Goodbye, and thank you."

Agnese watched as Giovanni grabbed his cart by the handles and began to walk away. She signed the cross as he got smaller in the distance, "Father, look after that child."

Giovanni made his way down the path, pushing the cart in front of him. The cart was heavy with everything that he had purchased that morning, causing a little extra strain on his sickly body. He knew he had to hold on until he was out of sight before he could let it out.

The young fisherman struggled down the dirt road as quickly as he could. The moment that the town disappeared from view, Giovanni knelt down next to his card and began coughing uncontrollably. Just as before, he struggled to force air into his lungs to end the coughing fit. The world went blurry for a few moments as he fought back the plague.

The pain was overwhelming and made Giovanni's throat raw. He couldn't take it anymore; it felt like his chest was going to explode if he didn't regain control on the next cough. *Lord… please help me. Save your loyal servant who places his trust in you.*

One last hard cough escaped Giovanni's lungs, sending blood spraying out all over his hands. He looked down at his shaking palms before wiping them on his trousers and getting back up to continue home.

As he began pushing his cart again, his eyes darted all around, making sure that no one had seen him. Blood slowly dripped from his lip as he looked around. He wiped it away and continued on the path.

Giovanni was relieved to see his house appear around the next bend. His lungs still hurt, but he was able to push the cart up against house and unload everything. He unpacked the fishing supplies and stored them in the shed

Divinity

next to his home before taking the food and dresses into the house.

Unsure what was waiting for him behind the door, Giovanni pushed it open very slowly. As the door moved out of the way, he could see that nothing had been disturbed. Everything was exactly as he had left it. To his relief, that included Adalyn, who appeared to still be asleep.

Giovanni quickly put away everything and then went to check on Adalyn. He set the dresses down on the table and slowly opened the door to the bedroom. The door creaked as he gently pushed it.

Once it was open, Giovanni peaked in to see Adalyn still sleeping on the cot in the next room. He was relieved to see that she hadn't woken up to find herself alone in the house. She had the same look of peace on her face from when he first found her. The bandages weren't bloody, indicating that her wounds had completely closed.

Satisfied that Adalyn was okay, Giovanni went to work on her clothes. He knew that she'd never be able wear them without slits for her wings. He picked up another knife from his kitchen and sat down at the table to go to work. He picked up the green dress first and gently cut a hole in the back on the left shoulder.

Giovanni knew he had to work slowly. If he ripped the dress instead of cutting a fine slit, it would continue to tear and eventually be ruined. He cut the second slit and then moved on to the next dress.

A noise from the next room stopped Giovanni in the middle of cutting the third dress. It sounded like someone was moving. The faint shuffles were then replaced by the same golden voice that he had listened to the day before, "Hello? Giovanni? Are… you still here? Hello?"

Giovanni dropped the knife on the table and went to the bedroom door, "I'm here, how are you feeling?"

Adalyn sat up and stretched her arms and good wing, "I'm… as good as can be expected. I still feel weak, but not as sore."

"Can you eat?" Giovanni asked.

Adalyn nodded, "Yes, I think that might help. My stomach hurts."

Giovanni turned back to the kitchen, "All right, stay put. I'll get breakfast going."

"Thank you." Adalyn replied as Giovanni made his way to the door.

Giovanni paused for a second and smiled, "You're welcome."

He fetched some water in the iron pot and once again hung it over the stove. The moment it was hot enough, he poured the steaming water into a bowl and mixed in some oats and milk to make a kind of porridge. It wasn't much, but it would suffice for now.

As Giovanni worked, he sensed another presence entering the room. He turned quickly to see Adalyn slowly walk in with her hands outstretched. She was trying to find her way to the table to sit down.

Giovanni got up and tried to take her hand, but she jerked it away, "Don't... I'm more than capable of finding my way on my own. I'd prefer it if you didn't touch me."

"Back to hating humans I see." Giovanni replied through an annoyed sigh.

Adalyn shook her head, ignoring Giovanni's remarks as she found the table and chairs. She sat down and leaned towards the fireplace for warmth. A more relaxed look appeared on her face as the warmth caressed her skin.

Giovanni placed a spoon in the bowl and pushed it towards her, "Here you go. It isn't much, but it should help you get better."

Adalyn took the bowl and picked up the spoon, "Thanks... I appreciate it."

Giovanni watched her slowly eat the food down. He still needed questions answered and had been patient, "Listen, about yesterday   you still haven't told me what happened to you."

The question made Adalyn flinch, causing her to drop the spoon in the bowl. She turned to Giovanni in annoyance, "Can it wait until after I finish eating?"

Giovanni sighed and got up to start his work. Adalyn heard him begin to leave and sensed the disappointment in his voice. She quickly changed her mind and spoke, "Fine...

I was expelled from my kingdom for supposedly falsely accusing another angel of treason."

Giovanni stopped in his tracks and turned back to Adalyn, "Angels commit treason?"

"They can…" Adalyn said through clenched teeth as she spoke. "Humans will never know the war that took place long before your kind was ever brought into existence."

Giovanni sat back down as Adalyn told her story, "One angel, Lucifer attempted to overthrow the Most High. He amassed an army of angels that had been bent to his will, blinding them with promises of power. He launched a full scale assault on the Celestial Temple. Our numbers were cut down to only a handful of what we once were."

Her face turned away from Giovanni as she continued the story, "At that point, I was a duty angel, ferrying lost souls from the battlefield to the underworld. I was tapped to join the fight not long after the fall of the Celestial Temple. It was late in the fighting and both sides were at a stalemate. The war had cost both sides greatly and had gone on for longer then you could comprehend…"

Giovanni didn't care for the condescending tone with which she spoke, but he remained silent the story continued, "After timeless fighting, we came up with a plan to capture Lucifer and force him to surrender. I was part of a small force that infiltrated his fortress, only three of us survived to drive Lucifer and his minions into the Nether World. Panic spread throughout his ranks as no one was giving them orders. With their leader gone, the rest of his forces fled. The war was over, but Michael suspected a few angels of conspiracy and ordered us to be on the lookout. I spent years after that splitting my time between guiding damned human souls to their final resting place and working with the choirs."

A sorrowful expression appeared on Adalyn's face, like it was paining her to continued, "Many years later, I uncovered a plot by another angel, but because it involved a very well respected one, I didn't think that I would be taken seriously. So I went straight to the Most High to try to convince him… I could not have made a worse mistake. They removed me and took my immortality away."

Giovanni had a hard time coming to terms with what he was hearing; a war on the Celestial Plain of existence? It was too much to take in for the young man. He wasn't sure he could handle it, but he wanted to hear more, "But you were a hero. Why did they send you here?"

She lowered her head so it was facing the floor, "They sent me here to die…"

"Truly?" Giovanni asked in a shocked tone. "That seems excessive."

"It's not," she responded, "I broke the Most High's decree, the punishment is appropriate. It was believed that I would encounter your people, only to be tortured and murdered. They knew my wings would be impossible to hide and that most people would come to the same conclusion that you originally had."

Giovanni shook his head, "Well you are safe here. No harm will come to you in my home. We'll just need to figure out what to do next."

A look of surprise came over Adalyn's features, "Truly, then you believe me?"

"Yes I do." Giovanni replied.

Adalyn was very confused by the young fisherman. He was trusting, kind, and gentle, unlike the other human souls she had encountered previously. The idea that she may have been wrong about humans concerned her, but she concealed it. She had only known the boy for two days and was unwilling to admit that she had misjudged him.

Giovanni turned back to the dresses as Adalyn struggled to keep her gown closed, "So your dress is dry, but…"

She turned in his direction, "What is it?"

"It's a mess." Giovanni replied. "If you want to wear it, I'll give it to you, but I thought perhaps something a little more comfortable might be in order if you're planning on staying here."

Adalyn sat back and tugged on the gown. She was suspicious of Giovanni's words, "What are you talking about?"

Giovanni turned to the dresses that he had been working on, "I went to the market to sell my catch and buy some supplies this morning. I also bought you some better clothing."

"You actually bought me a dress?" Adalyn asked in a surprised tone.

"Three actually," Giovanni replied, "two white ones and a green one. I know it's hard to remain decent in that gown, so if you want to try one of these out, feel free."

"May I see…?" Adalyn paused as she rethought her words. "May I feel them?"

Giovanni laid each of the dresses in front of Adalyn, allowing her to run her hands over them. When her hands rested on the green one, she stopped, "This one's different. The material is a lot softer."

"It's silk." Giovanni replied. "It's a little more luxurious than the others."

Adalyn stood up from the table. Her hands ran over the green dress as she tried to picture what it looked like. After feeling the neck lining, the sash, and the loose fabric on the arms, she smiled. She had a good idea of what it looked like.

Adalyn wanted to show her appreciation, but tempered it as she replied, "This is… acceptable, but how can I wear it with my wings?"

Giovanni took her hand and guided it to the slit in the back. She quickly pulled away, "Don't, please do not touch me."

Giovanni sighed, getting annoyed with her lack of trust, "Sorry, I was just going to show you that I cut slits in the back for your wings."

Adalyn ran her hands along the back of the dress until she found the openings, "I see… then it should work."

Adalyn stood up and turned to the bedroom to change. Giovanni stood up behind her as her hands guided her out of the kitchen. She struggled to avoid bumping into things as she found her way to the door.

Giovanni watched to make sure that she didn't hurt herself as she left the room, "Do you want some help?"

"I am quite capable of dressing myself!" She snapped back.

Giovanni frowned as he sat back down. *Why am I putting up with this? I've been more than a cordial host to her, but she is starting to try my patience. I know she's been hurt and is frightened but...*

Giovanni had his answer. He couldn't find it in himself to be mad at her, knowing what she'd been through. He'd put up with it for a little while longer and at least give her a chance to come to terms with things.

Adalyn felt the dress again and realized that she was treating the man who had rescued her very poorly. An intense feeling of shame came over her and she turned back to the door, "But thank you for offering... I... am very grateful for your care."

Giovanni looked up at her with a shocked expression on his face, "What did you say?"

She nervously forced a smile, "I'm grateful for everything you've done for me. I can tell that this dress is beautiful... thank you."

Giovanni nodded and returned the smile as it seemed like he was finally starting to get through to her, "You're welcome."

Adalyn nodded and disappeared into the next room to change. She quickly shed the gown and folded her wings behind her back as she lifted the dress over her head. She held her wings in place and let the dress drape down over her body. Her wings slipped through the slits in the back as she spread them and tied the laces to make it fit properly.

There was no way for her to tell how she looked, but the dress was a lot more comfortable than what she was normally used to. As the silk pressed against her skin, her mind filled with questions. *Why is this young man being so nice to me, especially after how I've been treating him? His people are savages. I've seen how bad they can be. What is so special about him?*

At that moment in the kitchen, Giovanni felt his chest seize. His lungs felt like they had collapsed and he started coughing uncontrollably. In an attempt to keep his balance, he leaned forward, but that only made the soreness worse. As the coughing got more painful, it felt like his chest was on fire. He became dizzy and fell to his knees.

Divinity

In the next room, Adalyn heard his intense cough and quickly shoved the door open, "Giovanni, are you okay? What's wrong, what's happening?"

Giovanni could not respond between coughs. He was unable to force enough air into his lungs to ask for help. The disease forced him to just keep coughing until he finally spit up blood. His knees gave out and he lay on the floor in agony for a moment.

Knowing that his guest was worried about him, Giovanni fought as hard as he could to force air back into his body. His chest ached and his lungs fought against him as he tried to suck in air. He closed his eyes and centered himself as much as possible as he worked.

After a few moments, he was successful and the squeeze on his lungs began to subside. His eyes blacked out for a moment, but then came back into focus. Adalyn returned to the kitchen and reached out her arms trying to find him, but couldn't, "Giovanni, say something! Are you okay? What's happening?"

When he finally came to, he picked himself up and sat back in his chair. In a hoarse voice, he began to speak, "I'm sorry, this happens now and then. There isn't much I can do when it starts. I'm okay now…"

"What ails you?" She asked while placing her hands on his forehead and chest.

Adalyn's head cocked to one side as she traced his illness. Giovanni didn't want to scare her, so he kept silent in hopes that she wouldn't be able to figure it out, but after feeling for a few moments, she gasped and pulled her hands away, "The White Plague… you carry a horrible illness!"

Giovanni nodded, "It took my entire family from me within the span of a few years; my father, my brothers… everyone. I've lost everything that I ever cared about, except this house and my ship. Even those now are nothing more than mere relics serving as painful memories of what I used to have."

Though unable to see the look on his face, Adalyn sensed pain in Giovanni's voice, "I don't understand why God would curse me this way. My family has always done

God's will. We have given all we could and treated our fellow man well."

Tears entered his eyes as he continued, "Why would this happen to me? I have always been a God fearing man, so why then am I dying while more wicked people live?"

Adalyn couldn't believe what she was hearing, "A God 'fearing' man? What reason do you have to fear him? To you, he is a loving father who has doted on you, protected you, and given you everything since you were created."

Giovanni shrugged, "Until you appeared in my path, my faith in him was almost irreparably shaken."

She placed a hand on his shoulder, trying to let him know that it was all right, "I can't fault you for that. It seems as though your kind has been given inaccurate teachings about the Most High. Much of what you have been told is mere myth that has been distorted as your stories were passed down by each generation."

She smiled as she sat down in the chair opposite where Giovanni was sitting. Her hand touched his and squeezed, "The Most High mourns for everyone who dies as though they were his own child, but he has nothing to do with things like this. He gave human beings free will. What you do with it is completely up to you. That is a gift that he has never given to my kind."

Giovanni wiped a small tear from his eye, "I see…"

He suddenly began coughing again, but this time Adalyn grabbed him and kept him from collapsing on the ground, "You have been kind to me without any thought of reward. Even after receiving scorn, you've continued to care for me. Let me help you… I don't know if this will even work, but let me try."

Giovanni forced a nod between coughs, wondering what she was going to do. Adalyn opened his shirt, exposing his chest, and kissed him right over his heart. There was a slight spark and an unusual feeling in his lungs as Adalyn pulled back.

At that moment, the coughing stopped. Giovanni could feel his lungs clearing out and he was able to take in a deep breath. Much to his amazement, he felt no pain as his lungs expanded. They filled with air and he was able to breathe in deeply over and over again. He looked down at his arms to see that his skin was also returning to its normal color.

As his body regenerated, he felt as though he was starting to gain more energy. "Wha… what have you done to me? I actually feel like I'm in good health again, like I could go for a run without worrying about shortness of breath!"

Adalyn gasped and braced herself as she sat back. The rush of energy fleeing from her body left her drained. She grabbed the back of the chair for support to prevent herself from collapsing on the floor. The little power she had clung to was now gone and the feeling of mortality was overwhelming.

Adalyn panted slightly as she spoke, "Do not waste that health. That was the last of my power… I healed you."

Giovanni shot up out of his chair without another thought. He left Adalyn sitting in the kitchen, flung the doors open, and ran outside. The moment that the sea air entered his nostrils, he took in a deep breath.

The sweet breeze caressed Giovanni's lungs as it filled them. As Adalyn sat back, trying to regain her strength, she heard him start running. His exhilaration made her smile for a moment before the reality of her situation set back in. The smile returned to a look of sorrow after a mere second.

Giovanni ran down to the dock, out on to the pier, and down to his boat. Upon reaching the end of the pier, he began to jump up and down cheering. There were tears in his eyes as he took another deep breath of sea air and dropped to his knees, "Lord God in Heaven thank you for blessing me with such a savior! My family will survive another generation! I promise that I will live well!"

Giovanni stopped for a moment to catch his breath. He then looked back at the house and realized that he had left his savior alone in the dark. He felt awful about running off so abruptly. His father had taught him better than to be so rude.

Giovanni shook his head as he began to run back to the house. He could feel his legs begin to pulse as he started running. He cursed himself as he moved. *What's wrong with you, you're better than this!*

Anxious to show Adalyn his gratitude, Giovanni charged back through the door. He was still breathing like he hadn't taken a breath in years. His body could once again feel the heat from the fireplace, yet for some reason, he broke out in goose bumps.

In his heart, Giovanni wanted to hug the blessed angel that had just saved him, but her injuries were still fresh and she was barely on the mend. So instead, he placed his left hand on her shoulder and gave it a gentle squeeze. His newfound exhilaration was so potent, Adalyn could feel it.

Giovanni was certain that she would pull away and once again repeat her request that he not touch her, but as his hand caressed her shoulder, she made no move to pull away. He breathed in deeply as he sat down, "From the bottom of my heart, thank you! You've given me back everything that I thought was gone forever."

She smiled faintly and nodded, "I don't know if I was wrong about you or not. Only time will tell, but you have shown me more kindness than I ever expected to receive. If I was wrong about you, then I owed you at least that much. I am happy that I was able to repay your kindness in some way."

VI

As weeks went by, Giovanni spent his time working endlessly to bring Adalyn back to health. At the same time, the young angel was beginning to notice that she was fond of Giovanni's company. At first, she kept her distance from him and didn't want him making any physical contact.

At night, she was unable to sleep and spent hours facing the door to the room where Giovanni slept. She had heard stories from evil souls about rape and the horrible temptation of the human species. She wasn't honestly certain whether or not Giovanni was capable of such things, but it was something that festered in her mind.

Adalyn still did not trust Giovanni. He was a human, corruptible as any other. As a result, on more than one occasion she stayed awake and huddled into a ball on the cot. She fully expected to be attacked, but it never happened.

After days of not getting much sleep, Giovanni noticed that she was having trouble staying awake. He had avoided fishing to stay with her for days, but was running low on food and supplies. No matter what, he had to go out and fish.

That morning, he got his things together and made sure that his ship was ready to go. As he packed his bags, he checked in with Adalyn one last time, "Are you all right? Do you need me to stay?"

Adalyn shook her head. She wanted him to stay, but she was too stubborn to admit it and would not take a strike to her pride by asking, "I don't need, nor did I ask for your help. I can take care of myself."

Giovanni sighed and walked out the door, "Very well. I'll be back before nightfall."

Adalyn nodded, "I'll be here…"

After Giovanni left, Adalyn found herself completely alone. She had nothing to do and was completely exhausted. Much to her shock, she found herself wishing that the young fisherman had not left. He may have been a human, but she had begun to grow comfortable around him.

**

Divinity

Hours passed as Adalyn rested on the cot. She fought her fluttering eyes, refusing to let them lull her off to sleep. She did not want to sleep on the off chance that Giovanni was still nearby. Eventually however, her body put up a fight and forced her to close her eyes and sleep.

After several hours of peace, the sound of wood scraping against the floor caused her to sit up quickly. Her head darted about the room as though she could actually see something through the blindfold. For all she knew, it could be a burglar or a priest that Giovanni had asked to deal with her. Regardless, she called out to see if it was the fisherman, "Giovanni?"

A familiar voice relieved the tension in the air, "I'm here. Sorry it took so long, but I managed to pull in a decent catch this time."

"I'm… glad you're back." Adalyn admitted.

Giovanni was surprised by her words, "Well, I'm glad to be home."

**

That night, Giovanni finished his meal early and stood up from the table as the fire died down, "It's getting late. I need to get to the market tomorrow."

He turned and looked at Adalyn, who was still finishing her food, "I'm afraid that I won't be very good company. I'd best turn in for the night."

Adalyn shrugged, pretending that she didn't care, "Do whatever you need to do."

Giovanni nodded, "All right, well have a good night."

"I'll try." The angel replied as she finished her food and headed for her bedroom.

Adalyn settled down on the cot as she heard the door to the master bedroom close. She sat up facing the door like she did every night. Her body was fatigued and once again fighting to go to sleep.

Trust did not come easily to Adalyn, especially not after everything she had been through. The notion of being able to trust someone from a species so easily driven to do evil was an impossible idea. She was almost certain that she would come to harm if she fell asleep. However there was something about this boy that had taken her in. He wasn't anything like what she had been taught to expect and definitely wasn't what she had come to believe humans were like.

By all accounts, Adalyn should already be dead at the hands of this violent race. Instead she had been cared for, dressed well, and was comfortably safe in the protection of a simple fisherman. Such a thing would have been impossible for her to comprehend beforehand and was hard to accept even as it happened.

Finally, Adalyn's weakened body gave out. She no longer had the strength to stay awake. There was no choice left; she would have to take Giovanni at his word. Before her eyes closed and her body went to sleep, she made herself a promise. If she made it through the night unmolested, she'd make more of an effort to be nicer to the boy who had rescued her.

*

The next morning, Adalyn's body jolted awake at the crack of dawn. This was the time that Giovanni normally got up to go fishing. She was still under the blanket, her body still in the same position it had been when she went to sleep. Her wings did not hurt as badly as they had previously, and the other wounds were almost healed. She still couldn't see, but she had learned to live without her eyes.

Adalyn sat up and folded her wings back. She was both relieved and surprised that nothing had happened to her. Had the stories she'd been told about humans been wrong? Perhaps her limited experiences guiding souls to the underworld had tainted her view of people.

Adalyn stood up and headed into the kitchen. She kept her hands in front of her as she found her way to the door. She'd spent days inside and was desperate for some fresh air. Her hand found the latch to the entrance after moving along the wall for a moment.

A gust of cool air entered the room as the door crept open a few inches. Adalyn sucked down a deep breath, allowing the sweet sea breeze to fill her lungs. The air energized her body and made her feel almost as well as she had before she fell to Earth.

Divinity

The momentary levity was interrupted by the sound of stirring behind her. A surprised voice broke through the silence, "What are you doing?"

Adalyn jumped as her wings spread and she turned in the direction the voice came from, "Giovanni?"

"You shouldn't be at the door." He replied. "Someone could see you."

Adalyn carefully closed the door and nodded, "You're right... I'm sorry, I'll be more mindful of that. I just really needed some fresh air."

Giovanni's eyes narrowed. He'd expected a more belligerent response. She was never this polite and he didn't know what to make of it, "Don't worry about it. Just be careful."

He was about to turn away and start breakfast when he realized how long she had been inside, "Look, if you want to get out that badly, maybe we can go out for a walk at night or something."

Adalyn smiled, "That would be nice."

Okay... what is going on here? Giovanni thought to himself. *She has been abrasive, angry, and holding all of humanity's crimes against me. Why is she suddenly being... civil?*

Adalyn sat down at the table and turned to face Giovanni, "Listen... I want to apologize for my behavior. Since you rescued me, you've been nothing but nice to me and I've repaid you with scorn, accusation, and rudeness."

Giovanni nodded as she continued, "I am truly grateful for everything you've done for me. I'd probably be dead now if it wasn't for you."

Giovanni smiled, "Thanks, I know that wasn't easy for you to say."

"It wasn't." She replied. "I've seen how evil your species can be. The way you are behaving and the way you've treated me, is completely foreign to the experiences I've had."

A frown appeared on her face as she sighed, "I'll be honest... it scares me a little."

Giovanni gently touched her shoulder, "That's understandable."

Divinity

Adalyn didn't react to his touch as she stood in front of the closed door, "No it isn't... You've done nothing to earn my scorn. I shouldn't hold you responsible for the crimes of your people."

Her face turned directly to Giovanni. For a moment, it felt like she was looking directly at him as she spoke, "I know you mean well, but I'm still having a hard time with this. Between healing and learning to trust a human, I'm being asked to do a lot."

"I understand." Giovanni replied.

Adalyn lowered her head, "Be that as it may, I just want you to know... If I am rude to you at any time, it's not because of anything you've done. Please don't take offense. I'll work on it... If you can be patient with an angel that's been stuck in her ways for millions of years, I promise I'll do better."

Giovanni laughed, "I'll do my best."

*

As more weeks slowly passed at Giovanni's cottage, Adalyn's apprehension slowly disappeared and she began to enjoy waiting for Giovanni to come home. She would listen intently to the stories that he would tell about his fishing trips, even if they were uneventful.

Gone were the days when Adalyn would cringe in fear when Giovanni entered the room. The coldness she used to greet him with became affection and feelings that she could not explain. All her life, she had been taught to be weary of these flawed creatures. So what was it about this young man that was different? Why was she drawn to him?

One day, Giovanni came home from fishing to a pleasant odor that filled the house. Something was being cooked in the pot which sat over his fireplace.

Adalyn was standing in the middle of the room when he walked in. He could not believe what he saw, "What is this?" He asked in a surprised tone.

"You've done so much for me," she replied, "I thought I'd do what I could to make your house a little more welcoming when you returned."

He was shocked, "It really wasn't necessary for you to risk hurting yourself to do this, you know."

Divinity

Adalyn nodded, "I know. I did this because I wanted to. I've been looking back on the first few days that we knew each other. I'm ashamed of how I acted. I wanted you to know how sorry I am."

"You've already apologized, many times over. I never blamed you for any of that. You were in pain and scared." Giovanni said in a comforting tone. "What I don't get is how did you do all of this when you can't even see?"

Adalyn's smile widened, "It was not an easy task and I don't know how good of a job I did. I used my hearing, my sense of smell, and feeling to do as much as I could."

"I'm sure you did just fine." Giovanni said contently. "This house has not been this welcoming since my mother tended to it."

Giovanni watched Adalyn put a bucket of water back next to the fireplace. She then walked over and sat back on the bed. Giovanni walked over to the pot, spooned out some of the stew that she had made, and brought her the bowl. She slowly ate it as he took a bowl for himself.

Once Giovanni was finished, he turned to check on her injuries, "I need to look at your eyes."

Adalyn nodded and removed the bandage. Her eyes were still dark red, and though they had long since stopped bleeding, there was no other sign of improvement. It didn't look like the damage could be undone.

Giovanni shook his head, fearing that her sight may never return, "It doesn't look like they're getting any better. They've healed over... but it looked like the damage could be permanent."

Adalyn nodded as she touched her face, "It could have been a lot worse... I'll learn to get by somehow."

As Giovanni reapplied the bandage, he couldn't help but notice Adalyn's shiny blond hair. She had managed to part it so that she could tuck one side behind her right ear, while the other side came down next to her left eye and touched her cheek. *My lord... she is beautiful...*

Somehow Adalyn sensed him staring at her and turned her face toward him with a warm smile, "I have to ask, Giovanni, what is to become of me? I am truly grateful for everything you have done for me, but I can't stay confined here forever. As long as I do, I am putting us both in danger. If anyone discovers me here, you could be placed in mortal danger."

"I know…" Giovanni sighed, "I wish I had all the answers for you, but I don't. We'll figure something out."

VI

As Giovanni became accustomed to having Adalyn living with him, he did everything he could to be proper like his father had taught him. He made the bunk room as comfortable for her as possible, but every now and then he would be awoken by the sound of shrill screaming coming from her room.

Each time, Giovanni would roll out of bed and rush to her room to see her clenching her blanket and crying into it. He spent those nights holding her and attempting to keep her calm. Being stripped of her immortality had taken a much larger toll on her then he had originally known. It was difficult to watch her suffer from mental anguish, but he did everything he could.

Adalyn's night terrors were becoming unbearable and began happening on a nightly basis. One night, as she finally calmed down, Giovanni began to move to go back to his room, but she grabbed his arm, "No! Please don't leave me. I know you are trying to be proper, but this is more than I can bear. I have not been able to sleep in days. I don't know what's causing this, but I can't stand it. Stay with me, please?"

"All right." Giovanni replied hesitantly.

He slowly lay back down on the large cot with her. She curled her wings back and lay on her stomach. Feeling his hand touch hers slowly lulled her off to sleep. He watched closely as her breathing took on a slow but steady pace.

**

Giovanni awoke early the next morning. His eyes felt heavy from being up half the night and his body fought him as he sat up. His back cracked as he stretched and stood up. By no means was he ready to start the day, but he had no choice. This was the height of the fishing season and he needed to haul in a catch.

As he stood up, Adalyn began to stir. She was still shaking from the night before and looked slightly pale. Giovanni watched her carefully for any sign that she might be sick, "Good morning."

Adalyn yawned and stretched out her arms, legs, and wings, "Good morning... what are you up to?"

"I have to get ready to go." Giovanni replied. "There should be some good fishing out there today. I can't pass this up."

Adalyn nodded as her face turned to the window, "I understand."

Giovanni saw the melancholy expression and realized that she'd only been outside for an hour here or there. The last time she'd spent a full day enjoying the outdoors or the warm sun was before he found her. He took her for a walk along the water's edge every few nights to get exercise, but he figured that she must be going stir crazy by now. He couldn't stand the look on her face and decided that it was time to do something about it.

Giovanni never liked the idea of keeping Adalyn cooped up in his home, and thought about what he could do about it. The sun had yet to rise, so the locals wouldn't be out yet. He quickly got his supplies for the day together and set them down at the door.

Adalyn sighed as Giovanni opened the door and stepped out into the cool night air that had not yet given way to morning. He looked down the pier to his boat and then back at Adalyn. He knew she couldn't see anything, but if she was outside, she'd at least be able to take in some fresh air.

Giovanni remembered Adalyn telling him about how she used to love gliding through clouds and about how refreshing it was. He finally made up his mind and turned back to her, "Are you coming?"

The expression on her face turned to shock as her head jolted in his direction, "Me?"

"Do you see anyone else around here?" Giovanni asked.

Adalyn shook her head, "Well no, but how do you intend to get me out without being seen?"

Giovanni smiled, "The sun isn't up yet. If we leave now, no one will see you."

"Are you sure?" Adalyn asked. "You know I can't help you fish. I'll just wind up getting in the way."

Giovanni walked over to her, "I'm sure. If you want to come, you can stay on the bow. I don't fish from there. You won't be in the way. It's a good chance for you to get out and stretch your wings."

The young angel immediately shot to her feet. She wanted to get out of the house for more than an hour and was not about to put up a fight to convince her savior that it was a bad idea. "All right, let's go."

Adalyn folded her wings against her back as best she could. However, she knew how big her wings were. Despite her best efforts, if someone was out and about, they'd be able to tell what she was. With wings that ran the length of her body when folded behind her, hiding them was impossible.

A soft feeling came over Adalyn's skin as she stepped outside. Giovanni had wrapped her in an old cloak to hide her wings. It wasn't perfect and she looked like she had a slight hump, but it would be sufficient to keep away prying eyes.

The two walked down the pier and boarded his ship. Giovanni released the moorings and began pushing against the dock with the guiding beam he'd kept onboard. The boat slowly pushed back, away from the dock. He leaned harder into the plank to get it to turn so that he was facing away from his house. By the time he was done, his face was red and he was breathing heavily.

Adalyn could hear him working and wished she could help, but without her eyes, she knew she'd just get in the way. She frowned as she faced his direction, "What can I do?"

Giovanni shook his head, "Nothing, it's probably best if you just go wait in the cabin until we get out into open waters."

Adalyn nodded and headed for the small cabin. Giovanni gave one more hard push and then brought the plank back onboard. The ship was slowly turning around and all he could do now was wait until he could drop the sail.

The horizon slowly began to turn a dark shade of purple as the sun approached. Giovanni's eyes alternated between it and the dock as his boat came around to the starboard. The moment it had cleared the pier, he pulled on the rigging to bring the sail down and then pushed the tiller so that it was hard to starboard.

The small ship slowly began to move forward as it continued to turn. Giovanni kept his hand on the tiller until the ship was facing the opposite direction, heading out of the harbor. He let out a deep sigh as he ran forward and lit the lamp on the front of the ship.

The moment they cleared the harbor, Giovanni turned his ship so that it was heading for the fishing grounds. As it glided through the waves, he placed the brace on the tiller and walked down to the cabin. He opened the door and called down Adalyn, "Okay, it's safe for you to come out now."

Adalyn immediately came to the door. Her head rose slightly as she smelled the sea air. A wide smile appeared on her face as she took it in, "This is incredible, I feel like I'm soaring through the clouds again."

Giovanni soon found himself guiding her to the starboard side and placing her hand on the walkway railing. The sea was slightly choppy that early morning as the sun came up. Fairly large waves struck the side of the ship as it cut its way through the sea. Giovanni wasn't worried about it though; his boat had been through worse.

A wave came crashing against the hull of the boat causing small drops of water to create mist in the air that caressed Adalyn's face. She breathed in deeply as goose bumps ran up her arms and down her back. She spread her wings, as far as her injuries would let her. They caught the air causing her to levitate a few inches off the ground.

It wasn't the same sensation Adalyn used to get when she would fly through a cloud, but it was similar. As the next spray of water touched her skin, she stretched out her wings a little further, allowing them to be cleansed by the sea. Giovanni saw her being lifted off the ground and watched to make sure the wind didn't carry her away.

As her wings folded and she touched back down, a content look appeared on Adalyn's face. She gently brushed wet strands of golden hair from forehead as she smiled. A deep sigh told Giovanni that he had done the right thing by bringing her along. It had been some time since she had felt so alive. Being out on the ocean had clearly helped raise her spirits.

Adalyn was about to turn around when a larger wave struck the boat. The sea crashed over the deck, drenching the unsuspecting angel. She stood completely still, breathing heavily for a moment in a state of shock before franticly flapping her wings in a futile effort to dry them.

Once the wave had passed, the young angel heard the sound of soft chuckling. Apparently, Giovanni had seen the wave approach the side of his boat and stepped back without saying anything. Adalyn's face turned red and she immediately spun around. Her legs bent as she began to charge at the fisherman, quickly knocking him down. She then dropped to her knees, and playfully beat on his chest, "You horrible little man!"

Giovanni lay back, trying to defend himself when the sound of laughter made him look up at Adalyn. Her soaked clothes were clinging to her body, but she had a wide smile on her face. It almost seemed like she was looking down at him as she smiled. He stared up at her for a few moments without saying a word.

Adalyn sensed him looking at her and bit her lower lip. Her heart raced and her body betrayed her. She thanked her lucky stars that she was shivering and could effectively hide her feelings.

Giovanni could see that they had arrived at the fishing ground and quickly pulled on the rigging to bring his sails down before throwing the anchor overboard. After the anchor sank, he threw the nets over the starboard side to begin catching fish.

At that moment, Giovanni noticed Adalyn's skin going slightly pale. The young fisherman worked quickly knowing that Adalyn would freeze if she didn't get out of her wet dress in someplace warm. The anchor struck the bottom, causing the ship to stop. Now that they were safe, Giovanni could turn his attention back to his guest.

Adalyn felt a pair of warm arms wrap around her and press on her back. Her trembling slowed, but did not

Divinity

completely go away. The cold was replaced by apprehension from being in Giovanni's arms.

This was a new feeling for Adalyn. A feeling of comfort and safety came over her that she had never experienced before. As her head pressed against Giovanni's chest, the sound of his heartbeat almost put her to sleep.

Giovanni quickly helped Adalyn to her feet and guided her back to the cabin. The inside was little more than a cell with a bed, one table and chair. It was Spartan, but more than enough for one fisherman.

Giovanni sat Adalyn down and lit a small flame in the stone fire pit on the side of the cabin. She stretched out her hands as heat filled the room. The chills on her skin were slowly disappearing as waves of heat passed over them.

Giovanni grabbed a dry sheep skin blanket and wrapped the angel in it to keep her warm, "You'd best get out of that dress and hang it up to dry. I need to go fish, but you should stay here until you dry off."

Adalyn nodded and rubbed herself with the blanket, "Just be careful out there. I've guided my fair share of fisherman to the afterlife."

Giovanni looked at her oddly and smiled. She was actually concerned about him. It was nice to see that she was finally warming up to him, "I will, don't worry."

Giovanni turned to leave but was halted by her voice as he reached for the cabin door, "Stop."

He turned back to see Adalyn jump off the bunk and quickly grab him. A surprised Giovanni found himself being hugged tightly. Adalyn rested her head on his chest and listened to his heartbeat.

Giovanni smiled as he gently placed his hands on her back. She relaxed a little more in his arms. He looked down at her with a warm feeling in his heart, "Are you okay?"

Adalyn immediately released him, "Yes… I'm fine."

Adalyn sat back on the bunk, biting her lower lip hard. Giovanni nodded, "I'll be on deck if you need me."

The moment that the door closed and Giovanni was out of sight, Adalyn gasped as though she had been holding her breath for days. She felt as though her body was betraying her in some way. Her lip was almost bleeding from how hard she was biting it.

What is going on with me? Is this a side effect of becoming mortal? She asked herself. *It's like I'm creating a bond with this boy. What does it mean?*

Adalyn's mind raced as she slowly stripped out of the wet dress and hung it over the fire. She quickly wrapped herself in the sheepskin and sat back down. She almost fell asleep from the softness of the blanket.

Out on deck, Giovanni pulled in the day's catch. He stopped for a moment, thinking about everything that had happened over the last few months. His lungs were working again, his strength had returned, and now he was apparently defying God by protecting a fallen angel.

Chills rolled down Giovanni's spine as the words crossed through his mind. He was defying God. He finished pulling the last net in and looked up at the clouds in the sky, "Dear God, please give me some sign that what I am doing is wrong. Your Church teaches compassion for all living things, but what of this creature that rests in my care? Does she not count? Is she exempt because she comes from your kingdom?"

Giovanni received no answer and that only served to frustrate him more, "If you won't answer me, then all I can do is continue behaving the way I was raised. I can only do what I think and feel is correct. You created me to have free will, but you also created me with a conscience and a sense of right and wrong. You gave me as a son to my father and he taught me how to live. Letting this creature die, or submitting her to the Church cannot be the right decision. I don't believe that's what you want. Why wouldn't you just send her to Hell yourself?"

The silence caused Giovanni to give up and get back to work. He rubbed his forehead as his eyes returned to the ocean. He still felt fear for his immortal soul and debated allowing Padre Antonelli to speak with Adalyn, but doing so could have ramifications that he could not live with. There was no way around it; he would have to do this alone.

Giovanni threw three more nets over the side, allowed them to soak, and pulled them back up. This time, his nets

were so full, that his boat was becoming weighed down. What should have been a full day's trip was quickly turning into a half-day's voyage.

Giovanni smiled, "Could this be your sign?"

**

That night, after the most successful fishing trip Giovanni had worked through in years, the young fisherman found himself relaxing after a good meal in his kitchen. The fish was on salt and he would need to deliver them early the next morning, but at the moment he was not worried about it.

Adalyn relaxed at the table, listening to the fishing stories that Giovanni had lived through. She suspected that many of them might have been slightly exaggerated, but she didn't care.

"I'm not kidding! The shark must have been close to the size of my boat!" Giovanni said in a boastful voice.

Adalyn nodded, "There used to be some sharks that got that big, but none that are particularly deadly. Are you sure you didn't see a whale?"

"No way!" He replied adamantly. "This thing had massive teeth. It was a shark."

"Oh okay." Adalyn said through a chuckle.

It was getting late and the fire was dying down. Adalyn was comfortable wrapped in a sheepskin robe that Giovanni had purchased for her. Its warmth was making her sleepy.

Giovanni stood up and stretched, "So it's getting late and I have to get up early tomorrow."

Adalyn nodded, "Then you should probably get to bed."

He turned and headed to the doorway and looked in at his bed. The master bedroom was a decent sized room with accommodations for two people, unlike the cot that Adalyn slept on. Knowing that he'd probably have to help her through another night terror if he let her sleep alone, he sighed and turned back, "Do you want to sleep in here tonight?"

Adalyn's head perked up with a surprised expression, "I beg your pardon?"

Divinity

Giovanni shrugged, "We always seem to wind up in the same bed anyway with how you've been sleeping. Why not just save ourselves a step? This way you might actually sleep through the night and in a bed big enough for you to stretch out a little.

Adalyn's brow furrowed as she thought about it. *Logically, it makes sense... but am I really considering this? It's not proper and it goes against what we are taught as angels.*

Giovanni's mind was in no better shape. He could picture his father scolding him at that very moment. The man would be screaming until he was red in the face. *Sorry dad, I know you'd probably be furious with me, but I am doing what I think is right just like you taught me. I may out of my mind right now, but the lines of right and wrong have been blurred beyond recognition.*

Adalyn didn't know what to do. Giovanni had left the decision up to her and she needed to choose. Finally, her mind gave in, *it's not like the choirs could hate you any more than they already do. This boy has proven himself trustworthy time and time again. You know you're not going to sleep without some comfort, so why not spare this boy from having to get up at night.*

Adalyn bit her lower lip as she replied, "Are you sure you're okay with that? Your bedroom is your personal space. I don't want you to feel as though I'm intruding."

Giovanni shook his head, "You wouldn't be. I offered it to you."

"Then yes." Adalyn said with a nod. "Thank you, this will probably help."

Adalyn followed him into the large bedroom and made herself comfortable under the blankets. Her eyes slowly began to close as Giovanni rested his head on the pillow. He lay on his back, staring at the ceiling while she drifted off to sleep.

Throughout the night, Adalyn shifted from her back to her side. She kept her wings folded, so that Giovanni never got hit. However he still couldn't sleep as he watched her struggle to get comfortable. Finally, she turned on her side facing him and rested her head on his chest.

Divinity

Giovanni's heart was in his throat as her watched her. The content look of peace finally came over her features as she stopped moving. She was now completely relaxed and sleeping soundly.

Giovanni stared up at the ceiling with his eyes wide open. *Oh God, what am I doing?*

VII

As Giovanni finally slipped off to sleep, he found himself in a dark room with blood splattered on the stone walls. When everything came into view more clearly, we could see Adalyn covered in blood and tied to a table, begging for mercy. His breathing rapidly increased as he tried to get to her, but some unseen force blocked his path.

Giovanni did everything he could to break through the unseen barrier, but no matter what he tried, it would not break. After a few moments of trying, Adalyn turned and looked in his direction, "Giovanni..."

The young fisherman could do nothing but watch as she stopped breathing and fell completely still. There was a sudden boom, causing Giovanni to wake up sweating with tears in his eyes. He looked next to him and saw Adalyn's wings flutter a little as she slept.

Giovanni got up and walked out of the house. It was late at night and the lamps were getting dim as they burned down. It was so dark that he could barely see his boat moored a few hundred feet away. The night air calmed him and the breeze dried the sweat covering his skin as he stood perfectly still with no shirt or shoes. Only his brown trousers protected him from the night air.

Adalyn began to rouse when she noticed that Giovanni was gone. Feeling the empty space next to her, she quickly sat up and called out, "Giovanni?"

She didn't receive a reply, telling her that he wasn't in the room. A cool draft coming from the kitchen made her realize that the front door was open. She guessed that he must have been outside for some reason. She stood up, tightened the sheepskin robe, and walked to the door. "Are you okay, Giovanni?" She asked in a worried tone.

She could hear Giovanni breathing so she knew that he was there, but still didn't get a reply. She walked up next to him and rubbed his arm, "What is it, talk to me."

"I'm fine," he said, trying to sound calm, "it was hot inside, I just needed some air."

Divinity

"You're lying," she said accusingly, "I heard you moaning in your sleep. Something is bothering you. Don't push me away, what's wrong?"

He closed his eyes, "I can't shake this feeling that something is on the horizon, something terrible. I'm afraid for your safety."

Adalyn experienced an odd feeling in her chest; her heart was racing and she was short of breath. She placed her right hand over her chest as she bit her lip, trying to breathe normally. *What is this?*

Giovanni noticed her labored breathing and looked at her, "What's wrong?"

"I... I don't know." She replied. "It's something about what you said, about fearing for my safety. It made me feel... happy… I know that sounds weird, but it's almost as though my body reacted to it."

Giovanni's eyes narrowed, "Can you describe it?"

Adalyn nodded, "Yes... it's like I feel warm inside. It's a mix of shock and delight, like nothing I've ever experienced before. I'm not sure what..."

Before she could say another word, another new sensation entered her world. She felt the skin of Giovanni's lips press against hers. Instantly, her lungs ached and wouldn't accept air, her heart raced even faster, and her knees pressed together as hard as they could. What had the loss of her immortality done to her?

Instead of wasting time thinking about it, Adalyn quickly responded by placing her hand on the back of the young fisherman's neck. She forced air into her lungs and closed her eyes, even though they were covered in bandages. Her whole body began to rise as she pressed herself into Giovanni.

When their lips finally parted, Adalyn let the air escape her lungs through her lips that were still puckered. Giovanni smiled as he watched her come to terms with what had just happened. She quivered as her face turned away from Giovanni, "Oh... I see... affection... that's what it is."

Giovanni looked at her oddly, "Angels don't experience love?"

"Not like that." Adalyn replied. "We are encouraged to love. We love one another, we love the Most High, we just love... but it's not like this. Loving affection is something only your kind is allowed to experience. Angels don't have the ability."

"Then how do you?" Giovanni asked.

Adalyn shook her head, "I... I don't know. Turning mortal must have had an effect on my physical being."

Adalyn began biting her lip as she smiled nervously. The feeling of euphoria was almost overwhelming, but it only lasted a moment. Her mind returned to reality, causing her to turn away from Giovanni, "I... I can't do this. It's wrong..."

Giovanni looked at her inquisitively, "What...? I don't understand."

"Come on Giovanni think about it." She said as she sobbed in to his shirt, "I know you care for me... and... I feel it too, but what would come of this? I cannot hide here forever. I fear someday soon I may be found out. My wings will give me away, and when that happens, I will be taken from you."

Giovanni shook his head and grabbed her shoulder so that he could look at her face, "I will never let that happen. If anyone comes to take you, I will stop them somehow. I promise I will not abandon you."

"How can you prevent it?" Adalyn asked.

Giovanni shrugged, "Maybe we could try removing your wings?"

Adalyn backed away with the hair on the back of her neck standing straight up, "No, you can't do that!"

"Why not?" Giovanni asked.

A frightened Adalyn grabbed his hand, "The removal of an angel's wings would strip her of immortality, since I'm already mortal, who knows what it could do!"

Giovanni nodded, "I guess."

"Giovanni, you have no idea how many people I've guided to the afterlife that died during failed amputations!" Adalyn replied.

"I understand." Giovanni said softly. "It was just a suggestion anyway. I didn't like the idea as it was."

He looked at the nervous expression on her face and touched her cheek, "I promise will figure this out somehow."

Adalyn smiled, "I believe you. For the first time since I was exiled, I'm not afraid. I have you to protect me... and somehow that makes me feel like everything will be okay."

"I won't let any harm come to you. You've made my house a wonderful place to live and I care about you too much to see anything happen to you now." Giovanni admitted.

Adalyn rubbed his arm slowly, "I care for you too Giovanni. I thought for sure that I would be dead by now, that I would find nothing but pain and sorrow in this world. Instead I found you. I will always be grateful for everything you have done for me."

The two embraced in a warm hug as they watched the sun creep up slowly over the horizon. Giovanni rubbed Adalyn's back and arms while he held her. She rested her head on his chest and watched the sky turn pink, "Um… you do know that I'm quite a bit older than you, right?"

"How much older?" Giovanni asked, feigning concern.

Adalyn thought for a moment, "About… six billion years older, give or take a millennium."

Giovanni smiled, "Well then I guess it's a good thing that I've always been attracted to older women."

As the sky got lighter, Giovanni could see her face more clearly. He moved his own closer to her, hoping that this time he wouldn't have to surprise her. His heart raced as little by little he closed the space between their lips.

Giovanni was unsure if she could sense his intentions and stopped a mere inch from her. *Should I try it again, or would such an act push her away,* he asked himself.

The question was quickly answered when Adalyn pushed her lips the rest of the way and kissed him. It only lasted a moment, but it sucked the air from Giovanni lungs as he stood completely still in a state of shock. She pulled her face back a little with a smile and hugged him tightly. He held on to her for as long as he could, "This is going to be complicated isn't it?"

Adalyn smiled, "You have no idea…"

BOOK 3

The Darkness to Come

I

Padre Antonelli had become extremely worried about Giovanni. The boy who used to frequent the church on a weekly basis was now nowhere to be found. Night after night, the priest looked out towards outskirts where the fishermen lived, but never saw the boy except when he sold his catch at the market.

Remembering that he had promised the boy's father that he would look after Giovanni, Padre Antonelli began to rethink the past month. Everything that seemed significant passed through his thoughts as he sat in one of the side pews nearest the altar.

Padre Antonelli thought back to the last time that Giovanni had come to him with questions. The boy did seem somewhat excited and unable to wait for answers until the next day. He also seemed somewhat apprehensive about being questioned.

It didn't help matters that Antonelli later saw Giovanni at the market, buying women's clothes. Anyone else, and the old priest might have suspected infidelity, but not from this boy. He knew the Patrisi family too well to believe that Giovanni was capable of such a sin.

Unable to put together exactly what was going on, Antonelli knew that he only had one option; to investigate. It was very early in the morning and the town was mostly still asleep. The old priest was used to getting up that early to prepare for early morning sermons before the fishermen went out, but he had none planned for that morning. *It can't wait. If that boy is in trouble, I have to know.*

The old priest exited the church, slipped on the pair of sandals that he left at the entrance, and made his way to the small Patrisi house. The road was long and dark, so Antonelli grabbed the torch which kept the entrance lit. It wasn't a long walk, but he felt better having something to light his way.

The priest made his way up the dirt path. The entire area was deserted, making the trip that much quicker. All the while Padre Antonelli wondered what he would see when he arrived. Could he be worrying needlessly and Giovanni had simply been busy? It was possible.

Divinity

The old priest breathed heavily as he moved faster. It had been years since he'd held this pace and his legs were out of shape. It didn't help that he was running through dirt and sand instead of a solid road. *Good lord... I haven't gone this fast in years. Of course when I did, I was used to running over a stone path that was smooth.*

The priest could hear the sounds of the ocean in the distance as he neared the fishing residences on the outskirts of town. His mind raced with questions. He began to pray for Giovanni. *God, please let my young friend be safe. I promised his father that I would do everything I could to keep him well. Please let him be safe.*

All of Antonelli's questions were about to be answered when the house came into view. Antonelli rounded the nearest bend and stopped when he saw Giovanni standing out in front of his home, wearing only his trousers. Antonelli quickly put the torch out in the dirt as he watched to see what would happen next under the cover of darkness.

As the sun slowly started to rise out in the harbor, Antonelli quickly ducked behind a nearby bush. That was when he saw her. A woman dressed in a sheepskin gown appeared at the door. She stood next to Giovanni and was partially obstructed by the house.

Who was she and why were her eyes bound? Antonelli had never seen this woman before and she clearly wasn't from the area. Everything about her seemed foreign, and somewhat mystical. The old priest crept out from behind the bush and moved closer to the house to get a better look. He couldn't hear what they were saying, but he could tell that it was of a serious nature given the looks on their faces.

Padre Antonelli almost screamed when the woman stepped away from the house. He could clearly see the damaged wings on her back. He could not believe it. *Dear God boy, you've taken a fallen angel into your care!*

The alarm in the priest's heart increased exponentially when he saw the two of them kiss. He shook his head and realized that this was well beyond anything he had ever encountered before. *This is very bad... Dear God, that demon has the poor boy in her grasp.*

Divinity

The priest began to lay out what needed to be done as he abandoned the bush and quickly made his way back to the Church. *I'm going to need help. I'll need to let the archbishop know. We'll need an exorcist here, and anyone else that the Church can spare. Dear God, don't let me be too late!*

Padre Antonelli found himself running until he reached the town and arrived at the doorstep of his church. He charged inside and sat down at his desk to write a letter. In it, he informed the Bishop and Venetian Patriarch, Antonio Contarini of everything that he had seen and asked for someone better equipped to come and investigate.

Antonelli knew that it would take several days to even get a response, given that the Bishop was currently in Rome, so he would need to get a good rider to take the letter. Once it was finished, he quickly folded it, stamped it with the Church's seal, and made his way into the slowly waking town.

The town messenger, a man by the name of Paoblo, was resting comfortably in his bed. He'd had a long day traveling back and forth from the main city, and was enjoying some much-needed rest. It was something he didn't get very often and it didn't last long when he did.

A sudden pounding at the door forced Paoblo out of his bed. The moment his eyes cleared, he looked outside at the rising sun, "Oh you have got to be jesting..."

The pounding continued as Paoblo threw his shirt on, brushed back his thick brown hair and made his way to the door, "All right, all right, I'm coming! Jesus, you'd think the rapture was..."

Paoblo stopped midsentence when he opened the door and saw an angry Padre Antonelli staring back at him. Paoblo's dark brown eyes widened as he spoke, "Padre I... forgive me. I didn't know it was you."

The priest shook his head, "Five 'Our Fathers' for the use of our lord's name in vein."

Paoblo sighed, "Yes, Padre... now what can I do for you so early on this blessed morning?"

The priest held out the letter, "You can take this to Rome, now!"

Divinity

"Rome," the man exclaimed, "but that's three days hard riding from here! Can't it wait a few days?"

"No it cannot." The priest fired back. "This is official Church business. I expect that you know what it means if you refuse?"

Paoblo straightened up, "Of course Padre. I'll get it there in three days, this I swear on the spirit of my departed mother!"

"See that you do." The priest replied.

Paoblo ran to the stable where he kept his horse. He picked up the saddle and threw it onto the mighty beasts back. The startled horse awoke with a loud cry. Paoblo nodded as he patted it on the neck in an attempt to calm it down, "I know... shh, it's okay. Sorry to wake you, but it looks like we've got urgent business to take care of with the Church. I hope they pay us well for this."

A low moan came from the horse. Paoblo nodded, "Well I agree, but we don't have much choice. We don't dare go against the Church."

After a few minutes of protest, the horse calmed down enough for Paoblo to jump on its back. It groaned as he climbed on. He got settled in as best he could and rode the horse out of the stable. Neither one of them wanted to do this as they were both tired from the previous journey but they had no other choice.

Antonelli called after him as the horse kicked up a large cloud of dust, "Go with God, Paoblo, I will see you back here soon!"

Paoblo didn't reply as the horse rode away with Antonelli's letter in his satchel. He was in no mood to talk and just stuck to the task at hand. *It sure is going to be a long three days* He thought to himself.

The old priest lowered his eyes as he turned and headed back to his church, "Father of mercy, I hope we're not too late."

II

After days of riding, Bishop Antonio Contarini received Padre Antonelli's letter. It was late in the evening and the bishop had all but retired for the night when a knock came at his door. The bishop had not yet lay down, so he decided not to ignore the house call. He yawned as he scratched his white beard and answered the door.

A guard stood next to an exhausted Paoblo, who had arrived with Antonelli's letter. Contarini's brow furrowed when he saw the man, "What is the meaning of this?"

The guard bowed, "A humble pardon milord, but this rider says he has an urgent matter that could not wait until morning."

Paoblo nodded, "Eminence, I bring important word to you from Padre Antonelli sir. He made it clear that this was to get to you as quickly as possible. He'd have my hide if I waited until morning to deliver it."

Contarini eyed the rider who looked like he was about to faint. The bishop sighed, "Come in my boy, sit down. Rest for a moment while I see what was so important that it merited disturbing what little rest I get."

The guard stepped out of the way, allowing Paoblo to enter the bishop's chambers. The door was closed behind him as the bishop beckoned to the nearest chair. Contarini nodded as a hesitant look appeared on the courier's face, "Go ahead young man, sit down."

Paoblo nodded as he held out the letter and took the chair, "Thank you, Eminence."

As the young rider sat down, Contarini opened the parchment and read its contents. Paoblo watched as his eyes darted back and forth over the page and then stopped right in the middle. The bishop's eyelids widened, revealing the white of his aging eyes. He lowered the letter and looked at the rider, "You got this directly from Padre Antonelli's hands, did you?"

Paoblo nodded, "Yes milord, he handed it directly to me."

"Was he of sound mind, or did he seem disturbed?" Contarini asked.

"Eminence?" Paoblo asked, confused.

"Was he of sound mind?" The bishop shouted. "Did he seem like he was all there?"

"Yes, Eminence!" Paoblo replied. "He looked stressed out, but I shouldn't wonder."

The Bishop nodded, "Then I doubt I have much time, but his holiness won't accept any excuses. I'll have to meet with him tomorrow after…"

He quickly turned and went to the door, "Guard!"

The startled guard stood at attention and nodded, "Sir!"

"Find the captain of my ship." Contarini ordered. "Have my ship made ready to sail. I make for Venice immediately after my meeting with his holiness!"

The guard saluted, "Thy will be done, milord! Your ship will be ready."

Contarini turned back to Paoblo as the guard disappeared into the dark hallway, "Do you have a moment?"

Paoblo nodded, "Of course, Eminence."

The bishop quickly scribbled down a note, folded it, poured wax on the folds, and stamped it with his seal. He then turned back to the rider, "Can you take this to Padre Antonelli?"

Paoblo looked at the letter and sighed, "Eminence with respect, I just road for three days. I'm…"

The bishop's hand appeared from under his robes, holding a small bag full of ducats, "Of course you will be amply compensated for your troubles."

Paoblo eyed the bag and nodded, "A… of course, Eminence. It would be my honor."

Contarini handed the bag to Paoblo, "Go with God, and be swift."

Paoblo nodded, "Thy will, Eminence. It will be there."

**

Days later, when the bishop's ship entered the Venetian harbor, Contarini did not even wait for them to drop anchor, "Captain, lower the launch. We need to get to shore, now."

Divinity

The captain shook his head, "Eminence, really… I am charged with your safety. Lowering a launch before the ship has been anchored…"

"Must be done." Contarini interrupted. "The Pope demands a report on the issue as soon as possible. Captain, in the name of God, lower the launch!"

The captain hesitantly nodded and turned to his crewmen, "Lower the launch."

The launch was moved over the side and lowered to the water per the captain's orders. Before the crew could do anything, Contarini was climbing down into the boat. A few guards joined him and helped row to shore.

Padre Antonelli was cleaning the floors of the church in town. He had received word from Contarini that they were on their way, but he didn't expect them to arrive as quickly as they did. He was startled when three knights threw the doors of the church open and the lavishly dressed regional leader walked in.

Padre Antonelli bowed before him and kissed the ring on his hand, "My lord, I am honored by your presence. Thank you for coming so quickly. "

The bishop disregarded his greeting, "Let us dispense with the pleasantries, Padre. I am here in response to your letter. You detailed finding an unclean spirit that had successfully physically manifested itself. You believe it's living in this town, yes?"

"Yes, Eminence, on the outskirts." The priest replied. "I've seen her with my own eyes."

"I want to see her," Contarini said in a gruff voice, "and pray you did not fabricate this story."

Padre Antonelli nodded, stood up, and began heading for the exit. He eyed the papal knights as he guided Contarini out the door. Each one was dressed in metal and armed well enough to deal with any enemy that came along. Antonelli knew that they would stick out like a gold coin amongst pebbles in the town. It was a fact that did not seem to bother them in the least.

As they exited the church, he stopped dead in his tracks and turned to Bishop Contarini, "Eminence, before I take you to her, I have one request to make."

The old man nodded, "I will hear it, but be quick about it."

"When you cleanse the house," Antonelli replied slowly, "leave the boy who lives there alive. On my responsibility, he is my student. I know him and his family well enough to be sure that he has not succumbed to evil."

Bishop Contarini's face twisted, "I make no promises until I see the situation for myself. I'll need to evaluate exactly what is going on. This may be out of my hands."

Padre Antonelli agreed and took the bishop to the Patrisi cottage. The old priest watched the knights as they marched up the road ahead of the bishop. The papal knights were a little-known, seldom called upon, organization that essentially functioned as a secret police force within the Church. They were both feared and respected by the clergymen and laypeople alike who actually knew of their existence.

Giovanni was out at sea fishing when they arrived. Quietly, the group looked through the windows until they saw the demon sitting in Giovanni's bedroom. The creature did not move and seemed almost as though it was in a trance, unaware of what was going on nearby. Bishop Contarini stood for a moment looking her over before turning to the knights, "Captain Gonzaga."

Captain Federico II Gonzaga, the tallest of the three knights stepped forward, and removed his faceplate to reveal a handsome man with dark, well-groomed, brown hair, a curled mustache and a thick beard, "My lord?"

The bishop nodded, "Captain, make for the ship, I want it ready to sail within the hour. We make for Rome."

The knight's eye's narrowed, "Back to Rome already, my lord?"

"Carry out your orders, Captain," Contarini said sternly.

The captain stood at attention and saluted, "It shall be done, my lord."

The obedient knight turned and ran up the dirt road back to the church to get his horse. He would then make for the port of Venice in order to get the ship ready. The bishop walked as fast as his feet would carry him. Padre Antonelli and the other two knights followed close behind, "Eminence, wait, are you just going to leave her here? She is alone, would it not be best if…"

Bishop Contarini did not stop moving, "This is beyond my power. It is truly worse than I ever imagined. There is no record of an unclean spirit powerful enough to manifest itself in this way. I must get aid from the Papacy. No letter will do it; I need to speak with him personally."

Padre Antonelli stopped dead in his tracks, "But eminence… the boy…"

The bishop turned and placed a hand on the old priest's shoulder, trying to reassure him, "We will do the best we can to save your young friend, this I promise you, but his holiness will need to determine the next course of action. In the meantime, I want you to keep an eye on them both. If there is any change, report it to my correspondent immediately. Understood?"

Padre Antonelli nodded as they continued walking, "Understood, Eminence."

Upon their return to the church, Contarini boarded his coach and bid farewell to the old priest, "Remember Antonelli, the boy is in your hands until we return. Trust nothing you see, and be on your guard at all times. Remember what you're dealing with."

"As always, your words are wise and true." Antonelli replied as he bowed and kissed the bishop's hand.

Once they were out of sight, old priest returned to his work. He knew that things around the town would soon become very difficult and began praying continuously for the life of his young pupil. However, even with prayer, the priest could feel deep down that the Papacy would do anything it could to rid themselves of this evil, even if it meant killing an innocent young man in the process. They would want all evidence of what happened removed from the eyes of commoners.

Questions and doubt began to fill the old priest's mind. Had he done the right thing or simply exposed Giovanni to even worse evil without thinking? His mind was now being torn and he knew that he would need to sort

this out, but for the time being he would carry out his orders and watch Giovanni closely.

**

Bishop Contarini made his way back to his ship. The carriage rode fast to the harbor until they reached the docked ship. As it stopped, there was a cracking noise in the wheels. They had ridden it so hard that the axles were on the verge of collapse.

Once onboard their ship, Captain Gonzaga approached, "My lord, the captain reports that we are prepared for departure."

The bishop nodded, "Full sail, I want us in Rome as soon as possible. The future of the Church may depend on it."

Federico nodded, "Thy will, my lord."

III

Evening fell on the city of Rome. In the Basilica di Santa Maria Maggiore, Pope Leo X sat on an ornate throne of velvet and gold, surrounded by the clergymen that he kept close to him as advisors. The group comprised of high-ranking bishops and cardinals from across the land.

The lights of the city outside of his window began to illuminate as the sun set over the horizon. The beautiful towers of the castle were large enough for it to look over the entire city. From his residence there, the Pope could watch over Rome and would know if anything was going on.

As the sun disappeared and the lights in nearby buildings replaced it, he turned to the group of men sitting in his council chambers. Captain Gonzaga and Bishop Antonio Contarini were included in this meeting having been witness to what was going on in Venice. The pope turned to the man who had brought word of the disturbance in Venice with him. His stoic expression did not change as he spoke, "Are you absolutely certain of what the priest told you?"

The Bishop had nearly lost his ship pushing it as fast as he could to get to Rome. Now he was trying to convince the Pope that what he had seen was more than a simple farce, "Eminence, I saw her myself. I even doubted Benito Antonelli's report, so I personally went to the fisherman's house. His report on the matter is accurate. Antonelli believes that this is something that can't be handled by a parish priest and I agree with him."

Pope Leo X's face twisted, "Yes, the stories about Padre Antonelli and his adventures for the Church are well known here."

Contarini smiled as the Pope turned to him, "He's been a loyal servant for a long time."

The Pope nodded, "Then we need to work quickly, Antonio. If word of this abomination is made public, God himself only knows what might happen. It could cause hysteria and riots amongst the masses, and if she starts preaching words that invalidate our teachings…"

Antonio nodded, "But sir, what if we are wrong? Texts on the attributes of angels are very limited. What if angels are not as infallible as we believe and she was simply injured on her way back to the Kingdom of Heaven? Would a demon not possess the strength to bring an angel out of the sky? Perhaps we should…"

Leo X sighed, "Perhaps, but what does it matter? Look around you my friend. We hold in our hands the power to crush empires, the will to crown kings, and make them shudder in fear of our wrath. I am the hand of God himself."

The Pope pointed out the window, "Look at all we have accomplished. The inquisition into Portugal has already begun to bring about positive results in the country. We give power to those who sit on the thrones of man and we can take that power away from them just as easily. So what happens if this angel is truly not fallen and invalidates everything our Church stands for? Yes, Antonio, what if we are wrong? Then the lavish lives we live, the power we have and everything we are will be lost, our Church will crumble and the world will be thrown into chaos. Uncountable numbers of lives would be lost in the chaos. It has happened before, and it will happen again, unless we maintain order."

He outstretched his hand as though presenting it to the bishop. The jeweled gold rings sparkled and shimmered in the candle light, "Look around you, old friend. The sales of plenary indulgences are down, people are starting to question our teachings, and these acts of terrorism by those that follow Luther's kin have already begun to make their mark on history. We can't allow them to get another advantage. If she is false, then we do the world a favor by exorcising her back to the dark realm from where she came. If she is not, then we must protect our interests from the damage she could cause."

"I agree…" Antonio nodded, "The only way to maintain order is to keep everyone in line. This new free exchange of ideas that is being brought about by the followers of Luther will throw the world into chaos. If it is an evil, then it is a necessary one. The creature must die."

Divinity

Leo smiled, "Excellent... but we must move quickly. Word of this will spread faster than wildfire, even if only a few have found out thus far."

One of the other cardinals spoke, "What are your plans then, Eminence?"

The Pope turned to the man who had spoken. His stoic expression had not changed as he spoke, "Summon the Papal knights, I want a full battalion to accompany us to Venice."

Bishop Contarini looked at the Pope oddly as he tried to figure out what he meant, "Us, Eminence?"

"Yes," Leo replied, "I will see to the apprehension of this demon personally. For the glory and the salvation of Rome..."

The bishop bowed, "It will be done Eminence, but if you intend to go personally, I ask that you take back the commander of your knights. Take Captain Gonzaga, he has served the Church well, and I believe that his wayward ways must come to an end. If he is ever to inherit his father's title in Mantua, then he must learn the ways of nobility. He is the best of our knights and I know that I will feel more comfortable if he goes with you."

"Very well, Antonio." The Pope replied before turning to the rest of the clergy. "You are all dismissed. I grow tired, and have a long journey ahead of me."

As Captain Gonzaga left the room, he began to wonder what the Church was getting itself involved in. Did they truly know what they were meddling with? Several thoughts raced through his mind as he walked; *what madness is this? They don't know for certain if she has fallen from grace or not. The Pope speaks for the Lord, but is he really willing to risk the Lord's wrath by going after one of his messengers?*

Federico did everything he could to put such questions out of his head. He had never had any reason to question the Church before and his oath was to protect the Papacy, not challenge it. He finally decided that his time would be better spent preparing the Pope's ship and made his way to the docks.

The clergy filed out of the room, leaving the Pope to sit alone for a moment before he retired. He remained motionless until everyone else had left. The door closed with a mighty thud as the last of his council exited.

Finally out of sight from the prying eyes of his council, the Pope leaned to his right and spoke into the white curtain on the wall, "So what do you think? Will this be sufficient for your plans?"

The Pope closed his eyes as the curtain began to move, "Yes I do agree, this could be a very serious problem. I thought you had assured me that her expulsion from the Celestial World would not cause our plans any further complications. You promised that we would be strengthened, no weakened."

The curtains began to tremble and a harsh whisper emanated from them. The Pope nodded, "I apologize. You are right, it's not for me to question your decisions, but do not forget our arrangement. I will help you, and in return, I am to be granted the power to throw down this resistance. Soon the Church will have regained control and a new age of peace will be ushered in."

IV

Padre Antonelli spent days watching Giovanni's home, but nothing seemed out of the ordinary. Giovanni would leave to go fishing, return home, take his fish to market, and then spend the rest of the evening indoors. He would occasionally go outside at night to take the demon for a walk or work on his rigging.

This was the normal behavior for a fisherman, which brought to light why there had been no suspicion surrounding his movements. The only reason Antonelli realized that something was different was because Giovanni had been missing the Sunday sermons that he so often attended. Otherwise people just went about their business without thinking twice about his behavior.

The following Monday, Antonelli returned to Giovanni's home to observe further. Once again, the two were outside as the sun came up. He slowly moved closer to the house, trying to keep quiet. He had no idea just how far the demon's temptation had gone, but he needed to find out. The boy's life could depend on it.

As Antonelli took another step towards them, the demon's head suddenly perked up. She turned in Padre Antonelli's direction as though looking for the source of a sound. Antonelli froze in place even though he knew she couldn't see him.

After a few moments, the demon turned back to Giovanni, whispered in his ear, and disappeared back into the house. Giovanni sat quietly for a few more minutes, not moving. He just stared at the rising sun off in the distance and sighed.

Antonelli smiled, knowing that at the very least, Giovanni wasn't suffering. He at least seemed comfortable, more so than he had in a long time. Still, this could have very easily been a ruse.

Padre Antonelli knew that he had to intervene if he was going to discover just how far the perversion had gone. Spying obviously wasn't the answer, so he decided to try a more direct approach. The old priest quickly made his way to the front door where Giovanni sat. He appeared at the

Divinity

side of the house and called out to his young friend, "Good morning to you, my boy."

Giovanni was startled and jumped to his feet at the sound of the familiar voice. His face quickly went from shock to concern. The priest could see that Giovanni didn't view his visit as timely when the boy spoke, "Padre, what brings you here this morning?"

"I haven't really seen you since we spoke of angels." Antonelli said in a hurt tone. "You have been somewhat distant since your brother died. I had to make sure everything was okay."

Giovanni nodded, "My apologies Padre, things have been... complicated around here lately. I haven't had much time to myself."

"No doubt." The old priest replied. "Bringing an angel back to health must be taking up quite a bit of your time."

Giovanni suddenly went pale as the hair on the back of his neck stood straight up. How did Padre Antonelli know? Had he been watching the house, or had someone else seen them. The boy stammered as he tried to speak, "P... Padre?"

Antonelli smiled and opened his arms revealing that he was unarmed. "I would like to talk to her, if that would be all right? I promise I will not try anything."

Giovanni didn't know what to do now. He had been caught red handed and struggled to find an easy solution, but all that came to him was questions and worry. Should he bring the priest before her? No, he couldn't risk the Church finding out about her. He knew full well what would happen as a result.

Adalyn had already asked him not to bring her to the Church. He trusted Padre Antonelli, but at this moment, he would have given anything for a way out of this. No plan or words became immediately evident as he stood struggling to protect her, "Padre... I do not know what you are talking about. An angel... what...?"

The old priest's smile turned to an angry scowl, "Do not lie to me, my boy. I've been watching you and I know what you're hiding here. You are just making things worse for yourself. You must let me talk to her. I can't help you otherwise."

Divinity

Giovanni took in a deep breath before responding. He could feel beads of sweat appearing on his back. There was a detectable level of frustration in his voice as he again denied Antonelli's accusation, "I'm serious Padre. I do not know what you are talking about! There is no one here but me. I don't mean to be rude, but I think it's time for you to leave. I have much work to do and no time for these accusations. Now if you don't mind…"

"It's alright Giovanni," Adalyn's voice appeared from behind the door, "I don't sense any danger from him. If he wants to speak to me, I'll listen to what he has to say."

Giovanni closed his eyes and sighed as his head dropped, "Please follow me Padre…"

"Four Hail Mary's for lying." Padre Antonelli said as he smiled triumphantly.

The old priest followed Giovanni into his home, through the kitchen and into the bedroom. An unusual aroma entered the room as the second set of footsteps became louder. The smell was of incense often burned in a church. She furrowed her brow as she heard his footsteps, "This must be the Padre Antonelli you spoke of…"

Giovanni nodded, "Yes… I'm afraid so."

She turned to him with an accusing expression on her face, "Tell me, priest, how long have you been watching this house?"

The priest stopped in his tracks, shocked, "How did you know?"

"I recently felt a presence nearby, watching us." She responded.

"Then why didn't you say anything to me?" Giovanni demanded.

"I felt his fear," she said softly, "but I felt no danger from him. I did not think we had anything to worry about. It was best that he come to us on his own."

Padre Antonelli was impressed, "You seem to be aware of much of the world around you. Even though you appear to have been blinded, you seem to still be able to see much."

She turned her head away from him, "Perhaps too much. I also know the Church you serve. You should know

Divinity

that the Most High is deeply saddened by the way you have corrupted your purpose."

The priest frowned, "I beg your pardon?"

She tried to strengthen her voice, but a small amount of fear still bled through, "The Church you serve. You keep the masses naïve and you concern yourselves with personal gain over religious truth, not unlike the money changers at the Temple of Jerusalem. The Kingdom of Heaven rests not within the walls of an ornate building, in the crucifixes you carry, not even in the hollow words you speak. The Kingdom belongs not to one specific person. Nor is it for any mortal to decide who is worthy to pass through the gates. A man toiling endlessly in the mud all day has as much of a right to it as a king who sits upon a throne of Gold, maybe more in some cases."

Adalyn raised her head so it appeared as though she were looking straight at him, "Or a priest speaking of things he does not know. Look upon me, I am no demon, but the teachings of your Church would tell you that I am an unclean spirit. For no other reason than because I am no longer protected by the grace of the Most High, I should be tortured and murdered. Know that those who try to hide the truths of the Most High will be brought into the light and will never see his Kingdom!"

Padre Antonelli was shocked. He had no idea how to respond to such a harsh accusation. It took him a moment to regain his composure before he spoke again, "I am not the Pope, young lady, nor am I member of his council. I left Rome years ago to get away from all of that. I am a simple community priest. I preach the word I have been taught to anyone who will listen. I have no such aspirations of power, nor do I try to deceive anyone. If what you say of my teachings is true though, then I would be one to ask for forgiveness."

Adalyn breathed deeply and sat back, relaxed. "I see, then perhaps I owe you an apology for my outburst, but much of the war and torture in this world has been caused by the religious teachings of a corrupt few."

Padre Antonelli nodded, "I can only speak of what I have been taught. I would be interested in hearing your view of things though."

"There are some things that you are not meant to know in your lifetime," Adalyn replied, "but I will share with you all that I can."

**

Padre Antonelli spent the next few hours talking to Adalyn. He tried to understand why she was there and who she was. The old priest was unsure about the truths that she told which challenged his faith. As far as he knew, this could all be the deception of a dark creature, but he listened intently. There was nothing satanic or unholy in the words she spoke.

As the time grew late, Padre Antonelli's mind was full of new ideas, new teachings, and new sets of rules. The old priest didn't know what to make of any of it. As the day slowly came to an end, he stood up, "It is getting dark. I should be getting back... Giovanni, be careful, and keep her out of sight for now."

Giovanni walked Padre Antonelli to the door, "So now you know the truth... now what?"

Antonelli shook his head, "Now I go home and pray. I have much to think on my son."

The priest turned back to him and spoke, "I mean it, keep her out of sight. We'll need to figure out what to do next."

Adalyn called to him from the other room, "Goodbye Benito Antonelli."

Antonelli stopped in his tracks at hearing his name, "Oh... peace be with you Adalyn."

The door closed behind the old priest as he headed home. The moment they were alone, Adalyn let out a long sigh and put her right hand to her head as she stood up, "I apologize for my rudeness. Perhaps I should not have been so quick to judge him the way I did. I have watched too much tragedy befall those who blindly follow the Church, committing genocide in the name of a God they do not even understand."

Divinity

Giovanni nodded, "I'm sure he's not holding it against you and at least I now understand your feelings about the Church a little better."

Adalyn sighed as she sat down by the stove, "I need some time to think…"

Giovanni nodded and headed to the door, "I understand. I'm going to go work on my nets. If you need anything, let me know."

Adalyn nodded as he closed the door behind himself and sat on the work bench. As it got dark out, two lanterns hanging next to his door and illuminated the docks to help Giovanni continue to work. He needed to have the nets done for the next day, so he worked diligently on them.

A gentle breeze blew as the fires danced in the night keeping the darkness away from his home. He stopped for a moment and closed his eyes as he remembered his favorite sea-going tune,

"Sing loud,

Let your soul run free,

Horizons calling,

Adventure lies ahead,

Danger in the distance,

It won't touch you,

Don't be afraid,

Release the fear in your eyes,

It will pass you by,

And all will be all right,

--

How could it be,

That our time has come,

As the winds change their course,

On invisible wings,

My sails will fly,

To take you away…"

Suddenly a golden voice from inside his home stopped him before he could repeat the verse. It continued with a second verse that he'd never heard before.

"In the dark,

Calm turns to fear,

In the cold of night,

Trembling with tears,
Sleep now,
Nothing will harm you,
Hear the sounds,
Let peace surround you,
Safe and sound,
Sleeping in my arms…"

Giovanni turned to see Adalyn walk up behind him, smiling. She sat down on the bench and listened to him work, "That's a nice song."

He furrowed his brow as he thought about the words, "I never knew that verse."

She nodded, "It's a very old song from the days when your people first took to the seas. It is a shame your father died before he could teach you all of it."

"How did you know that he taught me?" Giovanni asked with a shocked look, "I never told you about my father."

"I'm an angel, remember?" She answered, "I watched over people, that was part of my job. I also helped guide his soul to the gates of Heaven. He didn't want to leave you boys to fend for yourselves."

"You shouldn't be out here," Giovanni sighed, "It's not safe…"

Her eyes were still bandaged, but a look of sadness could still be seen on her face, "Do you wish me to leave?"

Giovanni looked down, "No… I don't. I am tired of being alone."

"I'm sorry," She said sympathetically, "… thoughts of your family are sources of pain for you aren't they?"

"Yes," he replied sadly, "I don't understand why God would take them all away from me, why would he ever make me suffer so… why?"

Adalyn could hear the sorrow in his voice. The amount of bitterness she sensed weighed heavily on her heart. He had been rewarded for his steadfast worship and kind-hearted nature by having his entire family stolen and was rightfully angry at the world.

She wrapped her arms around him and squeezed, "What I told you before wasn't false. The Most High did not

Divinity

take them away from you. He gave your people life, the world, his teachings, and prophets. You have the teachings and the tools. Now it is time for you all to stand on your own. Can a child truly grow if a parent continues to dote on them? I know the Most High grieved for the death of your family. He feels every death as though it were his own kin."

"But why," Giovanni demanded, "why grant us life and then allow us to lose it so easily? If it is so precious, then why is it so fragile? Why could he not make us more like you, immortal and pure?"

Adalyn was silent for a few moments, thinking of how to answer. When she finally found the words, she sucked in a deep breath before speaking, "Is that what you think life is for us? I'm sorry, but the reality is just not that simple, Giovanni. I wish it were, believe me. Angels are omnipotent and immortal, this is true, but we do not have any freedom of will. Our lives are nothing more than servitude. We have been and always will be what we were made to be; attendants to his will."

She rested her hand on his shoulder, "Your life on the other hand may be finite, but you have the freedom to do with it as you see fit and the Most High shows you unyielding patience and compassion. There are many angels that would gladly trade immortality for freedom. All we can do is watch and dream. Sometimes it can be a very hollow existence. To never feel for someone the way you do, to never make my own choices..."

She placed a hand on her stomach as her lips began to quiver, "Or ever have the ability to create life."

Giovanni placed his hand on her arm, "That's something you've always wanted, isn't it?"

She nodded, "Such desires are forbidden for me, but I would gladly trade my wings without hesitation for such a gift."

She sighed, "I guess that's part of the reason I was so prejudiced against your kind. Your people waste the gifts that my kind would die for."

"If given the choice," Giovanni said slowly, "I might consider going the other way... to live for only so long and make little to no impact on the world."

Divinity

Adalyn pulled away from Giovanni and placed a hand on his cheek, guiding his face so that he was looking at her, "No impact? You cannot be serious, that is simply not true. Every human being makes an impact on those around them, whether they realize it or not. If the Pope can wave his hand to issue a new order that will affect millions, can a beggar on the streets not utter a plea to the Pope that would touch his heart and prompt him to change such a decision?"

She kissed him on the cheek before continuing, "You are more significant than you know. Your lives may be brief on this world, but death is not the end for you. When night falls and your time here ends, you will take what you were given in this world and start a new journey. Think of this corporeal existence as a training ground. Your actions here will determine where you will go and what you will face when your time comes. What happens at the end does not truly matter. What matters is what you do with the time you are given."

Giovanni looked at her; it almost seemed like she could see him even through the bandages and her damaged eyes, "Where does the journey lead to? What waits for us at the end?"

She smiled, "There is no limit to where the journey can lead. What happens and where you go is in your own hands completely. You determine your fate. No one else can ever take that away from you. Never underestimate your worth; all life is precious in the eyes of the Most High. Those that live an honest life will be rewarded in the end."

Hearing her words, Giovanni felt as though a heavy weight was being lifted off of his heart. At least he could rest easy knowing that his family had been well attended to, "Thank you, Adalyn... your words mean more to me then you could ever know. I'm happy that you came into my life. I mean that."

Giovanni's words warmed her heart. She smiled as she gave him a squeeze, "Me too. The moment I was told that this would be my exile, I was sure my existence was at its end. I thought all humans were corrupted, primitive, and violent."

Adalyn lowered her face as she sighed, "I was wrong about you and I'm sorry. The Most High must have truly decided to show me some mercy by leading me to you. I refuse to believe that there is any other explanation. Even with my injuries and loss of sight, I've managed to find happiness in a dark place."

She leaned back into him and relaxed on his shoulder. A moment later, Giovanni felt tears on his arm that had fallen from her eyes. He looked at her, "Why are you crying, what's wrong?"

She fought to regain some composer, "I've spent so long being hard on my own existence. Angry for the treatment of my kind, angry at your kind... I can't believe how naïve I was. I feel like I deserved what I got."

Giovanni frowned, "You don't mean that. No one deserves the pain you went through. No one deserves to be put through what you were. Sending you here to be tortured and killed is excessive."

Adalyn didn't respond. Giovanni could see that he wasn't getting through to her, so he decided to change his tone, "I mean, look on the bright side, we met as a result."

Adalyn smiled slightly, "Yeah..."

The fires of light outside of Giovanni's home dimmed down to nothing and the darkness of night took over. The two sat outside until Giovanni could not see her anymore. The sounds of the tide going out drifted them both off to sleep.

**

Meanwhile, Antonelli had returned to his church. He spent most of the night trying to come to terms with what Adalyn had told him. His mind was going around in circles, thinking about the accusations that she had made against the leaders of his Church. *She speaks the word of God like she knows it better than the Pope himself.* He thought about it for a few more moments.

At that moment, reality set in, "My God, she's no demon... she really is... an angel... and the Church now knows of her existence. What have I done? Once Contarini speaks to his holiness... They will be coming... they will want to see Adalyn and most likely kill her."

His mind was filled with questions, "What must I do? Do I try to save her, or do I follow the Church's orders? If I let them come and investigate, would I be able to live with the consequences?"

The priest's thoughts were interrupted by a knock on his door. Padre Antonelli got up and looked outside. There was no one around. The old priest noticed a letter sitting on the doorstep. It had the Pope's seal pressed into wax on the back. He removed the folded piece of paper and looked it over. He was about to tear it open, when he heard the sound of soldiers marching in the streets. Realizing what he had done, he put a hand to his head, "It's already too late, they're here…"

Padre Antonelli ran inside to grab a few supplies before heading back to Giovanni's home. As he worked, he noticed the mural on the wall depicting the angel guiding lost souls. Recognizing Adalyn's face, he dropped everything and ran out the door. He could hear the loud pounding of shoes and knew that he didn't have much time, "I've got to get to them now. I'm out of time."

V

The sun was barely peaking over the horizon as Giovanni and Adalyn were roused by screams coming from the town. It sounded like the whole area was under attack, but from what? Who would want to come after a small fishing community?

Adalyn stood up quickly, "Something is terribly wrong… someone is coming this way."

Giovanni opened his eyes and quickly scrambled to get to his feet, "They aren't friendly, whoever they are. Go inside, Adalyn, quickly."

Gunshots could be heard in the distance and they were getting closer. Adalyn did as she was told without a word. She found her way back inside with her hands outstretched and shut the door behind her. She sat down on the cot and kept quiet, silently praying for whatever was coming to pass them by.

A shrill voice appeared from behind the house, "Giovanni!"

Giovanni turned to see Padre Antonelli running towards him, "Padre, what is going on in town?"

"Never mind about that." The priest replied, out of breath. "Giovanni, where is Adalyn?"

Giovanni looked at the priest trying to catch his breath as he stood hunched over, "Padre Antonelli, answer me, what is going on in town?"

"Forgive me my boy… forgive me…" The old priest said as his lungs finally caught up with him. "When you first told me about her and asked all those questions, I became suspicious and when I saw her in your home, I panicked. I thought you had been possessed or controlled by an unclean spirit…"

Giovanni grabbed him by the shoulders, "Padre, what are you saying, what have you done?"

The priest looked away, "Giovanni… Forgive me… I informed Bishop Contarini, who in turn informed the Pope. He has personally involved himself in this situation."

Giovanni's eyes widened, "You did what? God help us. You old fool, you may have condemned us both!"

Giovanni quickly turned back to the house, "Come on, we have to get Adalyn out of the house. She can't fall into their hands. We'll take her somewhere she can hide. Get her to my boat, we're leaving town."

Padre Antonelli lowered his head as he looked back at the town, "It's too late. They are already on their way here. You will never get her out in time. The Pope brought a battalion of his best Papal knights with him. Even if you could get her out of the harbor, they would hunt you to the ends of the Earth. You would not be safe anywhere."

Giovanni had heard enough, "I don't care, get out of my way you son of a bitch! I made her a promise that I'd keep her safe!"

Not a second after he had spoken, a large group of knights bearing a red cross on a white banner lined the road and surrounded the small cottage. They brandished swords and arquebuses as they stood in perfect formation, awaiting orders to attack.

Giovanni looked around trying to find some way out of this, "What is the meaning of this? The Patrisi house is a friend to the Church. Why have you come here brandishing weapons?"

"You know why we are here." A voice from behind the line of soldiers responded. "Where is the demon?"

Giovanni turned and saw a large man dressed in clothes so luxurious that they would rival those of a royal. His red and white robes waved in the breeze. Padre Antonelli dropped to one knee, "Eminence…"

Giovanni took a step back as his eyes widened, "His holiness…"

The Pope smiled, "Padre Antonelli, you have done a great service to the Church and are to be commended."

The priest nodded though his gaze never met that of the Pope, "Thank you sir."

Giovanni looked at Antonelli as though he were about to kill the old priest. The Pope noticed this and turned to him, "Young whelp, you have harbored an unclean entity here. That is a crime of heresy. For which the punishment is, most regrettably… death."

Pope Leo X pointed with two fingers at Giovanni. Captain Gonzaga and two other knights tackled the young man to the ground. He wrestled back, but was no match for the captain and the battle-hardened troops.

Once they had Giovanni subdued, his hands and legs were shackled and weighted to the ground. He tried his best to fight back, but the three knights were more than a match for one lone fisherman who'd never been in a fight other than with his brothers.

Federico stood back up and drew his sword, "Surrender now, and this will be a lot less painful. Things will only be that much more unpleasant for you if you continue to struggle against us."

Giovanni saw the shining blade and stopped moving as it was held close to his face, "Don't harm her! She's one of God's servants! If you bring harm on her, you risk your own souls!"

The Pope scoffed, "Do you presume to tell me of Gods will? You think you know more about the will of God then me? She will be taken and exorcised from this world. Fear not young man, you will see her soon."

Pope Leo X nodded at the closest knight who aimed his sword at Giovanni's neck. At that moment, Padre Antonelli stepped forward from behind him, "No, Eminence I beseech you, leave him with me. He is still young and can be reeducated."

The Pope narrowed his eyes, "He has been found guilty of heresy. Reeducation takes time and is not known for being successful. It would be better to execute him and be done with it."

"With respect, Eminence," Padre Antonelli replied, "the Patrisi family has been contributing alms to the Church for years. They are a decent, hard-working people, and he is the last of that family. If you kill him now without allowing me to try, you end his line. I could think of no greater a tragic end to this story."

"The boy's story is indeed tragic," the Pope admitted, "but, are you sure he can be helped?"

"On my honor, Eminence," he swore, "I will personally reeducate him."

"And if you cannot?" The Pope asked.

Padre Antonelli looked at Giovanni, lying beaten on the ground with his nose bleeding, "Then I will kill him myself."

The Pope shook his head as he sighed, "I wash my hands of this. I still think that it is a waste of time, but because of your service to the Church, I will release him to you. Just know, if he causes us any further trouble for the Church, you will be held responsible."

Padre Antonelli nodded, "I understand, Eminence. Thank you."

"Good," the Pope said stoically, "let it never be said that the Church cannot be merciful with a penitent soul. For his own safety though, you'd best hold him here until we leave."

The priest nodded as he knelt down next to his friend, "Remain still, this will be over soon."

Now that they had settled Giovanni's fate, the Pope turned his attention to his men, "Knights of the Church, you have sworn an oath to serve the faithful in life and death. I cannot tell you what horrors this demon has in store for us, but remain strong, and together we will save our Church from this blight."

The Pope stepped aside and let Captain Gonzaga lead the way into Giovanni's home. He followed close behind as the knights kicked the door in and entered the first room. In the kitchen, they found nothing. It wasn't until they turned their attention to the bedroom that they saw the wounded angel huddled up in the corner.

Federico saw her balled up with a look of fear on her face. He had his sword poised, but did not draw it when he noticed that her cheeks were soaked from tears. His hand let go of his sword's hilt and it slid back into its scabbard. This was not at all what he was expecting. Where were the horrors the Pope spoke of?

Federico wanted to say something to make the horrible look of sadness on her face go away, but he knew that the Pope would have his head for it. There was nothing the knight commander could do, but wait to see how this played

out. A sudden feeling of apathy and regret poured over him. *Could she really be all that dangerous?*

Adalyn had heard a lot of screaming and metal clanking, and was terrified by what might have happened. The knights began to topple furniture and tear the house to shreds. She began to breathe heavily and reached out, "What is it, what is happening? Giovanni, where are you?"

The Pope drew his sword and pointed it at Adalyn's throat, "Silence!"

She opened her mouth, about to utter one last scream, but when she heard the metal blade being unsheathed, she froze, too scared to move. The Pope glared at her, "Demon, you have fallen from the grace of God and been cast out of his kingdom. We have come to fulfill his will!"

When she didn't move, the Pope's voice became even angrier, "Do you not have anything to say in your defense, or is your silence an admission of guilt?"

Aside from a slight tremble, the angel's body remained perfectly still, too scared and unwilling to move. Angered, the Pope stabbed her in the arm, "Speak!"

Adalyn cried out in pain as blood dripped down her arm. When Giovanni heard it, he began to struggle. His mind was no longer concerned with self-preservation. He wanted to get to Adalyn, and nothing else mattered at that point.

Padre Antonelli did what he could to stop him and keep him calm, "Be still, you can't save her if you're dead."

Adalyn lay on the cot, holding her arm, "I have done nothing wrong. If the Most High wished me dead, I would not be here right now. Do you think that the he is not capable of carrying out his own decree without the aid of mortals?"

The only thing her words accomplished was angering the Pope even more, "I am no mere mortal. I am the Pope of the Holiest Church of God. I speak for the Lord my God."

She shook her head, "You speak for yourself and your gluttonous colleagues. Your actions do not reflect the true word of the Most High."

Divinity

Outraged by Adalyn's words, the Pope smacked her across the face with the back of his hand, "Silence, fallen one!"

She fell backwards hard into the wall. The Pope brought his hand back to deliver another blow, but Captain Gonzaga grabbed his arm and prevented him from striking her again. "All right, that's enough!" He said sternly.

The Pope looked back at his knight, "What is the meaning of this, Captain?"

The captain's young face bore a look of disapproval, "I have taken an oath of honor and chivalry. I will not stand by and watch you assault an unarmed woman."

The Pope sneered, "Unhand me, how dare you impede my actions! I am not bound by such a code."

"I am," the knight said as he placed his free hand on the sword he carried, "The Papal Knights have served in your wars for Christ. We have upheld your laws for centuries, but our first duty is to uphold the honor of the Papacy. Your actions will put a black mark on the office you serve. We cannot allow this, so you will cease this brutal treatment, or I will order my knights to stand down."

"This is insanity," the Pope shouted, "she is not a woman. She is an evil abomination and nothing more!"

"It matters not," the knight replied calmly, "as long as she holds the form of a woman, she is under the protection of the code. We will take her, but she is not to be harmed until she has been properly condemned."

The Pope sighed, "Oh very well... take her. It is not safe to keep her here anyway. Her spirit must be exorcised and her body cleansed. It cannot be done here. We must take her to the sanctified grounds within the city of Rome, only there can the proper ritual be performed."

"That could be difficult." The knight admitted. "Your ship took heavy damage on the way here from how hard we pushed it. She won't be ready to sail for..."

"Then we leave it behind and travel by carriage and horseback!" The Pope shouted. "Either way, we need to leave now. Make for the Contarini residence. He should have the necessary accommodations for us."

"Very well, Eminence." Federico replied.

Divinity

The Pope returned his sword to its scabbard, "Captain, we make for Rome, and once underway, you and I will have a long talk about what is defined as honorable and where it crosses paths with your duty."

Captain Gonzaga smiled, "Your will be done, Eminence. I look forward to it."

As the Pope exited the house, Captain Gonzaga was confronted by his Lieutenant, "It is unwise to confront his Holiness sir, especially if you hope to stay alive."

Federico nodded, "There are some things more important to me than my life, Lt. Piangi. Honor, Chivalry and duty seem to be notions that are dying out in this day and age. Also, something is amiss here. If she was a demon, why did she not fight back? She looked genuinely scared of us. This is not what we are taught about demons. They are supposed to be deceivers, dealers of pain and corruption... I didn't get that from her."

Lt. Piangi shrugged, "It is not what we are taught about angels either. I do agree that this is a most unusual case, but his holiness has proclaimed it the will of God that she be taken. Is that not enough?"

"Yes..." Federico sighed. "The will of God... very well, take her."

Adalyn was shackled, caged, and carried out of the house. She reached out of the bars looking for a sympathetic hand to give her comfort. She was hoping Giovanni would be able to reach her, but no touch came and no one was there to help her, "Where is Giovanni? Please do not harm him, he has done nothing wrong."

Federico turned to her as he helped carry her cage, "You need to worry about yourself now, keep quiet."

Adalyn turned to the voice, "Why are you doing this? I know your voice. You are not like the others."

"I am honor bound to serve the Church," he said softly, "but for what it's worth, I pray the Pope is right about you. If he is not, no amount of prayer may save me from my fate."

Even after hearing Captain Gonzaga's words, Adalyn was certain that these brutal people had killed Giovanni. She sat back in the cage as tear wet the bandages over her eyes.

Though she was certain her words would not reach him, she called out anyway, "Giovanni... I'm so sorry."

Adalyn's words drained the strength from Giovanni's muscles and he no longer possessed the will to fight against his captors. He knew that his renewed life came at the price of her divinity or what was left of it. So for him to squander it pointlessly fighting to get free would have been selfish. He could do nothing except helplessly watch as they carried her away.

The guards finally released Giovanni from his chains and left him lying on the ground to keep up with the Pope's caravan. He was still shackled, but now he could move around a little. As the last of the knights began to leave, the Pope turned to them, "Light torches and cleanse this cursed place. Leave nothing left standing."

Giovanni cried out, "No!"

"Keep quiet!" Padre Antonelli said softly as he tried to muffle Giovanni's scream. "Once they are gone, I promise I'll release you."

Giovanni quieted down and watched the knights do as they were ordered. They lit torches, threw them in the windows and doors, and watched as his house burned. He was filled with rage, but knew that if he tried to resist, he would be killed and unable to do anything to help the one he loved.

Giovanni's heart froze as the word passed through his mind while he lay on the ground. '*Loved,*' could it be possible? He thought to himself, *I care for her deeply... is it possible that I love her? God... I wish I had realized it before now. I have to get her back!*

Giovanni became even more enraged at the realization of his true feelings. The knights finished their work and ran to catch up with the main group. Captain Gonzaga looked back at the poor fisherman lying on the ground. The look on the young man's face was a clear indication that if he had even the slightest chance to run Federico through, he would take it.

Federico looked apologetically at the younger man before turning back to his duties, "Live better than this."

As the knights disappeared from view, Padre Antonelli stood at Giovanni's side and released the last shackles holding him in place. "How could I have been so wrong?" He said as he watched the Patrisi home burn. "Come, let's get you out of those cuffs and figure out our next move."

The moment Giovanni was set free, he came to life and lunged onto Padre Antonelli, knocking him to the ground, "You bastard, how could you? I trusted you, my family trusted you, and you betrayed us! All this time, what did you think you were doing, protecting me? I will kill you for this."

Giovanni ran his hands around Antonelli's neck and began to squeeze. The old priest fought back as much as he could, "Giovanni, please, you have every right to hate me, but don't give in to that rage. It only leads to Lucifer!"

"I do not care!" Giovanni hissed. "You took from me the last person I cared about in this world. She was the last shred of light that made me feel alive. She gave me the strength to keep living, now you've stolen that!"

"Giovanni, come to your senses!" Padre Antonelli yelled. "If you kill me, you destroy your only chance of saving her and in essence, ensure her doom."

Giovanni reluctantly loosened his grip on his former mentor's neck only slightly to allow him to speak, "What are you talking about? I won't abandon her to anyone, not even to the Church. I made her a promise. I'm going after her!"

Padre Antonelli scoffed, "So you intend to make headway for Rome, defeat the armies of the Pope single handedly, and fight all the way through the maze of dungeons to rescue her? Is that your plan?"

Giovanni released the priest and stood up, "What do you suggest I do then, let her suffer and die at their hands? I have heard about what happens to those who challenge the Church. I would not be able to live with myself if I left her to that fate."

Padre Antonelli got to his feet, "No of course not Giovanni, but think clearly on what you are planning to do. The Basilica di Santa Maria Maggiore is more than a simple residence for the Pope. It is meant to act as a fortress to protect him and his council, but even it has an Achilles heel."

"And what would that be?" Giovanni asked.

"The palace is built over a maze of tunnels and dungeons that led almost anywhere in the ancient parts of the city. If you know where you're going, they will take you deep into the city without being detected. Only men of faith are supposed to know of their existence. I discovered its secret when I was there for my training and vows."

"So we break into the Pope's home through those tunnels? Sounds like a good plan to me." Giovanni replied, anxious to get going.

"Even with this information, with just the two of us, we still stand no chance." Padre Antonelli said sorrowfully.

"Great... what else?" Giovanni replied. "Speak quickly."

The old priest thought for a moment, "Fortunately time is somewhat on our side. The Pope came here on a ship that can no longer sail. He is now forced to go back by horse-drawn carriage. It will take them at least 2 or 3 days to get back to Rome if you factor in the time they will need to rest their horses and make camp. I know the Pope will push his people as hard as he can, but even he will need time to rest."

Padre Antonelli sucked in deep breath as he continued, "Also, if I remember correctly, the Pope has an appointment with the Bishop of Versailles regarding a recent Lutheran uproar. He's already late for it and will need to leave as soon as he returns to Rome, which means he won't be able to cleanse and execute her until he that is resolved. That will give us a matter of weeks to get to her. During that time, she will be assigned to the inquisitors."

Giovanni shook his head, "How do you figure? He could just assign someone else to perform whatever ritual they have planned."

"No, my son." Antonelli replied. "I know Pope Leo X. This is something that he will want to personally oversee. He won't leave it in the hands of an inquisitor. He'll let them draw a confession from her, but he'll want to perform the actual ritual."

"I am no simpleton, Padre. You are not telling me everything. You have a plan. How are we going to get into the basilica, past its forces, and into the dungeons, all without being detected?" Giovanni asked, getting annoyed.

"That will not be easy." The priest admitted. "The Pope is a very cautious man, so he will no doubt take as many of his forces with him as he can when he makes his move on Versailles. So the basilica won't be as heavily defended."

Padre Antonelli paused for a moment, carefully choosing his words, "I also have some friends in Rome who can help us get in. They know the city better than the Pope himself. If I can convince them to trust us, they will be able to get us in and out without incident. The only problem is finding a way of getting to Rome without being noticed."

Giovanni looked down the pier, "My fishing boat, they didn't burn it."

"Yes…" The priest nodded as a smile slowly began to form on his face. "That would be sufficient. It is small enough to get by unnoticed in Rome's harbor city of Ostia. Get her ready for travel; I must go to the church to gather some charts and supplies. I will return in one hour and we will depart."

"Wait!" Giovanni said sharply. "Do you honestly expect me to trust you after what you've done? I would sooner run you through then trust you!"

"I know that," Antonelli replied, "but you need me to get into the basilica."

Giovanni did not look convinced at all. Padre Antonelli noticed it, looked him in the eye, and spoke earnestly, "Giovanni, I am aware of my sin, and I wish to repent for it. I will not be able to do so until I can personally ask her for forgiveness. Be suspicious of me all you want, but know that every minute we waste puts her life further in jeopardy."

"Fine, go," Giovanni said, "but know this; I will use you to get her out, and then you and I are finished. My ship leaves in one hour, with or without you."

The priest nodded sorrowfully, "I understand, see you in an hour."

Padre Antonelli had a slight feeling of nostalgia as he looked at Giovanni's boat. *I was quite the mariner in my youth. It will be nice to feel the deck under my feet again.*

BOOK 4
The Torment of Rome

Divinity

I

Giovanni dashed down the pier to where his boat was moored. He quickly got onboard, went below, and grabbed a much stronger cloth then the stitched one he normally had as a sail. It was intended for harsher weather should the old one fail. It was heavy and hard to carry, but he managed to get the folded cloth up on deck with a brief struggle.

Giovanni climbed the mast and removed the old sail. Using amazing speed, he rigged up the new one and then checked his hold to make sure that they had enough supplies to make the trip. He counted his blessings that he still had a batch of salted fish and preserved food still on the boat. There was also oil for the lamps and kindling for the fire pit in the cabin.

Once Giovanni had finished preparing the ship, he went back to the cottage to salvage what he could. There was not much left; what was once the home he'd grown up in was now mostly rubble. However he was able to grab some half burnt sheets he might be able to use to patch the sail if it got damaged during the trip. He managed to find one or two other items, including knives, which had miraculously survived.

Giovanni was about to run back to the ship when something shiny caught the corner of his eye. The crucifix that had hung over his door had miraculously not melted from the intense flame. He looked at the old cross for a moment, contemplating taking it. *All of creation is against us now, it seems. I doubt having that with us will make any difference.*

After a few moments of thinking about it, he remembered Adalyn's words. Whether or not God agreed with what they were doing, Giovanni hoped that it would at least be a forgivable offense. He hesitantly grabbed the cross, fearing it was still hot, but when the gold touched his skin, it did not burn him.

Giovanni quickly boarded his ship again, ran down to the hold, and stored his supplies just below the main cabin on the small shelves. He then walked up the small stairway

Divinity

to the cabin and nailed the cross above the entry way and quickly whispered to himself, "Lord grant us a safe journey... show us aid and mercy as we try to rescue one of your faithful. She is not guilty of what she has been accused of, I know that in my heart."

The young fisherman was not sure that God was listening or even cared, given the situation. As far as he knew, he was attempting to aid someone who had fallen from God's grace. *Would God leave them to it, or block their passage to Rome?*

It was a question that only time could answer. Above his head, Giovanni heard footsteps. He grabbed a knife and cautiously headed back on deck. Could Antonelli be back, or did he send the knights to finish the job after Giovanni had threatened to kill him?

Giovanni was ready if the knights were on deck. He would not let himself be taken so easily this time. He had nothing left to lose if the knights had come back and was prepared for a fight. He quietly tiptoed up the steps and pushed the door open.

Padre Antonelli was waiting for him with charts, food, and a couple of old swords. As the cabin door opened, Antonelli turned, "Come, my boy, help me."

Giovanni grabbed what he could and quickly stored the swords behind the door of the cabin. He noticed that Padre Antonelli had brought a table from the church to set up on the deck. He used the cart that Antonelli had brought the supplies on to wheel it on deck and secured it next to the cabin door.

The ship was fully stocked and ready to depart. Giovanni was shaking with eagerness to get going. The moment Antonelli stepped onboard, Giovanni ran along the rail, cutting loose the mooring lines. He then pushed against the dock with his plank. His arms ached as he pushed harder than ever before.

The ship responded by turning slowly away from the dock with the tide. As soon as it was far enough, Giovanni then set the sail while Padre Antonelli manned the tiller. The ship lurched forward as the sail instantly caught a gust of wind.

Giovanni watched as the ship began to move them away from the dock. It cleared the markers of the harbor in record time and made its way into open water. He watched as the remains of his house faded into the distance while they picked up speed. It was at that moment when he realized that, besides the cabin of his boat, he was now homeless. He felt a warm tear fall down his cheek as the anger began to take over. He turned away with his teeth clenched and began to curse under his breath.

Padre Antonelli noticed his anger and frowned, "I cannot apologize enough for this. I know that I have hurt you and committed a terrible sin that I may never be forgiven for. If I could undo the past, I would, but you must understand that I did not know what to make of her until I met her. Years of dogmatic law have taught me that any heavenly creature is incapable of being injured unless they have fallen from the grace of God."

Giovanni sat down, "It was not necessary for you to spy on us. You should have come to our door and spoken to her yourself. It did not have to be this way."

The priest was about to argue about how Giovanni had lied to him, but decided that the boy was angry enough. Instead, he just bowed his head, "Of course you are right, and I am sorry."

Giovanni shrugged off yet another meaningless apology. There was no point in accepting it as he doubted that he could ever trust the old priest again. Because of him, Adalyn was on her way to face unspeakable horrors before her own slaughter.

Part of Giovanni still wanted to kill Padre Antonelli for his crime, but he ignored the urge. He needed the old priest to get him in and out of Rome in one piece, if that was even possible. The thought was in the back of his mind that he was going to be caught and killed, but he knew that he had to try.

Giovanni stepped up onto the aft castle and placed his hand on the tiller, "I'll take over here, you should probably take a look at those maps. I can't read them for the life of me, so..."

Antonelli nodded, "A good thought, my boy."

Divinity

The priest relinquished the tiller and walked over to the table that Giovanni had set up. His eyes scanned over the hand-drawn image of the Mediterranean Sea as he began examining the old charts. Giovanni could tell that he was running estimates through his mind as the ship slowly turned south.

After a few minutes, Antonelli looked up, "It appears that if we steer a course south, south-east, and stick close to the coast…"

He pointed to the chart he was holding and his finger downward, "Then we should be able to reach Messina in about three days. We should resupply there before making our way to up the coast. From there, weather permitting, we can reach the harbor city of Ostia another three days after. Once we're in Ostia, it should only be a few hours by carriage to get to Rome. The entire trip should take no more than a week."

Giovanni sighed, "No good… that will take too long! God only knows what will happen to her during that time!

The priest nodded in response, "I know… it will only take them about half that time. The Pope and his caravan will be returning on horses."

Giovanni shook his head, "Maybe we should have just followed them on land."

Antonelli sighed, "We definitely would have gotten their faster, but think clearly on this… We're planning on taking on the Church. When we rescue Adalyn, we will need to make a quick escape. Attempting to run across the countryside with the full force of the Church coming after us is way too risky. We'd be far more exposed and easier to pick off. Retreating to the open sea would give us a better chance of getting away."

"What?" Giovanni exclaimed. "I've seen the ship that the Patriarch travels on. I know what kind of force Rome can summon on the water. We'd have a warship on our heels in no time."

Antonelli shook his head and replied in a reassuring tone, "No Giovanni, it takes some time to get a ship ready to depart and the large warships you're referring to are expensive to maintain. By the time they get underway, we'll be long gone and they will be hard-pressed to figure out where we went."

Padre Antonelli noticed the worried look on Giovanni's face, "Don't worry; they will not harm her until they are within the walls of hallowed ground. Then…"

"What does it mean that she'll be cleansed," Giovanni interrupted.

Antonelli took a deep breath, "She'll be interrogated according to the laws of the Church. This means if she refuses to cooperate, she'll be tortured. Whether or not she confesses to being an unclean spirit, she will be most likely burned at the stake. It is the general code of conduct for dealing with heretics and witches laid out for inquisitions, but I am sure the Pope will use those teachings against a suspected demon as well."

Giovanni breathed in deeply out of fear, "I can't let that happen… I won't. If she dies, I'll have lost everything."

"Don't worry," Antonelli said in a reassuring tone, "we're not going in their blind, and not without help. Additionally, we will have the power of the Lord on our side."

"How can you be so sure?" Giovanni demanded.

The old priest turned to him, "What do you mean?"

"Part of what the Pope said was true." Giovanni admitted. "I found her on the rocks, bleeding to death. She is no longer immortal, and is definitely a fallen angel. She no longer carries the grace of God."

Antonelli nodded, "Yes, I assumed as such. Yet knowing that you may risk your very soul, you are still willing to go after her, why?"

Giovanni put a brace on the tiller to keep the ship on its course and then walked to the railing where he stood for a few moments, looking in the direction of Rome, "Two reasons I guess… one because I believe she is innocent of the crimes she's been expelled for and two…I had the White Plague…"

"What?" The priest exclaimed as a look of shock came over his face. "You 'had' the White Plague? You mean you're infected with it?"

"No longer…" Giovanni responded.

The priest could not believe it, "How is that possible? There is no cure for the plague and no one has ever recovered from it. Yet here you are claiming to be in perfect health? How?"

"She did it." Giovanni said softly. "Adalyn saved me. I don't know how, but when she kissed my chest, it was like my body healed itself of all injuries. She said afterwards that she had used the last of her powers."

Padre Antonelli looked at him in disbelief, "So she gave up her last shred of divinity to save you… I cannot believe how poorly I judged her… She sacrificed her last defense to give you a second chance at life."

Giovanni sighed as he closed his eyes and looked the other way, "I should have done more… I should have been more careful…"

The old priest saw the look on Giovanni's face and came to a shocking realization, "My word… I can't believe I didn't see this before… You fancy her, don't you?"

Giovanni remained silent for a few moments. He didn't want to say anything. A lecture from Padre Antonelli was the last thing he needed at that point.

The young fisherman twisted his lips, "Listen, Padre… I…"

"Do not try to deny what is obvious to me." Antonelli interrupted as he pointed an accusing finger at Giovanni. "Your feelings betray you. I see the look in your eyes and hear the speed of your breath. You love her."

Giovanni's face tightened into a scowl as he responded, "Yes… I do. I will go against God and his Church to save her. I will risk my very existence, my eternal soul, and see Rome burn to the ground to get her back. I will do whatever it takes… anything. If that is love, then God as my witness… I truly do love her."

"She is not a human being like us, you know that." Padre Antonelli said as he contemplated his former pupil's words. "This is highly unusual. I really don't know how to react to this. I just worry that this could end badly."

Giovanni nodded, "I know, and I do not care. I have to take that chance and make this right. If don't at least try, then the price will be my own soul. How would I be able to

Divinity

go out fishing and look at my reflection in the water with anything other than disgust?"

"She was kicked out of Heaven for a reason. You don't know for certain that she's innocent." Antonelli reminded him.

Giovanni took a step closer to the priest as he spoke, "Yes I do. There is no doubt it my mind. She gave me a second chance at life and the will to keep on living. In doing so, she cost herself the last shred of immortality and her only defense against the world. She made me happy and brought light to where there had been only darkness. How could I do any less than risk my life to save her? I cannot believe that one who has done so much good could have done anything evil enough to merit her punishment. I truly believe she's innocent."

"I see." The priest sighed. "Though I was no stranger to love during my youth, I am not sure I agree with this. However my personal feelings on the matter are irrelevant. I have committed a terrible sin and I cannot allow her to be slain at the hands of the Pope, not for my mistake. We'll save her. This, I promise you."

Giovanni agreed, "I never thought the Church was evil… but now…"

Padre Antonelli turned and cut him off sharply, "The Church is not evil. Please do not hold us all responsible for the misdoings of a few. There are many good people within the Church, more then you know. They outnumber those in power, even if their deeds are not recorded by history, they are there."

It was clear Giovanni had insulted the old priest, "I can only judge based on what I see as I have nothing more to go on."

He didn't entirely believe Antonelli after everything that had happened, but he kept quiet to avoid a fight. He focused his energy on making course adjustments as needed to the tiller. The wind had shifted the ship's course slightly so he made what corrections that he needed to.

Once they were heading in the right direction, Giovanni sat back against the tiller. His mind filled with the memories of his lost love. Their time together was too brief,

and he would give almost anything for even just a few more minutes with her.

Giovanni's heart ached with that realization and he knew that he would never be able to live with himself if anything happened to her. He could feel the pain from his chest spread throughout his body. He wanted to cry out, but it would do no good.

As Giovanni's mind returned to the present moment, he vowed that no matter what the personal cost was, he was going to get her back. *I will bring the world to its knees if I have to,* he thought to himself. *I have to get her back.*

Hours passed and it began to get dark out. Giovanni found himself falling asleep at the helm. Padre Antonelli looked up from his navigating as he felt the ship alter course a few times. He saw Giovanni dozing off and moved to the back of the ship.

The young fisherman could barely keep his eyes open. Antonelli smiled as he extended his hand, "I'll take over. You need to be awake to pilot this ship, go rest for a few hours."

Giovanni looked down at the handle and back up at Antonelli. He hesitantly nodded and handed the tiller over to the priest, "Thank you, I am very tired."

The young fisherman left Padre Antonelli to handle the ship, climbed down from the pilot's deck, and opened the door to the cabin. Warm air rushed out as the door flew open. He walked through the doorway and closed it behind him.

Once Giovanni was inside, he looked at the state of his cabin. The small fire pit had long since stopped smoldering and his blankets were only half on the bunk. He relit the flame with some flint to warm the small room and lay down on the messy bed. The mattress was barely comfortable, but he did not care.

It wasn't easy for Giovanni to fall asleep as he knew Adalyn would soon be in Rome. He tossed and turned but knew there was nothing he could do at the moment. His breathing slowly decreased as his body gave out. He finally slipped off into a painful, dark, sleep.

Divinity

II

Night fell on the world once again, but from the dungeon, Adalyn would never have been able to tell. She was hidden away in a windowless chamber deep within the bowels of the dungeon below the city. She had spent three days in a small cell, praying.

During that time, she had been offered food, but refused it. She did not want to eat and knew that it was only being offered so that she'd stay alive long enough for the Pope to kill her. It was satisfaction that she didn't want him to have.

Another day would pass before Adalyn was moved from her cell to a new room in another part of the dungeon. There were only two torches to light the entire room. Sharp objects and infernal mechanical devices lined the wall. Each one had a single purpose; to cause as much pain as possible without mortally injuring their victim. The entire room was covered with dried blood and wreaked of rotten flesh.

In the center of the room, Adalyn was tied on a table with her arms stretched out to the sides by old leather straps in a crucified position. Her ears strained for any sound as her breathing increased. She tried to struggle, but did not have the strength to break the straps.

The sound of approaching voices made Adalyn quiver. She could not make out what they were saying as their voices were still somewhat distant, but they were becoming clearer with each moment. She was certain that they were coming for her.

A moment later, three men entered the room. The first man wore luxurious red and white robes, clearly a cardinal giving the Pope's orders in his absence. The second man wore plain black robes with a thin golden sash. He was an older man with a mangled right hand. The third man was dressed in all black with a hood over his face, so he could not be seen, not that it mattered, given Adalyn's blindness. For all she knew, they were all dressed in rags.

Adalyn listened into their conversation with a quiver on her breath as the cardinal spoke, "Remember, Father Nevelson, you are free to use any methods at your disposal

Divinity

to force a confession and acquire any identifying information that may be pertinent to the exorcism. Just remember that she is to remain alive."

The cardinal looked Inquisitor Nevelson directly in his eyes to emphasize the point, "If she is allowed to shed her mortal entrapments before being exorcised, she may be allowed to return to our world in another form. This must not happen. I cannot stress this enough; she is to be kept alive."

Nevelson nodded, "I understand, my lord. You needn't worry; I know how to handle these interrogations."

"Of this, I have no doubt." The cardinal said in a reassuring tone. "I know your record. You have the Papacy's full confidence in this matter, but the point bore repeating."

"I understand, my lord." Nevelson said again, anxious for the cardinal to leave so he could get started.

The cardinal nodded, "God be with you, my friend."

"And with you." Nevelson replied as the cardinal turned to leave the room.

As soon as the door was shut behind them, Nevelson went to work. The Pope had assigned him especially as he was the most experienced inquisitor in dealing with cases of confirmed heresy and probably the only one who would be able to get any information from this creature.

Inquisitor Nevelson was a shrewd, stoic, elder clergyman within the Church. He had devoted his life to weeding out its enemies by any means necessary. He had often been called in on cases of heresy where the Church knew that the accused was guilty or the accused had committed a heinous crime. If anyone could cut a confession out of a sinner before they died, it was this man.

There was quite a stir in the Church when his right hand was horribly mangled during a session of torture. Nevelson had been operating one of the machines when part of his sleeve was grabbed by the gears which quickly crushed his hand. He stopped the machine, but the damage was done. The Church's healer did what they could, but Nevelson had permanently lost the use of his right hand as a result. He was now forced to rely on the monk standing in the room with him to continue his work.

Nevelson stood over Adalyn and shook his head, "Unclean spirit, you should know that I have been assigned to identify you, interrogate you, and prepare you to be exorcised. Your time on this planet is at its end, and not a moment too soon."

Adalyn turned her head away and refused to speak. Nevelson had seen this kind of defiance before and it was of no concern to him. He had broken people with strong wills many times over his career.

The tone of his voice was almost boastful as he spoke, "Let me explain to you what is about to happen here. You are going to suffer under my hand, horribly. Cries for mercy will be ignored unless they come with a confession, and the pain will not subside. You are already condemned. Why not save us the time and effort, and yourself the pain?"

Adalyn sneered, "I am fully aware of what is going to happen. I've escorted my fair share of torturers, who enjoyed what they were doing too much, to their final judgment. I have done no wrong and have nothing to confess, not that it matters to you."

Nevelson sighed as he stepped back and looked over at his hooded assistant, "Oh very well... begin..."

The hooded man pulled a large knife off of the wall and brought it over to the inquisitor. Using his good hand, Nevelson took the knife and stabbed it into the green silk of Adalyn's dress without cutting her skin. He ran the blade over the shoulders and down the side.

Adalyn did everything she could to hold on to the dress, but in her position, there was no way to prevent it from being pulled away. She fought to keep the tears from falling down her cheeks as she felt her skin being exposed and breaking out in goose bumps. Her breathing increased as she did the best she could to remove herself from the scene.

Adalyn's mind pictured Giovanni, Ariel, and Roselyn. She forced her happy memories forward to try to take away her sadness, but it was not working. Her jaw quivered as she sucked in a breath and released a whisper, "Most High... please..."

Nevelson and his assistant stepped back when they saw her skin. She was pale without a single blemish and her skin looked like it was glowing. The assistant turned to Nevelson, "Inquisitor... perhaps we should at least allow her..."

"Yes, brother..." Nevelson agreed, slightly unnerved by her appearance, "I think we still have some rags from a previous session, cover her, but only enough to preserve some decency."

The robed man stepped away to fetch some of the rags as Nevelson circled Adalyn's table, "So tell me demon, what is your purpose here? Why were you staying with that fisherman in Venice?"

Adalyn shook her head as tears streamed down her cheeks, "I have nothing to say to you, wicked creature. I have done no wrong... that is more than you could ever say."

Nevelson scoffed at her words, "I will not be judged by one so fallen as you. I have heard these claims before. They mean as much to me now as they did then!"

Adalyn nodded, "Yes Augustus... I know that. I've heard your name before in my travels."

A chill went down Nevelson's spine as his first name was uttered, but he shook it off, "Don't think that because you know my name, you hold anything on me."

"You weren't always this cruel." Adalyn continued, ignoring his words. "You joined the Church to get away from your father and the way he treated you. He was a savage man..."

Nevelson took a step back from the table, "How... how do you know about that?"

Adalyn's voice lowered to almost a whisper, "My job as an angel was to guide souls either up or down. I made sure that your father found his way to Hell."

Nevelson shook his head as Adalyn continued, "He now suffers for his crime!"

Divinity

Nevelson took another step back and glared at her, "I... I... You are a deceiver. You will not deter me from my work."

"Has the pain gone away?" Adalyn asked. "Have you found comfort in subjecting others to the pain that was wrongfully brought upon you? Has it finally silenced the cries from your youth?"

Nevelson's heart froze in his chest. He clenched his jaw and brought his good arm around, striking Adalyn on the cheek, "Silence, demon!"

Adalyn's head jerked to the side from the blow. Blood dripped from her nose as she lay motionless. She was still conscious, but chose not to say anything else. Clearly, she was not getting through to this man.

Nevelson's assistant walked in just in time to see Nevelson strike. He dropped the rags and ran to the inquisitor's side, "Master, are you all right?"

Nevelson's good hand was shaking as he looked at Adalyn, "Yes, I'm fine..."

"Perhaps that's enough for now." The assistant suggested. "It's been a long day and you should rest."

Nevelson nodded, "Maybe that's best."

He turned and looked at Adalyn with a sneer on his face, "Give her the rags and some food. She needs to stay alive until his holiness returns."

The assistant nodded as Nevelson left the room, "It will be done sir."

Adalyn didn't move as the assistant pulled at her chains and released her from the table. He handed her some old rags to wear so that she would no longer be so exposed, "Here, put these on."

Adalyn felt the material, which was a little better than burlap. She frowned as her head turned to the assistant, "Sir, please, grant me death. I have done no wrong, yet my very presence has condemned me to torture and resulted in the execution of an innocent fisherman."

The assistant shook his head, "If the Church deemed it necessary to kill him, his blood is on your hands. Now put those on and start walking."

Adalyn quickly threw on the shirt and makeshift skirt. A piece of rope was the only thing holding everything on. She tied it tightly like a sash and then nodded at the assistant, "You do not seem as cruel as the others… why do this?"

"It is my duty." The assistant replied. "Now get moving!"

Adalyn felt a wooden staff push against her spine and began to walk. Her thoughts focused on Giovanni and everything that had happened to her since she was thrown out of Heaven. Her heart grieved as she still believed that her friend was dead.

A few moments later, Adalyn heard the clicking of a metal lock and a door creek open. The assistant grabbed her by the arm and pushed her into the cell. Before closing the door, she heard him pull something off of the table, "Here, eat this, you need your strength."

Adalyn was handed a bowl with some sort of mush in it. It was little more than paste and its smell was unappealing. It was nothing like the food she'd been served while living with Giovanni.

Adalyn held it for a few minutes before throwing it in the direction of the assistant, lying down on the bed, and turning away. She would not eat the slop and just wanted to be left alone. Her eyes filled with tears as she lay on the bed with her arms and legs tucked in.

The assistant managed to close the door before getting hit. He sighed as he looked back through the small window in the iron door, "Fine, don't eat. You're only weakening yourself."

Adalyn didn't respond. Humiliated and in pain, she slowly lay on her back to face the heavens, "Most High, take me into your arms… or condemn me to the Well of Souls, but please do not leave me here. I beg of thee. You have already made me the reason a wonderful young man is dead. That alone is more than I can bear… please… help me."

Adalyn's prayers went unanswered as she lay staring up at the ceiling without any hope of being rescued. The only people who would know that she was there either didn't care or wanted her dead. There was no way out and she knew it.

The skin on Adalyn's cheek had stopped aching, but her nose still dripped blood. She couldn't have cared less about it though, as the pain of losing Giovanni was even greater. She couldn't believe her change of heart. A short time ago, she would have been okay with eliminating the human race and starting over, but now she actually cared for one of them.

Adalyn closed her eyes as she slowly dozed off, "God…"

III

A clanking noise the next morning roused Adalyn from a dreamless sleep. She turned and listened as someone entered the room and spoke, "Time to go. The inquisitor would like a word with you."

Adalyn recognized the voice as the assistant from the day before, "I have nothing to say."

"No?" The assistant asked. "Shall we find out for certain?"

Adalyn lowered her head, "Am I such a despicable creature that you must treat me with such scorn? Have I harmed you in some way? Have I done anything to make you hate me?"

The assistant sneered, "You're a demon…"

"Spare me your narrow-minded view." Adalyn said, cutting the man off. "Just take me to the inquisitor if that is what you so desire."

The assistant nodded and grabbed her chains. Adalyn heard the metal clanking and felt the tug as she stood up. She was led back to the chamber where she had been stripped the previous night.

As Adalyn moved, the sounds of pain and anguish filled her head as others who had been accused of heresy were being held in nearby rooms. The sounds brought her back to the time when she ferried damned souls to their fate. The difference was that she was certain that at least some of these people were innocent of their crimes.

The squeaking sounds of a nearby rat that had been startled made her jump as she entered the chamber. The assistant tugged on the chain and began pulling her over to the table in the middle of the room. She immediately recognized the rank odor.

Once again, she was strapped down and chained in place. Her wings were forcefully spread and strapped down as well. It hurt, especially because they still hadn't fully healed, but she was not going to give the inquisitor the satisfaction of knowing that she was in pain.

There was a loud sound of metal scraping against stone as the inquisitor entered the room. His assistant stood in the corner sharpening his blade as Adalyn began to quiver. She knew what was coming and did the best she could to hide her fear, but she was shaking and biting down on her lip.

Inquisitor Nevelson walked over next to the bed and spoke in a smug tone, "So here we are again. Any chance you've changed your mind about talking?"

Adalyn pressed her lips together and locked her jaw shut. She then turned her head away from the inquisitor's voice as a sign of defiance. The inquisitor sighed, "Oh very well then…"

Nevelson signaled his assistant to begin. The assistant let out a sigh as he looked at the creature. Nevelson didn't hear the cranking sound he expected and turned to his assistant, "Brother, begin!"

The assistant snapped out of it and began turning the crank on the wall. A loud mechanical sound entered the room as the machine began to work. The whole room groaned as he continued.

Adalyn felt her arms and legs stretch as sharp, pointed, objects dug into her skin. She gasped for air as sharp pains ran throughout her extremities. Every fiber of her being wanted to cry out, but she would not give the inquisitor the satisfaction. She managed to find the strength to remain silent.

Nevelson pulled the bandages off of her eyes so he could see the expression on her face as the table worked. Her eyes clenched shut and filled with tears as she gasped a second time and bit her lower lip in an attempt to absorb the pain.

The inquisitor watched for a few more moments before nodding to his assistant, "That's enough, brother. Let's see if she has anything to say."

To his frustration, Adalyn remained silent. Nevelson stood over her and shook his head, "You are strong. Not just anyone can endure this level of pain, but it's so pointless. No matter how much you fight, no matter how strong you are, you will tell me what I want to know. I will tear the confession from your flesh if I have to."

Adalyn turned to face the inquisitor and tried to spit in his eye. Nevelson grimaced as he wiped the saliva from his face. He was becoming angry with the creature in front of him, "So that's how you want to do this? Very well then, I'm through being mild."

The inquisitor picked up a blade off of the nearby stand and sliced away the rags that Adalyn had been wearing, "Only those who stand in the light of the lord deserve to be treated with dignity."

Adalyn lay on the table completely naked with her head turned to the side. She forced air into her lungs and spoke, "You speak of things you do not know. How dare you talk to me about the light of the lord! It is something you have never even seen!"

Nevelson shook his head as he turned to his assistant, "Again!"

The monk looked at Adalyn for a second. Doubt entered his mind about what they were doing, but he knew that he needed to carry out his duty. He nodded and turned back to the machine, "Yes sir."

The loud mechanical sound echoed through Adalyn's ears as the sharp pain entered her arms and legs again. Tears streamed down her cheeks as her head shook back and forth in agony. Her mind began weighing its options and she was actually considering just telling the inquisitor what he wanted to know. So many others had done the same and there was no shame in it. However this did not sit well with her own personal honor, so she endured the pain once again.

Nevelson shook his head as more blood dripped from the angel's body, "All right, stop. Let me have a word with her."

The monk stopped the machine and watched as the inquisitor looked over Adalyn. Nevelson looked like he was almost fixated on her as he worked. An eerie feeling entered the room as a look of frustration appeared on his face. It had been a long time since the old man had met anyone this defiant, but he had broken them all just the same.

Adalyn's arms and legs were covered in blood that dripped from her body and pooled on the table around her. She had been stripped of her dignity and violated by machines with sharp points. She could not move her legs as they were pulled too tightly and at least part of one of the spikes was still sticking into her right leg.

Inquisitor Nevelson took special pride in his work. He held no regret for punishing people who were convicted of heresy or treason against the Church. These cases were uncommon, but they were enough to keep him busy.

Nevelson was honored when he found out that he had been chosen for this assignment and decided to approach it with the utmost care. However he was becoming frustrated that she had not once asked for mercy or even cried out. He did not expect this much iron from a fallen angel, especially not on in her condition.

Nevelson paced back and forth around the table that Adalyn was strapped to, "Demon, why do you persist in keeping up this farce? Why do you still proclaim your innocence? You were not cast of the Kingdom of Heaven for no reason, confess! Speak the truth, and all of this will end. Confess, I say!"

Adalyn could feel the blood flowing steadily out of her leg. She had been brutally mutilated and was very weak, but managed to find enough energy to speak. It was barely a whisper, but she forced the words out, "Barbarian... what have I done to deserve such brutality? Your job is to maim and mutilate people in order to satisfy your leaders' lust for blood. My only sin was following orders. So why am I the one now being ripped apart?"

The inquisitor sneered, "I am a servant of God. If it wasn't his will that you be tortured this way, would you be here?"

"A... servant of God." Adalyn repeated as she scoffed. "If only you knew how much it grieves the Most High to hear you killing your own kind in his name. He loves you all equally, but you can't even see that..."

The inquisitor was barely even listening to her anymore. As far as he was concerned, her words were little more than another attempt to create doubt, "Silence, foul creature! If you will not confess on your own, then we will need to find other methods."

He turned to his assistant with a furious look on his face, "Begin the process again, brother."

Adalyn turned her head away from Nevelson and clenched her muscles as the monk slowly began to operate the machine cranks near where he was standing. She once again began to feel sharp pains throughout her body as though large needles were piercing her all over. The pain spread from her extremities to the rest of her body as she fought to keep herself together.

At first, Adalyn faced it without making a sound, but then she felt a hard digging sensation in her leg and the pain became so intense that she cried out, "Mercy, please, I beg of you… mercy…"

Captain Gonzaga appeared at the door of the cell, watching from the small window. He could feel a tear fall from his eye as she screamed out in pain. Part of him wanted to burst in and put a stop to this pointless inquisition. He was quite sure that this angel would not confess to anything because she most likely had nothing to confess to.

Listening to her screams pained the young captain greatly as he knew that there was nothing he could do. Interfering in an inquisition could cost him his own life, especially this one. He was forced to stand there and watch.

Inside the chamber, the sound of Adalyn's voice moved the old inquisitor, so much so that he raised his good hand to stop the torture. This was very unsettling to the old priest. He had heard similar cries of pain and agony many times in his job, but none of them had ever successfully reached his cold heart like this.

In other cases, it had been within his authority to grant mercy to those whom either confessed or he believed innocent, but he rarely exercised that power because of the people he dealt with. In this case, he had no choice. The Pope had ordered that she would need to confess. No mercy could be shown unless she cooperated. He couldn't quite place it, but there was something about the way she spoke that made him rethink what he was doing.

Once the machine stopped, Nevelson moved to her bedside once again. There were tears running down her cheeks and her body was quivering in agony. She wasn't sure how much longer she could hold on at this point.

The inquisitor could not believe that he was feeling pity for her. He decided to try to reason with her in an attempt to bring this session to a quick end, "Please, there is no need for you to continue to go through such pain. It is just two words you need to say, 'I confess.' Nothing more, I am not even asking you to give me any information. Just say the words, and I promise you that the pain will end and you will be granted peace."

Adalyn stopped moving and fell silent. The inquisitor grew nervous and examined her to make sure she was still alive. He knew what the penalty would be if she died before the Pope had a chance to perform the final ritual. There was a hint of desperation in the air as the inquisitor saw that she was still breathing.

He clearly did not want to take this much further, but what choice did he have? She still had not given him as much as a name, "Very well then, we have no choice but to move on to more… invasive methods."

Inquisitor Nevelson turned to the monk and nodded, "Sharpen your cleaver, and once it's ready… extirpate her wings."

The monk looked at Nevelson with a worried expression on his face. He didn't want to do this. His mind was already full of questions and like Nevelson, he was feeling pity for her. Cutting her wings off was not going to solve anything, the monk was certain of this, "My lord… shouldn't we wait…"

Nevelson turned back to him, "We have gotten nowhere with her. I don't like resorting to such methods, but we have no choice it seems... Brother, extirpate her wings."

At first, his threat did not generate a reaction, but when she heard the grinding of metal, she began to panic. As the monk sharpened his cleaver, she tried to pull her wings back, but they too had been strapped down. She struggled a little more as the grinding sound ceased and she suddenly felt the heat of a freshly sharpened blade near her skin.

Divinity

Desperate, Adalyn cried out, "No, please! Please do not do this! I have done nothing wrong!"

At this point, Federico had heard enough. He called to Nevelson, "Inquisitor, a moment?"

Annoyed, the inquisitor turned and left the injured angel's side, opened the door, and stood face to face with the knight, "What is it Captain?"

"You have failed to get any sort of confession from her." He said sternly. "End this."

The inquisitor glared at him, "How dare you, I do not take orders from you! You risk your own soul by interfering in this interrogation!"

Federico nodded, "I am aware of that. I also know that the Pope ordered you to keep her alive until he returns. Are you willing to gamble whether or not she has the endurance to survive such brutal mutilation after everything you've already done? End this now, for your own good!"

The idea that he had failed was too much for the inquisitor. His record for drawing a confession was flawless and he took great pride in that. He was not about to admit defeat to demon and a young aristocrat, whom the Pope had foolishly handed over command of his knights to.

"No!" Nevelson shouted as he turned and stormed back to the table.

Showing his intense frustration, he slammed his right hand on the wood next to her. The wood shook, causing some of Adalyn's blood to spatter as the inquisitor shouted, "Confess, damn you! Say the words and I will end your pain. What harm will it do you? You are condemned, there is no escape for you and no one is coming to rescue you. Tell me what I want to know, or I'll kill you myself!"

Federico's eyes widened as Adalyn fell silent again. It was as though she were daring the old inquisitor to try to pry a confession out of her. Nevelson could sense her defiance and it taunted him. He became enraged and pointed at her with his right hand, "Damn you, you will not, bring down my…"

Suddenly Nevelson noticed that something wasn't right. He realized that he once again had full use of his right hand and was pointing at her with it. The Inquisitor raised his hand to his face to inspect it.

The hand was no longer scared or mangled; in fact, it looked as though he had never gotten it caught in the machines in the first place. The inquisitor shook his head as his mind filled with questions. How could this have happened? What manner of witchcraft was this demon using?

At that moment, he noticed that he had brought his hand down into a small puddle of Adalyn's blood. The inquisitor wasn't sure how, but her blood had rejuvenated him. He staggered back, "What… how is this possible? What black magic is this?"

Captain Gonzaga's jaw dropped open when he saw what had happened. His heart skipped a beat and he slowly backed away from the door. The knight decided that he'd seen enough, turned away, and ran out of the dungeon. His faith had been greatly shaken over the last few days and he needed time to think.

Back in the dungeon as Nevelson looked over his hand, Adalyn clenched her muscles as she knew that her next words would most likely be her last. There was nothing left for her now and no one was coming to her rescue. She knew she was going to die and was going to make sure that the inquisitor knew what he was guilty of.

Adalyn mustered up her remaining strength and lifted her body a few inches off of the table. Nevelson thought that she was about to confess and breathed a sigh of relief. He leaned in to listen as her head reached his ear.

Despite taking as deep a breath as she was able, Adalyn's words were little more than a whisper when she finally spoke, "May God forgive you… for what you've done."

The shocked inquisitor breathed heavily as he stepped back and stared at Adalyn, "It can't be… you really are…no…"

The room began to spin around him so fast that he became dizzy and fell to the ground. The monk ran to his side, but Nevelson raised his hand for the man to get back, "Don't… don't touch me."

Divinity

It felt as though the walls were closing in as the inquisitor got back to his feet. *I've got to get out of here,* he thought as he staggered toward the door.

The monk looked at Nevelson with concern, "What about the prisoner?"

"Dress her wounds and find her some proper clothes." Nevelson called back as he stumbled out of the room. "Make sure she is fed, and on pain of death, make sure that she is kept alive until his Eminence returns. Do you understand me?"

The monk saw the look of sincerity in Nevelson's eyes. It was not fear of the Pope or anger that he had failed. It was a lifetime of regret for the souls that he had tortured which had finally caught up with him. The bewildered monk shrugged, "But my lord, she has been offered food, she refuses to eat."

"Then force it down her throat." Nevelson screamed as he continued walking. "I don't care how you do it, keep her alive, do you understand?"

The monk nodded, "Thy will be done my lord."

Nevelson left the chamber and headed up the long circular stair case. Each step was more agonizing then the one previous as he approached his chambers. No matter how hard he tried, nothing could remove the awful thoughts from his mind. *Dear God... what have I done...? What have I done?*

Over and over again in his mind, these words continued to haunt him. Finally, he reached the tower residence of the priests living in Rome. Upon entering his small chamber, he began talking to himself, "I have been doing what the Lord commands, right? Are the Pope's orders not the will of God? That is what we've been taught since I began my passage into the Church as a student. That angel... she is a demon, they said so... she has to be... is that not correct?"

Nevelson glanced at his restored hand again. There was no scarring or damage of any kind. It was as though she had given him a brand new hand, but this was not a blessing. To him this was a reminder of what he had done to Adalyn. He began to shake and tears fell down his cheeks.

Divinity

Looking at the abomination on his wrist, he heard her voice again in his mind, "May God forgive you for what you do here."

Nevelson fell to his knees and cried out. This time it felt as though he had been run through the chest by a soldier's spear. His eyes blurred in and out as tears fell, but they cleared long enough for him to see the specter of every single one of his victims staring at him.

The old man shook his head as he cried out, "Oh my God, my dearest God… I have tortured an angel!"

The inquisitor walked over to the window, unlatched it and looked down on the streets of Rome, "I'm sorry… I'm so sorry…"

Tears fell from his eyes as he looked to the Heavens, "Oh God, into your hands, I commend my spirit. Please accept this as my reconciliation… please God, forgive me!"

Nevelson took one final deep breath and closed his eyes, "In nomine Patris, et Fili, et Spiritus Sancti…"

When the inquisitor reopened his eyes, he stared transfixed at the heavens. In his mind, the only way to repent for the sins of ending so many lives was to sacrifice his own. With that last thought, he threw himself from the window of the tower.

A second later, the Inquisitor's body was little more than a mangled mass on the stones below. A large crowd formed around him to see what had happened. One priest looked up to the window and then back down at Nevelson. The priest sighed and pushed Nevelson's eyes closed, "Rest now ye tortured soul…"

IV

Giovanni lay in his cabin tossing back and forth. In the midst of a dreamless sleep of sorrow, he heard Adalyn's voice in his mind, "Mercy..."

His eyes burst open and he shot straight up, gasping for air and covered in cold sweat. His eyes darted back and forth around the room as he scanned for the source of her voice, "Mercy?"

The young fisherman rolled out of bed, hit the ground, and stumbled through the darkness to the deck of his boat. Padre Antonelli was on deck, attending to the tiller when Giovanni came running out. He looked at his old pupil with some concern.

Giovanni was pale and looked sick. His hair was a mess, his eyes were bloodshot, and he had dark circles under them, "My son, did you not sleep?"

"Not well." Giovanni admitted. "I was roused by a voice."

The priest narrowed his eyes, "Who's voice and from where?"

"I heard Adalyn." Giovanni said in a shaken tone. "Her voice came to me in my sleep. I heard it as though she was talking to me... it was so distant, and fading."

"I see." The priest said thoughtfully. "I admit to being ignorant of what powers angels possess, but perhaps she was calling out to you?"

Giovanni looked out on the sea towards Rome, "She was in pain... I could feel it. She was crying out for mercy."

A look of worry came over Padre Antonelli's face, "Then we must hurry. While I am sure the Pope wants her kept alive so he can perform the final exorcism rite himself, people have died accidentally during interrogations in the dungeons of Rome. If she is being tortured, she may be running out of time."

A sense of desperation came over Giovanni's features, "She's scared... I'll never forgive myself if she dies that way. I think I can get more speed out of the sail. Let me see if I can't extend it just a little more."

Giovanni ran to the mast, brought the sail down, and stretched it as far as he could. Before he knew what was happening, the ship responded by pushing forward. The sudden jolt of speed sent the young man flying backwards. Padre Antonelli pointed to the mast as it began making a cracking sound, "Be careful lad, it will do us no good if the mast comes down. We don't want to be adrift out here without a sail."

Giovanni got back to his feet and adjusted the rigging to compensate for the amount of stress on the mast. The rigging held, but he was not sure how much longer it could take the stress. His boat was a simple fishing boat that wasn't even designed to travel long distances, but here it was passing every test they put it through thus far, "How much farther? We've pushed this boat to its limits."

"A matter of hours." The priest replied. "It shouldn't be long now."

Once the rigging was secured, Giovanni took the tiller from Antonelli. The priest walked slowly to the front of the boat and began to pray, "In nomine Patri, et Fili, et Spiritus Sancti. Heavenly father, guide us through the darkness, know that we believe we are doing the right thing, and if we are wrong, then guide us to the path of righteousness. Guide us now as we face the full fury of Rome… in your name Lord Most High, Amen… In nomine Patri, et Fili, et Spiritus Sancti."

"I hope he heard you…" Giovanni hollered from the back of the boat.

"He always hears you…" The priest said sternly. "You just may not always get the answer that you desire. I would think that after meeting Adalyn, your faith would be less shaken."

Giovanni shook his head, "My faith in the existence of God has been restored to me. Faith in his infallibility and in that of the leaders of the Church is what I am losing."

Padre Antonelli nodded, "Alas, I am as well, my son."

"I'm also not sure whose side God is on at this point." Giovanni added. "Adalyn swore that she was innocent, but God said she isn't… yet I find myself on her side. I can't believe she's evil… I can't."

Divinity

Antonelli sighed, "Only time will tell on that one."

**

The ship pushed forward as hard as Giovanni and the priest could get it to go. For the next few hours, they continued to make adjustments to keep the mast from breaking until a large settlement came into view. Other small fishing boats also appeared on the horizon.

In the distance, Giovanni could see large buildings on land. They had arrived at the city of Ostia. Giovanni's eyes widened as he looked on, "The harbor city of Rome... Ostia's incredible."

"Wait until you actually see Rome." Padre Antonelli replied boastfully. "It is very large to those who have seen little of the world outside of our small town. You're lucky; no other member of your family has been outside of our little town for two generations."

Giovanni looked at the large port, "I can't believe we sailed the length of the coast in that short a span of time."

"God has led us here," Padre Antonelli said confidently, "and he has blessed our journey."

Giovanni shrugged, "You still truly believe that don't you?"

The old priest turned to Giovanni, "Yes I do."

Giovanni hesitated for a few moments as the city grew larger on the horizon, "I'm glad."

Padre Antonelli took the tiller from the young fisherman and changed course to head into the harbor, "We must be cautious. The Pope has eyes everywhere in this town and we don't want to draw attention to ourselves. I'll dock us at one of the smaller ports, they tend to go unnoticed."

"Are you sure that's safe?" Giovanni asked.

"Yes." Antonelli replied confidently. "They don't care who docks at their peers. They don't ask questions as long as the person has the money to pay for it."

Giovanni nodded and tugged on the rigging, bringing the sail up slightly to reduce speed. The old priest piloted the boat towards a rather rundown looking pier. Considering the condition of Giovanni's boat, which had taken a harsh

Divinity

beating from the long trip; it looked like the most appropriate place to moor.

Giovanni pulled the sail up the rest of the way and tied it in place as the ship pulled up alongside the wooden pier. The boat slowed even more as they passed the outermost point. Low thuds emanated through the hull as the boat scrapped along the dock.

Giovanni grabbed a mooring line, jumped off the deck of his boat, and landed on the old wooden planks of the pier. He then tied his boat to the nearest post, bringing it to a stop. Padre Antonelli threw the second line over the side for Giovanni to secure on the aft end of the boat. Once they were done, Antonelli lowered the ramp and disembarked.

The travelers did not have to wait long for an older, gangly looking individual to come walking out from the boathouse. He smiled a near toothless grin as he scratched his gray beard, "Good day to you both. The fee is two florins to moor your boat here. The fee also includes maintenance work… which it definitely looks like you need."

The dock master looked at the shabbiness of the boat in disgust, knowing that his fee would most likely barely even cover the costs of the repair work on the hull. It was the same as always; another peasant fisherman coming into port, needing to make quick passage to Rome. It had gotten so bad recently that he had debated closing the port or raising the docking fee.

Giovanni had no money and was about to untie the boat when Padre Antonelli stepped forward, "Here, 5 zecchinos should cover any inconvenience you may have. I would love this boat to be in much more acceptable condition when we return."

He then flashed the gold crucifix from underneath his robes, "One more thing, we were never here, make sure of that."

The dock master's eyes widened as he was handed the money. Finally it seemed as though his fortunes were turning around, "Welcome to Ostia, the harbor city of Rome, Padre. Your boat will be fit for a king when you return, I will see to it personally."

Padre Antonelli put his hands together and bowed, "God bless you sir."

Giovanni looked around as the dock master ran back to the boat house, "Well we are here, now what?"

"Now…" the priest said hesitantly, "we find my contacts here."

The two men proceeded into town, but did not need to go far. They left the port and turned to one of the smaller market areas on the outskirts of the main city. It did not take them long to find what they were looking for.

Antonelli stopped at a fruit stand and spoke to the young man behind the counter. The man was about the same age as Giovanni, but he had a much sterner look on his face as though he had led a tough life. Judging by his demeanor when he saw Antonelli approach, he was expected to be courteous, but he had no love for the clergy.

As Padre Antonelli looked him over, the man spoke, "Yeah, what do you want?"

Antonelli smiled, "Jacob, I have not seen you since you were a small boy. I doubt you remember me, but I was good friends with your father."

Jacob fell silent for a moment, studying the old priest's face, "You… you do look familiar, but what difference is that to me? If you're not here to do business, then move along."

Padre Antonelli didn't move, somewhat let down by Jacob's lack of manners, "I need to speak with your father."

"Not possible." Jacob said shaking his head. "He is in dispose and does not wish to be disturbed."

"I think he will make an exception for me." Antonelli said smiling.

"And what makes you think that?" Jacob asked, making no effort to hide his annoyance.

The old priest leaned over the counter and whispered something into Jacob's ear. Jacob's eyes lit up, surprised, "You know of the cause?"

Padre Antonelli nodded. Jacob narrowed his eyes for a moment as he looked at them both, most likely sizing them up and trying to figure out if he wanted to cooperate, or try

to kill them. He knew that they could just as easily be Church spies that were tipped off and sent to kill them.

After a brief silence, Jacob rolled his eyes as he spoke, "Wait here."

The man quickly turned to the building behind him and went inside. The two waited a few moments while Jacob spoke to his father. Giovanni turned to the old priest, "What is your business with these strangers? How do you know they can help us?"

Antonelli had a look on his face as though he did not want to answer, "Do not ask out here. Wait until we are behind closed doors."

Giovanni nodded, but watched the priest suspiciously. What was Antonelli up to and who were these people. Why did he want their help?

Moments later, the door flung open and an older man came running out calling to them, "Benito Antonelli, how good to see you my old friend! What brings you to my humble home after so many years?"

The priest smiled, "Hello Father Anselm, I come bearing information that may aid you in your cause…"

The smile disappeared from Anselm's aged face. His dark eyes darted up and down the street, "I'm not a priest anymore Benito, you know that. Come inside, quickly."

Anselm opened the door wide and beckoned them both to get in the house quickly. Giovanni followed close behind the priest as he eyed Anselm suspiciously. His mind now had even more questions. *No longer a priest, does that even happen?*

Once they were inside the house and the door closed behind them, twelve more people appeared brandishing swords. Alarmed, Giovanni pulled a small dagger out from under his tunic and pointed it at the nearest swordsman.

Anselm smiled, "You are a brave one, but that will not help you here, drop it."

Giovanni looked at Padre Antonelli for instruction. Antonelli nodded to assure him that everything would be all right. He knew that if the young fisherman tried anything, they'd be dead in a second anyway.

Divinity

Giovanni dropped the dagger on the ground. He eyed the swordsmen carefully, ready for any attack. His eyes darted around the room as the armed men stood perfectly still, returning his looks.

Once disarmed, Anselm turned back to the old priest, "Forgive me old friend, such security measures are necessary in this day and age. Share what information you have and we will decide whether or not it is important enough for us to act on."

The priest looked at the sharp blades pointed at him, "I have a favor to ask of you. It is of an urgent nature."

"Speak," Anselm said calmly.

Antonelli began to tell the story of what had happened in Venice. He spoke of Adalyn, Giovanni's work to save her, and of what the Church had done to them both. The group listened intently as though they were children gathered around their parents during a bedtime story.

Giovanni listened to what Antonelli had to say too. He was curious to hear Antonelli's version of things, but was disappointed by the story. There was so much that the priest missed out on. He would be hard-pressed to convince these people to help on such a bare-boned story. *I hope Padre Antonelli has something up his sleeve,* he thought. *We may not get any help otherwise.*

Once Antonelli finished telling the tale, he turned and directly faced his old friend, "Anselm, I beg of you. We need the help of you and your men, we need to get into the Basilica di Santa Maria Maggiore and get her out before they kill her."

Anselm scoffed, "Benito... after all these years, you come to me with this? You expect us to believe that the Pope is now holding an actual angel captive? Even if it were true, what does the life of a fallen one matter to us?"

"Do not be a fool, Anselm." Antonelli said sternly. "You know as well as I do that an angel going about telling truths about the Kingdom of Heaven that do not coincide with the Church's teachings would only further your cause. Why do you think they want rid of her so badly?"

Giovanni's ears perked up after hearing him speak. *What cause would he be referring to? Who are these people?*

Giovanni became suspicious of the people he stood in front of. Anselm smiled, "Benito, you have not changed. I still love the cunning tone with which you speak, but still, she would only be one voice against the might of the Church. Even the words of an angel would not do the damage you speak of, if she actually exists."

Antonelli stepped closer to Anselm, even with a blade pointed straight at him. The look on Padre Antonelli's face turned from determination to desperation, "Anselm, we have known each other for many years. I stood with you no matter what and I have never once given you false information. I am asking this as a favor for myself. In all the years we've known each other, through all of the adventures you and I shared, have I ever asked you for anything?"

"Never, you've always been a good man who wouldn't take more than he needed." Anselm admitted. "However I am curious Benito, what does this angel mean to you?"

Antonelli lowered his eyes and let out a deep sigh before he spoke, "I am responsible for her persecution. I brought the Church down on that innocent soul when I saw her with Giovanni. This is a sin that I cannot be forgiven for... not unless I can ask her myself. My own honor will not allow it."

Anselm looked at the men on either side of him. It appeared as though they were speaking to one another without talking, if that were even possible. After exchanging looks, Anselm turned back to Antonelli and nodded, "We will speak of this in council. Wait here."

Anselm took his people into the next room to decide what they were going to do. The wooden doors closed behind them, leaving the two visitors alone in the room. They were now alone in the quiet space.

Giovanni moved closer to Antonelli as he overheard muffled arguing from the next room over, "Padre, what are we doing here, who are these people?"

Divinity

"Anselm is an old friend of mine and a former priest." Antonelli responded. "He was amongst the most intelligent men that I had ever met. It was said that one day he would take his place as a leader of the Church, possibly even Pope. He was a favorite of the Council of Cardinals for many years."

"What happened?" Giovanni asked.

"He watched his sister's home burn." Antonelli said softly. "The Church killed his family for heresy after his sister was found to be healing people against the will of the Church."

Antonelli sighed, "Since then, Anselm became disillusioned… he became obsessed with alternative views of Christianity and began reading texts that were considered forbidden by the Church. In time, he discovered the teachings of Luther, and began studying his writings. Now he leads this sect out of his own home."

Giovanni snatched his blade from the ground and stepped backward towards the door, "Lutheran revolutionaries!"

The startled young fisherman glared at Antonelli, "You mean that you are one of them?"

Padre Antonelli shook his head, "Keep your voice down. Don't forget where we are. To answer the question; no, I am of the Church, but I do lend them aid from time to time."

"You would ask these people for aid?" Giovanni said in disbelief, "They're heretics!"

"No Giovanni," the old priest said softly, "I thought so too at first, but that is not the case. They have interpreted things differently from us, this much is true. However the simple fact that they have found new ways of practicing and living their faith does not make them wrong, nor are they heretics, they are just different."

Giovanni sighed, "I do not feel comfortable with this. These people ransack churches, they kill towns of people for their beliefs and they have waged war against good faithful people!"

Antonelli nodded, "Who better to help us stand against the Church?"

Giovanni turned away, "This will lead to bloodshed. I am sure of it, I do not approve…"

"No, I did not expect you would," Padre Antonelli replied, "but you said you were willing to do whatever it took to get her back. We will not be able to do so without their aid. They know the city better than anyone. So will you now stop at only words or are you willing to accept their help?"

Giovanni fell silent and lowered his eyes. A moment later, Anselm came back into the room, "Come with me please, both of you."

Antonelli nodded as he beckoned to Giovanni to stay close. They were led into an enclave chamber. The twelve men sat in old wooden chairs in a circle, all watching Giovanni as he entered the room.

Anselm took his seat at the head of the meeting, "The council has decided. We are going to help you."

Padre Antonelli smiled, "Thank you my old friend, I knew I could count on you."

Anselm sighed as he continued, "We are going to send three scouts and seven of our best soldiers to help you get into the basilica and rescue her. We will also arrange for a hooded carriage to meet you outside the city to ensure your safe transport back to Ostia."

Giovanni stepped forward and scoffed in disapproval, "Ten, you are giving us ten people to take on the Papal Knights?"

Anselm frowned, "Yes, ten. Your story is still an extraordinary one that is hard to believe. Yet here you are asking for help, and I've never known Benito to be a liar. We have also heard a limited amount from our contact in the dungeons about an unusual interrogation going on that resulted in one of the senior-most inquisitor's death. We don't know what to make of any of this, but we are willing to help you."

Anselm looked at the man to his right for a moment before continuing, "That said, at the moment, we do not have the resources or the man power to launch a direct attack on Rome. I will not order my men to certain death.

Divinity

We are giving you ten men to get you inside the basilica, retrieve this angel, and get you back out."

Anselm looked Padre Antonelli straight in the eye, "My old friend, I pray that this isn't the time you would choose to lie to me."

Padre Antonelli smiled, "Blessed are those who have not seen and yet still believe."

"You never gave up the old ways." Anselm smiled. "Still... I find it odd that the Church would risk harming a divine creature, even if they thought she was fallen. It seems like an awful risk."

Another member of the enclave spoke up, "It would not be the first time. People in general have a long history of slaying possible prophets of God."

Anselm shook his head, "Perhaps, but that is the basis for all of our beliefs. Lest we forget how our savior died."

The room fell silent for a few moments. The air hung around them and the tension was almost visible in the room. The men looked at one another, waiting for someone to speak.

Finally, Anselm broke the uncomfortable silence, "We have people on the inside that work in the dungeons. They should be able to locate the angel's cell. Once we have that information in hand, we will create a diversion to draw away the attention of the guards. That's when you will move into the city by way of the south tunnel. Our scouts know the way. They will take you in."

"Thank you," Giovanni said graciously, "I am in your debt, but may I burden you with one additional favor?"

Anselm nodded, "Go ahead, I will hear it."

Giovanni shuffled his feet nervously as he spoke, "Please have your men tell her that Giovanni is coming for her. She will most likely be badly injured. Tell her, so she'll hold on until I can get to her."

Anselm smiled, "I'll ask our informants to pass the word on when they find her. You have my word that she will know that you are coming for her."

Giovanni smiled, "Thanks... I appreciate it."

V

In the dungeon of the Basilica di Santa Maria Maggiore, Adalyn had been returned to her cell and given another bowl of food. She was still refusing to eat as both physical and mental agony took over. All around her, the distant sounds of men, women, and children asking to be let out of their cells, echoed through the walls. They each cried out begging for mercy in the name of God.

Adalyn tried to block out the sorrowful sounds, but it was impossible. Her own pain had weakened her too much to focus. Azrael's teachings had failed her and all she could do for comfort was continuously pray, "Lord Most High, please do not forsake me anymore, grant me death... I beg of thee. I have been punished for the crimes I have committed against you. Please do what you will with my spirit, but take me away from this awful place. I can endure no more of this..."

"And endure no more you shall." A calming voice said from the door.

Using the last of her strength, she sat up and pressed her back against the wall for support, "Who is it? Who is there?"

"My name is Brother Paul," he responded hesitantly, "I am the monk who has been participating in your torture... the late Inquisitor Nevelson's assistant."

Adalyn cringed and curled up in the corner as tightly as she could. The pain was too much for her and she was too weak to put up a fight. She wrapped her wings around herself as her only means of defense.

Knowing that her life was in the monk's hands, she tried to appeal to his humanity in the hopes that he would show mercy, "Please, no more... I beg of you, grant me death! This is more evil than I ever wanted to see. I have guided damned souls on their way to the Nether World, but never experienced the pain they inflicted. I hated humans for what they've done to one another. Then I met the boy in Venice, and he made me realize my unreasonable prejudice. I... I thought that maybe I was wrong about humans and began to rethink my own worldview... but he's most likely

Divinity

dead now, and it's my fault. Please sir, end my suffering. Send me to where I belong…"

He shook his head, "I'm sorry, I cannot, but I am not here to torture you anymore either. I can't… because I do not believe that you are an unclean spirit."

She didn't move, "Then why have you come to me?"

He lowered his head, "I have committed a terrible sin. I guess I just wanted you to know that I regret ever being a part of it… and to ask for your forgiveness."

"You are not worth forgiving." She replied sharply as her head turned away. "Your people are savage! You prey on the kind and the just, corrupting them, and bending them to your will."

She turned to face him with a pleading expression on her face, "Please, be the one person to show me mercy and end my suffering."

The monk looked at the ground as he spoke, "I am sorry for the pain I caused… but I can't kill you. It's not your time."

At first, she didn't respond. There was nothing but silence and the monk began to wonder if she believed him. He was about to walk away when she responded, "Then leave me be…"

Her voice was so soft; it was barely more than a whisper. The monk knew she was weak and nodded, "As you wish… but first, I have a message for you."

Adalyn sucked in as deep a breath as she could, "A message from whom?"

Brother Paul smiled, "Your friend, the boy from Venice."

"Are that cruel?" Adalyn asked as blood soaked tears ran down her face. "After everything I have lived though, you still feel the need to taunt me?"

"I am not taunting you." Brother Paul insisted. "Your friend still lives! Giovanni is in Rome. He has found some allies in the local resistance cell and is coming for you."

She raised her head at the sound of his name and her heart skipped a beat, "Truly, he is here?"

Brother Paul nodded, "Sign of the cross."

Divinity

"I believe you." Adalyn said convincingly, "Make sure he knows… I'm holding on for him."

"I will tell him for you." Brother Paul replied. "We are going to get you out of here. Please be patient, and try to eat something, you need keep your strength!"

Adalyn nodded as Brother Paul quickly stepped away from the door to avoid being seen. He looked around to make sure that no one had been watching and left the dungeon. His mind raced as he climbed the stone staircase back to the world, *so fragile, it is hard to believe that she really is an angel.*

From the door of her cell, Brother Paul heard a single whisper, though he was not sure how he could hear it, being so far away from her, "I forgive you for this…"

A tear fell down his cheek as he closed the dungeon door behind him, "Thank you."

**

The next few hours remained very quiet for Adalyn as she tried to rest and await rescue. For the first time in days, her heart felt warmth where there had only been fear and sadness. She wanted to be in his arms again more than anything at that point. There was a chance that Brother Paul was deceiving her, but she was certain that she would have detected it in his voice. She decided that it was best to take him at his word.

As the moon reached its zenith, Adalyn sensed another presence in the room with her. It was as though someone was standing over her, watching as her head darted to the side. Her damaged eyes were once-again covered by a bandage, but she didn't need them. Somehow, she knew who was in the room with her, "Azrael…"

Out of the corner closest to her bed, a dark figure appeared and faded into a winged man dressed in a gray tunic, "Adalyn… my friend… "

She sneered at him, "Come to finish me off, or just watch me die?"

Azrael was visibly pained by her words. He still didn't understand entirely what was going on, but he was determined to get to the bottom of it, "Adalyn, I don't know what you saw in the Asphodel Woods, but I wasn't there. I was away on business. Gabriel was with me the entire time, which is why Michael refused to listen to you. He knew where I was."

She could not believe what she was hearing, "If that is true… then how is it possible that I saw you there? Who was using your face?"

Azrael scratched his head, "I don't know, but I've suspected that someone was plotting to move against the Most High myself. I was looking into it and had a feeling that our culprit may be someone high up. I knew that if I got too close, I'd end up being betrayed. That is why I tried to distance myself from you and keep you in the dark as much as I could. I was hoping that should I be expelled, you would be able to continue my work. I have informed Gabriel, but I don't think he believes me."

Azrael looked behind him as though checking to make sure that they were still alone before he continued, "Still… he did promise to keep this between the two of us until I found some proof. He said he would bring it to Michael if we did. So far, all I've heard is that the circumvention of authority is increasing in the Celestial World. There were quite a few objections to your exile and some of the other angels have formed a small group to investigate behind the backs of the Seven Archangels. I honestly thought it would be me who got exiled once I stumbled on something I shouldn't have. If that happened, I wanted you to continue my work. I have a feeling that whoever is behind this knew about what I was doing and set you up either to send me a message to back off, or to remove any allies I might have."

"Do you suspect anyone?" She asked.

"No, I have no hard evidence against anyone at this point," he responded, "but such a deception would have taken a lot of power to accomplish. If I had to guess, I would suspect one of the Archangels, but I can't be certain. Whoever it was that arranged all of this is now working with the Church, I suspect. They are trying to plunge the world into a war that will turn all of existence into a slaughter house."

Adalyn's mouth fell open as she pieced the plot together, "Such a war would weaken the Most High enough to be vulnerable to attack!"

"Yes… We came to the exact same conclusion." Azrael sighed. "With the Most High out of commission, Lucifer would have all the push he needs to return and claim the throne."

Adalyn shivered at the thought, "You need to get me out of here, and we need to put a stop to this. Everything depends on us now. We need to find out who is behind all this."

"Adalyn… I can't," Azrael said in an ashamed voice, "Michael told us that the Most High has decreed that no angel can interfere in matters concerning you. If I save you, I risk blowing my cover and drawing attention to myself and the resistance movement currently trying to figure this out. As you said, all existence depends on us now. I am sorry my friend, but I cannot afford to help you with this much at stake."

"Excuses." Adalyn shot back as she turned away. "You coward, why should I believe anything you have to say? It's because of you that I am made to suffer now."

Azrael looked at her injuries with disgust. His heart grieved for what had become of a friend that he had held dear, "You don't have to believe me. You are right. It is my fault, and if I could trade places with you, I would without hesitation. Unfortunately that isn't possible."

He looked at the wound on her leg and ran his right hand over it. The palm glowed as it passed over the massive tear in her flesh. She winced as it shrank slightly and the bleeding slowed.

Azrael nodded as he finished, "This should keep you from bleeding to death for a while. That friend you made in Venice knows how to tend to injuries. He'll be able to help you as soon as he gets here."

"Thank you..." Adalyn said softly as she looked away, "but it's too late to earn my forgiveness."

"Yes I know," Azrael replied, "but what you should know is that Giovanni wouldn't have gotten here in time if it weren't for the extra wind that entered his sail… where do you think that wind came from?"

Azrael sighed as he continued, "Adalyn, you don't have to trust me or believe a word of what I told you. I'm not sure I would if I was in your place, but I will prove it in the end. For now, I will continue to guide your friend here. I know it isn't much, but once he gets here, I promise that you will be safe."

Adalyn remained silent. Azrael could tell that she didn't know what to make of any of this, "My friend, if you can't believe I'm innocent, please believe me when I say that I did not want to see any of this happen to you."

She nodded slowly, "All right… I will trust you on your word."

Azrael forced a smile as he turned away, "Thank you."

He said nothing further and vanished into the night. Adalyn breathed in and contemplated what would happen to all existence if this plot was not found out. *What is happening? Is all of existence really falling apart?*

Her thoughts were cut short as the pain took over. Azrael had treated her wounds, but not even his power could protect her from the pain. She could feel the sting of a thousand needles run through her skin. It became so intense that she lost consciousness.

Meanwhile, Giovanni and Padre Antonelli had successfully arrived at the Holy City. Their trip had taken hours and they were both worn out. Fortunately, they were allowed a brief time to rest outside the basilica's walls. The small force of revolutionaries that Anselm had promised to send, met them outside the walls and brought them to their small encampment.

Much to Antonelli's surprise, they were a lot younger than he had thought soldiers would be. Some were Giovanni's age, but a few of them were barely in their adolescent years. *Far too young to fight in a war… but then it is their world too.* The thought of children dying on a field of battle was almost more than he could bear, but it was the world he lived in.

Suddenly, a sound from a nearby bush put the group on alert. Their leader, a man that was a few years younger than Giovanni and clearly a foreigner turned, "Men, to arms, to arms!"

Giovanni was amazed by the speed with which the group reacted to the situation around them. They quickly dropped down behind the brush with their weapons ready to go. Even he reacted as though he was a trained soldier. He ducked down and pulled out his knife as he awaited the attack.

The men grabbed their arquebuses, lit their wicks, and aimed at the bush where they had heard the sound. The young man raised his hand, "Steady men, no one fires until I say."

As the men stood by, ready to fire, a tall man with dark hair and skin, who was clearly not from the area, appeared in front of them. He was a thin man with light brown hair looking to be in his early 30s. His accent was also a clear giveaway to his heritage. Giovanni concluded that he was from further east.

The man raised his hands, showing that he was unarmed, "Nicolas, don't shoot! It's me, Cyrillus, I bring news."

The leader, Nicolas, lowered his hand and signaled his troops, "Stand down men, its Cyrillus. Thank God he made it out."

Nicolas walked over to Cyrillus, with Giovanni right behind him. Cyrillus was out of breath and holding his knees as he tried to pull himself back together. He could barely speak through huffs of breath.

Nicolas put his hand on their scout's shoulder, "Good job making it back, do you have any news?"

The man was struggling to speak as he had not yet caught his breath. Nicolas nodded, "It's okay, take your time."

Seeing the anxiousness in Giovanni's eyes, Cyrillus pulled in a deep breath and spoke, "I've spoken to Brother Paul. He sends word that she is alive, but…"

Giovanni stepped forward, "What is it?"

Cyrillus looked at the young fisherman in the eye as he cleared his throat. His pause lasted only a moment, but to Giovanni it felt like a lifetime. His response did not relieve

the tension building up inside the young fisherman's chest, "She's been tortured badly. Brother Paul has seen to it she's received food, but she's refused to eat, and she's bleeding out. Paul does not believe she will survive another session with an inquisitor."

Giovanni became frantic as he turned to Padre Antonelli, "We must hurry! She'll die if we wait much longer!"

"I agree," the priest said with alarm in his voice, "we will have to wait until the cover of nightfall, but then we must get her out."

Nicolas nodded, "All right, we'll get our things together."

He then turned back to Cyrillus, "Where is Quintace?"

"He didn't make it." Cyrillus said sadly. "I saw him get shot as he was trying to escape."

"God rest his soul." Nicolas said quietly before turning back to the group and pointing to three men that were standing to the side. "I want you three to go scout out the guard compound. The rest of us will wait until nightfall over by the south tunnel."

One of the men turned to Giovanni, "Anselm told us about that entrance when he first joined us. It's little more than an ancient drain for the bath houses in the basilica. This will not be pleasant, but it is the quickest way to the dungeons."

Giovanni nodded, "I've come this far. Adalyn, I'm coming for you, please just hold on."

Padre Antonelli closed his eyes, "Keep speaking to her, my boy. Even if your words cannot reach her, your heart will."

As the group took refuge in their small encampment, Nicolas sat down next to Giovanni on the grass. He didn't know what to make of this Venetian fisherman and wasn't sure he trusted him. As far as Nicolas was concerned, Giovanni was an outsider whom he intended to keep at arm's length.

Nicolas had always been a man of reason, but he also preferred to be cautious. He knew that he would need to find out more about whom they were going to rescue and why

Divinity

this person was so important, "So this is the real thing? There is absolutely no doubt in your mind that she is an angel?"

Giovanni shook his head, "None, unless you can come up with another explanation for why someone would have wings on their back."

Nicolas chuckled as he thought about it. His face then quickly turned back to a serious expression, "Giovanni, I heard the Papal army burned your home to the ground just to get to her. They did the same thing to my family's home.

Giovanni nodded, "I was the last of my family. Everything I had of them was in that house. Now… I still have my family ship, so maybe I can get enough money to rebuild it at some point. For now, I need to focus on saving Adalyn. Otherwise it's all been for nothing."

Nicolas looked at the walls of the Basilica di Santa Maria Maggiore as the sky slowly darkened, "How long was she with you?"

"Not long," Giovanni said glumly, "A few months, just about? I found her on a rock in the harbor near my home. She was soaked and covered in blood from her injuries. I did what I could to care for her at that point. She was on the mend, but her wounds were only beginning to heal."

"So that's why she's blind?" Nicolas asked.

"Yeah." Giovanni replied. "When she was kicked out of Heaven, she landed face first into the ocean and damaged her eyes. They were really bad, and I'm not sure that they'll ever heal."

Nicolas frowned, "What do you think happened to her? Why do you think she was expelled? I was always taught only evil, fallen, angels could be hurt like that. What if we're wrong and wind up helping a demonic creature?"

Giovanni shook his head, "I don't know, she was expelled for treason, but she swears that she's innocent. She broke the lord's decree and had to suffer the worst of punishments for it. She was stripped of her divinity and sent here to die."

Even as he spoke, Giovanni could tell that it was the second part of the question that Nicolas truly wanted

Divinity

answered. He looked Nicolas directly in his eye as he spoke, "As for whether or not she's a demon... I spent months with her, and she never once tried anything. She was extremely cautious and untrusting of humans, but she didn't exhibit any of the signs that the Church tells us about demons. She wasn't bothered by crucifixes, she prayed, and she even taught me things about God that I never knew. I don't know about you, but that doesn't sound like a demon."

Nicolas nodded, satisfied with his answer. Giovanni turned his attention away from the basilica to find out more about the people helping him, "So what about you? You don't look like you're from around here and your accent is a clear giveaway."

Nicolas thought back to the days before he joined the revolutionaries. He remembered a time before violence was reality and life was far simpler, "My family lived in Athens. They still followed the philosophies of the ancient forefathers of my country, in direct opposition to the Church. It was the source of a lot of scandal in our hometown, but we were still happy."

Nicolas shook his head, "We were arrogant enough to think that because our family had status, that we could stand up to the Church and expect to survive. The Church concocted suspicions of hedonism against us and thus we were declared heretics. They came to my home just as they did yours. My family was questioned for days by the Church. In the end, the inquisitor made a full report to the local governor that we were unrepentant. Not long after, soldiers surrounded the house. They cleansed my family by burning them alive our own home. "

A shocked expression appeared on Giovanni's face, "How did you survive?"

Nicolas shrugged, "I guess you could say that I was the lucky one. I was just coming home from the market when I saw the house burn from a distance. There were soldiers all around so I hid in the nearby woods. Sometimes I can still hear my family's screams in my sleep."

The look on his face was one of seriousness and anger as he spoke, "The day I watched them burn, I died as well."

Divinity

The look on his face turned from anger to sadness, "I fight for the revolutionaries, but to be honest, I no more share their beliefs than I do those of the Church. I cannot begin to fathom how a loving God could allow things like this to happen. Such evil…"

Giovanni lowered his eyes, "Adalyn told me that God grieves for every death as though it was his own child, but the time of prophets and teachers is over. Like any parent, eventually the child must eventually leave home. It's the only way they grow. As a result, the Most High only interferes behind the scenes."

He looked up into Nicolas' eyes again, "I know it's not much comfort, but once the suffering ends, Adalyn told me that the good go to live with God and the angels in paradise. She told me that an incredible journey lies ahead of us."

Nicolas smiled, as the sadness disappeared from his eyes, "I look forward to meeting this angel. She sounds incredible."

Giovanni looked back up at the basilica walls, "I know what she'll say… You are the last of your family. Don't allow it all to end in a blaze of hatred."

Nicolas shook his head, "I fight against the Church. I am not suicidal, but I do not want to bring children into a world where things like this happen. I want peace and that can only be achieved through struggle."

Giovanni frowned, "I have heard reports of what sects of Lutheran attacks have done. How many families were burned in their homes by the people you have sided with? How many people are homeless on the streets because of them… how many?"

Nicolas sighed, "Yes I know, but I have never been party to that. Sometimes you have to side with the lesser of two evils. That is the only way we will end this."

"No," Giovanni said wholeheartedly, "you only achieve peace through vigilance and self-purity. Struggling is a part of life, but should never consume it to the point where there is nothing else. There are other more important things you miss out on by allowing that to happen."

"In a perfect world," Nicolas sighed, "that might be true, but this is not a perfect world. In the end, fighting is all I have left."

"I'm sorry for your losses, Nicolas." Giovanni said empathetically. "My family was all claimed by the white plague. I had to care for them as one by one, I watched them all fall away from me. So believe me, I know how you feel; you're alone in the world now. The dread that you may lose your sanity in a quiet house that was once filled with activity and life is always with you, but are you really willing to throw away your family history for revenge?"

Nicolas looked up nervously, "The white plague? Your entire family was claimed, yet somehow you were not infected? How is that even possible?"

Giovanni looked toward the drain which led to the tunnels that they would need to traverse in order to rescue Adalyn. Water dripped between the rusted old iron bars, creating a stream of brown water. He sighed as he revealed the truth of his condition, "I was infected. When I found Adalyn, I was already having a hard time. I was coughing more and more every day."

His eyes scanned the basilica walls as he continued, "Do not ask me how, but when I saved her she apparently had one drop of divinity left. She used it to rid me of the terrible disease. She cured me when I was in the middle of coughing so badly that I thought that I was going to die."

"I see…" Nicolas said thoughtfully. "So you're doing this for her so adamantly because she saved your life? You want to repay your debt?"

"No, not exactly." Giovanni hesitantly admitted. "Although that is part of it, I also made a promise to her… I told her that I would take care of her and protect her… I failed to do so when the Church arrived at my doorstep. I can't live with that."

Nicolas narrowed his eyes in a rather suspicious way. Something about the way that Giovanni spoke was very telling about how he felt, "You sound almost smitten. So you love her?"

Giovanni looked at him seriously, "Yes… I realized it too little too late. I just hope I survive long enough to tell her."

VI

Night had finally come over the land. Rome was covered in darkness, but each house had its own set of torches to combat it. A faint aura rose from the city as though the sun was dwelling amongst the buildings, keeping the streets lit.

The group began to work on the old metal drain cover. It had been some time since the revolutionaries had used this entrance due to it not being of much strategic value to them. The drain led anywhere that they wanted to go in the city, but it was on the far side of the basilica and passed through the dungeons first. Freeing people being tortured for heresy by the inquisitors was extremely risky and often not worthwhile unless it was one of their own.

The revolutionaries' swords scraped against the old iron bars as the cover slowly began to come loose. When the group finally pried it off, they squeezed through one by one. They found themselves in a dark hallway that had been carved out of solid stone.

Nicolas lit a torch and cautiously slid through the narrow opening. At first it burned bright, but once he stepped inside, the fire dimmed to only half of its original brilliance. He quickly turned his back and blocked the wind to keep the flame burning.

The walls were moist, the air was humid and smelled of must and mold, and everything looked like it was covered in slime. Giovanni had never endured such an offensive odor and began to cough. It took him a moment to regain his composure, and he fought back the urge to gag. He buried his face in the sleeve of his shirt and took a few breaths through his nose.

Once he felt better, he turned to watch the rest of the group struggle through the small entrance. Padre Antonelli was the last one through and to Giovanni's surprise, the only one not to grimace at the smell. The old priest smiled as he looked around, "Ah yes, I remember this smell... I think it may have actually gotten better than it was when I was young."

Divinity

The group moved down the tunnel with Giovanni and Nicolas at the lead. Padre Antonelli followed close behind them through the darkness. No one knew what lay ahead as the sound of movement echoed through the tunnel.

As the group walked, the priest's eyes suddenly shot to the left. He swore that he saw someone moving around, perhaps following them. The shadow kept to the corner of his eye, but when he turned to face it, the shadow disappeared before his eyes could focus.

Antonelli kept looking to the side every few minutes just in case. Giovanni noticed it and placed his hand on the priest's shoulder, "Padre, what is it?"

Not wanting to alarm anyone, Antonelli shook his head, "Nothing, but we'd best be on our guard."

"Always." Nicolas replied, looking back. "The last thing we need right now is surprises."

As they marched deeper into the basilica's underbelly, Giovanni's eyes narrowed. He'd never seen or heard of such tunnels under the Holy City before. He quickly turned to his old friend for answers, "Padre, where are we? What are these tunnels?"

Padre Antonelli pointed down a right fork and beckoned everyone in that direction as he replied, "In the last years of the Western Roman Empire, the Emperor feared invasion and these tunnels were built as a precaution. That way, if the need arose, they would be able to evacuate the clergy, as well as any relics from Rome as quickly as possible. However, by the time the Roman Empire fell, only the Church still knew of their existence. Now they're little more than forgotten passages, but they still lead everywhere that you would need to go within the city."

Nicolas nodded, "Including the dungeon where she is being kept."

Padre Antonelli nodded, "Yes, there is an underground dungeon beneath the papal residence that is reserved for only the most serious heretics. Since the revolution began, those cells have been all but filled. No one who goes in there as a prisoner has ever come out alive and no one is supposed to know it exists, except for those within the

Pope's own council. I'm told even most priests don't even dare enter that area."

There was a sudden creaking noise as though someone had disturbed the nearby rubble. Two of the men drew their swords and scanned the area with their eyes wide open. Padre Antonelli turned to them, "What is it?"

One of the men looked back over his shoulder, "I'm sorry Padre. I swear I saw something there, just for a moment."

Antonelli nodded, "I saw it too, everyone spread out and be on your guard. I think it's clear that someone may be watching us. Giovanni, I want you to take point, Nicolas, you're with him."

The two men nodded and moved to the front of the line. Nicolas drew two swords and handed one to Giovanni. The sword was very ornate, but had much wear and tarnish. Still, Giovanni held it out in front of him should he need it.

Giovanni had never used a sword before, but had experience with other blades. He was proficient with carving knives and cleavers. This was not much different in principle and he was certain that he could manage. His life could have very easily depended on it.

The group kept their eyes opened on all sides as they marched down the next tunnel. This unusual maze appeared to go on forever and the smell of must grew worse as the air became thick with moisture. Giovanni stayed to the center of the path, not wanting to touch the rank stone.

**

In the distance, the group could hear the sound of dripping water as they moved in. They had been walking for roughly an hour when Padre Antonelli decided everyone needed to take a break. He planted his torch in the ground, "Okay, everyone rest here for a few minutes."

The group sat half on one side of the tunnel, half on the other side. Each person took a moment to find a dry area between the puddles to try to relax for a moment. It wasn't easy as no one wanted to lean against the moist walls.

Nicolas and Giovanni sat facing each other in the hall. Nicolas peered down the tunnel as the walls stretched on into darkness and shook his head, "There is no end to this

God forsaken labyrinth. Padre, I mean no disrespect, but are you sure you know where we are going?"

Padre Antonelli turned to face him and nodded, "Quite certain, your master taught me these paths back when he was still part of the Church. It may have been some time, but I still remember the way. I have not gone totally senile just yet."

Nicolas lowered his eyes, "Apologies, Padre. I meant no disrespect."

Giovanni looked at the priest oddly, "Why did Anselm feel the need to show you all of this?"

"You know," the priest replied, chuckling, "I have no idea now that I think about it, perhaps for just such an occasion?"

Giovanni frowned at the absurdity, "Or perhaps to recruit you for something like this?"

"Possibly." Antonelli agreed.

Another shadow passed overhead as the group rested. The men drew their swords and searched the area, suspecting attack. They panned out and kept their swords pointed, ready to strike anyone who jumped out at them.

After a few moments of silence, Padre Antonelli heard a crumbling sound down the next tunnel, "I think it's best if we keep moving. The more time we spend in one place, the more exposed we are and all the more likely we'll be to fall under attack. Come on, let's go."

Giovanni again took point as the group stood up and took their positions. He was now growing impatient, knowing that Adalyn was in pain. Time was running out for her and he was determined to get there before it did. He marched hard and fast as though he had God's own determination.

The bewildered group followed Giovanni as he led them down tunnel after tunnel. At times, they had to run to keep up. Antonelli called out a couple of times to him, but his words were ignored.

Giovanni's persistence paid off when they reached the hall where Antonelli had heard the crumbling noise. In front of them was a fragile wall that appeared to have once been a doorway to another room. Another stone fell as he touched it.

Padre Antonelli inspected it for a moment before looking back at Giovanni with surprise, "You were marching as though you had been down here before. What happened?"

Giovanni shrugged, "I can't explain it. It was as though I was being guided here by something, or someone. I felt like my feet were leading me down the correct path."

Padre Antonelli nodded, "Pray your guide is on our side this night."

Nicolas pushed hard against the wall to see how solid it was. The poorly lain bricks began to fall away and crumble, "This wall looks new. It seems like it may have been constructed in a hurry. The stones are not sealed into place."

The group continued to push until they cleared a path big enough for everyone to get through. Giovanni moved frantically to get them down. Antonelli placed a hand on his shoulder to get him to calm down, "My boy, you're going to hurt yourself or alert someone to our presence if you keep acting like this."

After prying and pushing for a few moments, the wall came crashing down and the group moved into the next chamber. Dust and debris was kicked up all around the group, further impeding their vision. Giovanni waved his arms as he tried to figure out where they were.

In this room, they encountered a whole new foul odor. The air was so nauseating that the group was forced to cover their noses and mouths to stop themselves from vomiting. As the dust and debris settled, it became clear as to where the smell had come from.

The floor was littered with poorly made wooden sarcophaguses that were haplessly strewn about the room. Some had been stacked on others to save space. Many had fractured planks and decaying human remains were hanging out.

Padre Antonelli looked around, "This place... from what Anselm told me is where they kept the worst offenders. These people were murderers, sadists, and

adulterers. Their crimes were so numerous and so horrific that the Church did not even grant them a proper burial."

Nicolas shook his head, "I've never even heard of anything like this."

"It's not exactly something that the Church wants people to know about." Antonelli replied. "These people and their crimes have been all but forgotten about in recent years and the Church would like it to stay that way… Given the stories that I've heard… this is one area that I agree with them on."

Giovanni grimaced in disgust, "We need to keep moving. This place is disgusting. I will live a happy life if I never see it again."

Nicolas touched the brick wall on the opposite end of the room. To his surprise, it also began to give way. Startled, he jumped back and turned to the others, "These walls are not sealed, if we take the bricks down quietly, we should be able to clear a path. Come on, everyone get to work."

Giovanni shook his head, "I don't like this at all, why put up a wall like this, why not just bury them?"

Antonelli shrugged, "I would say that the old leaders of the Church didn't want them to be afforded the dignities that they had denied their victims."

Giovanni sighed as the group began to pull bricks down. They worked quietly, pulling bricks down one at a time to keep anyone who could be on the other side from hearing them. Small beams of light appeared through the darkness as each brick was removed from the wall.

Finally, they had cleared a hole into the next room. Giovanni was able to pull one last brick from the wall before it collapsed. A gust of wind blew past him as the foul odor disappeared. The rush of air extinguished the torch he carried, leaving him at the mercy of a few smoldering torches that were hanging from the wall in the next room.

Nicolas stepped into the next chamber first. His eyes were wide, fully expecting to be rushed by a group of guards. He was poised and ready to strike if there was any movement, but to his surprise, the next room was completely deserted.

Giovanni followed right behind Nicolas with his sword at the ready. He found himself in a large room with doors on every wall. Each one was solid wood that had been reinforced with iron bars.

The entire room looked as though it was carved out of solid rock many hundreds of years ago. Escaping from such a place was near impossible. Torches were hung above every doorway, but most of them looked like they had long since burnt out.

Giovanni shook his head, "No wonder they don't have many guards here! This place pretty much provides its own defense against escape!"

Nicolas frowned, "It also helps that no one knows about it... or so the Church thinks."

It was very dark and cold in the chamber. As Giovanni walked past the nearest cell, he once again recognized the rank odor of rotting flesh and covered his nose. Nicolas came up behind him, "How are we ever going to find our way from here? She could be in any one of these cells!"

One of the men peered into the first dark chamber on the right and quickly pulled his head back in disgust, "Ugh... this one is definitely dead."

Nicolas nodded, "Just from the smell, I think you'll be hard pressed to find many that are alive."

Nicolas hated being the bearer of bad news, especially when he knew how the recipient felt. The idea of shattering someone's hope of finding a loved one weighed heavily on him, "Giovanni, I hate to say it, but I fear this may be a lost cause. It's pretty obvious that no one survives very long down here."

"No, she's alive, I just know it." Giovanni replied confidently as he closed his eyes.

His mind raced a mile a minute as he looked over the cell doors. *Adalyn, where are you?*

In her cell, Adalyn heard his voice and turned her head to the door, "Giovanni?"

At the same moment, Giovanni's eyes opened wide. He couldn't explain how, but he heard her voice as clear as day in his head. The room where she was kept lit up like a beacon in his mind. He pointed to the door at the end of the last row and smiled as his face lightened up, "She's in that one. I can feel it!"

Nicolas nodded, "Men, you heard him. Get over there and get that door open!"

Giovanni ran ahead of the rest of the group as they moved to the end of the hallway by the staircase. He banged on the door frantically, "Adalyn, are you in there?"

Adalyn's heart jumped as she heard his voice. Her ears tingled at the sound. For the first time since she arrived in Rome, she felt joy, "Giovanni, is that you? I'm in here, please get me out!"

No one had the key to unlock the door and there wasn't a guard nearby for them to attack. Nicolas signaled for everyone to stand back and bashed the ancient lock with the butt of his sword. It made a loud clanking noise that echoed through the prison, but it would not break. He tried again, hitting it on the side, but it would still not budge.

Giovanni sighed, knowing that every minute they spent fiddling with the lock was leaving them open for attack. His hand went into his trouser pocket where it was poked by a sharp metal object. He quickly withdrew his hand to see two fishing hooks. He smiled as her bent the hooks straight, "I think I can get the lock off."

Nicolas looked at him oddly, "How?"

Giovanni showed him the two straightened hooks, "My older brother showed me how to pick locks when I was younger. It's how we used to escape being locked in our room. You should have seen how angry our papa was when he found out!"

Nicolas chuckled as he backed away, "I can imagine. All right, have at it."

Giovanni knelt down so his eyes could look right into the keyhole. He inserted the two hooks and began slowly turning them. He heard a click, but he could tell it wasn't the sound he was looking for. He began to sweat as he moved the hooks in the opposite direction. Slowly, he could feel the mechanism pushing back as it finally gave way.

There was a faint click before the old lock released and fell to the ground. Giovanni pushed on the door, but it

Divinity

wouldn't budge. He turned and looked at Nicolas, "I can't get it open."

Nicolas nodded, "Look at it, the thing is ancient and probably not open very often. It's probably going to take a few of us to do it."

Nicolas signaled a few of the other men to help. Cyrillus came up next to Giovanni and put his shoulder into the door while Nicolas pushed from the top. As they applied pressure, the door slowly creaked open. Dust and debris fell from the doorway as it finally opened enough for them to look in.

Giovanni could not wait another second. He could tell from her labored breathing that she was in pain. Once the door was open enough for him to squeeze through, he ran to her bedside.

Adalyn rested her head on the slab as he inspected her wounds, "Giovanni... you came for me."

He smiled, "Of course I did. I made you a promise. Did you think I was lying to you?"

Adalyn frowned, "No... I thought you were dead."

"I almost was." Giovanni admitted. "I may still be if we don't get moving."

She reached out for Giovanni to pick her up, "Please help me, I can barely move."

Giovanni quickly placed his arm under her to support her legs as her arm limply rested on his shoulder, "Rest easy, I have you. We're going to get you out of here."

Adalyn grabbed his chest with her other hand and gently kissed him on the cheek. Giovanni noticed that her grip was very weak as she held on. A petrified look came over his face, "Padre, she's barely breathing, I think she may be dying."

Padre Antonelli looked at her injuries. It was almost sickening to see just how badly she'd been beaten, "This isn't good my friend. She's impoverished and whoever her inquisitor was, took special care to inflict as much pain as possible. This is sadistic... what animal could have done this?"

The old priest's thoughts were interrupted as Adalyn struggled to breath. He could plainly see how dire her situation was, "Giovanni, we have to get her out of here, now. She requires rest and some decent food. She'll die if she doesn't get the care she needs."

"Do you think she has any chance?" Giovanni asked in an almost defeated tone.

Antonelli nodded, "Her wounds need to be treated before they can heal. Once that's been taken care of, she'll just need time to let her body repair itself. That will happen with rest and some decent food. As long as she gets those, with any luck, she should be okay, I hope."

Giovanni nodded and quickly exited the cell with Adalyn in his arms. He was desperate to get her out of there as quickly as he could. Not a second could be wasted if she was to survive.

Adalyn did the best she could to keep her wings tucked back so as not to obstruct Giovanni's vision. She pressed her head against his chest as he moved. His heartbeat comforted her and helped take away some of the sting from her injuries. She smiled for the first time in a week as she spoke, "I missed you."

Giovanni nodded, "I missed you too. There is something I need to tell you, but it will have to wait. We can talk once I get you somewhere safe."

"Hold me tight, Giovanni," Adalyn pleaded, "and don't let go."

Giovanni smiled, "Never…"

As the group was about to head back the way it came, they began hearing voices in the distance. Five Church guards were investigating the caved in wall in the distance and blocked their escape. The guards had confused looks on their faces as they looked through the debris. They were heavily armed, making attacking them unwise. Someone had apparently seen that the flimsy wall had caved in and called the guards.

With their escape route cut off, Giovanni's group began to look for another way out. Nicolas shook his head, "No good, we'll never get out of here the way we came. What do we do now?"

Padre Antonelli sighed, "It looks like we don't have much other choice but to head up. We're going to have to make our way out through the city."

The group looked at each other with a sense of doom about them. Each of them knew that they were no match for the entire force of the Church, but it was either fight their way out or surrender. They all knew what surrender meant; they would be questioned, tortured, and eventually executed.

"This is suicide!" Nicolas insisted. "There must be another way!"

Giovanni shook his head, "Antonelli is right, it looks like heading up is our only option."

Cyrillus smiled, "Well today is as good a day to die as any and we'll probably be able to take a few of them with us. I say we go!"

Nicolas nodded as he turned to his command, "All right men, this is it. Keep your swords out and follow us. It's either fight or die now. Everyone head up the winding staircase."

Giovanni took Adalyn in the opposite direction of the where they entered and headed over to the long staircase that would lead them up through the basilica. It was a long climb, and heading right into the Pope's residence was a dangerous proposition at best, but Giovanni knew it was their only option.

As they made their way out, a figure appeared out of the darkness behind them. It had been standing off to the side pretty much since they opened the door. It was watching their every move without making its presence known.

As the figure came into the light, Captain Gonzaga's face appeared. He had heard a rumor that someone was going to attempt to break her out, but he never fully believed it. Though it was his duty to stop them from defying Church law, he was still confused by everything that had happened since the angel had arrived in Rome.

The Captain's mind filled with questions as he watched them move. *Why would the Church want to kill a divine spirit? Unless she was an unclean one... but then why*

would these people risk all to save her? What is it about her that has everyone in an uproar? Fallen or not, what information could she possibly have to force the Pope to risk the Lord's wrath?

Federico's mind returned to reality and he realized that he could no longer trust the information that he was given. He would need to find out the truth on his own. *I can't let this go. I'll need to keep an eye on them for now. I will find the answer.*

For now, it seemed, allowing them to escape and keeping an eye on their movements would generate more answers than another inquisition would. The Pope wasn't present, so there would be no way for him to know that his captain had let them go. It didn't seem like the Pope fully trusted him anyway as he rarely took him along on any missions.

The group pressed on through the darkness until they reached the door at the top of the underground dungeon. Giovanni was tired and his legs were screaming for a break, but they would have to wait. They were still in danger and could not stop any time soon.

After slicing through another door, the group forced it open and ran out into the lowest level of the basilica. Nicolas shook his head as he looked around, "This is probably the lowest level anyone knows about who doesn't live here."

Antonelli nodded, "Yes, but we're nowhere near out of danger yet, we've got to keep moving."

Giovanni let Padre Antonelli walk in front of him as the priest led them to a large iron door on the far side of the basement chamber. It wasn't locked and easily opened when the latch was pulled. The moment it was released, Giovanni gave it a solid kick, sending it flying open.

The young fisherman took in a deep breath of fresh air as he stumbled out into the moonlight. A full moon shined over Rome, giving off a tranquil glow. He looked back at the large palace that they had just exited in complete awe of its size.

The scene was spoiled when they noticed that the entire city was in a panic. In the distance, large plumes of

Divinity

flame appeared that were generated by thundering explosions. One of the basilica's guards brushed passed them, not even giving them a second glance, "Everyone, take cover! We are under attack! Lutheran rebels have set fire to the city!"

Padre Antonelli turned to Nicolas with an unhappy look, "Nicolas, what exactly have your men done?"

Nicolas shrugged, "We promised you a diversion and this was it. We've had powder bombs set up all over Rome for just such an occasion, although we'd hoped to use them as a diversion to attack."

Antonelli shook his head, "I wish you'd found a better way of doing this. You're causing a panic!"

"What better way to cover our escape?" Nicolas asked in an annoyed tone. "No one has been hurt. They've just been frightened a little. It's enough to get us out of here alive. That should be good enough for you, priest."

Giovanni ignored them both and began to move toward the gates to the city. So far, they hadn't encountered any resistance, but as the group entered the courtyard leading away from the basilica, they heard the clicking of metal behind them, "Hey you, hold up there!"

Giovanni turned to see a soldier pointing a smoking arquebus at them. He froze in place while Nicolas reached for his sword. Before anyone could react to the guard's words, a sword's tip appeared in the middle of the guard's chest, pushed through from behind.

One of the revolutionaries had successfully snuck up behind him and ran him through. The guard fell limp without even having a chance to cry out. The revolutionary let the guard fall to the ground as he rejoined the group.

Padre Antonelli was outraged, "He hadn't done anything wrong, was that really necessary?"

The man sneered, "He's working for the Church, that's enough of a reason for me."

Padre Antonelli was about to give the man a piece of his mind, but Giovanni cut him off, "Padre, we don't have time for this. Deal with that man once we're all safe. If we don't get moving, more people will wind up the same way!"

Padre Antonelli released his breath and nodded as the group moved out of the sanctuary and into the courtyard. He was well aware of the crimes that the Church had committed, but that did not justify murder. He was not about to let this go and went over exactly what he was going to say to the revolutionary once they were safe.

BOOK 5
Into Exile

I

The group pressed on through the city and made their way closer to the exit. The city guards were busy dealing with the flames and preparing for an attack that would never come. They were beginning to think that the danger was past, but that quickly changed as they neared the gates.

The moment that Giovanni placed his fingers on the iron bars, a winged figure appeared out of the darkness and blocked their path, "Well done men, for a small peasant group, you have come quite far. Now place Adalyn on the ground and step away if you value your lives. There will be no more loose ends once she's dead."

Adalyn's head jerked, surprised by the voice. An expression of intense horror came over her features as she spoke, "Michael… no, it can't be. You are the traitor?"

Giovanni's eyes widened, "Michael, as in Saint Michael, the general of God's army?"

Adalyn nodded as the figure stepped out of the darkness. He smiled maliciously as he pushed his curled hair back, "I should have killed you when you were unconscious on the rocks. I didn't count on someone like this boy finding you. You have been a thorn in my side for too long… You defied orders on a constant basis during the war, but always made it out okay. You were a brilliant fighter, but at the same time you were too naive. You should have known that I can assume any form I wish… including my dear friend Azrael."

"And the feelings of sadness and death from him?" She asked with a tight fist.

"That was easy," Michael replied, "I just amplified the energy already present in Asphodel."

Adalyn clenched her jaw, "But why deceive me and frame your best friend? Why go to such great lengths to have me killed. I don't understand. I am not even a member of one of the Choirs! Compared to others, I would think you'd view me as insignificant!"

Michael moved closer to them, "You were far from insignificant. An otherwise unknown and uncelebrated angel

who rose to become the hero of the Celestial Wars, it was a story unlike any other. You may not have found your place amongst the Choirs, but you have shown unwavering loyalty to the Most High. I knew that it would be impossible to persuade you to see my side."

Michael shook his head as he continued, "Think of it, removing you would have hurt morale amongst the legions of angels. It would be enough to make them question each other's loyalty. I could easily use such doubt in my plan. If we were able to remove enough of the lower class angels through false accusations of treason, I could convince the Seven that there was a central force behind these acts. Before long, no one would trust anyone and the Choirs would be in chaos. At that point, the legions that had once flocked to the Most High during the Celestial Wars would not be there."

Giovanni shook his head, "You're completely insane. Are you are seriously going to declare war on God? What kind of madman are you?"

The angel clenched his teeth as a look of hatred appeared on his face, "Mad... man? I am no man! I am far superior to anything you could possibly fathom. How dare you compare me to a being of such insignificance?"

Adalyn's face twisted into a scowl, "Do not criticize him in front of me! You speak of something that you do not know! Your teachings about humans have been nothing short of a deception!"

"Have they?" Michael asked in an almost amused tone. "I have existed a long time. I have dwelt amongst these creatures and seen them tear one another to pieces. Yet still, they receive the undying love of the Most High. No matter how much they turn against him, deny his existence, and maim one another, he favors them! You yourself saw it. I heard your words when you spoke of it to the Most High. This is something that I can no longer tolerate."

"There is truth in your words." Adalyn admitted as she turned her head away. "No Angel knows of their evils better than I do. I was the one who made those evil souls answer for what they have done."

She raised her arm, showing him the wounds that she had received, "And I've experienced their evils first hand, thanks to you."

Michael fell silent as she pressed herself tightly against Giovanni, "But I have also seen their potential to do good. I understand now why the Most High loves them so. While their leaders continue to practice cruelty and barbarism, there are still good amongst them that hide in the shadows. They work behind the scenes and while the evil regimes topple, they continue their work. Those are the people that will someday inherit the world, as it has been written! I didn't understand then, but I do now. This was the Most High's plan all along!"

She pressed even harder against Giovanni as she spoke, "No amount of torture or torment can destroy that. While the old regimes topple, people like Giovanni and Padre Benito Antonelli will continue fighting for what's right."

"You truly believe that, don't you?" Michael asked in an exasperated tone.

She nodded confidently, "I do."

Michael shook his head and sneered, "Then you are nothing more than a fool! I was right to have you removed. You are of no further use to me!"

"Michael…" Adalyn said sorrowfully. "He trusted you above all others. You were his favorite amongst the Choirs. He made you his general. What more could you have asked for? Why do this?"

"A leader of servants is still himself a servant." Michael replied. "The dominant sheep in the flock must still bow to the will of the shepherd. Soon, Lucifer will take his place on the throne and when he does, angels will no longer be servants and stewards. We will rule as kings, as it should be!"

Padre Antonelli could not believe what he was hearing. He had read stories about the Angel, Michael, but his words did not match the angel's deeds. To the old priest, these were words that no man of faith should ever have to endure, "You are truly insane… this can't be real. St.

Michael is a hero of God, called upon when all else fails to defend the weak."

Adalyn shook her head, "No, he is both demented and blind with the promise of power, but not insane. The stories that you have heard are not false… but it seems they are just history now."

The old priest could not handle these revelations, "But how… God is omnipotent, he can't be harmed. It is not possible."

Michael laughed, "Spout your ignorance and falsehoods to those who will listen. Do not presume to do so in the company of those who know more about him then you ever will. The stories you've heard are lies and your teachings are flawed!"

Adalyn turned her head towards Antonelli, "It is possible. Every time you fight and kill one another, you weaken the Most High. If the killing gets worse, Lucifer will be able to move in and do what he wants."

Padre Antonelli stepped back, "My God…"

Adalyn sucked down a deep breath as she turned to face Michael. Even though she couldn't see, she knew where to point her mouth, "You actually think Lucifer will share power with you? He is the lord of the Underworld, the master of darkness and deception. He will kill you before he gives up anything!"

"Lucifer is a revolutionary seeking to aid his brothers and sisters." Michael responded, "He pushed for the fair and equal treatment of all angels. If you don't believe that, then I'll send you to hell to ask him!"

The tension was shattered by the sound of thunder before another voice appeared on the scene, "So it was you... All along, you had us all fooled. Michael, my old friend, how could you? You stand to be counted with the people we fought and sacrificed so much to destroy so long ago."

Everyone turned in surprise to the strange voice. Adalyn recognized the voice and a relieved smile appeared on her face, "Azrael!"

Giovanni turned and looked at the figure stepping out of the shadows, "Another angel?"

Divinity

Adalyn nodded, "He was my friend and mentor during the war. He's on our side... I hope."

Azrael stepped out in front of the group with a sword of flame in his hand. He stood between Michael and Adalyn, intent on protecting her from any attack that Michael had planned, "Who was next old friend? Were you planning on having me taken down next, or perhaps another member of the Seven? Uriel implicitly trusts you, is he next on the chopping block?"

Michael frowned, "You wound me, Azrael. Do you think that I had forgotten our friendship? I had hoped to bring you with me, to share with you the change to come. I could think of no one more deserving of Lucifer's rewards."

Azrael scoffed at the absurdity, "You actually that think I would have followed you into madness? The very idea that I could turn on my friends and betray those who had given their lives to protect all of existence, it's unthinkable."

"Perhaps," Michael sighed in a disappointed tone, "but I would have at least offered you that chance. At least you would have survived that way."

"Never," Azrael shot back, "and now the Choirs will know what you have done. I'm taking you in Michael, you're broken now."

"I don't think so. The Choirs will never know what happened here!" Michael hissed as he drew his own sword. "Not until it's too late to stop it. I'm going to end this, here and now."

Azrael shook his head, "So what then, Michael? Are you going to kill us, and then lay waste to the Celestial Temple? I can't allow that to happen... I'm going to have to bring you down... old friend."

Michael's smile was full of malice as he stood face to face with his former comrade, "I see... so here we stand as I suppose we were eventually meant to... Will it be my doom that we face this day, or yours? Either way, by the heavens, you will not find an easy opponent in me. I will not hold back."

Azrael nodded, "I would expect no less from the Most High's most beloved general."

Divinity

Michael bowed respectfully as he wiped a tear from his eye. He put on a strong face, but he genuinely did not want to fight his oldest friend. He knew what he was going to have to do as he spoke, "Well... Shall we begin then?"

Azrael quickly turned to the group still standing behind him in shock, "Giovanni, go! Take Adalyn far away from this place. Keep her safe, and this might all have been worth it."

Giovanni nodded, "I will, you have my word, but what about you?"

"Don't worry about me." Azrael replied with his eyes locked on Michael. "This is the price I have to pay for allowing Adalyn to suffer. You are a good man, I'm glad she found you."

Giovanni frowned, he knew what Azrael was saying, and did not want to just abandon him there. Azrael sensed Giovanni's hesitation and glared at him, "Go, now! I'll buy you as much time as I can."

Adalyn realized what was happening and began to struggle in Giovanni's arms, "No, Azrael, I won't leave you here!"

"You don't have any other choice." Azrael replied with a voice full of sorrow. "Don't be afraid... I will always be with you, but this is how it has to be. You were right when you said that it was my fault. You were kicked out of the kingdom because of me. I should have told you more when I had the chance."

He frowned as he looked at what she had become and what she would now have to live through, "I thought I was protecting you by not giving you fair warning. Now you have suffered because of me. That's a strike against my soul that I cannot live with. Michael has to be stopped. He is too powerful to be left unchecked. Go, warn the choirs, save the world, save each other..."

Azrael closed his eyes as he heard the group run by, "... save yourselves..."

"Such noble words, Azrael," Michael scoffed, "I didn't think you had it in you, very well spoken indeed."

Giovanni held on to Adalyn tight as they ran towards the outskirts of Rome. To their relief, the gates were open.

Divinity

Azrael watched as the group disappeared into the darkness. He looked at Giovanni one last time and nodded, "Take care of her…"

Giovanni turned back and looked at Azrael in the eye with a reassuring nod, "Always…"

The gates closed and the two could no longer see one another. Adalyn screamed out in panic as she struggled in Giovanni's arms, "Azrael please, there is no need to do this, come with us, please! Don't die…"

All Azrael could do was ignore her as he turned back to face Michael. A hot tear fell down his cheek as he circled close to his opponent. The two stepped closer to each other with each move until their swords crossed. They stared each other down for a few moments, their eyes glowing from the flame of their blades. It was as though the battle had already begun in their minds.

Finally, Azrael pulled his sword back above his head and brought it down on his opponent. Michael was able to dodge out of the way and take flight. Azrael looked up and watched as Michael spread his wings.

Once Michael was high enough above the city, he raised his own sword, turned it over, and plunged downward. His wings curled around his back to pick up more speed. He quickly became a blur as he moved.

Azrael knew this dive attack well and deflected it with amazing strength. He then raised himself off of the ground with a mighty flap of his wings and shot straight at Michael. The moment he was close enough, he swung his sword and grazed Michael's chest.

Michael felt the burn as Azrael's blade crossed him. He put his hand over his heart, "Well done old friend, it has been a long time since last I actually felt pain."

Azrael smiled, "You have been my master, but I have grown since your teachings. I have learned a few moves of my own over the years. This won't be as easy a fight as you hoped."

"Excellent," Michael said smiling in approval, "This should be fun!"

Anyone viewing this battle would be reminded of two fireflies frolicking in the night sky. The white feathers on their wings were illuminated by the blaze of their swords as the two clashed. They glowed as the two circled around each other.

Each strike created a sizzling sound as the blades connected. Azrael attempted a high risk dive successfully connected with one of Michael's wings. Michael fell to the ground in pain. He had been cut deeply, but had not lost his wing. He had not felt pain like that in a long time and had forgotten how to cope with it.

Azrael landed and stood over Michael, "How sad for you, old friend; you have lived beyond the boundaries of time, yet can't see past your own lust for power. The Michael I've known over the years would never have been brought down this easily.

Michael got to his feet, nursing his wing as he slowly backed away from his old friend defensively. Azrael sighed and shook his head, "It's over Michael. You have lost this time. Surrender and come back with me. You must stand trial for what you have done. The remaining six Archangels should have some questions for you. If you stop this madness now and admit the crime, they may yet show you mercy."

Michael sneered, "Not this time!"

He immediately thrust his arms forward creating a field of energy that pushed Azrael away. The blast sent Azrael flying backwards, but he was able to remain upright. He dropped to a knee to balance himself as the blast passed him by.

Once Azrael found his feet again, he countered Michael's attack with beams of light from his eyes. Michael dodged out of the way of the first one by doing a tumble. He then countered with his own beams, which deflected off of Azrael's.

The two angels fought with a spectacular display of light. The energy was so bright that it illuminated the entire city block. Giovanni and the others could see the aura over the city walls as they ran for the carriage that was waiting for them on the outskirts.

Adalyn sobbed as she feared for Azrael's life, "Azrael… no…"

Giovanni didn't like seeing her like this. She was already in pain, and now that her friend was putting his life on the line, her condition was even worse. He was desperate to cheer her up, "Don't count him out just yet. He could win."

Adalyn shook her head, "Azrael is an incredible fighter, but Michael was his master. He taught Azrael how to fight, and he is the Most High's steward. Now that the Most High is in rest… Michael is even more powerful. Azrael is knowingly sacrificing himself for us."

Giovanni shook his head as he looked back at the city. The aura continued to glow as people fled the area. He didn't know what to say as part of him feared that Adalyn was right.

After a few moments of stalemate fighting with white beams of light, they stopped and just stood in place staring each other down. Both fighters were exhausted and breathing heavily. They were both covered in sweat which was a new feeling for them both.

Azrael wiped his brow as he stared down Michael, "Such a strange world."

Michael nodded, "I know, fighting here is so much different than in the clouds. The gravity here is so much more intense. It's obvious that we can't stay in the air for too long."

"That's probably why humans have such strong legs." Azrael replied with a chuckle. "This could be stressful if the Most High ever decided to have us try to work here more regularly."

Michael shook his head, "Soon… that won't be a problem, for either of us. Join me Azrael!"

Azrael frowned, indicating that Michael already knew his answer, "You know I can't do that. I'm sorry old friend. It ends here for you."

There was almost no movement, as the two angels were locked into one another's eyes. Finally, Michael let loose with his most powerful blast yet. Azrael dodged out of the way and responded in kind. Their beams connected causing a large explosion that threw them both back against

the walls. Azrael regained his footing quicker than Michael could, flew over, and kicked Michael in the head.

The blow knocked Michael backwards, stunned. Azrael nodded, breathing heavily, "That is enough, it is over!"

"No," Michael said as he sat up, "I will not be judged by you or any of the others."

Azrael raised his sword again, ready to strike, "Then… I'm sorry Michael; it's the Well of Souls for you."

Using split second timing, Michael pulled a small dagger out from under his armor and thrust it into Azrael's chest. Azrael dropped his sword and tried to cry out, but was unable to draw the breath to do so. His eyes widened as he tried to cry out.

Michael held Azrael close and whispered into his friend's ear as the blade moved deeper into Azrael's chest, "You first old friend."

Michael let go of Azrael and let him fall to the ground. Azrael teetered for a moment as though trying to fight it, but it was a futile struggle. He fell to his knees and began to cough. Blood poured out of his side as pain shot through his body.

With his last ounce of strength, Azrael grabbed his sword. Before Michael could stop him, Azrael threw it into the air. The sword shot away into the clouds and disappeared.

Azrael turned back to flash one final look of anger towards his murderer. As he closed his eyes for the last time, his body turned to ash and was whisked away by the wind. Before he completely dissolved, Azrael closed his eyes and whispered, "Adalyn… stay safe…"

Michael wiped a tear from his eye as Azrael vanished. The full moon provided him light as he looked towards the heavens. He knew that with Azrael gone, there was no one left who could stop him.

Now it's your turn Adalyn, Michael thought as he prepared to take off.

The angel quickly turned to take to the air, but his injury was worse than he thought. Michael felt a sharp pain shoot through his wing as he tried to spread it. Unable to fly due to this injury, he knelt down and shrouded himself using his healthy wing. He quickly vanished from the ensuing chaos as Church guards finally appeared on the scene. His teeth clenched in anger as he spoke, "Adalyn, you will live today, but this is not over between us…"

II

The group finally arrived at the carriage that was waiting for them on the city outskirts. They quickly untied the horses from their stand. As Giovanni loaded Adalyn on to the bed of the carriage, they could feel that something had happened. The courtyard had fallen silent and was no longer glowing.

Adalyn gasped as she suddenly felt a sharp pain through her heart as though she was being stabbed. She immediately knew what had happened and cried out, "Azrael no, please God… no!"

Giovanni placed his right hand on her forehead and tried to calm her by caressing her skin, "What happened, Adalyn?"

"He has fallen." Adalyn said as she fought through the tears. "He's dead…. Azrael is dead!"

Antonelli lowered his eyes, "Adalyn, I'm so sorry."

"Michael…" She sobbed. "What did you think this would accomplish? You had everything…"

Giovanni tried to comfort her as he jumped into the carriage, "I am sorry Adalyn. What can I do for you? Just tell me what you need and take the pain from you."

"I've had to watch my entire world die in the night." She replied as she curled up in Giovanni's arms. "Giovanni please… you are my last hope. Please just get me out of Rome."

Giovanni nodded and turned to Nicolas, who had grabbed the reigns in the driver's seat, "All right, you heard her. Let's go, we need to get back to Ostia as quickly as we can. The sooner we make it to my ship, the better."

Nicolas snapped the reigns and the horses began to move. He quickly snapped the reigns, causing the horses to pick up speed. The carriage shot quickly through the night as they made their way back to Ostia.

Padre Antonelli sat in the back with Giovanni while the rest of the group rode horses. He looked over Adalyn as Giovanni cradled her in his arms, "All right, my friend, we need to do something about these injuries."

Giovanni nodded, "I know this is going to sound crazy, but it's like the wounds reopened the moment Adalyn sensed that Azrael died."

"Strange indeed." Antonelli admitted. "Thoughts for another time perhaps."

Giovanni saw that her blood was dripping all over him and began to panic, "She's going to bleed to death if we don't do something."

Padre Antonelli noticed some rags that had been left for them in the back corner of the carriage, "We should use these to dress her wounds. We may not be able to stop her bleeding, but at least we can slow it until we get her somewhere safe."

Giovanni nodded and began to wrap the rags around her legs and arms. She winced in pain as he pulled them tight, "Giovanni…"

He began to breathe heavily in a state of panic as her skin slowly turned pale, "Hold on Adalyn, you'll be okay, I promise. We'll go somewhere that you'll be safe from all of this. Evil will never touch you again as long as I draw breath."

Adalyn nodded as she lay back and lost consciousness on Giovanni's lap. Once they finished wrapping her injuries, Antonelli sat back with a troubled look on his face. Giovanni looked up at him with a stoic expression, "Surprised to find out that the Church's teachings are flawed?"

Padre Antonelli shook his head, "Anyone capable of, and not afraid of, thinking for themselves can plainly see that a lot of what the Church's leaders do is flawed. That being said, I at least thought that I would pass into the next life and meet with an infallible God and father who was completely omnipotent. Now I find out that this isn't exactly the case."

Giovanni sat back as Adalyn rested on his lap, "You know, she told me that God loves all of his children, that no matter how far we turn from him and even forget him, he still loves us. The father you knew may not be everything you thought he was, but isn't it enough to know how much he cherishes us and that his promise of paradise remains true?"

Padre Antonelli thought about his former student's words. He finally smiled faintly and sighed, "Yes... yes, I suppose it is. Well said, my boy. You really have grown up."

The carriage went over a bump, causing Giovanni to turn and look out of the front opening. Ahead of them, he saw the ocean. He smiled as the sounds of the sea began to fill his ears, "It looks like we've arrived. Good, the sooner we get out of here, the better."

The carriage slowed down and proceeded into the town at a crawl so as not to attract attention. Antonelli kept his eyes on the harbor as he spoke, "Tell me boy, you said that you plan on taking her somewhere that she would be safe. Do you know of such a place?"

Giovanni shook his head, "No... no I don't, but there has to be one somewhere."

Antonelli frowned, "I hate to say this, my boy, but there may not be. The Church has eyes everywhere, even in the new lands that have been discovered. Besides, even if you do escape the Church, there are still people out there who would see her as an unclean spirit. People are not very forgiving of things they don't understand."

Giovanni rubbed his forehead, trying to think, "Admittedly, I hadn't gotten that far, Padre. I've been too focused on rescuing her."

"You might want to start thinking of a place." Antonelli replied. "You can't sail your little ship to the ends of the Earth."

Giovanni didn't respond as his mind was now deep in thought. Antonelli was right, there may not be anywhere that she would be safe as long as there were people nearby. What could he do? There was no doubt in anyone's mind at this point that she was innocent, but that meant nothing when the person who condemned her was the very person that they were fighting against.

Giovanni quickly put it out of his head when he noticed that a small platoon of papal knights had beaten them to the harbor and alerted the local garrison. Knowing that Ostia was no longer safe, the group needed a new plan. Nicolas looked back at Giovanni, "What are we supposed to do now? We can't risk taking her back to the market, even if they don't see us, the houses will be searched."

Giovanni nodded, "Head for the harbor, we'll get her out of Rome on my ship. Look for the southern-most dock."

Nicolas nodded and snapped the reigns, making the horses turn south as they headed for the docks. The horses whinnied as they picked up speed. Giovanni continued to caress Adalyn's forehead, "Hold on my love... hold on."

Adalyn's eyes shot open briefly, "Wh... What did you call m...?"

Before she could finish her sentence, her eyes fluttered and she lost consciousness again. Giovanni shook his head, "I'll tell you later."

As they arrived at the pier, Giovanni could see that the old dock master had been good on his word. Giovanni's ship had been cleaned and resealed. It almost looked brand new. The lamp oil had been replaced and everything was polished up nicely.

Giovanni did not have time to admire the fine handy work as they were still in danger. The moment the carriage stopped, Giovanni carefully picked Adalyn up and jumped out of the back. He was relieved to see that she was breathing more normally as he approached the gangway to his ship.

The group got onboard and prepared the old ship for departure. Nicolas made sure that everything onboard was secured. Cyrillus joined him and attempted to throw off the lines. Giovanni did the best he could to prop Adalyn up against the railing next to the ramp.

Padre Antonelli and the others worked on the mooring lines from the dock. The lines that could not be untied were quickly cut. Giovanni continued to look back at Adalyn, who was slipping in and out of consciousness as they worked.

The lines had almost all been cut when suddenly there was a large flash of light and a thundering boom. Padre Antonelli grabbed his chest and dropped to his knees. Behind him, a local guard was pointing an arquebus in their direction. Smoke poured from the muzzle and breach as he dropped it to grab his sword.

Giovanni cried out when he saw his mentor fall, "No!"

One of the revolutionaries pulled out a small blade and threw it at the guard. The point of the blade hit the guard in the neck, causing the guard to gag and lifelessly fall backwards.

Nicolas and the scout from earlier, Cyrillus, finished getting the ship ready while Giovanni ran to Padre Antonelli's side. The priest coughed as he began to fall backwards. Giovanni got to him in time to catch the old priest before he hit the wooden planks, "You're okay, hang on Padre, we'll get you on the ship and everything will be fine."

Antonelli shook his head, "I fear that the Lord has other plans for me this time, my son."

The old priest frowned, "I'm sorry, Giovanni..."

"Sorry for what?" Giovanni asked in a confused tone.

Antonelli coughed as he slowly responded, "For the trouble I caused and the loss of your home. I cost you everything."

Giovanni shook his head, "Padre, that wasn't your fault. I didn't mean what I said. I was angry."

"I know that." Antonelli replied. "I would have reacted the same way, but the fact is that you were right. I should have tried talking to you. I'm paying for that mistake now..."

Tears welled up in Giovanni's eyes, "No, please, come with us. We still need your help. I still need your guidance. This is not over."

"No." The priest said softly. "No it's not... but my part in this adventure has ended. I have helped lay the groundwork. Now it is time for you to stand on your own. Adalyn needs a hero to watch out for her... that's not me. I'm just a foolish old man."

Giovanni shook his head, "You were more than that! A fool would never acknowledge that he didn't have answers when asked a question. He would just parrot the answers told to him by the powers that be. That wasn't you. Your mind was open. You are one of the good ones."

Divinity

Antonelli smiled, "Thank you, my son. You were always my favorite pupil. I very much enjoyed our talks. I just wish I could have done more to answer your questions. After a lifetime of studying, I thought I knew so much. Only now at the end do I realize how little I really knew."

"You knew enough…" Giovanni insisted. "How am I supposed to go on now? I'm not ready for this…"

Padre Antonelli reached into his robe and pulled out the golden cross that he kept on his person at all times. He held it out to Giovanni, "You can do this Giovanni… I know you can, and so does she. Take my cross… keep it close to you and never forget that no matter what, the lord God is with you, and so I am."

Tears flowed down Giovanni's cheeks, "I will… Padre…"

Padre Antonelli fell silent for a moment before his face turned to sadness, "I got you this far and helped you save her… I'm content that my sacrifice made a difference. My one regret… my only sin…"

Giovanni shook him gently, trying to get him to respond, "Is what, what is it?"

Padre Antonelli coughed a little as he struggled to speak. Blood dripped from his lips as he tried to clear his throat, determined to speak one last time. He could feel the life draining from his body.

Adalyn regain consciousness and sensed Antonelli's pain. She weakly turned to face him from the top of the ramp and listened for his breathing. Using what strength she had left, she called to him, "I forgive you Padre Benito Antonelli. You have repented for your sins. Thank you for the part you played in my rescue. Please rest easy now and go join our kingdom… where you so rightly belong."

At hearing Adalyn's words, Antonelli's face brightened up and he was able to smile one last time as his consciousness began to fade. It was as though a giant weight had been lifted from his heart. He looked up at the sky with wide eyes and a smile on his face, "Adalyn… thank you…"

After one final deep breath, it was all over. Padre Benito Antonelli fell limp. Giovanni rested his old friend's head on the dock and closed his eyes, "No…"

Both Nicolas and Cyrillus stopped working and looked down in silent reverence. Feeling his pain, Adalyn rested her head on her knees as she balled herself up, "I'm so sorry…"

Nicolas watched from the boat and quietly folded his hands, "I am the resurrection and the life, so says the Lord: he that believeth in me, though he were dead, yet shall he live: and whosoever liveth and believeth in me shall never truly die, rest in peace."

"Amen," Adalyn whispered in response.

The commotion on the dock summoned three more guards. The remaining three revolutionaries that had not yet boarded the boat saw them coming and ran off to confront them. One called back as they moved into the darkness, "You two, we'll create a diversion to cover your escape. See Giovanni and the angel safely out of Ostia! Once they're safe, report back to Anselm!"

"Understood." Nicolas called out as he turned to his companion, "Cyrillus, get the sail down, we need to get this ship moving."

Cyrillus nodded, "Yes sir!"

Nicolas then turned, ran past Adalyn down the ramp, and grabbed Giovanni, "Come my friend, it is time for us to go."

Giovanni didn't want to leave his friend, but he knew that he there was nothing more that could be done for Antonelli. Nicolas tugged Giovanni back on the boat and sliced the last two mooring lines. He then turned to Cyrillus, "Let go the sail!"

The sail came down and the boat jerked forward as it began to move away from the docks. Giovanni ran to the side and kept his eyes on Ostia as the boat sailed in to the distance. gunshots could be heard amongst the buildings and fires in the city could be seen for miles.

After a few minutes, Giovanni put his head down and slammed his fist on the railing. His anger had taken over and he was unable to fight back the tears in his eyes. He was simultaneously enraged by what had happened to Padre Antonelli, and regretful for his behavior over the last few days.

Adalyn heard the loud thud and struggled to drag herself closer to him. When she was close enough, she rested her head against his leg and reached for his hand. Giovanni felt it and clasped his hand around hers, locking their fingers together.

Tears fell from under the blindfold as Adalyn spoke, "I am sorry about Padre Antonelli. I can't believe I misjudged him as badly as I did. He was a good man."

She tugged his hand a little as she continued, "Please don't worry about your friend. His sacrifice saved our lives... He did not die in vain. The Most High will recognize this when he awakens... Padre Antonelli is at peace now..."

Adalyn had run out of energy. Her breathing became more labored and she let out a deep sigh before collapsing on the rail. Giovanni picked her up as she fell. He squeezed her gently in his arms, "Thank you."

Nicolas saw her collapse as he was checking the rigging, "Giovanni, she's badly injured. Those bandages won't hold her blood back much longer. They're already stained."

Giovanni nodded, "I know, I'll get her below deck and do what I can. My father taught me how to close cuts when he was teaching me about fishing. I just hope I still have everything I need."

Adalyn was still covered in blood and the tight bandages were the only things keeping her grievous injuries from bleeding out. Her body had been ripped apart and she was too weak to move on her own. Everyone could clearly see that she needed to be cared for immediately if she were to survive.

Giovanni positioned himself under her arm, supported her wings as best he could, and led her below to the cabin. Before the two disappeared through the door, Nicolas called to Giovanni, "My friend, do we have any plan on somewhere to hide? Which way should we go?"

Giovanni looked back at Ostia in disgust, "I don't care... just put more distance between us and Rome. We'll figure out where to go as soon as Adalyn is tended to."

Nicolas turned to Cyrillus as Giovanni went below, "You heard him, steer us a course south and hold us to it. I'm going to get the sail down a little more. All of Rome will be in an uproar soon enough and we don't want to be anywhere near Ostia when the warships appear."

Cyrillus pulled on the tiller as he watched the stars to get his bearings. The night sky turned as the ship began to change course. Nicolas walked to the mast and began coaxing the sail to stretch a little more. The sail flapped a few times before finally catching the full force of the wind. The ship was now going at full speed.

Once Cyrillus was confident that they were going the right way, he called to Nicolas, "So she is really an angel? She seems so much more fragile than the other two we saw."

Nicolas nodded as he tugged on the line, "From what I understand, she was stripped of her powers, and badly injured when she was kicked out of Heaven. The other two were at full power."

He quickly tied the line down before joining Cyrillus at the tiller, "Even if she hadn't been injured, I'd be willing to bet that she'd still be vulnerable. Imagine living with immortality and the power to do almost anything, only to have it all stripped away and then be left defenseless in a world you don't understand. I think any of us would be the exact same if something like that were to happen. That is probably why she seems so weak."

"We risked a lot to save her," Cyrillus said in a doubtful tone, "perhaps too much; our surprise attack is gone, we've lost men, and now the Church will crack down on the city. Rome will no longer be an easy place to hide. How could she possibly be worth everything we've sacrificed?"

Nicolas shrugged as he turned to tend to a support line that had come loose, "I don't know, my friend, but the leaders of the Church saw her as enough of a threat to keep her existence quiet, and then they try to execute her. No doubt they believe that she has knowledge about God that could do them damage. Any solid proof that conflicts with their teachings would be sure to cause strife. That is a good enough reason to risk what we have as far as I'm concerned."

III

Down in the makeshift cabin, Giovanni carefully placed Adalyn on the single bunk so that he could tend to her wounds. She was still in pain, but was able to briefly relax as Giovanni got everything he needed. He quickly lit the lamps hanging from the ceiling and then did the same with the fire pit off to the side.

The moment that the cabin lit up from the glow of the fire pit, Giovanni went to work. He used a piece of the clean cloth from the chest under the bunk to clean as many wounds as he could. First he washed the wounds using the bottle of grog that his father had kept in storage, and then he wrapped each wound with the long pieces of cloth.

Adalyn lay back with her head on the small pillow and clenched her jaw. A piercing sensation entered her leg with each drop of grog that was dabbed on her wounds. Giovanni saw it and frowned, "I know it hurts. I'm doing the best I can to be gentle."

Adalyn nodded, "I know you are… just please try to hurry…"

Giovanni nodded and wrapped the injury on her left leg. He looked her over carefully as he finished up the small wound on her arm. The bleeding had stopped and her skin was slowly healing.

All but one of her injuries was dressed and it was the one that Giovanni dreaded dealing with. He was hesitant about touching her right leg. It was the most serious of all her injuries, even more so than the one on her wing from when he had first met her.

Giovanni had never seen an injury so grievous. It was the result of the final interrogation, and needed a lot more care than any of the others. This was going to be difficult; he'd never worked on a wound this serious before.

Giovanni sighed as he prepared another cloth, "This one on your leg is really bad. It will not close on its own. This won't be pleasant."

As he touched it with the cloth, Adalyn flinched, "Please don't, it hurts too much."

Divinity

"I'm sorry Adalyn," Giovanni said adamantly, "if I leave this one alone, you will bleed to death. It needs to be sewn shut. I promise that I'll be as gentle as possible, but I have to do this."

Adalyn grimaced and squeezed her eyes closed as tears poured down on cheeks, "Then do whatever you need to… There is nothing worse than what I've already gone through."

Giovanni got up, went into the storage hold, and grabbed a small bait hook and some rope. He brought the supplies back to the cabin and began to work on making a stitching tool. Using his knife, he cut the rope down to a single hair and threaded it to the hook.

Once it was ready, he bent the hook until it was straight and turned back to Adalyn. His heart clenched as he washed his homemade needle and thread in the alcohol. He then turned and looked at Adalyn with a sympathetic expression.

Giovanni knew that what he was about to do was not going to be pleasant, but it had to be done. He braced himself, knowing that her cries would probably haunt him forever after this. His mind blanked as he stared at the needle for a moment.

Once Giovanni was sure that it was ready, he brought the threaded needle over to the wound on her leg, "Here we go"

Adalyn nodded, giving him permission to proceed as she grabbed the thickest piece of rope she could find and bit down on it. Her eyes clenched shut and she braced herself for what was coming. She didn't think it was possible to experience pain worse than the torture she had already lived through, but it was still going to hurt.

Giovanni breathed in deeply as he made the first incision into her skin and pulled the string through. The piercing sensation shot through her leg, causing her to gasp for air as she winced in pain. He did it again on the other side, and then back and forth down the wound on either side.

Adalyn lay on the small bunk with tears welling up in her eyes as he carefully worked on her leg. Every single

muscle in her body was tense as they absorbed the pain. She fought every urge to pull away or kick, knowing that Giovanni was only trying to help her.

With each stitch, the pain became more intense until it finally became too much for her to handle. Adalyn's wings stretched out as far as they could in a futile attempt to alleviate some of the pain. When that didn't work, she pleaded with Giovanni, "Stop, please stop! It's too much!"

Giovanni's heart got heavy as he listened to her pleading cries. It made working on her leg more difficult, but he had no choice, he knew that she would not survive if he didn't finish, "I'm sorry Adalyn, this needs to be closed or you'll bleed to death. Please just try to hold on."

Adalyn nodded and held her breath as Giovanni did two more stitches and pulled on the string to tighten them. The wound finally closed and the bleeding slowed. He cut and tied the remaining string, hoping that it would stay in place.

Giovanni knew that there was still one more thing that he had to do. He placed his knife into the fire pit next to them. The wound had to be cauterized if it was to heal properly. All he could do was watch her sob as he waited for the blade to get hot enough to make a difference.

Once the dagger was ready, Giovanni picked it up with a wet rag. After a few heart wrenching moments of staring at the searing metal, he brought the knife back over to her, "Adalyn, this is really going to hurt, brace yourself."

Adalyn frantically shook her head, "No, please... you can't!"

"I have to." Giovanni insisted as a tear escaped to his cheek.

He hated himself for what he was about to do to her, but there was no other choice, "I'm really sorry, but it'll be over in a few seconds, I promise."

Adalyn gripped the bed and nodded that she was ready to continue. He slowly placed the knife on the bleeding wound. Part of her wanted to try to move away, but she fought the urge harder than she had ever fought anything. She could feel her skin heat up as the blade got close, causing her to breathe more heavily.

Divinity

Giovanni took a deep breath and quickly pressed the blade against her leg. The blade let out a loud hiss as it sizzled against her skin. She opened her mouth, dropping the rope, and tried to scream. The agony was overpowering and choked all sound out of her voice. She was completely paralyzed for a brief second before she could release the scream.

On deck, both of the men tending to the ship could hear her cries. They wanted to help, but they knew how painful healing could be. If Giovanni didn't tend to her injuries, she would quickly bleed to death. Having no other choice, the men ignored her pleas.

Giovanni finally pulled the blade away from her skin and tossed it in a bucket of water. The heat had done the trick; the bleeding had all but stopped. There were a few small drops still coming through, but at least the wound had a better chance of healing now.

Giovanni grabbed two clean cloths, dipped one in his grog and wrapped it around her leg. The cool cloth soothed the pain as she lay on the bunk quivering. Her body was in a state of shock from the pain, and she could not move.

Giovanni took the dry cloth and placed it on top of the one soaked in grog and tied it around her leg to hold the dressing in place. She lay on the bunk breathing erratically, barely able to stay conscious as she fought through the agony. Waves of pain continued to shoot up her leg as Giovanni worked.

Finally, she cried out, "Please, no more, I can't stand the pain anymore. I beg of you, stop… please… stop."

Giovanni nodded, lay down next to her, and started brushing her hair away from her face in an effort to calm her, "It's okay, we're done now. The wound is closing and with a little luck, it will be healed up in no time. We just have to pray that you didn't lose too much blood."

Giovanni grabbed the last of his clean cloths and began to wipe the dirt and blood from her face. He didn't get very far before she grabbed his arm and held on tight, sobbing endlessly. He began to wondered if her tears would ever dry after everything she had been through.

Divinity

When Adalyn finally calmed down and the pain became more manageable, she was able to speak, "Giovanni... thank you. Most people don't know how to do all of that. Where did you learn to tend to wounds that way?"

Giovanni smiled, "My family has been fishing for many generations. When you are out on long trips for days at a time, you need to learn these things in case someone gets hurt, so my father taught me how to do it."

She nodded, "I see, truly remarkable."

"Thanks." Giovanni replied as he looked at her.

Adalyn looked slightly skinnier than she had before she was taken. Clearly refusing to eat for days had already impacted her appearance. He frowned as he looked back into her eyes that were slowly fading, "Can I get you something to eat or drink? You'll need some nourishment in order to heal."

Adalyn shook her head weakly, "Later. For now... I'm just so tired..."

After everything she had been through, she couldn't even hold her head up anymore. Her body finally gave out and she collapsed into Giovanni's arms. He rested her heard on the pillow and stroked her arm as she slept. *Poor girl, it's a miracle that she was able to stay conscious for this long. I should give her some time to rest.*

Giovanni let her sleep and walked back up on deck. He shut the cabin door behind himself to make sure that their voices didn't carry into the cabin. Nicolas was now handling the tiller while Cyrillus was dealing with some fouled rigging.

Nicolas saw him come out on deck and placed a brace on the tiller. He walked up next to Giovanni with concern in his eyes, "How is she?"

Giovanni's hands and arms were covered in blood. He still had a worried look on his face as he spoke, "Well, she's alive. I've done everything I can for her. Now we just have to wait and see if her body can repair itself."

He looked at them both as Cyrillus stopped working to listen in. The look of worry turned into one of thankfulness as he spoke, "You both have my everlasting

Divinity

gratitude for helping to get her out of there. She'd most likely be dead right now if it wasn't for you."

Nicolas and Cyrillus both nodded appreciatively as he continued, "You've kept your promise and helped me get Adalyn out of Rome. I don't know where I'm going to take her, but we can drop you off at a nearby port so you can make your way back to home."

Nicolas' eyes narrowed as a hurt look appeared on his face, "Now just one moment, if she is an angel, then the Church and Michael will stop at nothing to get her back, correct?"

When Giovanni said nothing, Nicolas continued, "You are not going to be safe anywhere you take her, the Church has eyes in nearly every city. Even if you were lucky enough to evade the Church's eyes, you could never get away from Michael and a legion of angels. Like it or not, you will need our help and I think you know that. So I am not leaving."

Nicolas turned to Cyrillus who also chimed in, "Our lives were forfeit long ago. We have nowhere to go and no one is waiting for us to come back. At least by fighting on this front, our lives will hold some meaning. If by aiding you we are able to strike a blow against the Church's leaders, I will remain by your side as well."

Giovanni smiled, "Thank you both, I'm glad to have you with us."

Cyrillus finished the rope and walked over to the group, "What's our plan then? We are getting low on supplies and cannot sail on like this forever."

Nicolas thought about it for a moment, "We have two choices; we can either run as fast as we can and take her to the ends of the Earth, away from the reach of the Pope, or we can try to put up a fight."

Giovanni lowered his eyes, "The reach of the Church has no limit that I have seen. No matter where we run, we may never be safe. The Pope has the powers of the angel, Michael helping him, though I'm fairly certain that Michael is the true architect here. He has to answer for his crimes, somehow, and I'm certain that the Pope's power would disappear without him."

"Then we're doomed," Cyrillus sighed, "Adalyn may be mortal and capable of being killed, but I doubt Michael is."

"I know," Giovanni agreed, "but there must be a way. Perhaps Adalyn has the answer to such a riddle. If she can be stripped of her powers, there must be a way Michael can be as well. When she wakes up, I'll ask her."

Giovanni frowned, "If she wakes up…"

"I'm sure she will." Nicolas said confidently. "Until then though, what course do we follow?"

Giovanni shrugged, "Just keep putting distance between us and Rome. For now, that should be sufficient. We don't want to stop somewhere and wind up having a warship on our heels."

Giovanni yawned as he stretched out his arms to steady himself. The stars were bright in the sky and it was several hours past when Giovanni usually went to bed. Nicolas put his hand on Giovanni's shoulder, "When's the last time you've slept?"

Giovanni smiled as he tried to picture the last time, but was unable to, "It's been a while."

"You have worked so hard to get her back." Nicolas replied. "Go be with her, I can attend to the sailing of this ship for now. You've earned some time."

Giovanni nodded, "Most kind, thanks."

He left the deck without another word and returned to the bunk where Adalyn was resting. Cyrillus walked the length of the ship until he found a spot that suited him. He lay down near the cabin and watched the stars, "Such a blessed night this is with a clear, starry sky."

Nicolas smiled as he held the ship on its southern course. The lamps on the boat flickered and danced as the ship rocked over the waves. He hummed a tune to himself as they sailed. In the distance behind him, they could still see the lights of Rome as an aura in the night sky.

In the cabin, Giovanni watched Adalyn as she slept. Her wings fluttered every few moments as the boat gently rocked her from side to side. He noticed that some blood had soaked through the bandage on her leg. The wounds were fairly large and, even with his care, some blood was still going to seep through. This was to be expected and didn't concern him much as he went to work redressing the wounds.

Giovanni gently unwrapped the bandage, being careful not to wake her. He slowly pulled the old rag off before picking up two clean rags. He dipped the first one in grog, and carefully placed it on the wound to keep it from getting infected. Then he repeated what he had done earlier by tying the dressing down with a clean bandage.

Once her leg was taken care of, Giovanni lay down next to her. He didn't want to risk waking her, so he moved gently and was careful not to touch her until he was comfortable. As his eyes slowly began to flutter, he wasn't sure, but he thought that he had heard her whisper, "Thank you."

IV

"It would appear then your plan has failed, my lord!" Pope Leo said with an angry look as he stood in his council hall with his cardinal advisors.

All three of them watched as Leo himself spoke with the figure of an Angel in the window. He pointed his finger in an accusing manor as angry words flew from his lips. The angel's demeanor was more annoyance than anything else. At best, he was tolerating the Pope's words.

The figure hissed as it spoke, "My plan has hit a snag, nothing more. I did not count on Azrael interfering, but I have yet to be exposed to those who would stop us in our tracks. The only one left who stands in our way is blind and near death. Even if she survives, her only protection, are the rabble that rescued her."

The figure blurred as it spoke, "She will not be a thorn in our side much longer. Do not fear, Eminence, soon the final loose end will be tied up, and you will have gained total control over the known world. Things will once again be as they were during the days of Rome's greatness."

The Pope shook his head, "I'm afraid that I no longer have faith in your ability to deliver on your promises. Perhaps this was a mistake all along."

The figure pulled itself from the window and took form right in front of the Pope. The form quickly turned into a very angry Michael, "The Most High has decreed that these revolutionaries need to be taken out. If you go against his orders, then not only will Rome never reclaim greatness, but it will burn to the ground as you watch. Sodom and Gomorrah were nothing compared to the destruction that will be brought down on your people!"

The Pope lowered his eyes, "Very well, we will keep up our end of the bargain. The powers of the Church are at your disposal, Saint Michael, as they always have been. In the name of our Lord, I pray it will be enough."

An air of satisfaction came over Michael as the Pope bowed to his wishes, "You are most gracious Eminence, and you will be rewarded in the end. There is nothing to be worried about, you will all see."

Divinity

Pope Leo X turned away from Michael as the angel began to fade from the room. His shadow propelled itself upward, out of Rome. The clergy was left with one word as the angel disappeared, "Patience."

Once Michael was gone, one of the cardinals spoke, "Eminence was it truly wise to make this agreement? I know he is the Archangel Michael, but I feel as though we may have made a pact with the devil himself. Who is to say that Michael truly speaks for the one true God as he claims? Have other angels not fallen from grace?"

The Pope turned and glared at him with a menacing look, "You will be silent! I do not wish to hear any more of this heresy, and you would do well to remember that words of that kind will draw the attention of the inquisitors. So I will say this to you only once; keep those thoughts to yourself. We dare not go against the might of Saint Michael."

The Cardinal bowed, "Forgive me, Eminence."

Leo X looked out the window, "You are all dismissed. I grow tired of this. I need some rest and time to think."

The three cardinals bowed left the room as the Pope gazed at the smoldering ruins of the buildings that had been damaged by the Lutheran revolutionaries. He shook his head as he watched the smoke rise, "How could it have come to this. Attacked on our very doorstep? I must put these rebellions down... for the good of all."

After a few minutes of deep thought, Leo summoned the captain of his knights. Federico had been standing guard near the Pope's chamber during the meeting. He responded promptly and appeared before the Pope as requested, "You summoned me, Eminence?"

The Pope nodded, "Yes, I need you to reinforce the lines around the basilica and bring in more guards for the city. I don't want anyone getting in or out without us knowing about it."

Federico nodded, "I understand Eminence, and it will be done immediately."

"You don't totally understand." The Pope said hesitantly. "I also want you to keep an eye on my advisors in the clergy as well."

This request was unusual and troubled the captain. Spying on other members of the clergy was outside of the knights' normal mandate. His sworn duty was to protect the honor of the Papacy, not go around on secret missions for the Pope. He needed to know more about what was going on, "Does his eminence suspect that we have a traitor in our midst?"

Leo X frowned, "No, I don't suspect them of any wrong doing, but I prefer to be absolutely certain. I know that I will feel a lot better knowing that if one of them tries something, I will hear about it first."

Federico nodded, "Your will, eminence."

The Pope looked into the captain's eyes as he continued, "I wanted it understood, Captain… This is not to be spoken of outside of this room. If you suspect any of them of wrong doing, you are to report to me immediately. Speak to no one else."

Captain Gonzaga nodded as the Pope issued his orders, "Rally your men Captain, we may need them."

Captain Gonzaga bowed, "It shall be done, Eminence."

The Pope bowed and bid his knight captain farewell. He was tired and needed rest. Pushing himself to consider his situation and the alliance with Michael was not going to solve anything that night.

Captain Gonzaga turned and closed the door behind him. *What is going on here? First he orders the torture of a possible divine spirit without investigating the matter. We captured her, interrogated her, and find no evidence of her being an unclean entity. After that, he orders the occupation of Versailles and now this? He is even beginning to suspect his trusted allies of misdoing. I don't even know where we stand anymore. What am I supposed to do?*

Once Federico was back in his office, he met up with Lt. Piangi, who had been waiting for him, "Captain, do you bring orders from his Eminence?"

Captain Gonzaga nodded, "Lt. Piangi, we are to reinforce the basilica's guards and make sure that there are no more incursions within the city. This attack at our doorstep must have no repeat."

Divinity

The young lieutenant saluted, "I understand sir. I will take care of it personally."

Federico raised his hand to stop the enthusiastic young officer from leaving, "Wait… close the door."

The young man did as he was told and then turned back to Federico, "Sir?"

The captain sighed as though giving into something he didn't want to do, "What I am about to tell you does not leave the room. I have a private matter to speak to you about and it could send us both before the inquisitors."

Lt. Piangi looked oddly at his commander, "Uh… of course sir, what is it?"

"The Pope has further ordered us to keep the Church's high clergy under surveillance for possible treason." Captain Gonzaga hesitated as he spoke. "By telling you this, I am violating a direct order from the Pope to keep it secret."

Those words appeared to freeze time momentarily for the lieutenant, "Sir, I can understand why he would want to keep this quiet. That order goes against our mandate. You are telling me that the Pope himself really asked us for this?"

Federico nodded, "Yes, he personally asked me to do this… which is a sign of a paranoid dictator, not the head of a Church of God. This is very disturbing."

Lt. Piangi nodded, "I agree with you. What are you going to do sir?"

Federico frowned, "Exactly what the Pope has asked me to do. What other choice is there?"

Lt. Piangi shrugged and was about to reply when his captain continued speaking, "That being said, I believe that the Pope should also be watched. Something is out of place here and has been for some time. I need to figure out what it is."

Lt. Piangi nodded, "I understand sir, what are my orders?"

Captain Gonzaga stood and smiled unenthusiastically, "We follow our orders. I want the walls reinforced, the clergy watched, and…"

Federico placed a hand on his lieutenant's shoulder to bring him close before responding, "I want you to

Divinity

personally keep the Pope's dealings under surveillance. You're the best investigator I have. I want you to report anything strange directly to me, understood?"

A look of shock came over the young officer's face, "But sir, is this not treason?"

The Captain shrugged lightly, "Technically no, we took an oath. We owe our loyalty to the Papacy. We are to protect it against all enemies... even if said enemy is the Pope himself. The office of the Pope must not be dishonored. That is our mandate."

Lt. Piangi shook his head, "I doubt the Pope would accept that as justification for such actions."

Federico nodded, "No doubt, which is why I am not ordering you to do this. I am asking you as a friend. Surely you must see that something has been out of place recently. We must be vigilant in finding out if the people we currently fight for are the people we were sworn to protect in the first place."

When Federico saw the uneasy look on his lieutenant's face, he sighed, "If we turn out to be wrong, I will personally submit myself to be judged before the clergy and bear the brunt of the responsibility alone... if I am wrong. You will simply have been a solider following his orders."

The Lieutenant frowned, "You do realize that most likely means that at best, you will never see the light of day again."

Federico nodded, "That's the chance I have to take. I can't let this go."

The young man did not like Federico's answer, but nodded slightly, "Yes sir. I will carry out your request."

Federico looked at him in the eye, "One last thing... I want to remind you that this must not be spoken of outside this chamber. As far as anyone is concerned, this conversation never took place, understand?"

It took him a few minutes, but finally the young man agreed, "I figured that would be the case, Captain. You can count on me."

Satisfied with his instructions, the lieutenant turned and left the room. Federico watched the city lights of Rome

Divinity

through his window as they began to dim. *How has it all come down to this?*

V

Adalyn awoke in the cabin onboard Giovanni's ship. The sound of waves breaking against the hull had broken her slumber. Almost immediately, she noticed that she didn't feel as disgusting or sore as she had before her rescue. Someone had cleaned her, her wounds had been redressed and were healing, and she wasn't in as much pain as she was when Giovanni worked on her leg.

To her surprise, the stitches on her leg had been removed and replaced with a tight bandage. *My leg healed? How long have I been out?*

After sitting on the small bed for a few moments, trying to sort out her memories, she put her hand on the wall next to the bed and pushed herself into a standing position. Her legs almost immediately gave out as she grabbed on to the post in front of her for support. She stumbled for a moment before finding her footing.

When Adalyn regained her balance, she stretched her legs and slowly began walking to the door. She opened it slowly and stumbled out on deck where the men were tending to the ship. She was still unable to see, so she reached out with her hands to keep from bumping into any walls.

Giovanni could hear stirrings coming from the cabin door and noticed that Adalyn was up and about. His heart was in his throat as he ran over to her, "Adalyn!"

The loud voice startled her as she turned in its direction. The pounding of feet on the deck echoed in her ear as she put out her hand to him, "Good morning Giovanni."

Giovanni wrapped his fingers around her hand and pulled her close. The two came within an inch of kissing, but stopped when they realized that they were not alone. They contained their excitement and casually turned away before their lips touched.

Adalyn smiled slightly and bit the right side of her lower lip before speaking, "Um, how long was I asleep?"

"A few days." Giovanni said quietly. "I was worried that you would never wake up. You lost a lot of blood and

Divinity

only woke up to eat. Even then, it was like you were in a hypnotic state. You never spoke, and just gave everyone a lifeless stare."

"He didn't leave your side except to tend to the boat." Nicolas added as he walked up next to them. "He just kept tending to your injuries, and talking to you. It seemed like it helped you sleep."

"I don't know what to say." Adalyn replied as she turned red in the face. "I'm sorry that I worried you, but I do feel much better thanks to your care."

Giovanni could see that she was still struggling to find her feet and stumbled as she walked. When it looked like she was about to collapse, he quickly grabbed her by the shoulders. A worried look appeared on his face as he held her, "Are you okay?"

She nodded, "Yes I will be, just don't let me fall, all right?"

As Adalyn righted herself, her stomach started to groan. She lowered her head and placed her hands over it. Nicolas handed them some dried, salted fish that he'd brought up on deck, "You really didn't eat much, you must be hungry."

"I'm starving!" Adalyn replied. "My stomach feels like it's screaming at me... it's kind of an odd sensation."

She took the fish, bit off big pieces, and swallowed them. Giovanni chuckled as he watched her, "Easy, you don't want to choke. The fish isn't going anywhere."

Within moments, Adalyn devoured the entire fish. She covered her mouth and licked her lips as she finished, "Thank you..."

Nicolas nodded, "It isn't much, but it will help you get your health back."

Giovanni smiled, "Not that you needed much help. The wound on your leg healed incredibly fast. I thought you'd be off your feet for a month, but when I redressed the bandage a few days ago, it was little more than a cut. I just removed the stitching before rewrapping it."

"I can't explain that." She admitted. "Angels aren't supposed to be able to be hurt, and there are very limited

Divinity

ways we can be killed. I am no longer immortal, so I can be hurt, but I am not sure how healing works."

Nicolas looked her over as she talked to Giovanni. *It's incredible, a real angel. I didn't believe it, but here you are.*

Even blindfolded, when Adalyn turned to him, Nicolas felt as though she was looking through him, all the way to his soul. He stood frozen for a moment as Adalyn began speaking to him in his native tongue, "*Your name is Nicolas, yes?*"

He felt his heart clench as she spoke. He was shocked to hear her speaking Greek and had trouble replying, "*Y... yes, milady.*"

"*Do not despair for your family.*" She said in a comforting tone, "*They now walk with the Choirs of Angels in paradise. They are happy, and they miss you.*"

Nicolas froze in place, not knowing how to respond. He had been completely caught off guard as a tear fell from his cheek. Unnerved, he quickly turned away and headed to the back of the ship, "Thank you milady."

She then turned to the tiller where Cyrillus stood and frowned, "And you, Cyrillus... your wife misses you greatly, she is sorry that your time together was cut short, but she is deeply saddened by your choice to spend your life out looking for revenge."

Cyrillus nodded, "I'm sure she is, but I cannot change what I have become. I've seen too much evil to not stand and fight."

"I was there when she joined us in the kingdom." Adalyn said in earnest. "She would not want you to suffer the same fate as..."

"Please leave me alone." He interrupted. "I'm sure you mean well, but there is nothing left in me but hatred for those who took her from me."

Adalyn sadly nodded, "As you wish... you poor man."

She turned and let Giovanni guide her over to the railing on the port side of the ship. He placed her hand on the railing and looked out on the ocean, "We're pretty far from Rome, we've been sailing for days, but we are running low on supplies."

"Where are we going," she asked, "back to Venice?"

Giovanni shook his head, "No there is nothing in Venice for us now. My house was destroyed. The knights burned it as you were taken away. If we go back there, they may be waiting for you. I was hoping you might have some idea of where we could go next."

Adalyn's heart sank as she realized what she had cost him, "Because of me, you have lost your home, your friends, and your entire world. I'm sorry that I ever washed up in your harbor, please forgive me."

He touched her face and raised it so that he had her attention, "You put those feelings out of your mind, do you hear me? I'm not sorry that you found your way into my harbor at all. Without you, I'd be living alone and dealing with an illness that would have killed me in a few months. You gave me a second chance at life and the will to go on living. Thanks to you, my family's legacy won't be cut short. It will live on for many more years. What I have lost pales in comparison to what you've given me."

Tears came out from under the blind fold, "Your words are bittersweet. I know you care for me but..."

"What?" Giovanni asked.

Adalyn placed her hand on Giovanni's cheek and felt his face, trying to picture it in her mind, "I... I can't be certain, but I could have sworn that I heard you call me something... that night when we escaped Rome. It was before I lost consciousness in the wagon."

Giovanni nodded, "Do you remember what I said, exactly?"

"... my love." Adalyn replied as more tears fell from her eyes. "Is that what you said?"

Giovanni smiled as he replied, "Yes."

Adalyn shook her head, "You can't... you just can't. Don't let it happen, Giovanni, please... for your own good!"

"Why not?" Giovanni demanded as a confused look appeared on his face.

Adalyn leaned on the railing and put her left hand to her face as she sobbed, "It's not right. You are a kind and gentle soul who has been caught up in something that you never should have been. I... I care for you too much to see you get hurt and that's where loving me leads."

Divinity

"How do you figure?" Giovanni asked.

Adalyn lowered her head, "I'm condemned, remember? I am grateful for your rescue and care, but we can't sail on forever. Eventually we have to stop. You'll either wind up being cut off from your own kind, or killed by those who would see me put to death. Either way, you risk your immortal soul in protecting me."

"I don't see it that way." Giovanni replied, "God's decree was that you be banished here. You yourself said the reason for that was for you to meet your death."

She nodded, "That was Michael's plan."

"But was it God's decree that you be killed?" He asked.

"No" She replied.

"Well I don't want you to die and I don't consider sabotaging an implied intention as a violation of God's decree." Giovanni said, smiling. "So why don't you let me decide for myself what's good for me?"

Adalyn twisted her lips into a grimace. She did not like his answer and she made no secret of it, "A technicality? That is a pretty poor argument for defying your God, you know?"

Giovanni chuckled, "I know, but it's the best I can conjure up at the moment. As soon as I think of something better, I'll let you know."

She sighed as her head rested on Giovanni's arm, "Are you absolutely certain you know what you're doing?"

"No," Giovanni replied honestly, "but in these situations, who does? Being with you could be the biggest disaster I've ever encountered, but how will I know that if I don't try? You're too wonderful to not take a chance. I'd rather try and deal with anything as it comes up instead of spending my life wondering what might have been."

Adalyn could feel her cheeks turned red as she spoke, "Caring for me this way will wind up resulting in pain. I don't want that."

"I don't either." Giovanni replied. "So let's be careful not to let that happen."

"And if Michael sends a legion of angels after us?" Adalyn asked.

Giovanni shrugged, "He hasn't yet, and we were able to escape him once. It doesn't seem like he's willing to go that far."

"That could change very quickly if he gets desperate enough." Adalyn replied darkly.

Giovanni placed his hand on her shoulder as he continued, "Look, there is risk in all things. When someone gives their heart to another person, there is always the chance that it will be broken. That's why you need to be careful who you give it to… and I think I've made a good choice."

Adalyn felt her entire body warm up when she heard his words. She could feel her face turning even brighter red as she smiled. Though she wished Giovanni would listen to reason, part of her was glad he was so stubborn.

Once again, she brought her hand up and touched his cheek. As she ran her fingers across his face, she did the best she could to picture what he looked like again. Her mind raced with possibilities, "It is truly a cruel twist of fate that I cannot see the face of the one who has cared for me so… the one who is now fighting for my life… and my heart."

When Nicolas finally regained some of his composure, he joined the two of them near the bow, "I really hate to interrupt, but we need to know where we are going. We've been sailing south for what seems like an eternity and we'll probably end up in Carthage or worse if we continue on this course."

Adalyn turned away, "Michael is behind all of this; the wars on your planet, my expulsion, everything. There is no doubt of that anymore. He is the reason I'm here, and he killed Azrael. I sought to have a close friend and mentor punished for crimes that he didn't commit. I hated him for no reason. That's something that I'll now have to live with forever. Michael deceived me into believing that Azrael was a traitor. He has to pay for what he's done. I won't be able to rest easy until he stands before the Most High with his crimes revealed."

Giovanni nodded, "I agree, but Michael is pretty much God's most trusted servant and he is immortal. How are we supposed to kill him?"

As though responding to Giovanni's question, a thundering boom overhead parted the clouds. A small shiny object fell from the sky and landed on the deck. Adalyn turned when she heard it hit the wood planking, "What is it?"

Giovanni did the best he could to inspect the object without actually picking it up, "It looks like a sword. The hilt is very ornate, but the blade is only about six inches long. It almost looks like it's glowing."

Adalyn gasped, "An angel's sword of flame? It can't be... Those are only given to angels who have earned them. I had hoped that the day would come that I would earn one when I joined the Choirs."

She then realized where it may have come from, "Tell me, are their rubies on the hilt?"

Giovanni nodded, "Yes, one on each end, as well as one large one in the middle where the handle meets the guard."

"It was Azrael's." She said sorrowfully. "He must have used the last of his strength to prevent it from falling into Michael's hands. These swords are extremely powerful, even an immortal can be brought down by them. No angel should ever hold more the one. The blade merges with the essence of its owner."

"Well that's wonderful!" Giovanni said with a sense of relief in his voice. "That means we now have the tool we need to kill Michael."

Adalyn shook her head as she knelt down and picked up the hilt, "No we don't."

She focused on the hilt with her mind. The blade glowed yellow as her face hardened. Smoke began to float away from it as it got hotter.

Giovanni's eyes narrowed as he slowly backed away. Her face turned red as she focused harder and harder. No one on deck knew what was about to happen, but they could feel the heat from the blade.

After a few moments, Adalyn released her breath in a deep sigh as a defeated expression appeared on her face, "It's useless. I don't have the power to wield this any longer."

Giovanni frowned as he rubbed her arm, "I don't understand why Azrael would give you such a weapon if you couldn't use it."

"Safe keeping from Michael perhaps? Otherwise I have no idea." Adalyn admitted, feeling the hilt. "I've known Azrael for countless millennia… He would never do something without good reason. Maybe he thought I could still use it or maybe he knew something I don't."

"Wait; there is something I don't understand." Nicolas said, turning to Adalyn. "You were near death when we found you. How were you turned mortal?"

"There are ways to rip the immortality from a divine being," she replied sadly, "though we do not speak of them in the Celestial World. I was stripped of my immortality and my powers when I was sent here. The idea was that I would be mortal, but still have my wings so someone would find me, think I was a demonic creature, and have me killed. Had it not been for the three of you… the plan would have worked."

She clenched her teeth as she continued, "The Most High instituted such punishments, never thinking that they'd ever need to be used. Lucifer suffered a similar fate, but he survived because the Most High took pity and allowed him to keep some of his power. The lengths he was willing to go to survive perverted him beyond recognition. I was not willing to make the same sacrifices and Michael showed no such pity with me, not that I would have accepted it if he had."

Cyrillus placed a brace on the tiller and walked up to the group to get some answers. He was tired of listening from afar. Part of Adalyn's story had been bothering him and didn't add up, "Can I ask you something Adalyn?"

She nodded, "Please."

"Where is God in all of this?" He asked. "I don't understand, surely this type of thing is within his power to fix with the blink of an eye. He should be aware of what is

going on. Why does he not simply smite Michael himself? Almost certainly all he would need to do is speak the words and Michael would be blinked out of existence."

Adalyn nodded, "You are correct in that this is something the Most High could put an end to, though not that easily… if he were awake."

Giovanni's eyes narrowed, "What do you mean awake? Is God not always watching us?"

"No, in a way he is," Adalyn replied, "but do you remember the creation story? When the Most High created all things both corporeal and celestial, he became fatigued. I believe the passage goes 'By the seventh day, God had finished the work he had been doing; so on the seventh day he rested from all his work.' The story is partially true though it is far less glorious."

"How so?" Giovanni asked.

Adalyn leaned back as she spoke, "The Most High doesn't recognize time the same way you and I do. Your seven days were actually several billions of years. He created the Heavens and the Earth, but the way he did it took a very long time to come to fruition exactly how he wanted. When he was done, the Most High was exhausted and had to take rest."

"What do you mean?" Nicolas asked, "Is it possible for God to be vulnerable?"

Adalyn frowned, "It is possible, and sadly, it is caused by your kind."

"What?" Giovanni asked in surprise.

"It is because of your wars and strife." She replied. "I was not speaking metaphorically when I said that the Most High felt each death as though it were his own. In a way, you are his children. A small piece of the Most High rests within each of you, like a child carries a piece of their parents."

Adalyn could sense their unease as she continued, "Imagine feeling the sorrow of millions of lives cut short. Picture it; innocent men, women, and children being caught in the crossfire of constant warfare. Each cry of pain, each plea for mercy, and each unheard cry for help weighs on his heart. He tires from all the animosity, the killing, and the depravity going on in his world and thus now he slumbers."

Giovanni put it all together, "Michael means to use the Church to make God even weaker and in doing so, open the door for Lucifer to reenter the Kingdom of Heaven with almost no resistance. The Choirs of Angels would be overrun without a leader."

"That's right." Adalyn said darkly. "I'm positive that Lucifer is just using Michael. Once he has what he wants, he'll kill Michael along with anyone else who tries to share power. I cannot believe Michael is so blind that he does not realize it."

Nicolas didn't know what to think. His head was still spinning. Everything he'd known from when he was a child was false. The reality was far grimmer than he could have imagined, "Okay, so how do we kill Michael?"

Adalyn turned to him, "That is a difficult question to answer. Angels can be killed, but it is not as easy as killing a human. The first way is to remove him from existence, which is something that only the Most High can do. Since he is unable to help us, the second way would be to use the angel's sword of flame."

"Which will not work for you." Giovanni added. "So what does that leave us with?"

"You have to turn him into a mortal." She said, though she did not like this option. "Then and only then can a human kill him."

Nicolas and Giovanni exchanged glances nervously. Something about the way Adalyn spoke made a chill run down their spines. Cyrillus stepped forward, "I'm all for it, but how do we accomplish such a goal?"

Adalyn turned away so that she was facing the ocean before raising the tattered rags that she was wearing and showing them the bite marks on her ankle, "The same way I was turned; venom from the Serpent of Eden."

A look of shock came over Nicolas as he spoke, "Are you referring to the same beast that is responsible for our expulsion from the Garden of Eden?"

Adalyn nodded, "The very same. It is the only one of its kind. Cursed for convincing Eve to eat the apple and then share it with Adam. Even a drop of the creature's venom is enough to bring down any immortal."

"I know I'm not going to like the answer to this question…" Nicolas said nervously. "Where do we find the Serpent of Eden?"

Adalyn didn't turn to him as she responded, "It resides deep in the Netherworld. There is a small Oasis between Lucifer's castle and the punishment grounds. The serpent took a liking to the single tree there."

"What?" Giovanni said as his eyes widened, "You mean we have to go to…"

"Yes," Adalyn replied in a dark voice, "we have to go to the Nether World, Tartarus, Sheol, Hades, The Valley of the Damned, the Pit… Hell."

"Are you insane?" Nicolas demanded. "You want us to travel to the land of the damned? Why can't we just find a way to alert the Choirs of angels?"

"They will not hear us." Adalyn retorted. "You may pray to them for help if you must, but do not expect any sort of reply so long as Michael lives. If there were another way, believe me, I would go for it in a heartbeat."

Both Giovanni and Nicolas looked at her as though asking what she meant, so she explained, "Michael is one of the highest ranked angels within the Choirs. He is one of the Seven Archangels all of whom are very well thought of and respected by the rest of the Celestial World and much of the Mortal World. Michael himself is the leader of the Most High's army and his most trusted general. Many of the other Choirs are unquestionably loyal to him for his heroics during the first war. Even the Most High has almost limitless trust in him. As a result, there is nothing the Choirs or the Most High will do. No one is willing question what Michael does. They'll need absolute proof."

Giovanni nodded, "Okay, so it looks like our course is clear then. How do we reach the underworld?"

"Wait a minute!" Cyrillus cut it. "Before we go off on some wild journey, may I point out one obvious problem?"

Adalyn nodded, "By all means."

Cyrillus continued speaking, "Killing Michael won't end the wars on this planet. Even if we stop him, God will still be weakened and Lucifer may still find his way into the Celestial World."

"Yes…" Adalyn admitted in a defeated voice. "I have actually been thinking about that quite a bit. The truth is that there is no way to know if killing Michael is the solution, but it is a start. One consistency about war is that it is unsustainable. If Michael's influence disappears, then the wars can progress to their conclusions. As the fighting dies down, the Most High will regain strength."

Giovanni nodded, "Okay then, it looks like finding the Eden Serpent is our only option. So what's the plan then?"

"There are a few entrances that can't be found unless you know where to look." Adalyn said, trying to remember back to her old lessons. "Also… they are not without risks, and you may find yourself in the Underworld with no way back. The best way I know of to get there…"

Giovanni moved closer and put his arm around Adalyn when he saw her shudder, "What is it?"

She breathed in deeply, really wishing she wasn't recommending this. She would rather they turn the ship around and run in the other direction. Finally, she spoke, "Charybdis…"

Nicolas' eyes widened, "The magnificent whirlpool? I know of that legend. We were told stories about the days when my countrymen were divided and pagans. One of our ancient kings defied the God of the sea and was forever blocked from sailing back to his homeland. He encountered the massive whirlpool, and chose to avoid it, but that story was a myth. No one has taken it to be a factual account in hundreds of years."

"Very true," Adalyn said, "but every story, every rumor, and every myth has some basis in reality. Your king did in fact get lost and encounter the massive whirlpool. My guess is that the story made its way back to your people, who then passed it on over time with their own folklore. I am telling you Charybdis exists."

Cyrillus's eyes narrowed, "No one is doubting you Adalyn, but what would create such a massive whirlpool in a random location like that?"

Adalyn's breathing increased as she continued, "Once there was an island north of Crete. It exploded thousands of years ago and was sucked into the sea. The people living on that land had become so corrupt with sin that the Most High ordered the Angel of Death, Samael, to destroy it in a manner that would wipe out any evidence of their existence."

Adalyn sighed as she continued, "Samael did as he was commanded. He created the giant Maelstrom by diving beneath the waves and spinning around at incredible speeds. It swirled so quickly that the center became a vortex and pulled all life on that cursed land down into Hell. The awesome power pulled the entire island down. Unfortunately, that whirlpool is still there. It was the only way to prevent the island from resurfacing. During the crimson sunset on the sixth hour of the evening, the vortex opens briefly."

Nicolas shuddered, "I've heard the stories about the island that you speak of. There were rumors of an advanced civilization that lived in isolation in that area, but there has never been any evidence that it truly existed."

Adalyn nodded, "Yes and that is no accident. The people of that land had become so corrupt and wicked, that if their ways ever left their isolated land, they could have poisoned the world. The Most High commanded that the island be destroyed. For mankind's own good, those people, their sinful ways, and their infernal technologies were wiped out of existence. The Most High protected his children from ever being corrupted by them. I will not reveal to you his reasoning. Men have gone mad searching for the mysteries that the island possessed."

Hair stood up on the back of Nicolas' neck from listening to Adalyn. A sense of terror came over Nicolas and Cyrillus as they looked at each other. Nicolas did not want to go through with this, but as it seemed to be their only option, what else could he do. Cyrillus looked at Nicolas as though asking for orders.

The young revolutionary nodded as he spoke to Cyrillus, "Well… you heard her, back to the tiller, hard to port. We sail for Crete."

Divinity

Cyrillus promptly obeyed and brought the ship around. The three men took shifts at the tiller and kept the sail in one piece. Adalyn stood at the bow during the entire voyage to Crete.

**

Giovanni took the last watch before sundown and was eventually relieved by Nicolas at the end of the day. After being freed from his post, he joined Adalyn at the bow and put his arm around her, "It will be at least two weeks or so before we reach Crete. We'll try to resupply near Messina for the long voyage and then make one final stop at Crete before we head out. The Church's influence there is not what it is on the mainland. We should be able to resupply without any issue."

Adalyn faintly smiled, "You've always been optimistic. It's a good quality, Giovanni. Hang on to it. The Church is not what I'm worried about right now though."

"Then what is it?" Giovanni asked.

She sighed, "This journey will not be as easy as simply sailing through a whirlpool and entering the Underworld."

She calls sailing through a maelstrom into the world of the damned easy? Giovanni thought to himself.

He did the best he could to pay attention as Adalyn continued, "It is a cursed place where not even angels dare go. There are temptations that we will have to face and corruptions that could easily take any one of us. While we try to do good, we could easily be manipulated for evil."

"I see," Giovanni replied hesitantly, "and how will we know?"

"We can't know." She conceded. "We just have to keep our wits and our faith. It's the only way we'll make it through."

Giovanni nodded, "As long as we have you with us, I'm confident that we'll make it. You know this place and you know what to watch out for."

Adalyn lowered her face, "I'll do my best not to disappoint you."

"As if you ever could." Giovanni replied.

Nicolas and Cyrillus had also been listening in. Nicolas called out to Adalyn before she could say anything else, "You can count on us too!"

Adalyn nodded, "We will need each other, and it will take all of our strength to survive this. The trials of the Netherworld will not be easy ones."

"I'm not afraid." Giovanni said adamantly.

Adalyn smiled, "I'm not either... some would say that makes us fools... but there has been no room for fear in my heart since I found out that you hadn't been killed."

Giovanni returned her smile, "I couldn't think of anything other than getting you back. My life was a shell without you. Now that I've got you back, I'll never let you go again. Keeping you alive is my only priority now."

Adalyn didn't respond, she just continued to lean on the railing as though she were looking out on the ocean. Giovanni turned away and looked at the mast, "I'd better check the rigging one more time. We don't need anything coming loose."

Adalyn heard Giovanni's footsteps as he walked away. She sighed as she relaxed her shoulders. *I'm sorry Giovanni... I know what you want of me... In a different time, in a different place, I would give it to you, but right now I cannot afford to make you the focus of my attention... not so long as our worlds are in danger.*

A tear fell from her eye as a smile formed on her lips. *I hope in some way that you know how much you mean to me. I know that I haven't really said it... but you've become dear to me, more so than I ever thought possible. My heart beats for you... you are the greatest incentive I could ever have to do everything I can to save our worlds.*

Divinity

Part 2

THE DESCENT

BOOK I
The Infernal Voyage

I

ays of traveling along the coast of the mainland began to wear heavily on the brave travelers. They had been given the blessing of good weather and a high wind speed, which got them to the city of Messina ahead of schedule. The smell of dry land in the distance tickled their noses as they passed the large port.

Adalyn was in the cabin asleep, still recovering from her injuries when she heard irritated voices up on deck. She immediately got up and stumbled up the stairs to see what was going on. She knew that she had to hurry as it sounded like a fight might break out.

On deck, Giovanni was having it out with Cyrillus. There seemed to be a big disagreement over where they should go next. Nicolas stood at the tiller, trying to ignore the argument as Giovanni glared at Cyrillus as he spoke, "We can't just sail on by! We're short on food and supplies. The sails need some work, and we can all use some time ashore."

Cyrillus shook his head, "I know that, but Messina is not the answer. The Church has too much of a presence there and with the knights chasing us, we'd be smart not to stop anywhere we couldn't quickly escape from!"

"I know that," Giovanni replied, "but Adalyn is still weak. She needs good food and medicine if she's going to regain enough strength to help us in the Underworld."

"So what do you propose we do then?" Cyrillus demanded. "Sail into port, get stopped by the Church and held until the papal knights catch up? You're a fisherman, what do you know about strategy?"

Cyrillus's condescension only served to push Giovanni even further over the edge, "I know the difference between being cautious and a suicide mission! You may be on a suicide mission, but don't drag the rest of us down with you."

Divinity

Cyrillus clenched his fists, "What was that? You take that back!"

Giovanni also clenched his and was about to respond when Adalyn came running out, "Hey, hey, hey! No no... stop this! You're both going crazy! Look, we've been pushed to the limit over the last few weeks. We've lost good friends, our homes, and a lot worse."

Giovanni let out a deep sigh as his features softened and his fists unclenched, "You're right..."

He turned back to Cyrillus, "Look, I'm sorry. You deserved better than what I said."

Cyrillus also lowered his fists, "Maybe you're right, we have been at sea a long time."

Adalyn nodded, "I think we're all on edge. Cyrillus is right, we can't go to Messina, it's too risky."

She turned towards the starboard side, "However there is a smaller port on an island not too far from here."

Cyrillus snapped his fingers, "That's right, I completely forgot about them, and they don't ask many questions either."

He then nodded and turned to Nicolas, "You know the way, steer us to the island port."

As Giovanni and Cyrillus returned to their work, Adalyn headed for the aft castle. She stood next to Nicolas and whispered to him quietly, "How close were they to coming to blows?"

Nicolas sighed, "You showed up just in time. I'm sorry I didn't try to stop it, but I have to admit that it was getting to me as well. I think I probably would have just made it worse."

Adalyn nodded, "It's okay, I think we all need a respite. If only we could have stopped at Messina, but it's just too risky."

"Giovanni looks like he needs you." Nicolas replied. "I can handle things here, but those two still look like they're on edge."

Adalyn nodded and leaned on the railway as she made her way to the bow of the ship, "I'll do what I can."

Giovanni was tending to some fouled rigging when he heard soft footsteps behind him. He quickly turned to see Adalyn smiling nervously at him, "Are you okay?"

Giovanni nodded, "Yeah, this is just the longest that I've ever been at sea. Don't worry, I'll do my best to keep it together, how are you?"

"All right." Adalyn replied. "My leg still hurts a little and I feel dizzy every now and then, but I am healing."

"Good." Giovanni replied. "Very good… so…"

Giovanni was about to say something when Nicolas cut him off, "I see the post in the distance!"

A small town appeared a few miles down the strait of Messina from the main city. There were only two piers and a few small buildings. Cyrillus nodded as he came up next to Giovanni, "This will work out better."

Giovanni nodded as he placed his hand on Cyrillus's shoulder, "I agree."

He then quickly turned to Adalyn, "You'd best go below."

Adalyn nodded and turned away, "I know the drill, don't worry."

Nicolas steered the small ship towards the open pier on the left as Cyrillus and Giovanni worked on the rigging to bring up the sail. Unable to catch the wind, the ship slowed to a crawl and bumped gently against the wooden dock.

Giovanni hopped over the side and caught the lines that Cyrillus threw over to him. The dock groaned as the ship was secured against it. Cyrillus ran the ramp down the side of the ship as Nicolas secured the tiller.

With the ship safely docked, Nicolas and Giovanni headed for the main shop with what money they had for some goods and food. There wasn't much money and Giovanni had nothing onboard to barter with. They had no idea how much they would be able to purchase, but hopefully it would be enough to hold them over for the remainder of the trip.

The merchant's house was little more than a hut with a rag door. Inside, the old merchant kept neither crucifix nor any religious symbol in his shop. The whole room was very plain.

Giovanni leaned forward to inspect some of the supplies they were picking up. As he did, the cross that Padre Antonelli had given him fell from his shirt. The merchant saw it and shook his head, "If you truly want luck in your travels, you'd be better off either melting that and using it for money, or tossing it overboard into the seas."

Giovanni glared at him, "That cross was given to me by a departed friend. Are you not a believer in the lord God almighty?"

"No," the merchant said plainly, "not after God decreed that my wife should be burned at the stake for caring for a man who was later found to be a heretic."

Nicolas nodded, "I feel your pain, good sir. The Church killed my family as well."

"The Church?" The merchant scoffed. "I'm referring to those damned followers of Luther. Just as bad as the Church I say. They ransack our towns and their churches. They murder the faithful citizens and pervert the young to their blasted ways and all in the name of God. These cursed holy wars will see the end of us all."

Nicolas could not believe what he was hearing, "It's a lie. You speak falsely. The followers of Luther are a revolutionary people fighting for religious freedom."

Divinity

The merchant spat back, "They fight to take over, so convinced that they are right."

"The Church is the evil one!" Nicolas shouted, "We fight to end their oppression!"

The merchant laughed, "Barbarians all, Luther's followers have done as much, if not more damage than the Church could ever dream of!"

Nicolas reached for his sword, but he felt Giovanni's hand blocking it, "Forgive us sir, we have taken up too much of your time. Thank you for your business."

The merchant nodded as Nicolas and Giovanni collected their goods and left. Once the two men were out of earshot, the merchant stood and turned to the curtain in the back of the room, "They are on the move…"

**

On their way back to the ship, Giovanni noticed that Nicolas was deep in thought. After a few moments of sorting out his thoughts, he finally spoke, "That peasant merchant lied, he must have. Is it possible that we have become the very evil that we have been fighting to rid the world of?"

Giovanni looked at him sympathetically, "Father Antonelli told me that this has been going on for a long time. After fighting for so long, sometimes the cause can be lost under hatred and bitterness. It's easy to lose sight of your goals when confronted by sheer madness."

Nicolas couldn't believe it. Their cause had to be just. If not, then his whole life since his family died had been wasted. "I watched my family's home burn. I heard them scream. I fight to rid the world of the Church, but I've never killed anyone who didn't deserve it. I wouldn't…"

"I know." Giovanni said in a reassuring tone. "Put it out of your head for now and let's just get back to the ship."

Nicolas nodded, "Perhaps… all right, let's go."

It took the group some time, but they managed to load the ship's cargo hold with everything they could. Once the cargo space below deck was full, they stored the rest on the deck. The ship was so loaded that the ship was at least a foot deeper on the draught. Once everything was tied down and secured, Giovanni turned to Cyrillus, "All right, grab one of the planks and help me shove off."

Cyrillus nodded, "I'm on it."

The two pushed the ship out while Nicolas hopped on the tiller and pushed it hard over so that the ship was turning away from the dock. They could hear the wood groan as they continued to apply pressure. It was slow work, but the ship was giving way as they worked.

Giovanni minded the bow as they pushed. The moment it was facing out enough, he nodded, "That's good, let's get the sail down."

Cyrillus nodded as Giovanni turned away and looked at Nicolas, "Keep her hard over until we catch the wind."

"I know, I know…" Nicolas said in an annoyed. "I'm not going to run your precious boat aground."

Giovanni pulled on the rigging until the larger sail fell. He then moved on to the smaller mast and began working the rigging there as well. The sails flapped a few time before catching the wind and carrying the boat forward.

Nicolas and Cyrillus watched as Messina faded into the distance. The narrow inlet between the islands and the mainland slowly faded behind it. The land grew smaller and smaller as the ship picked up speed.

Cyrillus sighed as the last strip of land was enveloped by the horizon, "It would have been nice to sample the bounty of the Kingdom of Sicily."

Adalyn appeared from below deck, "I take it from the movement of the floor that it's safe to come up now?"

Giovanni smiled, "Yeah, we're out of sight."

The young angel stretched out her wings and arms, "Finally, I really hate being cooped up like that."

"I'm sorry." Giovanni said sympathetically. "We just can't risk you being seen."

Adalyn shook her head, "No, I know. It's not your fault. I know it's important that I remain unseen. If we were discovered, I doubt that I could protect you. My wings are still slightly sore."

Giovanni chuckled, "I thought that I was protecting you."

"Not for long." Adalyn said with a grin. "Just wait until I get my eyesight back."

If you get your eyesight back, Giovanni thought to himself.

**

Over the next few hours, Adalyn noticed that Nicolas had gone from being an inquisitive young man to being a quiet and bitter person. He stayed away from everyone as they worked on the ship, opting to stare out to sea from the bow.

Adalyn decided to see if she could help him, "What troubles you Nicolas?"

He sighed, "Adalyn, who's on the right in this war?"

"Are you asking me which side God would deem as morally correct or righteous?" She asked as she leaned on the railing.

He nodded, "I've recently heard some troubling news about what some of my brothers in arms may be guilty of."

"Yes…" she said sadly, "unfortunately my friend, as with all things, if you are looking for the truth, then you may not like what you find."

"Please tell me," he insisted, "I must know if I have been wasting my life."

"Wasting?" She said surprised. "No I do not believe that you are wasting your life by any stretch of the

imagination. You fight for what you think is right. Some of your people have lost their way, but your purpose has remained true. One cannot fault you for that. You fight for ideology, not revenge or greed. The Most High sees that."

"Thank you." He said quietly.

She sighed, not looking forward to breaking his spirit, "However, if your people were to win, and the Church were to collapse, what do you think would happen? Do you really believe that people would be allowed to practice faith on their own, or would a new regime with different rules and practices take over and eventually cause the same pain you are now fighting to end?"

"But we are fighting for the good of all." Nicolas said, now fighting back his anger. "We want to end oppression!"

"Truly?" She asked. "The good of all you say, and how many has your cause killed? How many children no longer have a father, how many wives watch the shores for a ship to bring back their husbands that will never come? Tell me how many, my brave revolutionary. How many families has your cause burned alive in their homes?"

Nicolas staggered back, "I…"

She shook her head, "It's okay, Nicolas, you still have most of your life ahead of you. The Most High grants you the ability to atone for sins. I know you're not guilty of the horrors that some of your allies are. Still, you are living in a dream if you think that either side has the moral high ground."

He shook his head, "How… if I have truly squandered the time I have been given thus far? How can I expect him to forgive me?"

"Because that's what he does." She said as she grasped his arm. "So the question I now have for you Nicolas is what are you going to do with the time you have left?"

Nicolas couldn't find the words to answer her. After a moment of silence, Adalyn smiled, "When you get a chance, think about it, you still have time."

II

The ship pulled out into the open sea and began its way to the island of Crete. The trip had taken its toll on Nicolas more than the rest. In addition to seeing more of the world then he ever through possible, he had also learned terrible truths about those who he fought with. "I never thought I'd see so much. I was just a local boy with no aspirations of travel. The family life had its appeal to me before the Church ever got involved in our lives. Now here I am. I feel like we will be traveling the world in its entirety."

Giovanni stood next to him leaning on the tiller, holding their course, "I know, but this task has been given to us, and if we are not victorious, the entire world will suffer for sure."

"But we didn't ask for this…" Nicolas sighed.

"No we didn't," Giovanni admitted, "but I don't think Adalyn asked for what happened to her either. I will stay on to the end, but if this is becoming too much for you and you wish to leave, please feel free to do so. What we're doing is very dangerous and no one would blame you for wanted to quit."

Nicolas looked hurt, "I gave you my word, and I will stick with you until this is over, but it seems that I have a lot to answer for. Maybe in some way, helping Adalyn will help me atone for my actions"

Giovanni nodded, "I appreciate that."

It wasn't long before the ship was covered over in a veil of darkness. The sun set on the horizon, leaving Giovanni to navigate by the stars. This was nothing new and even though he was in unfamiliar waters, he still knew which way to go.

Nicolas took a lookout post at the front of the ship and lay down while Cyrillus took his turn in the cabin. Giovanni was resting at the tiller trying to stay awake while he was steering the ship towards Crete. It was his turn to face the chilled air while the others slept, but he enjoyed sailing at night.

Above the ship, thousands of stars twinkled in the night sky. As Giovanni watched them, a shooting star blazed past and disappeared as quickly as it came. Light from the moon and the lamps onboard illuminated the water around him.

Giovanni rubbed his arms as the chill caused him to break out in goose bumps. It wasn't too bad, but the air was just cool enough to make him uncomfortable. His clothes were old and torn and he had found no replacements in the merchant shops that they had visited.

"Are you cold?" A voice asked from the darkness.

Giovanni had been so distracted that he had failed to notice that Adalyn had come up on deck. She was carrying a wooden bowl with her. Steam flew from the bowl that was visible, even in the night sky.

"What is this?" He asked as she approached.

Adalyn smiled, "I boiled some fish in the leftover alcohol and made a broth. It isn't much, but it should keep you warm."

The aroma of hot food entered Giovanni's nose as he took the bowl from Adalyn. Without much thought, he sipped the soup down slowly. The broth tasted of fish that had been in salt for way too long. A dry sensation entered his throat as he drank it down, but continued drinking. He did not want to insult Adalyn by pushing it away.

Once the bowl was empty, Giovanni looked at her, "Thank you. That does help."

Adalyn could tell he was still shivering from the movement of the deck below him. The rags that she had been given in prison didn't provide any protection against the elements either, but she at least had her wings to keep

Divinity

her warm. She couldn't imagine that he was in any better shape.

As Adalyn sat down, she took the bowl from Giovanni, and placed it on the deck. With her wings spread, she quickly cuddled up next to him and wrapped them around her's and Giovanni's bodies. His cold skin sent chills through her body as she leaned into him.

Adalyn's feathers were so soft and warm that Giovanni nearly fell asleep. He was happy to see that most of the damage to her wings had healed and her feathers were no longer stained. The two watched the stars go by as their ship glided through the water.

*

As the days passed, the group began to notice that their supplies were getting low again. They had purchased plenty of food, but much of it was spoiling. Salted fish could hold for weeks, but fruit and fresh meat would not. There was also not enough salt left in the hold to store any of it.

By the end of the week, their food stores were down to nothing. Cyrillus and Nicolas were sitting on deck discussing their next move, "If we don't stop soon, we'll starve to death. There are a few small islands between here and Crete, I say we make a break for one of them and pick up more supplies."

Giovanni joined them, "It would be impossible. We don't have any money left and don't even know if any of them are inhabited. We also don't have much in the way of hunting tools if we did come across an island."

Nicolas agreed, "I know, it's not possible, but fishing isn't getting us anywhere, and our food supply is almost gone. What are we going to do?"

Adalyn could hear them from the cabin below. She worried that soon they would wind up starving to death if they did not come up with a solution. Feeling the unrest in

Divinity

their voices, she dropped to her knees and prayed, "All-knowing father, I know not if you can hear me, but I need your help. I have no right to ask, but it's not for my sake. The people I travel with are still beloved to you. We are running low on supplies and food. I know you are at odds with me, but please save my friends, they have done nothing wrong."

Darkness fell and as Adalyn expected, no response came. She lowered her head sat back, "Please…"

**

Another day went by and the last of their food was gone. The ship they were on was larger than an average for a fishing boat, but it was not large enough to sustain four people for a long voyage. They began to contemplate heading towards the closest island, when out of nowhere, Cyrillus spotted another ship on the horizon, "Sail ho, looks like a merchant vessel!"

Giovanni nodded, "Let's head for it, maybe they have some extra supplies."

As they drew closer, they were able to get a better view of what they were dealing with. The ship was almost three times the size of Giovanni's little fishing boat. It was clearly a cargo ship of some kind, but definitely of foreign design.

Giovanni noted that it resembled a carvel that he had seen in Venice many years ago. It had an aft castle, as well as a fat hull for cargo. The ship was painted red and blue and did not appear to have any sort of weapon ports on it. Three masts poked up from the hull, one of which was square rigged, and looked to belong to some wealthy merchant.

Perhaps most alarming was that the ship appeared to have fire damage on the masts and whatever sails it once had were long since burned away. The masts were pitch

black, as was most of the visible deck. No one onboard Giovanni's boat knew what to make of this.

Cyrillus lit the signal fires, but no one responded. The ship batted about on the waves and appeared to be drifting with no sails down. Nicolas watched it from a distance, "What do you think Giovanni? It appears that the ship may be derelict. There may be supplies on board we can use."

Adalyn shook her head, "Just because they do not respond, does not mean that there is no one on board. It may simply mean that they wish to be left alone."

Giovanni nodded, "That may very well be, but look at the damage. I think it's a safe bet to say that whoever owned it, abandoned it long ago. Either way, we can't afford to just sail on by. We're too low on food and supplies. I think it best if we check it out."

Adalyn nodded, "Very well, but please be careful."

As she disappeared below decks, she quickly said a prayer of thanks. She was certain that it was no coincidence that they had found the ship. *Praise be to you, Most High.*

Nicolas turned to Cyrillus, "Get us in alongside that ship, we're going aboard."

"No problem," Cyrillus replied as he pulled the tiller to turn toward the strange ship. As they got close, Adalyn put her hand on the rail and guided herself to the cabin, "I think it might be best if I remain out of sight."

"Probably not a bad idea, I'll check on you when we get back." Giovanni said as he watched her disappear into the cabin before turning back to see them closing on the other ship.

Nicolas called out, "Ahoy there, is anyone on board?"

When no response came, the three of them threw grapple lines on to the other ship and pulled it close. They then extended the ramp, and went aboard. Giovanni drew his sword and went over first, followed by Cyrillus. Nicolas was left behind to guard the ship, despite his objections.

Divinity

As they walked up the gangway, Giovanni noticed a soaked piece of paper posted on the side of the hull. It was written in Latin with the symbol of the Papal Knights on top. Nicolas could not read it, but Giovanni had learned some Latin from Padre Antonelli. He read the note to himself and shook his head.

Cyrillus looked at him anxiously, "Well, can you read it?"

Giovanni nodded, "This ship and crew have been condemned by the Church for their heresy. It looks like the crew has been taken to Rome to be interrogated, and the ship was to meet the same fate as my house. This message serves as a warning to anyone who would board the ship before it sank that they would face the same condemnation."

Cyrillus laughed, "I would say it is a very good thing we are already marked men within the Church, otherwise this might actually worry me."

Giovanni nodded, "The ship must have encountered a storm or rogue wave that put out the fire. The deck is charred, but it also looks soaked. I can't come up with any other reason for its survival."

"Who cares?" Cyrillus asked. "Let's just see what we can find!"

The ship was rather ornate with multiple carvings and murals painted on what was left of the inner hull. The captain's cabin was also quite luxurious with silk curtains and a soft bed, having been untouched by the flame. By the looks of it, the ship had come from the east, possibly from the Balkan region or even further out.

They went below decks and found an abundance of supplies, including preserved food, clothing weapons, and tradable goods. Giovanni shook his head and crossed himself as he stared in awe at the holds, "This was definitely a merchant vessel of some kind."

He was extremely relieved that they would no longer need to stop off for supplies on their way. "Now we have things to barter with when we reach Crete, as well as enough food to sustain us for the trip."

Cyrillus looked at his tatter clothes, "And fresh clothes for us."

The two travelers grabbed everything that they could carry and returned to their own ship. Nicolas helped arrange everything in the hold while they brought the supplies over. He was eager to see what they had managed to find.

It took them a few trips, but they squeezed as much as they could on their smaller ship. Even doors, windows, spare rope, and wood were not overlooked. Their holds were full and their ship was once again much deeper on the draught. They piled a few more things on deck but realized that they could not take everything. After assessing what they had taken, it was decided that part of the wardrobe and bartering goods would need to be left behind.

Cyrillus shook his head, "Why not just trade ships? That one is designed for longer voyages."

Giovanni shook his head, "That vessel cannot be crewed by three men. Even if it could, I don't think that we have enough cloth to replace the sails."

Nicolas pointed to the masts, "Considering that they'd even withstand the force of high wind, they look pretty well charred."

"Exactly." Giovanni replied. "It's probably best if we just continue on my ship. It's in better shape and much smaller. A small fishing ship will attract less attention than a large merchant vessel."

Adalyn came up on deck when she heard Giovanni's voice and chimed in on the conversation, "I agree with Giovanni, it's way too risky."

Once the group had secured all their supplies both on deck and in the hold, they cut the lines and pulled the ramp back on deck. The group thanked God as the larger ship slowly began to disappear on the horizon. The final few days of their voyage would be a lot easier now that they had managed to outfit Giovanni's ship with much of the supplies they had found, including enough durable cloth to replace the main sail, tools to navigate the seas, maps, preserved food that would last longer, expensive arquebus matchlocks, new swords, clothing, and the décor that they had ripped from the other ship. Giovanni had even taken some of the lead plated lamps with colored glass and added them to the railing of his own ship.

Once they had nailed the new additions in place, Giovanni began to think to himself, *look at my boat! It's more of a luxury yacht now then a fishing boat. I wonder if I will be able to use it to fish ever again or if our lives even have a chance of returning to normal. Is it even possible at this point?*

Giovanni's thoughts were interrupted by Cyrillus and Nicolas ripping the door off his cabin and throwing it overboard so they could replace it with the door to the captain's cabin off the other ship. It was an ornate door with stylish carvings and a plated window.

Giovanni sighed, "You two really stripped that ship to the keel didn't you?"

Cyrillus shrugged, "Their crew is most likely dead by now, and no one is going to be using that ship again. Why not put what's left of it to good use?"

Giovanni shrugged and went about sorting through everything they had brought on board. He spent a few minutes sorting through boxes of ammunition, clothing, and carpentry tools, until he found a small wooden box with ornate carvings on it. Cyrillus smiled, "We may find a lot here that we can trade. I should have been a pirate!"

Adalyn rolled her eyes and headed for the cabin, "On that note, I'm going to try to clean up a little. I saw some perfumes amongst the goods you brought onboard."

Giovanni laughed at the thought Cyrillus raiding ships on the high seas as he opened the box. Inside was a shimmering white dress made with soft cotton and fine silk. It looked similar to the dress Adalyn had been wearing when he found her, but this one was clean and much more luxurious. He packed it back into the box, "Not this one, this goes to Adalyn."

Nicolas looked through another stack of supplies and found a few more boxes of clothes. These ones contained an assortment of men's clothes, "Not these ones either, I think we should use these to look a little more presentable when we stop in various ports."

"Not a bad idea." Giovanni replied. "I'm getting tired of being looked at like a peasant."

The group began changing as they found shirts, trousers, and sandals. Once they were done, the tattered rags that they had been wearing for weeks were thrown over the side. Giovanni liked the feel of brand new clean clothes. It had been a while since he felt fresh materials on his back. The moment that he was presentable, he stood up, took the ornate box and walked to the cabin.

Through the window on the new door, Giovanni could see that Adalyn was struggling to clean herself. She decided to take advantage of the perfumes and new handkerchiefs that were found onboard the merchant ship. She had obviously been uncomfortable with her appearance during the voyage.

After lighting a fire in the small pit, she boiled a small pot of water, let it slightly cool, and tried to wash herself with a wet cloth. She then filled a cup with water and mixed in some of the perfume. Once she was ready, she leaned her head outside the cabin window, and with one hand over her

face, rinsed her golden blonde hair. The cool breeze quickly dried her as Giovanni made his way into the room. It wasn't much, but at least she felt clean. Her wings were a different story, she tried to clean them, but it took too long to wash each individual feather. She would need to immerse them in water if she had any hope of completely cleansing them.

Giovanni knocked on a post in the doorway. The sound accidentally startled her and she quickly turned around, "Giovanni?"

He smiled, "Sorry, I didn't mean to scare you. I found something amongst the goods from the other ship. It's something that I think would look good on you."

Before Giovanni handed her the box, he noticed what she had done while they were restocking the ship, "You cleaned and organized the cabin? This is wonderful, now we can get to everything we need. I still find it amazing that even though you are blind, you can still do so much."

Adalyn smiled, "Eyes are not everything. We have other senses that we really do not give enough credit. Azrael trained me to be able to function without the use of my eyes and I am tired of being useless around here while everyone else does all the work."

Giovanni shrugged, "I don't think you've been useless at all. You've raised all of our spirits since the day we rescued you."

He looked down at the box, "Here, take a look. It was part of the haul we brought onboard to trade, but I'd rather you have it."

Adalyn took the box from Giovanni, opened it, and felt the dress inside, "Oh thank you! Finally I have some decent clothing. What a relief, they took my dress from me when I was captured and left me with just enough to stay decent."

Giovanni saw the expression on her face as the painful memories once again filled her mind, "What happened to you in there?"

Adalyn felt the scars on her arms and legs as tears began to drip out from under the blindfold. Her lips quivered and she could not speak. She turned to the side and tried to hide her face from Giovanni as she fought to regain her composure.

At that moment, Giovanni realized that not all of her scars had healed. While her physical injuries had been attended to, the emotional ones were still wide open. Giovanni rubbed her shoulder to comfort her, "It's okay, Adalyn. I'm sorry; I shouldn't have brought it up."

"No," Adalyn replied, forcing the words out, "we never really talked about it and you deserve to know."

She took a deep breath and sat down on the bed. Giovanni sat down next to her and took her hand, "Take your time."

Adalyn took in one more breath and began to speak, "That inquisitor, Nevelson I believe his name was... he was a monster. He thoroughly enjoyed his work as though it gave him some retribution for a youth he was forced to suffer through. They strapped me to the table, tore away my clothing, and my dignity, and ripped me apart. There was no limit to what they would try in order to force a confession. The brutality, the violation, and the humiliation were more than I could bear. By the time I heard you were still alive, I had stopped eating and was praying my body would just give out. I wanted to die."

Adalyn's voice faded as tears began to fall down her cheeks. She covered her mouth with her right hand as her lips quivered. She tried to be strong, but the pain from her memories was overwhelming.

Giovanni couldn't believe what he was hearing. He didn't know how to respond, but that wasn't important at that moment. She was visibly in pain and he hated seeing it. He quickly put his arm around her and pulled her close. She rested her head on his shoulder and took a few minutes to calm down.

Adalyn shook her head, "This is pointless, I'm sorry…"

"For what?" Giovanni asked. "You didn't do anything wrong."

"I know…" Adalyn replied. "It's just hard, but I know that I should be better than this. What happened, happened and thanks to you, it won't happen again."

"You're apologizing for being in pain?" Giovanni scoffed. "There is nothing for you to be sorry for. You held out a lot longer than most people probably could have. Many would probably have just given in and falsely confessed just to end their pain."

Giovanni lowered his eyes as he continued, "I should be the one saying sorry. I should have done more to protect you. We should have had some kind of escape plan in place in case something like that happened."

Adalyn raised her head with a shocked expression on her face, "There was no way you could have prevented the Church from taking me, just as there was no way to fight off the guards at your house. The moment you were freed, you came after me and got me out of there. You kept your promise and rescued me from death in that awful place. I owe you everything."

Giovanni shook his head, "Even so, I did everything I could to show you the goodness in humans. I wanted to change your perception of my people so that you would see that even though we can do horrible things, we are just as capable of doing great things. I feel like I failed you."

"Failed me? Is that what you think?" Adalyn asked as a comforting smile appeared on her face, "Is that really what you think? Giovanni, before I met you, I was extremely

prejudiced against humans. We were taught to be weary of humans. We learned to avoid and distrust you. Those teachings and my job as a guide for the damned made it very easy for me to hate humans. I was so foolish… I thought being banished here would have been the worst thing for me. In truth, I expected I would be dead by now, but you saved me. You restored my faith in the good of people."

There was a brief silence that was beginning to annoy Adalyn, so she broke through it by picking up the dress, "Well, let's see how this looks on me."

She paused and thought about her words for a moment, "Correction, I'll let you do the seeing. I am just so relieved to have something new to wear. These rags leave little to the imagination."

Giovanni refused to respond as she picked the dress up, got a feel for it, and adjusted the sash to fit her figure. Once she was ready, she used Giovanni's dagger to cut two holes in the back for her wings and then closed them around her hips to get a little privacy.

Giovanni quickly turned to face away from her as she changed. They had lived together for a while, but he knew it was still inappropriate for him to watch her change. He was about to head up on deck, but the sound of her fidgeting with the dress made him stay put in case she needed help.

Adalyn heard him turn away and quickly untied the rags, letting them fall to the ground. She fitted the dress over her wings and brought it down to cover the rest of her body. It was a bit of a struggle, but she managed to get the dress on fairly quickly. She flapped her wings a few times to make sure that they were comfortable as she tightened the sash around her waist.

Once she was decent, Adalyn reached out and tapped Giovanni on the shoulder, "Okay, how do I look?"

Divinity

Giovanni turned around to see her clean and, for the first in a while, dressed in clothes that were not torn, bloody, or filthy. He stood by for a moment, looking at her as though seeing her for the first time. She could sense he was looking her over and felt goose bumps break out across her skin, "Well?"

"Beautiful." He replied, barely able to breathe. "As always, beautiful."

Adalyn blushed as she slowly stepped up to Giovanni and hugged him, "Thank you."

She sat down on the bunk as she straightened out, "I made the bed with a new set of sheets from the other ship. The old ones were starting to irritate my skin."

He nodded, "I kept the good sheets in my cottage, these are little more than burlap."

Hearing Giovanni's words, reminded Adalyn of what he had lost because of her, "I still can't believe the Church burned your home. It's hard knowing how much saving me cost you. The guilt when I thought that you were dead was worse than any pain the inquisitor inflicted on me."

Giovanni put his hand on her shoulder as she sat on the bed. He placed his other hand on her chin, and raised her face to his, "Enough, we've been through this already. No one blames you for what happened. I would have sacrificed a lot more to be where I am now. Before you came along, I was lonely and sick. My only daily activity consisted of fishing. Padre Antonelli, in all his wisdom, wasn't going to be around forever so what in the world was I supposed to do after his death, considering I even outlived him?"

Adalyn's expression did not change, so Giovanni continued talking, "You came into my life and changed all that. You gave me a second chance at life and a reason to live it. For you, there is nothing I wouldn't do. I would follow you to the ends of the world and I will never stop fighting until you are safe. I love you."

Divinity

Adalyn's heart seized in her chest for a brief moment. She was completely caught off guard by Giovanni's words, "What did you say?"

He placed his hand gently on her cheek, "You heard me. I said I love you."

Adalyn's heart froze and she had trouble breathing when she heard those words. For her, they were bittersweet. She was aware of how he felt and reciprocated those feelings, but she didn't know if they stood any chance of having a future together.

Knowing that she had no way of making him retract his words, she bit her lower lip, "You really meant that didn't you? You won't ever leave my side?"

He shook his head, "Not a chance."

Once again Adalyn found herself wishing that Giovanni would listen to reason, but knowing it was pointless to try to convince him, she vowed to do everything she could to protect him from pain. From that point on, it would be as much her job to protect him as he was protecting her.

"Then... neither will I," She said smiling, as she finally allowed herself to completely give in. "I'll stand by you through everything. Whatever I can do to make you happy, I will. You need only ask."

Divinity

III

A few more days of sailing brought them to Crete. As the island finally came into view, a sense of relief came over everyone on board Giovanni's boat. The island continued to grow larger on the horizon until the large port city of Heraklion came into view.

Cyrillus looked on, "Will we be safe mooring here?"

Nicolas nodded, "Based on our most recent information, the Church maintains a presence here, but it is constantly mired by the diverse community on the island. This land was originally the property of the Aegeans, but it has changed hands a few times over the years and is now held by the Venetians. Different religious sects and various ethnicities make it difficult for the Church to get a hold on the area."

Giovanni smiled as he pulled on the tiller, "My countrymen, we should be safe here."

The small ship pulled into port and Nicolas helped tie her to the nearest post. As Giovanni helped bring up the sails, Adalyn suddenly appeared behind them, "I'm coming with you this time."

Giovanni turned to see Adalyn dressed in a long cloak. Using a tight strap, she somehow managed to restrain her wings and them against her back. It wasn't a perfect solution, but she would be able to pass as a human. Nicolas shook his head, "This is not a good idea. If you are discovered, it will be hard getting out of here."

Adalyn frowned, "Please, I need to stretch my legs for at least a little while. I promise not to get in the way."

Giovanni had to chuckle a little as she resembled a hunchback, but at least she was now passable as a human, "I agree with Nicolas, this isn't a smart move at all."

He was about to tell her to go back inside, but he saw the look on her face as she spoke, "Please?"

Divinity

Giovanni sighed, "Oh very well, come on, let's go."

Once they disembarked, it took the party a few minutes to regain their land legs. Adalyn also needed a moment to get used to continuous walking. She had spent years relying almost completely on her wings. She had gotten used to using her legs during her stay with Giovanni, but the time in prison and on his ship had undone most of that. To have to walk so much now was an adjustment, but she managed to keep up with the group.

The four of them travelled the streets of the small harbor community until they reached the main market. The town was larger than the village Giovanni was from and far more built up on. This town resembled Venice, but the buildings were considerably smaller and far less ornate. They were also more spread out over the land.

Cyrillus and Nicolas were out picking up extra supplies wherever they could. They were determined to make sure that they'd have everything they needed for the final leg of their voyage. Nicolas had taken down a list of everything they would need and didn't give up until he found every last item.

Adalyn took the time to listen to the people in the crowd. With her eyes still covered by bandages as they healed, her ears had to take over. It took her some time to filter out the background noise to make sense out of everything. She could hear families worrying about feeding themselves, two men arguing over the price of goods, and children playing in the street. To Adalyn, these sounds were quite tranquil in comparison to the quiet rocking of the ship or the mournful cries of the prison.

As Giovanni guided her down the main path, she heard something in a nearby alley that drew her attention. She moved closer to the sound and leaned into the dark area just off the street. It was a young boy coughing and gasping for air. She stopped in her tracks and listened carefully as the little boy continued to cough.

Giovanni also felt sympathy for him. For a moment, he could see himself sitting there alone and in the dark. It was not so long ago that he was in the exact same condition. This was the same scene that played out from him when he first realized that he was sick.

Adalyn listened to the boy sympathetically as he began to cry, "Why God, why did you leave me like this? Why did you take mommy and daddy away? Won't you please help me, I'm hungry and hurt. Please send me my angel."

Adalyn could not stand to hear any more of this. A tear fell out from under her bandages and streamed down her cheek. She quickly turned to Giovanni, "Give me one of the loaves of bread that we brought."

Giovanni nodded, pulled one out of the sack, and handed it to her. She turned around and brought it into the alley where she heard the little boy. Though she couldn't see him, she did hear his hoarse breathing.

Once Adalyn was close enough, she knelt down near him and held out the loaf of bread, "Here, please take this and eat. It isn't much, but it should help."

The boy eyed the bread for a moment before grabbing the bread and taking large bites. He consumed the entire loaf as quickly as possible. The boy sounded like a ravenous wolf as he ate.

Adalyn heard the loud gulping and feared the boy would choke, "Careful, there is no rush!"

The boy finished up and looked up at Adalyn, "Thank you kind lady, I was so hungry."

Adalyn nodded, "You are quite welcome. I just wish there was more I could do for you."

The boy forced a smile, even though he was still hurting inside, "I always wondered why God would let this happen to me. My mother always told me that I should pray to my guardian angel if I ever needed help, but I guess God didn't think I was important enough to have one."

She knelt down next to him, "Now you listen to me, the Most High cares for you as much as anyone else on this Earth. He grieves when you hurt like you were his own son."

He looked up at her, "Then why hasn't my guardian angel answered me? Where could she be?"

Adalyn didn't know how to answer him. There was no explanation she could give that a boy his age could accept. She didn't want to further break his spirit, but knew that he deserved an answer.

Finally, she got an idea, "Well maybe she has answered you…"

Nicolas and Cyrillus realized what was about to happen and obstructed the view of the alley from the street while Giovanni kept a lookout. He tried to protest, but Adalyn didn't give him a chance to do so.

A second later, Adalyn removed the cloak and spread her wings out to their full magnificence. The boy's eyes widened, "You… you're… my angel?"

He reached out and touched the white feathers on her wings, "You're… you're real. I can't believe it. My mother told me how beautiful angels were…"

Adalyn smiled, "Just remember, the Most High always cares about you and that no matter what, when you pray to him or ask him for something, he'll always answer. That doesn't mean you'll always get what you want, but you will get an answer."

"But why would he take my family, milady?" The boy asked in an almost demanding tone.

Adalyn shook her head, "It is no more my job to interpret the Most High's will than it is yours. Just know that he took them for a reason and that they are now living with him in paradise."

"But what should I do now?" The boy asked as tears continued to flow down his cheeks.

"Go and live your life." Adalyn replied. "The world ahead of you is wide open with limitless possibilities. Explore your options, learn how the world works, and then decide how you wish to live it. Whatever you decide to do, do it well and live an honest and righteous life. If you can do that, you will see your parents again one day."

The boy nodded, "I… I think I understand."

He quickly got to his feet and brushed off his trousers, "I guess I'd better get started then, but how will I find you if I need you again?"

Adalyn shook her head, "The Kingdom of Heaven is within you. Look to your heart. Your angel will always be there."

The boy covered his chest and nodded, "Thank you… I will never forget what you did!"

"Just be sure to keep our meeting a secret." Adalyn replied cautiously. "You don't want anyone thinking that you're seeing things."

"I know." The boy replied. "Don't worry, I will never tell."

Adalyn nodded, "Peace be with you boy, the Lord expects great things from you."

As the boy quickly left the alley in search of a way to survive, he carried a renewed sense of faith with him. There was a spring in his step that even the blind angel could detect as she listened to his feet hit the ground. Adalyn was sure that he now stood a better chance of survival.

Once the boy was gone, Adalyn tied her wings back again and pulled the cloak back over her dress. With her identity safely concealed, she quickly walked out of the alley and looked at the group, "Thank you for being patient. We can go now."

Divinity

Nicolas looked at her in disapproval, "Why would you do something like that? Would such a small token truly help the boy or just give him false hope. Would making him think that there is more out there for him then just living in his own filth improve his life?"

Adalyn's brow furrowed as she responded, "If at the very least it gives him some hope, then I believe it was worth it. Remember the Most High's teachings, 'What you do unto the least of your brothers, you do unto me.' Those teachings were meant to be taken literally. Some people say that the Most High never appears to them. Those people have spent their time staring into the sky rather than looking at the world around them. If they did, they'd see him in themselves, as they were meant to."

"But what if someone had seen you and our cover was blown?" Nicolas insisted, "What if, by giving him such a token, all you are doing is postponing the inevitable and making him suffer even further. Perhaps it's best to just let things happen as they may."

"I disagree, Nicolas." Giovanni chimed in. "That is a lesson I pray is lost on Adalyn. I do not think it is true. That boy has the same chance anyone in this town has. It's just a question of how hard he wants to work for it."

Nicolas shrugged as everyone continued walking, "Fine, I guess I can't argue with you. Just know that we can't afford many more delays."

The group continued through market, bartering for as many supplies as they would need. Once they were fully loaded, they made their way back to the ship. It was slow work as they purchased a lot of preserved food and drink for the trip.

As they crossed back through the town and eventually arrived at the docks, Giovanni froze in place. Adalyn felt the tug of his arm as he jerked to a halt. His heavy breathing

made her nervous, "What is it Giovanni, is something wrong? Why have we stopped?"

He didn't respond, and quickly turned to Nicolas, "Do you see that?"

"Yes… It's massive," Nicolas exclaimed nervously, "and it looks like it's heavily armed."

Giovanni nodded, "We need to leave, now."

Nicolas grabbed Cyrillus's arm, "Let's go, we need to get the ship ready!"

The two left Giovanni to guide Adalyn back with some of their supplies. Adalyn was getting scared by the change in atmosphere around her. The voices of the townspeople became more intense and turned to panic. She could hear the sound of wood and stone as doors and windows closed. Mothers pulled their children off the streets while shopkeepers struggled to bring their stands down.

Adalyn tugged on Giovanni's shoulder to get his attention, "Heavily armed? What are you seeing, talk to me, what is it?"

"It's a warship, Adalyn." Giovanni responded. "I've never seen one that big. It has enough armaments to take on anything, and it's bearing the sign of the Papal knights."

She pulled close to Giovanni, "They must have traced us here somehow. They'll be sending troops ashore soon. If we are not out of here by then, I fear we may never leave."

Giovanni agreed, "I know, they'll block off the port and hold all shipping, both in and out. If that happens, we're finished."

As the two made their way to the ship, Nicolas called to them, "We're all set, get aboard now! It looks like they just dropped anchor, so we don't have a minute to spare!"

Giovanni guided Adalyn up the gangway as Cyrillus cut the mooring lines, pulled the ramp up, and ran back to the tiller. Nicolas brought the sail down as the ship began to move.

Divinity

Giovanni turned to Adalyn as they got underway, "Go below, and no matter what happens, stay quiet."

"Okay." Adalyn nodded and made her way to the cabin.

Once she was out of sight, Cyrillus turned the boat toward the harbor exit. As their ship moved, they passed close to the anchored warship. Nicolas realized just how close they were getting and began to panic, "I don't like this! Veer away you fool, they'll see us!"

Giovanni shook his head, "Quiet, no! Keep us steady as she goes. If we veer away now, they'll get suspicious."

Cyrillus nodded, "I sure hope no one on that ship recognizes us."

The small fishing vessel slowly passed by the papal warship. The massive hull had enough armaments to rival the large fortress that could be seen at the harbor entrance. This was a newer warship that resembled a large caravel. In addition to the row of gun ports in the hull, she was also loaded down with smaller guns on deck.

There were armed soldiers brandishing arquebuses marching up and down the deck. The large vessel was square rigged on the foremast, with lateen sails on the mizzen and Bonaventure mizzen masts. Armed lookouts could be seen in the crow's nest on the foremast.

Giovanni knew that if they were recognized, there would be no way to outrun such a large ship. Nicolas watched as they lowered their first launch full of soldiers into the water. They both tried to hide their nervousness and keep a casual look about them.

Adalyn huddled in the back corner of the cabin. She stayed away from the window and kept her head down, waiting for the cannon fire to begin. She feared for the one she loved and whispered a small prayer as the ship continued slowly out of the harbor.

As the small fishing boat moved alongside the warship, Giovanni noticed that several of the crew gave them odd looks. Nicolas tried to keep anyone from seeing his face by looking off in the other direction, but he wasn't sure if it helped. The moment passed incredibly slowly for everyone on board.

Once they had passed it the warship, Giovanni wondered if anyone had recognized them. He was extremely nervous as they pulled out into open waters. His eyes remained pinned to the papal ship's sails, waiting for them to drop again.

Nicolas had momentarily disappeared below deck and returned with a pair of the arquebuses they had found on the merchant ship. He loaded them and lit the wicks just in case. He was about to bring them to the railing, but Giovanni shook his head, "Keep them out of sight. Let's not give the knights a reason to attack us."

Nicolas agreed and kept his eye on the massive warship as it grew smaller in the distance, "Not much good those guns would do us anyway."

The small fishing ship began heading north toward the forbidden island. Giovanni ran to the back of the ship for any sign that they were being followed. To his relief, there was no movement from the island port. The warship remained anchored and its sails were tied up. He turned back to tend to his own ship as the port finally disappeared on the horizon. He was convinced that at least for the moment, they were safe.

From the deck of the warship, Captain Federico stood near the helm, watching the small fishing boat pull away. One of the lookouts came up to him, "Sir, a few of the men claim they saw two people matching the description of the fugitives who made it out of Rome. They are on that fishing boat."

Divinity

Federico watched as the boat quickly began to disappear on the horizon, "I see…"

The man stood by, "What are your orders, sir? Do you wish to pursue?"

Federico shook his head, "No."

"But sir…" The man protested

"Our orders were to hold all traffic at this port and prevent anyone from coming in or going out." Federico said, cutting the man off, "Not go chasing after fishermen. So begin your occupation, that's an order."

Knowing better than to question the captain, the man nodded and turned back to the crew to carry out his duty. He still felt like Federico was making a mistake, but what could he do. It was not seemly for a soldier to question his commander.

Federico, now free of distraction, shook his head as he watched the small boat disappear, "What is it about you that has Rome in such a stir? What are you, winged creature…?"

On Giovanni's fishing boat, Adalyn had come back up on deck when she heard the three men arguing with anger in their voices. Giovanni sounded furious, "What is going on here? I refuse to believe that it is sheer coincidence that a fully armed warship under the flag of the Papal army would just suddenly appear out of nowhere!"

Nicolas nodded, "I know, I just don't see how they could have caught up with us so quickly, or even know where we were heading. The Church must be so desperate to find us that they're sending ships out searching random harbors."

Cyrillus was not convinced that this was a possibility, "No large ship of war just randomly shows up anywhere. The resources just to put a ship like that to sea would be considerable. It would be to the point of bankrupting a lesser noble's house. Adalyn must really be important to the Church if they are willing to send a ship like that after her."

"No," Nicolas said in a convinced tone, "I suppose you're right… It is not possible, they knew we were here, which means they've either been watching us, or someone has been tipping them off."

Giovanni shook his head, "They've been watching us, for what purpose? If they knew where we were, then why not just kill us? Something else is going on here."

"It's Michael." Adalyn said as she appeared behind them. "There is no other explanation. He's spreading word about our voyage."

Cyrillus looked over at her, "I don't understand. If he's so all-knowing, what's preventing him from coming here and killing us outright?"

"That's not how it works." She said softly. "He's already tried that and failed. No doubt he's learned that if he tries to physically intervene, he'll be found out and subject to attack by those still loyal to the Most High. He can watch us, but he cannot directly interfere in the way of the world. To do so would bring his actions into the light. It would be far too evident that his actions were a clear violation of the Most High's decree. The remnants of the Seven Archangels would hunt him to the ends of existence. His only option at this point would be to rely on his allies in the mortal world."

"So how do we stay ahead of him?" Nicolas said, as he became frustrated. "We keep moving from place to place, but they always seem to be nipping at our heels. There must be somewhere we can disappear from his sight."

"The Nether World." Adalyn said hesitantly. "The Most High has no presence there. Lucifer has made perfectly sure of that. Thus Michael won't be able to find us there either. His range is just as limited."

She sucked down a deep breath as she continued, "We won't be able to stay down there forever, but it will be enough time for us to arm ourselves to fight him."

Giovanni looked out to the horizon as he spoke, "It may even give us the element of surprise we so desperately need."

Adalyn nodded, "True, if we survive the trip, that is."

Her words sent a chill down Nicolas' spine, "You mean when we sail into Charybdis?"

Adalyn turned away and leaned on the starboard railing, "The trip will not be an easy one. The whirlpool is extremely powerful. Ships have been dragged into it unwittingly and unable to escape. We must be very careful."

Cyrillus shook his head, "I still have a hard time believing that such a thing is able to exist."

"Really?" Adalyn said, slightly amused. "You've seen winged creatures, beams of light, and swords of fire, but a giant whirlpool is too much for you to believe?"

Cyrillus smiled after being caught off guard, "Well... okay, I concede, well played. So once we get to Charybdis, what is our plan?"

"I don't know that a plan would help us." Adalyn replied. "I know what perils we will face there, but each person must face different illusions and torments. All we can do is play this by ear and improvise as we go. As long as you stay with me, I can guarantee your survival, but I cannot guarantee we'll be able to return. Even the strongest and the wisest who have braved to sail the waters of the underworld have never been heard from again."

"Then what chance do we have?" Giovanni asked with a hint of worry on his voice.

"You have me." Adalyn said in a reassuring tone. "I have travelled the underworld before, back when Lucifer was forced out of the Celestial realm. I know what to expect and will keep you safe as best I can."

"You know I trust you, Adalyn." Giovanni replied with confidence. "If you say we can do this, I believe you."

**

Divinity

That night, Giovanni sat at the tiller once again while his comrades slept. He was cold and tried to wrap himself in a blanket he'd brought up from the hold, but it wasn't doing him much good. He was still shivering and the blanket didn't do much to keep the breeze away.

Relief came when Adalyn came up on deck. She slowly sat down next to him, and spread her wings around them both, "How ever did you keep warm before I came around?"

He shrugged, "I usually anchored the ship and slept in the cabin."

Adalyn relaxed as the two of them warmed up together, "You know, I have thought a lot about the first day we met and our journey since then. I suffered horrific evils and depravity, but the truth is… I would suffer all the pain and shame again without a second thought if given the choice."

Giovanni looked at her oddly, "You would, why?"

"Because that road would lead me back to you." She replied, resting her head on his chest, "The things I have lived through, no other soul should ever have to endure."

Adalyn let out a quivering sigh as she continued, "I had given up all hope. I thought for sure that I was going to die, but when Brother Paul told me that you were still alive and coming for me… It raised my spirits and I found the will to keep going. I no longer wanted to just give up and fade away. As long as I got to see you again, I was willing to endure the pain."

She smiled as she looked at him, "Since then, I have seen the kindness that humanity is capable of. You showed me mercy, compassion… and love. It made me realize that being abandoned here is not the worst thing that could have happened, being forced to live without you is."

"I won't let that happen." Giovanni promised, "I am not going anywhere, and I don't die that easily."

"I sincerely hope not…" Adalyn said quietly, "but… once we reach the Netherworld, we will encounter things that will throw you off your guard. There are horrors there I can't even begin to describe. Giovanni, promise me that you will stand with me. If you get separated from me by so much as an inch, I can't protect you from what you may encounter."

He looked at her with a grin, "I thought I was the one protecting you."

"Not there." She replied seriously. "That cursed place is nothing but evil. I am the only one who knows what to expect. Please follow my directions exactly. No matter what I ask, no matter how much what I tell you may hurt, you must do as I command. Make me that promise."

Giovanni shrugged, "What could possibly be there that would cause you so much fear?"

Adalyn grabbed his shoulder, "Promise me Giovanni, as a former divine spirit, I should be protected from the forces of evil, but you will not be. Lucifer's minions have grown more powerful because of what is happening in the mortal realm."

Giovanni rolled his eyes, "Don't worry, I can handle myself."

Adalyn shook her head, "These creatures won't come at you with swords, spears, or gunpowder. They will attack you out of the darkness in ways that will torment your soul. Every pleasant memory, everything you love, everything you stand to lose, and everything you regret, will be pitted against you. The legions of Hell will use your own mind as a weapon. They will bend and twist your soul until you are so corrupted that there is nothing left of who you were. When that happens, even I won't be able to reach you. You will become one of his minions, forever enslaved to his will. So please, promise me that you will let me protect you when we get there."

Giovanni saw the urgency on her face and nodded, "Okay, I promise."

Adalyn breathed a sigh of relief. Though she trusted Giovanni at his word, she feared what they might encounter. In her heart, she worried that she would lose Giovanni there. At the very least, she knew that their attachment would be used against her.

IV

The small ship sailed for two more days into unknown waters. The four friends barely slept at all during that time as they were too anxious about what life ahead of them. What horrors would they soon face, and more importantly, would they all make it out alive?

Nicolas was at the tiller while Giovanni stood at the bow on lookout. Cyrillus's watch had just ended and he was below getting some rest. The ship had hit doldrums and had not moved in hours. What was more curious was that Adalyn sat in the middle of the ship, against the mast. She had refused to say a word since the wind died and would not even respond to anyone talking to her.

Giovanni was beginning to worry as her face was pale and lifeless. She was still breathing, but was as solid as a statue. The lack of movement seemed almost hypnotic as her face continuously stared out onto the open sea.

As the sun finally began to set, the sky turned red. Giovanni knew that this was it. He ran to the mast and tied the sail up. Adalyn didn't move or even react to his presence. Giovanni touched her face, hoping she would say something to him, but she still didn't move. He gave up, walked back to the bow, and continued looking.

Less than a second after Giovanni placed his hand on the railing, the four of them heard a distant crackle of thunder. The loud boom woke Cyrillus up. He had a bad feeling about what that meant and ran back out on deck, "Have we arrived?"

His question was answered by a flash of lightning that strangely seemed to come from the ocean floor. A second one appeared a few moments later, and a third. Muffled thunder quickly followed the three flashes as the men looked on.

Divinity

As the thunder dissipated, Adalyn raised her head and spoke in a disembodied voice, "It's beginning…"

The flashes of light from beneath the waves became more numerous and the water began to churn. To everyone's amazement, the sea floor began to cave in around the lights. Water started to twist and spin very quickly downward into the hole.

Adalyn stood up and turned to her friends, "Sail for it. Try to go with the current, sailing straight into it will guarantee that we won't have a boat to come back on."

Nicolas held the tiller stead and sailed closer to the vortex as he was told. The ship picked up speed as the current sucked them towards the vortex. Finally, they entered the massive whirlpool and started slowly heading in a downward circle.

Giovanni felt the current and turned to Nicolas, "Hard to port, we need to stay with it!"

Nicolas nodded and pulled the tiller back much as he could. The boat turned a little more and stayed with the pull of the massive maelstrom. They had been overtaken by the current and there was no turning back.

As the ship neared the abyss, two more ships emerged from the waters. They were both wrecked hulks with torn rags on their masts and cracked planking. Clearly these ships could not remain afloat on their own.

Giovanni could not believe his eyes, "Incredible… Adalyn, is this whirlpool so powerful that it can rip ships from the bottom of the ocean?"

Adalyn shook her head, "No, such boats would be torn apart. What are you seeing?"

Giovanni breathed heavily, "Two ships on opposite sides of the vortex. They seem to be adrift with the current."

Adalyn had a worried expression on her face, "The poor souls on those ships were dragged into the abyss and could not get out. Those who were judged as living a full

Divinity

and holy life, were taken by the Most High, those that were not..."

Giovanni watched as one of the ships passed by. On the deck were green and white apparitions. They appeared to be human, but they were heavily deformed. Their flesh was almost gone, revealing skeletons underneath. As the wrecked hull got closer, the entire crew abandoned their posts and ran to the side. They cried out for help, begging for mercy.

With no one manning the ship's helm, they lost control of the wrecked hulk. The ship jerked about violently before capsizing into the vortex. It immediately disappeared beneath the surface.

Giovanni wiped a tear from his eye, "Can't we do anything to help them?"

Adalyn shook her head, "No, they must reap what they have sewn."

Giovanni looked away, "Pray Lord is with us today."

"He always is." She responded adamantly before turning to the back of the ship.

Nicolas was holding on to the tiller for dear life. His heavy breathing let Adalyn know that he was scared. She called to him, "Steer us in a little more, keep with the current, it will take longer, but we'll get there intact."

Nicolas began to trembled and breathe more rapidly. She heard it and spoke in a comforting tone, "Do not be afraid Nicolas, do as I tell you and we will survive, I promise."

He nodded, and turned the ship to follow the current down into the abyss, "As you say, milady."

The ship began to tilt inward toward the heart of Charybdis. It was spinning so fast now that the group could barely see the world around them. Soon everything was a blur that was slowly fading to black.

Divinity

Adalyn grabbed the side railing, "Everyone, for the love of all, hold on!"

The crew grabbed on to whatever they could to prevent falling as the ship began to spin faster and faster, completely out of control. The tiller was swinging back and forth as Nicolas had given it up for something more stable.

Cyrillus grabbed the rail, but the section he got his arm around was fairly rotted and began to give out under him. Adalyn could hear it breaking as Cyrillus struggled to grab anything else nearby, "Cyrillus, look out! Move to another spot, quickly!"

As the railing gave out, Giovanni stretched out as far as he could and grabbed Cyrillus's shirt. Nicolas and Adalyn grabbed Giovanni to prevent him from going over as well. Adalyn screamed as she held the rail and Giovanni, "For the love of God, please pull him back, he mustn't fall in!"

Giovanni and Nicolas pulled with everything they had. Giovanni turned to his friend and nodded, "Come on Nicolas, heave!"

Giovanni noticed his hands were beginning to turn red and blood trickled out, still he kept pulling despite the pain, "Hold on, my friend. We've got you."

When Cyrillus was close enough, Giovanni tugged hard, bringing him back on the deck. Cyrillus grabbed his arm and steadied himself. Once back on the ship, he held on to a sturdier railing as much as he could. He was far too petrified to move.

Giovanni smiled at him, "Well that wasn't too bad was it?"

Cyrillus smirked a little, but otherwise did not respond. He chose instead to stare into the whirlpool as the ship continued to sink deeper into the vortex. The further they went, the more their world began to vanish from view.

Once they had reached the abyss, they were totally consumed by darkness.

For a few moments, Giovanni could not hear or see anything. He called out, but his voice echoed back and there was no response. He feared that he would be in this limbo forever. His thoughts focused on Adalyn and seeing her face in his mind quieted his fears.

BOOK II
Into the Breach

I

A loud splash of water broke through the silent void and Giovanni's vision slowly returned. Everyone came back into view. The ship was doused in water and equipment was strewn about the deck, but everything seemed to be in one piece.

Nicolas looked around, "Are we dead?"

"No," Adalyn said, trying to dry off her wings, "We are alive, but I suggest we get moving if we want to stay that way."

Giovanni looked around, attempting to assess their situation. The ship had touched down in very thick fog that made it impossible to see past the deck. It appeared that they were in the middle of a swampy dead wood.

The entire area smelled of mildew and was very damp. Around them, the landscape was littered with broken trees that were partially submerged in pitch black water. Everything looked as though it had been badly burned.

Giovanni wondered just how deep the water was, but quickly forgot about it when he noticed something that was out of place; the ship was moving. *What the...*

The young fisherman ran to the front of the boat to see if he could tell what was pushing the boat forward, but nothing up front was out of the ordinary. He called to Nicolas, who was standing at the tiller, "Nicolas, do you see anything strange back there?"

Nicolas quickly looked around and shrugged, "No, nothing. Why?"

Adalyn could hear Giovanni running around the ship, "What is it?"

He turned to her, "We're moving... but the sail isn't down."

"Yes..." She said softly, placing her right hand on her forehead. "Wind isn't what's propelling us forward."

Nicolas looked around, "Then what magic is this?"

Divinity

Adalyn shook her head, "Not magic… wait until we clear the trees. Then, if you dare, look into the water."

The ship moved forward slowly through the woods. As the trees began to clear, a low moaning noise could be heard from beneath them. Adalyn walked to the back of the boat and sat right in front of the cabin door. She covered herself with her wings and squeezed her legs in tight, trying to block out what was going on around her. Giovanni noticed the pained expression on her face, "Are you alright, what's wrong?"

Tears began to fall down her cheeks, "I can hear their sorrow. The cries of pain in their voices, it is so terrible."

Nicolas turned to her, "What voices?"

When he got no response, he turned and looked at Giovanni, "What is she talking about?"

Giovanni shrugged, "I have no idea."

Suddenly, Cyrillus's voice cried out, "Look, the water!"

Nicolas and Giovanni ran to the side, leaned on the railing, and looked overboard. At first there was nothing to see. It was the same blackness as before, but then in the dark, murky water, they saw a spectral green light go by. Then another and another until it the blackness was completely consumed by these lights. It appeared whatever these were, they were pushing the boat forward as they swam through the water. Giovanni squinted to get a better look at them. One began to take the form of a person. He could see the decrepit face in the water with a look of terror and sorrow.

Giovanni fell backwards, "What…"

Adalyn parted her wings slightly, "These souls did not lead full lives. They technically committed no sin, but did nothing positive either. They saw pain, and they ignored it, heard cries for help, and turned a deaf ear. They were completely indifferent towards their fellow man. To the

Most High, those that are aware of the pain and suffering around them, but do nothing, are just as guilty as those who caused it in the first place… but not even he had the heart to send them to the Netherworld."

Giovanni performed the sign of the cross and said a brief prayer for them, "God have mercy…"

Adalyn shook her head, "He won't hear it that is forsaken in this land."

The boat continued to move through the eerie glow. Adalyn looked like she was suffering as the spirits passed by. Suddenly, her head perked up, "No…"

She quickly got to her feet and ran to the side of the ship, "No!"

Giovanni grabbed her to prevent her from falling over the side as she reached out her arms. He looked at her oddly, "What is it? What's going on?"

Nicolas pointed at one spirit, "Look!"

The four of them watched as one bright spirit drew near. Giovanni's mouth dropped open, "Azrael…"

Adalyn shook her head, "I had hoped that it was a myth. I did not think that this would be where the Most High would send his servants when they died. Lord, this is too cruel."

She sobbed into Giovanni's arms as Cyrillus watched Azrael's spirit keep pace with the boat. He felt horribly about what he saw, "Is there anything that can be done to help him?"

Adalyn shook her head, "We cannot save those condemned to the well."

Giovanni did the best he could to comfort her as the boat kept moving. She continued to cry, but had finally calmed down, "He was my friend. He looked out for me. It's just not fair."

**

After an hour or so, a small wooden platform appeared out of the fog. Their ship moved alongside it and stopped. It was an ancient pier that looked extremely rickety. The group put the ramp down, but hesitated when it came to stepping off the boat.

Adalyn stepped down first and beckoned to them, "Do not fear, it will hold us."

Cyrillus shook his head, "I'm not so sure, it looks pretty unstable."

She turned to him with an earnest look on her face, "You have to trust me, come on."

The four of them walked cautiously down the gangway. The old pier creaked and moaned as they moved. Nicolas looked over at Cyrillus as the fog completely consumed the group, "My friend, we are pilgrims in a very unholy place."

Adalyn shook her head, "No, not yet."

Below them, the water rippled as more moaning sounds like the ones they had heard on their ship broke the surface. It sent chills down the spines of everyone in the group. The eerie feeling wasn't getting any better as they continued onward.

Cyrillus leaned over the side to look at what was making all that noise, "What in the world…"

Adalyn heard the dock where he was standing creek. "No!"

She spoke too late. One of the green spirits took form and jumped out of the water with an evil grin on its decrepit face. Its eyes glowed as it looked over its intended victim.

Cyrillus fell over and began screaming when he saw the creature coming at him. It reached out its boney fingers to grab him when Adalyn stepped in front of it, "Stop!"

The smile left its hideous face upon realizing that it was dealing with an angel. Adalyn furrowed her brow and clenched her teeth. It was difficult to appear angry with the

blindfold, but she did the best she could, "Back to the well with you, wraith, you will not claim a prize this day!"

The creature slowly retreated back into the water as it was told. Adalyn grabbed Cyrillus and helped him up, "Do not look into the abyss! It is not safe here."

As they moved, in the distance a very tiny strip of land appeared with a second pier leading out into the water. Adalyn stopped once they reached the land, "Everyone, make sure you have at least single zecchino with you."

Nicolas' eyes narrowed as he found the coin in his pocket, "Why?"

"For the boatman, he won't take you without pay." Adalyn said softly as though trying not to be heard, "Just be ready to hand it to him, let me do the talking."

They each stepped on to the second pier and walked to the end where a small docking station stood with horn attached to it. The horn was massive and looked almost like a military trumpet that had been coiled into a circle.

Adalyn stopped as she felt the wood under her feet, "Do you see the horn?"

Giovanni nodded, "Yeah, it's very old and looks like it came from the head of a massive ram."

She nodded, "I won't tell you what type of beast it came from. Pick it up and summon the boatman."

Giovanni did as he was told. He picked up the horn and inspected it. It was covered in dust and extremely heavy. He had to balance himself as he picked it up to prevent falling backwards. Without another thought, he blew into the small end.

The horn made a loud noise that echoed off into the distance. It was a very deep and hollow sound that resembled the sorrowful sound of a dying bull. The four stood by looking out on the water for any sign of movement.

Suddenly the fog began to clear and the creaking sound of old wood could be heard in the distance. Nicolas turned and grabbed Giovanni, "Look, out there, the boatman!"

A black boat slowly appeared out of the fog. Giovanni recognized it as being an older version of the gondolas that would taxi people through Venice, except that it was slightly larger. The boat creaked toward them. On the pilot's stand at the back of the boat, was a cloaked figure clad in all black. His face could not be seen under the robe as it was too dark. The four stood at the shore watching this odd vessel approach.

Once the boat arrived, the hooded man turned to the party, "Adalyn…"

His voice was little more than a whisper on the wind. Adalyn smiled, "Hello Charon, it's been a long time."

He nodded, "What happened to you? I had heard stories, but I did not believe them. I was told you were a traitor and that I should expect to see you soon. I cannot express my sorrow to see you this way."

Adalyn shook her head. "Don't grieve for me, old friend, I am not dead."

She turned to Giovanni, "And honestly some things have turned out for the better."

"Then why have you come?" He asked softly. "Do you desire entry into the Netherworld so eagerly?"

"What I said before the Choirs was not wrong." Adalyn replied. "We have a traitor in our midst and he needs to be flushed out, before it's too late."

Charon did not move, "You seek the Eden serpent…"

"Yes." Adalyn admitted. "There is no other way. I have been stripped of all my power. I cannot do anything more than act as a guide."

Charon nodded, "As you wish, however you know that I cannot take you across without payment. I make no exceptions."

With that, he extended his hand. To Giovanni's shock, there was no skin, no muscle, or tissue of any kind. Only dirty white bone appeared from under the black cloak. Charon was little more than a skeleton.

One by one, they each placed one zecchino into his hand as they climbed onboard the decaying gondola. Once everyone on board, Charon pushed with his oar and moved the boat away from the shore.

The boat was too small for anyone to sit down and the boat looked as though it were decaying slowly. Water was leaking through in some areas and a single lamp on the bow lit the way. The dark orange light let off an eerie glow, causing Giovanni to question whether or not it was actually a flame."

Giovanni had his arms around Adalyn to keep her from getting cold. The fog was gone, but when they breathed, they could still see it. Adalyn could sense the tension in his body as she leaned back, and rubbed his arm to try to calm him, "We'll be okay, I promise."

Finally, the boat reached a small beach on the other side of the river. On the land there was another wall of heavy fog which they could not see through. There was no way to tell what was ahead of them.

As they each stepped off the boat, Cyrillus and Nicolas drew their swords. Adalyn heard the metal being unsheathed and placed a hand on each of their shoulders, "No, don't show any aggression. It won't help you here anyway."

They both obediently put the swords away and walked a little further down a foot path. Adalyn stayed close behind Nicolas as they walked. Giovanni was about to follow when Charon stopped him, "You take care of her. Keep her safe."

Giovanni turned to him and nodded, "With my life."

He jumped off the boat as it pulled away and caught up with the group. He grabbed Adalyn's hand and walked

next to her as she kept the other hand out in from of her. As they walked, Giovanni turned and spoke, "Charon seems to be very concerned with you safety, did you know him well?"

Adalyn nodded, "Years ago, I was the guiding light for souls that had been lost at sea. It was my job to guide the wicked ones to the Netherworld. At times, I had to convince them to go using less than orthodox measures. I regretted forcing it on them every time. Charon helped me be strong through it until the choirs decided that my accomplishments during the war merited a better job. He is a good friend."

Nicolas looked at her oddly, "Wait… you were the reaper?"

Adalyn sighed, "There is no grim reaper. At least not in the way you perceive one. Several angels have been tasked with ferrying lost souls to different places. There are angels who guide souls to Heaven, Hell, and the Well of Souls. The closest we had to a grim reaper, was the angel of death. That was Azrael."

Nicolas nodded, "I see…"

The group moved along to a large, heavy, door. Adalyn placed her hands on it, feeling the cold stone. She shook her head as she turned to her friends, "This isn't going to be easy. It's going to take all of us to get it open."

Giovanni, Nicolas, and Cyrillus pushed against the doors as hard as they could. At first, the door didn't move. There was a low groaning sound and debris fell from the top of the door. They continued to put their backs into pushing until the door finally creaked open.

As the door moved out of the way, the group was greeted by a rush of intense heat. The air was so hot that they needed to cover their faces to prevent burning. The heat was accompanied by the smell of putrid, rotting, flesh and was so powerful that even Adalyn had a hard time holding her stomach. Sounds of sorrow and pain could be heard in

Divinity

the distance as they reached a deep canyon with an old rope bridge over it.

II

Adalyn put her hand on the side railing, "This is the final bridge to the gates. From here, let go of what you know, what you love, and what you hold closest to you. It will all be turned against you here."

They proceeded slowly across the bridge. Beneath them, was a river of lava flowing quickly downstream. Burning rocks from above plummeted into the stream from either side of the bridge. They moved quickly out of fear of getting hit.

Once they were back on solid ground, Giovanni heard a voice call to him. When he turned, to his amazement, he saw his father sitting on a small stone bench, "Papa, what are you doing here?"

His father smiled warmly, "Giovanni come, sit with me. I have not been able to see you since my death. Now that you have come, we can spend some time together."

Giovanni rubbed his eyes, "No… Papa, what are you doing here? You led a good life… what could you possibly have done to justify being sent here?"

Giovanni's eyes took on a red hue. Adalyn could feel him tugging away, "Giovanni, no, stop, it is not real. Your father is not here, I promise you."

Giovanni's father's face began to wither, "Come Giovanni, I do not have much time… come to me before it is too late."

Giovanni struggled against Adalyn, desperately fighting to get free, "Let go damn you! I just want a moment with him, just one moment!"

She shook her head, "Please listen to me, it's not him! Your mind is deceiving you! If you go to him, you will be giving in to the whims of evil. Please hear me!"

Finally, the ghost of his father corroded away and disappeared, "Giovanni… you are too late."

Divinity

Giovanni screamed out, "No!"

Enraged, he turned around to face Adalyn, jerking his arm free, "He was my father! He was wrongfully taken from me and I was not going to get another chance! All I wanted a single moment with him. Your loving God took him from me… Was that too much to ask? You…"

Adalyn lowered her head, "Giovanni I… I'm sorry…"

Without thinking, he brought his hand up with the intention of striking her. Cyrillus saw it and called out, "Giovanni, stay your anger! Think about what you're about to do!"

Giovanni froze in place. His hand was shaking and covered in sweat. He saw the frightened look on Adalyn's face. She cringed as though she were waiting for him to strike, but did not move to defend herself.

Giovanni's mouth dropped open. Breathing heavily, he lowered his hand, as his head began to pound, "What is wrong with me? Adalyn… I am so sorry."

Cyrillus kept very close to Giovanni just in case he lost it again. Adalyn waved in the direction she had heard Cyrillus's voice, "It's okay, Cyrillus don't worry. Even in his mental state, he wouldn't strike me."

"How can you be sure?" Cyrillus asked, clearly not convinced.

"Because I know his heart." She replied. "He would sooner cut off his own arm."

Cyrillus nodded and slowly backed away. Though Giovanni had regained control of his senses, he was still shaking. His heart squeezed tight as he fell to his knees, "I swore to protect you from harm, what have I done…"

She knelt next to him and shook her head, "Nothing, you didn't strike me, just as I knew you wouldn't. The rage you felt is not your fault. That is what this cursed place does to the human mind. It bends and twists you to its will until there is nothing left of the person you once were. When that happens, you become one of his minions. That is why you must be on your guard."

She tried to move Giovanni, but he would not budge, "Please, it is not your fault. I do not blame you. This just happened, put it out of your mind and it will never be brought up again, I promise."

After a few moments, Giovanni nodded, shook it off, and slowly got to his feet. He looked her in the face even though he knew she couldn't see him, "I'm sorry…"

Adalyn touched his cheek and smiled, "For what, nothing happened."

Adalyn extended her arm, opened her hand to Giovanni, and nodded. He forced a partial smile and grasped her hand tightly as though he were afraid she would disappear if he let go. Her fingers closed around his and locked them together.

The group proceeded deeper into the Netherworld. The fog began to clear revealing the chaos in front of them. There was a massive black castle in the distance that looked as though it had been carved from a violent volcano. In front of that, lay a city in ruins which surrounded a massive lake of fire.

The buildings looked to have been carved from marble; however instead of white and majestic, they were covered in soot and smashed to the ground. Fire spewed from the ruins and out of the ground all around them. What few buildings still stood, were also as dark as coal. Rivers of lava, streaming from the dark castle flowed slowly between the buildings in a straight path.

Cyrillus took a step backwards, "I recognize this place! What happened here?"

Adalyn could feel the heat and knew what he saw, "This is Rome."

They all turned and looked at her. Nicolas surveyed the area, "Rome, but how, Rome is not like this!"

"No, not anymore… at least not in a corporeal sense." Adalyn admitted. "You must understand that this place is, by its very nature, evil. The souls of the wicked, demons, and Lucifer himself have corrupted this place. It takes the form of the most evil aspirations of man. Here you see Rome as it was during the great fire. I can't even begin to measure the screams that were heard in the city that night, or the ones that followed when Rome tried to find a scapegoat. The ears of the angels that were present for it are still suffering."

They pushed forward through the smog and heat, the entire time with a sinking feeling flowing through them. In the distance, they could hear screams of horror and pain getting louder. The despair in their voices was incredibly painful.

As they neared the buildings, they noticed that bodies were strewn about everywhere. Some were lying on the ground, ripped apart, while others were hanging by hooks and nails on the sides of the buildings. The worst of the bunch were being burned in bonfires created by forces unknown.

Giovanni looked at the first husk they passed by. He wasn't certain, but he thought he'd seen it move. Unable to shake the feeling, he nudged it gently. The husk screamed out as though it had just been stabbed.

Startled, Giovanni took a step backward, "My God… this one is still alive, how is that possible?"

The body was horribly mutilated, no eyes, ears, or tongue. Maggots could be seen crawling through this husk's wounds. The being made a low, inhuman, moaning sound as they watched it.

Nicolas stared in disbelief, "So cruel."

Adalyn nodded, "Yes, very cruel, but no more so than this man was in life. He tortured people for his own pleasure and left their bodies like this. He was truly a depraved lunatic. So he must endure the same way as he left his victims."

She bit her lip, "I brought him here myself. I can still hear his voice echoing in my mind. I never forgot his plea for mercy. He wanted to repent... too late."

Giovanni put his hand on her shoulder, "It must have been hard."

"It was impossible." She said turning to him, "We are taught to love all life and yet I was tasked with this terrible job. I can still remember him. I remember them all, begging for mercy, asking me to just take them back... as if I had the power to."

She faced him, "I have never told anyone this Giovanni, but I realized that if I had that power to do so... I would have. The moment I realized that, I knew I couldn't do this job anymore. That was around the time I was mercifully called to join the Choirs."

Cyrillus took one more look at the husk, "I doubt anyone could blame you for that."

Nicolas refused to take his eyes off of the husks as the group continued down the path of volcanic ash. One of the husks hanging from a smashed wall saw them and cried out, "Living souls, leave this place or suffer our fate!"

After losing his family, Nicolas no longer feared death. No soldier or knight gave him any pause, but this place was different. He feared that if he died in this place, his soul would be trapped. In his heart, he wanted to heed that abomination's warning, but he had sworn an oath to his friends and would not abandon them. Everything depended on reaching the Eden Serpent and getting the venom they came for.

Giovanni passed another husk being hung by its arms over a pit of intense flame. It was unable to move away from the flame, but it could extend his arms slightly. As it saw Giovanni, it reached out and called to him, "Please sir, water… I am parched of thirst. Please, just a few drops of water, that's all I want. Won't you spare some?"

Nicolas looked at the husk in disgust, but Giovanni felt pity for the poor soul. He took a small pouch from his belt and was about to hand it to the burning man when Adalyn turned to face him.

The moment Adalyn heard the cantina, she quickly slapped his hand away, "No, no water for him!"

The burning man turned his attention to her, "You… I know you… Are you still that cruel, angel?"

"Still?" Adalyn asked suspiciously.

"Yes, I remember you." He said in a raspy voice. "You are the one who brought me here. I did everything I could to prevent it. When you realized that I was not fooled by your charm, you transformed into a monstrous beast and violently forced me down here."

He scoffed at her as he looked her over. She had been injured, blinded, and though she tried to hide it, was clearly frightened, "I see you now know what torture is like, yet you are still as cruel as ever. No mercy in you at all."

Giovanni was about to speak in her defense, but Adalyn cut him off, "I remember you too. In your life, were you any better? You burned people alive when it was in your power to spare them. If they begged you for mercy, you degraded them even more. You stripped your victims naked for all to see, cut them, stabbed them, and subjected them to far worse pains while they were burned alive. You did all that because some tyrant decided that certain groups of people were guilty of false charges and treason."

She spit in to the flame, "I know what that's like now and that is why I have no remorse over what I did to you! You enjoyed what you did. I just made sure you paid for it. How dare you now try to judge me? You earned your fate; there is no mercy for you."

Divinity

She turned back to the group and sneered, "We're done here, let's keep moving!"

As she began to walk away angrily, the burning husk turned back to Giovanni, "Be weary of that creature. She is not what she seems. Consider that before following her much further."

"Silence filth!" Giovanni shot back, "Whatever Adalyn did to get you here, no doubt you deserved much worse! I was willing to take pity on you, but I won't stand by and listen to you insult her. Stay here and burn for all I care."

The husk then turned back and lowered his head, no longer responding to anything. Giovanni shook his head and ran to catch up with Adalyn. She was clearly flustered as she walked. A single tear fell out from under her bandages.

Giovanni grabbed her hand and walked next to her, "Are you okay? You were a bit curt with him."

She nodded and quickly wiped the tear away, "Forgive me, Giovanni. That man was an executioner who was responsible for painfully ending the lives of many people. It was in his power to show them mercy, but he chose not to. Most of them weren't even guilty of the crimes they were executed for. Amongst those he burned, was one Jeanne D'Arc, or more famously known as St. Joan. Her death alone sealed his fate."

She lowered her head as she continued, "I lied when I said that I had no remorse over how I treated him. My time in that dungeon made me face what I had done to these souls. I thought I wouldn't feel any different if I had to face him again, but I did. I hate it."

Giovanni shrugged, "It's not the worst thing in the world to feel sympathy for someone who suffers, even if they themselves caused some."

Adalyn sighed, "I guess…"

Nicolas ran to catch up to Cyrillus and lowly whispered to him, "What do you think that thing meant when it said she turned into some kind of beast… is it possible that she's some kind of demon after all?"

Giovanni heard Nicolas and turned back, "How can you even ask such a question after all you've seen?"

Adalyn could sense the tension behind her so she stopped and turned to the two revolutionaries, "If you have something on your mind, then get it out in the open now. We can't be going forward with our minds in doubt. Not if we hope to survive."

Nicolas let out a long sigh, "Okay, what did he mean when he said that you transformed in to some kind of beast?"

She lowered her eyes, "As I said, sometimes my ways were unorthodox, but they got the job done. Metamorphosis is an ability some angels have. Given the job I was originally tasked with, there weren't many evil spirits that would follow the instruction of something that looked like me. I am not proud of what I did, but it was my job."

Cyrillus nodded nervously, "But how do I know this is the real you?"

Adalyn looked annoyed, "Don't be ridiculous, come on, let's go. The less time we spend here, the better."

An annoyed Adalyn turned without another word and moved forward with the rest of the group in close pursuit. As they cleared the city, the heat intensified. The four of them found themselves standing in front of the massive lake of fire.

Giovanni knelt down and looked in. To his shock, he could see hundreds of thousands of people within the flames. They squirmed about like a group of worms, trying to relieve their endless suffering. They were all naked and their skin appeared to sear and blister as they moved in the relentless flame. Some even began to tear the flesh from others nearby.

Giovanni could not stand to look at it anymore. He got up and stepped away from the flames, "What is this?"

Adalyn stepped forward and felt the intense heat on her skin, "It's simply called the pit. Only the most extreme of sinners have specific tortures, the rest are thrown into that massive fire pit, forever burning. Their fate is merciful by comparison."

She pointed out to the middle of the lake, "Look."

The three of them moved slightly closer and realized that there was a black tree standing in the center of the flame. A man hung from one of the branches. He was held in place by a rope that was tied around his neck. The burnt husk was trying to breath, but his broken neck made him gurgle. His feet were singed from the flames of the pit and he was so parched that his lips had been burned completely off.

"Who is that?" Cyrillus asked.

"The betrayer…" Adalyn said in a low voice, "Judas Iscariot. He turned on the people who cared the most for him. He was nothing more than a deceiver who committed the worst possible sin imaginable… decide. After that, he hung himself, which was yet another mortal sin to his name. His lifetime of greed finally caught up with him. His fate is to forever hang the way he did so long ago. He deserved far worse."

They moved around the edge of the pit until they came to a river of lava which ran above a large cavern. Adalyn shook her head, "I was afraid of this."

"Of what?" Giovanni asked.

She pointed to the cavern, "The only way across the lava is to go under it."

Nicolas shrugged, "It doesn't look so bad. It's only about forty feet to the other side."

"Don't be fooled." Adalyn said back to him. "Keep your wits about you and remember what I told you before: Let go of everything you fear to lose."

III

Giovanni and Adalyn entered the cave first, followed by the others. The entrance was pitch black to the point where Giovanni could not see anything. He even tried putting his hands up to his face, but was unable to see them.

After a few moments, Giovanni no longer heard the footsteps of his companions, "Adalyn, where did you go?"

There was no response. Giovanni started to get worried, "Adalyn, Nicolas, Cyrillus, where are you guys? Can anyone here me?"

Still not receiving a response, Giovanni ran straight ahead. He couldn't help but feel like something was out of place. *Why is it taking so long for me to get to the other side? The tunnel only looked like it was about forty feet long on the way in.* He began to wonder if he would ever get out.

After running for about ten minutes, Giovanni reached a large heavy door. This made no sense as it wasn't there when he looked in from the outside. Had he gotten sidetracked somehow?

Too worried to consider it, he pushed the door open and entered a larger room with torches lit on every wall. Much to his relief, he saw Adalyn standing in the middle of the room with her back to him. He quickly called to her, "Thank God, Adalyn, are you okay?"

Adalyn turned to Giovanni and smiled. He stopped right in his tracks when he saw that she was no longer wearing the blind fold. Her eyes were still black and red, but it looked like she was able to see him, "Giovanni, you made it this far, well done."

Something wasn't right. Giovanni could feel the hairs on the back of his neck stand straight up as he walked toward her. Something about the look on her face was malicious. He continued to step cautiously forward, "Adalyn, what is this place?"

Divinity

Before she could say anything else, Nicolas walked in with his sword drawn, "Giovanni, watch out, I have discovered a terrible truth."

He turned to his young friend, "What is it?"

Cyrillus entered from the other direction, also with his sword drawn, "Adalyn is liar. Michael isn't the betrayer, she is! She's twisted our minds to believe her story, but it is not the truth."

Giovanni's jaw dropped, "That's impossible, we saw Michael kill Azrael. We heard him openly admit to the crime!"

Nicolas shook his head, "It was all her doing, she made us see what she wanted us to so that we would save her from being cleansed."

Giovanni turned and looked at Adalyn, "I can't believe that. It's not possible."

She smiled and looked over at Nicolas, "You heard him, now let's get going. We have a job to do."

Nicolas pointed his blade at her, "Not this time, demon. Giovanni may be blinded by love, but we are not."

Adalyn sighed, "Well then you die!"

She pointed her arms at the two revolutionaries and emitted the same white beams Michael had fought Azrael with. Cyrillus and Nicolas were tossed against the wall, screaming in pain. Nicolas called to Giovanni, "My friend, help us, before it is too late."

Giovanni looked at him, and then back at Adalyn. He didn't know what to think, or what to do. His head began to hurt as Cyrillus cried out, "Giovanni, please!"

Adalyn turned and looked at Giovanni, "You have a choice to make, Giovanni. Whom do you believe?"

She smiled as the sash to her dress came undone and her body slowly began to reveal itself, "Don't you still want me?" She said seductively.

Giovanni shook his head as he closed her eyes, "Forgive me…"

He unsheathed his sword and ran at Adalyn. Before her dress could part any further, he ran her through with the blade. His teeth were clenched as he forced the blade deeper, "I'm sorry…"

Adalyn gasped for air as blood filled her mouth. Cyrillus and Nicolas fell to the floor and began laughing. Giovanni turned to them, "What?"

They both morphed into imp like creatures and flew into the darkness cackling loudly. Adalyn looked up at him. "Giovanni, you chose wrong."

She breathed in one last time and fell limp. Giovanni began to shake uncontrollably, "No… no, God please no!"

Giovanni cradled her lifeless body in his arms for a moment before it dissolved into ash. He felt his blood began to boil. His eyes turned red as he was filled with rage. He picked up his sword and headed for the door. His eyes flicked red, "Lucifer… you will pay for this!"

As Giovanni moved, another apparition appeared in front of him. This one took the form of Padre Antonelli. Giovanni stood in shock as he stared at his old friend, "Padre… no… what are you doing here?"

Padre Antonelli's features looked tortured and scarred, "I spent my life attempting to do good, but by spreading the lies of the Church, I was actually doing evil. My sin was perverting the minds of so many people, many of whom went off to fight against the revolutionaries. People have died and it is my fault. That is why I am now doomed to suffer."

Giovanni shook his head, "I can't believe that. You were a good man who always cared for the people you preached to. You were not evil!"

Then he realized what was going on, "Oh I get it, you're not really here. You're just an apparition sent to further torment me… as if that were possible."

Padre Antonelli shook his head, "No my son, I'm here, and I can prove it."

He reached out and touched his hand to Giovanni's shoulder, "One of those apparitions would need you to come to it in order for the trap to work and its touch would be lethal. It needs your consent."

Giovanni wasn't convinced, "Who's to say that you're not some demon, or possibly Lucifer himself?"

"My boy… you've changed." Antonelli replied. "The Giovanni I used to know was never this untrusting."

"The Giovanni you knew hadn't seen as much of the world as I have." Giovanni spat back. "Things have changed and probably not for the better."

A remorseful frown came over Antonelli's face, "That is something I share in the blame for. My boy, there is no way I can convince you beyond a doubt that I am who I claim to be… but if you look at this from a logical standpoint, do you really have much choice other than to trust me?"

He pointed a decrepit finger to the cavern, "You can try to find your way out on your own and spend an eternity trying to do so, or you can trust me and either find a way out, or die in the process. The choice is yours."

Giovanni sighed and lowered his eyes, "You make a good point… and you are sounding more and more like the man I knew. Forgive me, Padre…"

Antonelli nodded, "It's not your fault my son. This is my fate, nothing you did could have changed this."

He looked behind Giovanni to see the pile of ash, "I see that you failed in your mission to protect Adalyn. Truly a tragedy, one that Lucifer should pay for."

Giovanni clenched, "I want to kill him, he needs to be stopped."

"Yes…" Padre Antonelli said softly. "That would be the best course now. Without Adalyn to stop Michael, defeating his main ally would halt his plans. I will help you."

Giovanni hesitated in accepting Antonelli's help, "But Padre, if you help me, won't that result in further torment for you?"

Antonelli cackled, "What more are they going to do to me? I have seen the worst of the worst. Nothing they could do to me now would ever compare to that."

"If you're sure," Giovanni said sorrowfully, "I need to find a way out of here."

Antonelli opened his arms, "Very well, follow me, we'll get you out of here."

Antonelli floated a foot above the ground and led Giovanni out the next doorway. He noticed that Antonelli was taking him on a path that was no longer going straight ahead, but did not care. He trusted Padre Antonelli and kept pace with him. The two proceeded down another hallway that seemed to stretch on forever. Giovanni recognized the walls as they resembled the sewers under Rome, "Padre, where are you taking me?"

"If you want to take on Lucifer, you're going to need to get in to his castle." Padre Antonelli replied. "This is a back way that Lucifer would not expect you to take. It will give you the element of surprise."

The spectral image of the priest led Giovanni to a door that resembled one he had seen in the prison. Antonelli pointed at it, "Open the door."

Giovanni grabbed the latch and pulled. The old wooden door slowly creaked as it released from its frame. Suddenly, Giovanni was thrown backwards as the door blew

open and flames illuminated the room. Hands reached out from the flame trying to grab at anything they could reach.

"You've led me to the pit!" Giovanni said accusingly. "What are you playing at?"

Padre Antonelli looked at him with very serious eyes, "You are still alive. The flames will not burn you. Going through the pit will put you in a position to enter Lucifer's castle from the opposite side. He won't be expecting it."

"And how will I know the way?" Giovanni asked in an accusing tone.

"I will go with you." He responded softly. "I have learned to tolerate the flames so that they do not hurt me as much."

Giovanni wasn't sure how much he trusted Antonelli now, but he reached out his hand to the flame and sure enough, it did not burn him. Hesitantly, he took another step forward. As he entered the doorway, he could feel his body begin to heat up.

Giovanni closed his eyes as he entered the flame. It was hot, but his skin did not burn. He opened his eyes to see the blaze of yellow and orange light in his eyes.

Padre Antonelli joined him. Though Antonelli seemed like he was in pain, he beckoned Giovanni forward, "Come, we must be quick about this. If we spend too much time here, we may never be able to get out."

As Giovanni followed the specter of his old friend through the chaos, other spirits appeared and tried to grab him. Some tried to attack him, while others tried to reach through him. One of them even reached for his eyes, revealing that it did not have any.

Giovanni covered his eyes as he moved deeper into the pit. One spirit with a grotesque face, but a perfect body attempted to remove his shirt. Filled with anger and disgust, Giovanni pulled the cross that Antonelli had given him from underneath his shirt, "Back you demons, all of you!"

Seeing the blessed crucifix, they spirits screamed and backed away. Antonelli nodded, "They shouldn't bother you anymore, let's keep moving."

Giovanni nodded as he wiped the sweat from his forehead. His hand passed over the skin of his face revealing veins popping out and several bumps forming. He put his hand on his cheek and noticed the same thing happening there. Being in the pit was corroding Giovanni's very existence; he knew he needed to get out of there soon.

Padre Antonelli noticed it as well and shook his head, "We need to get you out of the pit, or you will turn."

He quickly led Giovanni to a small staircase. Other spirits tried to get out that way, but they were being blocked by an unforeseen wall. Giovanni climbed the steps to where they were being blocked, but when he put his hand, there was nothing blocking him. He stepped out of the pit and on to the ledge.

Giovanni felt a new source of strength as he stepped off the staircase. Before him stood a vast, barren wasteland with a small oasis and a single tree in the center. Without thinking, he began to walk towards it.

Padre Antonelli followed closely behind him, "Ah yes, the Eden Serpent, good plan."

It took some time for Giovanni to cross the barren land. The heat beat down on him every step of the way, but he ignored it and continued on with his sword in hand. Nothing was going to stop him from making the master of darkness pay for what had been done.

Giovanni kept his eyes on the small oasis as it grew bigger right in front of him. Slithering around the branches of the ancient tree was a large black and yellow serpent. The enormous snake was draped over almost every branch as it coiled itself around the tree.

Giovanni raised his sword to kill the ancient reptile, but the snake opened its mouth and hissed. The sound was an unusual whisper that sounded like a foreign language. It sounded extremely hypnotic to the young fisherman's ears.

Giovanni's arm froze. No matter how hard he tried to kill the serpent, he was unable to deliver the blow. Padre Antonelli began to cackle, "Not so easy is it? Do you really think a mere mortal could kill a creature of such power, especially in your condition? That serpent has existed for eons. It will not suffer the wrath of maggots!"

The serpent continued whispering in its odd language. Giovanni's head began to pulse as though it were about to explode. He fell to his knees and screamed. Antonelli's laughter echoed across the plains as he saw Giovanni begin to turn.

Nicolas and Cyrillus suddenly appeared on the scene. Nicolas knelt next to Giovanni and tried to figure out what was going on, "My God, Giovanni are you okay? What happened back in the cave?"

Cyrillus looked up at the specter of the priest in disbelief. How could that the priest would just let his old friend suffer like this? "Padre Antonelli, what…"

At that moment, the answer hit him, "Wait… you are not Padre Antonelli! He was Giovanni's friend. There is nothing but malice in your eyes."

The specter laughed even harder, "Young fools, do you seriously think any of you ever stood a chance against my master?"

Cyrillus shook his head, "We're not here for him. We came for the serpent."

"Bad bluff, young revolutionary." The specter cackled. "My master knows of your plans. You would bring down Michael and end the true Most High's ascension. I will not let you go any further!"

"You are not in a position to stop us!" Adalyn's voice appeared behind them. "We're not fooled by you or your cheap antics, Kaliban! Show yourself."

Divinity

The specter of Padre Antonelli disappeared to reveal a hideous imp-like creature with black wings that resembled those of a bat. He cackled in his true voice, which was in a much higher pitch, "Well well, Adalyn. I never thought I'd see your face again. I expected you to end up in the Well of Souls like your friend."

Adalyn clenched her jaw as she spoke, "Get out of here Kaliban, even in my weakened state, I am more than a match for you, and you know it!"

Kaliban nodded, "Trying to get rid of me so soon? Oh very well, but don't expect my master to let you out so easily, farewell!"

Kaliban disappeared without another word while Cyrillus knelt down to help Giovanni. He pulled Giovanni's face up and looked at his red eyes, "Oh no, Adalyn, you'd better get over here."

Adalyn turned and ran in the direction they were talking. It took a few moments for her hands to find Giovanni, but once she did, she could feel his body quivering. "What do you see?"

"His skin is turning gray and his eyes are dark red." Nicolas replied.

She placed her hands on Giovanni's cheeks and focused, "No... he's being turned."

"What does that mean," Cyrillus asked.

"It means his soul is being corrupted." She replied. "Whatever he's been facing since we parted has caused him so much despair that the demons were able to shatter his will."

She turned to Nicolas, "Hold him down. We've only got one chance to save him."

Nicolas got behind Giovanni and held his arms back as he continued screaming. Adalyn placed her hands on his forehead and chin, both were burning intensely. A fever that bad was usually fatal, but this was not coming from an illness.

Adalyn focused on Giovanni for a few moments. His eyes opened and he looked directly at her. The redness began to slowly fade and was taken over by a blue aura. The two colors swirled in his eyes as though good and evil were waging war and Giovanni's eyes were the battlefield.

Adalyn focused even harder, to the point where her body began to shake. A few tense moments of struggling went by before Giovanni's eyes returned to their natural color. He stopped screaming and let out a sigh as his eyes closed.

Adalyn nodded, "He's going to be okay. He just needs to rest for a few minutes."

Nicolas laid Giovanni down before grabbing his sword and turning to the Eden Serpent. The beast had been watching the entire time and now had a worried look on its face. As Nicolas approached it, he smiled, "Sorry beast, you have a lot to answer for. It's about time you were used for good."

The serpent hissed and turned to look behind the tree. Nicolas began to hear a familiar giggle. It sounded like his little sister was playing behind the tree. He called to her, "Antonia, it can't be!"

Adalyn turned and stood up when she heard what was happening. Antonia smiled, "It is me big brother. I followed you here. You need to stop what you are doing. It will only lead you to ruin."

Nicolas rubbed his eyes, "No, it can't be, I saw the house burn, you were killed. I heard your screams!"

"Please brother," She said pleadingly, "Please come see me, I have missed you for so long. You are the only family I have left. Please don't leave me here."

Nicolas didn't know what to do. He turned back to look at the group. Cyrillus was holding Giovanni's head

Divinity

steady as he began to wake. Adalyn faced Nicolas' gaze and shook her head.

Seeing the look on the angel's face made up his mind. Nicolas knew what he needed to do. Nicolas nodded back, breathed in, and returned to the Serpent. As he moved, his sister's voice continued to plead with him to stop.

Nicolas clenched his teeth, "Ignore it, ignore it…"

Antonia's voice became even higher pitched with desperation. He could feel his ears begin to throb as his sanity was nearing its breaking point. Finally, he took the last agonizing step toward the serpent. With his last ounce of strength, he raised the sword above his head and brought it down on the serpent, "For the love of God, be silent!"

Nicolas' aim was perfect. The blade cut through the serpent, severing its head. The large serpent hissed as its head fell to the ground. The rest of its body whipped around out of control for a few moments before slithering away. Nicolas quickly looked for his sister, but she had vanished. Even though he knew that specter was not really her, a tear fell from his eye, "Goodbye Antonia."

Without another word, Nicolas picked up the head of the serpent and stuffed it into a small burlap sack he carried.

Giovanni tossed and turned for a few moments before finally opening his eyes. He let out a loud sigh of relief when he saw Adalyn looking down on him. Tears streamed down his cheek, "Adalyn, there is no apology fitting for what I have done… but please forgive me."

"For what," She asked, "You haven't done anything wrong."

It took Giovanni a moment to muster up the strength to tell her, "In the cave, I failed you. I was given a choice on who to believe, on who was telling me the truth. When I saw what you were doing, I stabbed you with my own sword, after promising to protect you."

Divinity

Adalyn shook her head, "Giovanni, the images you saw there were designed with the specific intent of driving you insane. There was no way to succeed. No matter what decision you had made, no matter what path you chose, it would have made you pick the wrong thing."

Giovanni still would not look at her. Cyrillus got under his left arm and positioned himself to help his friend walk, "I don't understand this, we were all put through the same torment. How is it his was so much more awful to the point that it drove him to insanity?"

"I don't know." Adalyn replied. "Unlike you and Nicolas, Giovanni still has things he fears to lose. Perhaps that is what made him so vulnerable to attack. He also had Kaliban with him and believe me, a few minutes with that insect is more than enough to drive anyone to insanity."

Adalyn put her hands on Giovanni's cheeks, "Listen to me, what happened wasn't real. You did what you thought was right in the cave and no one here will blame you for that, especially not me. We all had to do horrible things to get through that nightmare."

Giovanni nodded as he finally found his feet and stood on his own. Cyrillus let go as Nicolas walked up behind them, "I have what we came for."

Giovanni smiled faintly, "Good work, you did a much better job than I ever could have."

Nicolas shook his head, "No my friend, I almost did it… I too almost gave in. I don't want to talk about it. Not now, not ever."

"Very well." Adalyn said as she lowered her eyes. "Let's get out of here."

IV

As the four of them walked back toward the river, they noticed something wasn't right. The tunnel was gone, and in its place was a stone bridge which led into a thick cloud of blackness. There was something eerie about how the cloud hovered, but did not move.

Cyrillus looked back to the field, but could not see the oasis anymore, "What's going on, what is this?"

"All we can do is move forward." Adalyn replied. "Please trust me, stay close and we'll make it out of here."

Giovanni looked down into the river of lava as the group proceeded over it. The stone was solid, but looked very much out of place. He was half expecting the bridge to collapse and send them into the hot lava, but it held together.

As they reached the other side, the bridge suddenly vanished. Nicolas looked back, "Something isn't right."

He barely had time to finish that thought as the darkness in front of them disappeared. Suddenly, the large castle they had seen from a distance appeared in front of them. By now, it was painfully obvious that they had been tricked into heading directly into Lucifer's lair.

Adalyn gasped, "I don't believe it. We have been deceived!"

Kaliban appeared at the entrance, "My master would not allow you to leave without first paying your respects! Step this way please!"

Adalyn became agitated, "Kaliban..."

They had thought they were heading out the way that they had come, but instead had marched right into Lucifer's hand. Cyrillus looked up at the mighty walls, "If we go in there, I don't think we'll ever come out."

Kaliban laughed, "You have no choice! You must go on!"

Divinity

Cyrillus turned and tried to follow the path back, but a wall of flame appeared in front of him. Giovanni shook his head, "It doesn't look like we have much of a choice."

"I can't believe I didn't see this," Adalyn said angrily, "We were going back the way we came, but somehow we have also come upon Lucifer's lair!"

Nicolas' tone turned to anger, "How is that possible?"

"He can do whatever he wants here." She said softly. "This was supposed to be a world of torment for him, but because he managed to hang on to some of his power he was able to feed off of the evil perpetuated by man. Over time, he turned this place into his kingdom. He now has full control of what goes on here. His powers have limits, but playing tricks on the minds of mortals is what he's good at."

Nicolas took the head of the serpent from his bag, "Everyone, hold out your swords."

Giovanni and Cyrillus put their swords together with Nicolas' as he smeared the venom from the serpent's fangs on them. The green liquid sizzled like acid as it struck the blades. The swords glowed green for a moment as the venom dried.

"You must be cautious with those weapons now." Adalyn warned. "They are cursed objects and if abused, they can do as much damage to the person who wields them."

Cyrillus looked at the blade of his sword and nodded, "Foul beast... what horror lies ahead for us."

Adalyn shook her head, "I do not know. This is as far as any angel has ever dared go. As I said, Lucifer can do whatever he wants here. No doubt anything we encounter in there will be designed to torment our souls. Keep your wits about you and stay close."

The group moved cautiously into the castle. With Kaliban still laughing behind them, "Yes, go on! Go, my master is waiting!"

Divinity

The entrance to the castle was ornately designed with grotesque images of pain. The group looked at the infernal designs on the walls of this massive structure. Everything was cobalt black and had scenes of horrific torture carved into them. It seemed as though Lucifer had decided to admire his initial work, introducing evil to humans. Each scene carved on the wall depicted evil deeds humans were guilty of.

Giovanni could see the tortures committed by the Assyrians, the burning of Rome, and the crusades. It was a sickening display that he could've gotten by without seeing. Now though, it would be something he'd have to put out of his head.

The massive doors slammed shut as the group stepped inside the main hall. They found themselves in a huge room with an ornate throne sitting at the top of a large staircase. The lava glowed in the windows like horrific red specters keeping a watchful eye on them.

Seated on the thrown, was a beautiful woman with brown hair and green eyes. She wore a silver evening gown that shimmered as she moved. Cyrillus froze in place and dropped his sword, "Menia, you're here? How can that be?"

She smiled as she stood up and walked down the steps towards him. Cyrillus turned back to the group, "It's my wife, she's here!"

Giovanni noticed that his eyes were turning red, "Cyrillus, I don't think that's her."

"What," he demanded, "Of course it's her, look with your eyes, there is no mistaking her. Even Lucifer himself could not mimic such beauty!"

Cyrillus left his sword on the ground and walked towards her. Giovanni tried to run to him, but something blocked his path. He slammed into an unseen wall and fell to the ground.

Divinity

Adalyn put her hand against the unseen force that Giovanni hit, "It's solid, though we can't see it, it's definitely there."

She shook her head, "It's no good, we can't get to him!"

"I have to try!" Giovanni insisted as he pulled his sword and desperately slashed at the wall. "We wouldn't have gotten this far if it wasn't for him!"

Giovanni's sword impacted against the illusionary wall with a mighty clank. The sword glowed green and left a green line on the wall. He slashed again, leaving a second one, and again.

Nicolas saw the breach marks on the wall and began slashing as well, "Cyrillus, come on man, snap out of it!"

Adalyn listened as Cyrillus distanced himself from the group. Desperate to stop him and having no sword, she cried out, "Cyrillus please hear us. I knew your wife well and that is not her! Please you must listen to me. I know you miss her, but what you're looking at won't bring you any peace!"

Cyrillus ignored her and walked closer to Menia, "My love, why are you here?"

Menia put her hand to his face, "When I died, this is where I was sent. I came here and was spared the tortures of those who are damned."

"How?" Cyrillus asked.

Menia's smile turned to malice, "I became his consort. I belong to him now."

At that moment, her stomach began to grow, revealing that she was pregnant. Cyrillus stepped backwards, "No!"

She laughed, "I was never waiting for you. You have wasted your life!"

Adalyn stepped back with her hands limp at her side, "Cyrillus…"

Giovanni saw what was happening and drove his sword into the wall, "Come on damn it, collapse!"

Divinity

Steam began to fly from Cyrillus's skin. He could feel his entire body begin to sear. At that moment, the invisible wall disappeared.

Nicolas saw what was happening and tried to ram the wall with his shoulder, but Adalyn grabbed him by the arm and held on tight, "It's too late, you can't save him, you'll only damage yourself!"

"Be silent." Nicolas shouted as he turned back to his comrade. "Cyrillus turn back, come on, we've got to get out of here! That is not Menia!"

Giovanni grabbed his other arm, held him in place, and looked away, "Adalyn is right. It's too late, we can't help him."

Nicolas watched as his friend's skin began to melt away. The flesh collapsed, revealing a hideous husk that pulled and ripped at the remaining semblance of Cyrillus' being. His scream turned into a demonic shriek.

Adalyn's mouth dropped open when she heard the cry. She knew what Cyrillus had become. The demon sprouted wings and began to fly about the room. Adalyn screamed when she heard the demon's voice, "No!"

Filled with rage, she grabbed Nicolas' sword and plunged it deeply into the wall. Her jaw clenched as she twisted it a few times. There was a flicker of green light before the wall collapsed.

With the illusion gone, Adalyn took flight. Giovanni watched in awe as her wings spread and she raised herself off the ground. One mighty flap sent her speeding towards the demon. She homed in on the sound of the demon's wings as it flew.

The demon tried desperately to get away, but it was not fast enough to outrun Adalyn's wings. She raised herself above the creature, then folded her wings behind her and dove down towards it. Her sword was straight out in front of her, ready to strike. A second later, she ran the demon

through. The sword began to glow green again as the demon shrieked in pain.

Adalyn could feel hot tears falling down her cheeks, "You have suffered enough, Cyrillus. I release you now. Go be with your wife where she really is."

Adalyn breathed in deeply and plunged the sword deeper into the demon's chest. It shrieked and began to shake violently before exploding into dust. Adalyn nodded as the dust fell to the ground, "Rest in peace my friend, and thank you for everything."

Once the demon was gone, Adalyn turned and brought herself down in front of Menia, "No more of your tricks Lucifer, I know it is you! No more of this!"

"Young fool!" The woman cackled as she began to spin in a circle. Her body began to spin so fast that the group could not see anything more than a blur that resembled a cyclone. Adalyn stood with her sword drawn, ready to strike as she waited for Lucifer to finish.

After a few moments, the spinning stopped. In the place of Cyrillus's wife, a dark skinned angel with tattered wings, unearthly yellow eyes, and blood stained clothes appeared in front of them. It glared at Adalyn with a malice-filled stare.

His eyes met Adalyn with rage, "It's been a long time, old friend. At long last, we see each other face to face as we did that day."

"Lucifer." She growled. "You were never a friend of mine. In my opinion, the Most High would have done everyone a much-needed service by simply blinking you out of existence."

Lucifer shook his head, "Azrael always spoke very highly of you before the war. If only he were still alive to see what has become of his star pupil!"

Nicolas picked Cyrillus's sword up off the ground, clenched his teeth, and pointed it at Lucifer, "You bastard!"

Nicolas dropped the bag with the serpent's head on the ground. He then brought arm back and charged at Lucifer. Seeing the young man coming, Lucifer rolled his eyes and reached out his hand as though to catch Nicolas in midair.

To Giovanni's shock, he didn't have to. The mere act of reaching out was enough to stop Nicolas in his tracks. Some unseen force held him in place as Lucifer closed his fist. Nicolas dropped his sword and began to gurgle. Adalyn could hear the labored breathing and cried out, "No Lucifer, no more!"

She summoned all of her strength, spread her wings, and blocked Lucifer's vision. As she did, Nicolas began to breathe again. Lucifer smiled, "It seems that even without your powers, you still have a strong force of will protecting you... Magnificent!"

Lucifer flapped his wings and took flight, "But that alone will not save you."

Lucifer had a harder time flying then any normal angel due to the condition of his wings. There was a lot less finesse about the way he flapped his wings. He looked like a fledgling just learning how to fly.

Adalyn crouched down and put all of her strength into her knees. She pushed with everything she had and sprung herself into the air flapping her own wings to catch up to him. Adalyn used Lucifer's heavy breathing to home in on his position, just as before. She chased him down and slashed at him with her sword.

Lucifer blocked her attack with the pair of gauntlets he wore. She slashed at him again and again, but he easily blocked each attack. As Adalyn began to tire, Lucifer laughed, "I'm not so easily beaten! This is not as it was before. Here I hold all the power!"

Adalyn lowered herself to the ground and tried to catch her breath, "Power at what cost, Lucifer? Look at what you had to become to return yourself to any semblance of your former self."

Lucifer laughed as he landed in front of her, "Young fool, you are finished!"

His inhuman laughing continued as he brought his hand back and struck Adalyn with his right gauntlet. She was thrown backwards stunned by the force of the blow, but she still managed to keep her sword pointed at him. Pushing with her feet, she tried to back away from Lucifer, "This is not over, fallen one. Other angels know of your plot. They will fight you."

"There are not enough of them to stop me this time," Lucifer scoffed, "and with the Most High so weak, they will be nothing more than a peasant resistance."

He flicked his wrist and a knife appeared in his hand. Using an unseen force, he grabbed Adalyn by the throat and held her down on the ground, "I will enjoy this."

As Lucifer was about to strike, he heard the scraping of metal behind him. He quickly turned and reached out his hand. Giovanni had tried to sneak up on him with a sword, but Lucifer had heard him coming. He used the same trick he had on Nicolas and raised Giovanni off the ground by his neck.

Adalyn whimpered as she heard Giovanni began to gurgle. She was struggling to stand, but still stunned from the hit. Despite her efforts, there was no way that she could save Giovanni.

Her noise made Lucifer stop for a brief moment, "What is this?"

Lucifer turned at looked at Adalyn struggling to stand. Seeing the tears began to flow down her face, he smiled, "Can it be, do you actually have feelings for this insect?"

He looked back at Giovanni and squeezed a little tighter, causing him to choke even more. Behind him, Lucifer could sense her reaction and smiled. "I don't believe

this." He said with his blade still pointed at Adalyn, "How could such a pitiful creature win the heart of one that should be counted as a God."

Adalyn turned her head away, "Please… don't hurt him."

"Hurt him?" Lucifer mused. "There must be something special about this boy if he was able to win the mighty heart of an angel. I would not harm something this rare."

The fallen angel turned to face Giovanni, "But I will turn you! You will become one of my most powerful servants."

Lucifer squeezed his fist tightly and dropped Giovanni to the ground. Giovanni could feel his body begin to boil as his skin emitted steam. He began to breathe heavily, but did not want to give Lucifer the pleasure of hearing him scream.

Adalyn could hear him struggle and cried out, "No, I gave him a second chance at life. You have no right to take it away, stop this!"

Her words only made Lucifer laugh harder, "I do not take orders from you! I will send you to the Well of Souls after I make you watch him turn!"

She turned her face in Giovanni's direction as his skin began to turn gray and his eye became red. Bumps began to appear on his forehead and back, and his face began to twist. She could feel the intense pain he was in and called to him, "Please, you have to fight this… I need you with me!"

Her words reached his ear, and suddenly Giovanni forced himself to rise to his knees, "No!"

He grabbed his sword and pushed himself off the ground with amazing strength. Lucifer's eyes widened, "It cannot be…"

Giovanni dove through the air at the bewildered angel and struck his arm with the sword. The young fisherman landed on his knees behind Lucifer. He knew that if he

missed, all would be lost. He sucked down a deep breath before turning around.

Lucifer felt a sharp pain in his arm. The sword began to glow green and Giovanni turned to face him, revealing that his features were returning to normal, "You won't be hurting anyone now!"

Lucifer sneered and grabbed Giovanni by the throat, throwing him back against the wall, "Such strength, you will make a fine addition to the legion, once I am done with her."

Lucifer turned back to Adalyn, ready to deliver a deathblow, but the knife suddenly vanished. The slash on Lucifer's arm began to sting and the intensity got worse with every breath he took. Having never felt real pain before, Lucifer staggered backwards and screamed his body began to emit a green sparkle.

The green specter left his body and exploded in one magnificent burst of power. The room began to glitter with specks of an unknown green substance shimmering down. Lucifer looked at his hands, "What have you done to me?"

Adalyn sneered, "You are mortal now. You will not harm anyone ever again."

She thrust out her hand toward Lucifer who began to sink into the ground. Lucifer watched in horror as his legs disappeared into solid rock and screamed out. Next, his arms began to sink until Adalyn was sure he was properly restrained.

With her last ounce of strength, Adalyn stood and dragged her feet over to him. She stood inches from where he was trapped with her sword ready to strike. She raised it and was about to stab Lucifer in the throat when she heard the quiver in his breathing. The strength to deliver the blow left her arm and she lowered the sword.

Unable to strike, she lowered her head to face him, "I see now why the Most High took pity on you. Evil as you

Divinity

were, even he did not wish to see you dead. You were one of his beloved. I don't wish to reverse his decision, so instead of killing you, I will leave you as you are. As time does not pass here, you will not have to worry about dying, but if you ever try to leave here again, your body will wither and turn to dust. This place will once again be as it was originally meant to be; a prison for you. You shall continue to perform your task here, but will never be able to live lavishly again!"

Lucifer cried out again, "No!"

Adalyn nodded as the ground around him finished hardening, "Let this forever be your prison, traitor!"

Lucifer spat at her, "You are weak, just like he was. This is not over Adalyn. You can't keep me here forever. I'll find a way to free myself and I promise you, when I'm free, you will pay! I don't care if I have to wait for an eternity, this is not over!"

Adalyn sighed, "By the time you get free, you will no longer be my problem."

Giovanni had recovered from his impact on the wall. He walked over and helped Nicolas to his feet. Nicolas picked up his sword once again and limped over to the angels, "Adalyn, if you will not kill him, then I will! This bastard has a lot to answer for!"

"No," Adalyn said, stretching her hand out to him, "there has been enough killing today. For the sake of your own soul, don't stoop to his evil. Let him rot here in his own misery."

Nicolas looked conflicted. He wanted revenge more than anything, but feared for his immortal soul if he took it. Having no other choice, he sighed and nodded that he had regained control of his emotions, "Very well..."

V

The three friends left Lucifer screaming in his new prison, unable to move. Nicolas wouldn't look at either of them as they journeyed out of the underworld. They exited the castle and looked for a way out.

Already, Hell looked a lot less menacing. The flames had died down a little and a tunnel opened up on the opposite side of the massive cavern from the tunnel under the pit. It looked far easier than facing the temptations of the cave again.

Giovanni's eyes narrowed, "That wasn't there before…"

"Yes it was." Adalyn replied. "Lucifer just kept us from seeing it."

Nicolas and Giovanni moved toward the cave and noticed skeletons and dismembered arms and legs from what looked like demons strewn about. Giovanni scratched his head, "What dwells here?"

"A horrific creature that you are probably familiar with from Revelations." Adalyn replied as she turned to Nicolas. "You probably know it better as Scylla."

Nicolas shuddered at the name, "A massive sea beast…"

Adalyn nodded, "Right, it escaped from here briefly before Charybdis was able to reclaim it. One of your kings encountered it on his journey home."

Giovanni peered into the cave but didn't see the creature in its pen, "It's not here…"

"Then we'd best move quickly." Adalyn replied. "Who knows where it could be."

The group made their way past the massive pen and headed for the old rope bridge that led them to the black doors. They immediately ran across the bridge, thinking nothing of the possibility of it collapsing. They wanted out and nothing was going to stop them.

Giovanni and Nicolas worked on getting the door open as quickly as they could. While they worked, Adalyn turned back towards the cavern and appeared to be disappointed about something. Her face homed in on the large pen that was Scylla's lair.

Giovanni looked back as the door creaked open and placed his hand on her shoulder, "Everything okay?'

Adalyn sighed and nodded, "Yes, I guess I was just hoping to see someone that I know should be here."

"Who?" Giovanni asked.

"It doesn't matter." Adalyn replied. "It was just someone who was a good friend of mine before the war. I guess I just wanted to tell her how sorry I was that things turned out the way they did, but I guess it's probably better that we didn't run into her."

Giovanni smiled, "Come on, let's get out of here."

Adalyn took his hand and followed him through the doors. The three friends took in a deep breath of cool, clean, air. Adalyn's however was cut short as she felt a disturbance nearby. She turned her head to the side as though she could see something off in the distance.

Giovanni noticed her unrest and turned to look at her, "What is it?"

Adalyn let out a gasp but did not respond. He gave her a second and then asked again, "What is it, what is wrong?"

"Someone… is coming," She said quietly.

Giovanni and Nicolas quickly drew their swords and scanned the area carefully. Moments of terrible silence went by without anything happening. Adalyn quickly gasped again as two rays of light suddenly appeared in front of them.

The bright specters quickly took the form of human-like creatures. Both were angels, matching Adalyn's beauty,

but they looked considerably different. They appeared to be slightly older than Adalyn and wore shining silver armor. The most striking difference was their wings. Instead of a pair of large white wings on their backs, these two had four bright red wings. They landed in front of Adalyn and folded their wings behind them.

To Giovanni's surprise an unusual golden aura emanated from their skin which illuminated the land around them. It grew brighter as they moved. There was something strangely majestic about the two as they stepped forward.

Adalyn smiled, "Ariel, Roselyn, it is good to…"

She let out a faint sigh as she spoke, "… 'see' you again. What are you doing here?"

Ariel stepped forward with her sword sheathed, "Sister… your absence has pained all of us greatly, and it breaks my heart to see you like this."

Roselyn had tears in her eyes, "Adalyn, forgive us for not doing more at your hearing in front of the Choirs. We should have put up more of a fight."

Adalyn shook her head, "There is nothing to forgive, had you continued to speak out, you would have shared in my fate. I could not have lived with that additional sin on my heart."

The two angels tried to move closer to Adalyn, but Giovanni and Nicolas stepped in front of her with their swords drawn. Neither were sure of what to make of the angels, but they had seen too many demonic creatures and they were not about to let either of these near Adalyn.

Ariel rolled her eyes at the two men blocking her path. Annoyed, she put a hand to her own sword, but did not draw it, "What do you intend to do with your swords, kill us? We are seraph angels and do not suffer the threats of mortals. Do you think that corporeal blade is going to do anything at all?"

Giovanni glared right into Ariel's fiery eyes, "These are no ordinary blades. They have been coated in the venom of the Eden Serpent. It can kill you now as easily as it can kill me!"

Ariel pulled her sword from its sheath. The flame ignited in a mighty blast, "Are you so devoid of light that you would wield such infernal weapons?"

Roselyn grabbed Ariel's hand, "Stop it Ariel, we should be more respectful then that. These people are the ones that kept our sister safe from harm!"

Ariel nodded and lowered her sword. With her sister calming down, Roselyn turned back to Giovanni, "Please, we intend no harm. There is no need for such hostilities!"

"No?" Giovanni shot back. "I found her on a rock in the harbor near my home, covered in blood and near death. Where was your concern then? She would have died…"

"Giovanni, please stop." He heard Adalyn say from behind him.

Giovanni tried to protest, but Adalyn silenced him by placing two fingers on his lips, "Shh, it's okay. I appreciate you trying to defend me, but it is not necessary. We are in the company of friends here. These two are a pair of seraph angels that I have known for years. They have watched out for me for a very long time."

Giovanni hesitantly lowered his sword and turned to Ariel unenthusiastically, "Forgive me."

Ariel placed her sword back in its sheath and the two angels returned his gesture. Ariel kept her eye on Giovanni as they stepped forward. Clearly she wasn't willing to give him anymore trust than he had given them.

Once Giovanni moved, Ariel placed her right hand on Adalyn's arm and gently stroked it, "You weren't alone, Adalyn. We had been suspecting that there was a higher raking angel guilty of treason within our ranks. You were simply the one unfortunate enough to stumble on the truth."

Divinity

Adalyn shook her head, "Azrael wasn't guilty."

"We know that." Roselyn piped in. "Many of us were highly suspicious of you being prosecuted for following Michael's orders, especially since simply looking into your claims with a little more care would have cleared everything up. So we started watching Michael closely and began our own investigation. Azrael led the charge and coordinated our efforts."

"Did you find anything?" Adalyn asked.

"Yes." Roselyn replied. "Michael lied, he never sent anyone to the location you told him. We found the grove exactly as you described it. That was when we started to suspect him of misdoing."

Ariel continued the thought, "But we weren't certain of anything until we saw what he did to Azrael. We know the truth now."

"Well that's all nice and good." Giovanni said angrily. "Azrael, Padre Antonelli, and Cyrillus had to die so you would finally open your eyes. Now what do you intend to do about it?"

The two angels looked at each other, and then back at Giovanni. Ariel hesitantly spoke in an apologetic tone, "There is nothing we can do. The Most High has decreed that we are not to interfere in the workings of the world without his express permission. To reverse his decree would mean death for us and more power for Michael."

Roselyn nodded and stepped forward, "Right now we're slowly gaining support, but with Azrael gone, many of the Choirs are hesitant to take a stand. Roughly half of the Seraphim are willing to believe us. Gabriel has said that if we can provide him proof, he will support us as well. A few others Choirs are also starting to come around, our list of allies is still small, but it is growing. Unfortunately, Michael still holds the support of the majority of the Choirs and they will not turn on him. Even in the current state of affairs, without solid proof, they will not even hear our case. Right now, we cannot afford to interfere outright. If we do, we lose everything."

Nicolas' eyes narrowed, "Proof? Your friend Azrael died at Michael's hand. What more proof do they need?"

"Michael sufficiently shrouded his actions so that they went unnoticed by the Choirs." Ariel replied. "He's good at doing things without drawing attention to himself."

Giovanni rolled his eyes, "Typical, we're here fighting and dying for your mistakes, and your short sightedness, meanwhile you hide behind procedures."

Ariel nodded, "I apologize, and I know we are wrongfully placing a heavy burden on you, but we are prepared to offer something in exchange."

Nicolas looked at them both suspiciously, "And what would that be?"

Roselyn smiled, "We're petitioning the choirs to overturn Adalyn's expulsion and return her to her brothers and sisters."

Adalyn's face tilted, "What trickery is this?"

"No trick." Ariel insisted. "No one will do anything as long as Michael is allowed to run amuck, but if you finish him, the Choirs will most likely allow you back. I'm sure the Most High will welcome you too."

Giovanni frowned and turned away from what he was hearing. Adalyn was dumbfounded, "I don't know what to say... I am very grateful."

The two angels smiled, "We will continue to do what we can on the Celestial side. With Lucifer now apparently out of the picture, Michael's options will be numbered. He still has the support of most of the seven archangels, as well as many other followers who refuse to hear what we are trying to tell them. Roselyn will continue to appeal to them while I dig up evidence."

Roselyn stepped forward, "But the Most High is in a weakened state, if Michael returns to the Celestial side, it could mean civil war without end."

Adalyn nodded, "Giving the Netherworld a chance to move in and take over. Lucifer may be out of the picture, but he can still lead from afar. Then again, if Michael remains in the mortal realm, he will hollow humanity out from the inside like a cancer."

"Yes, that is the reality of the situation." Ariel sighed. "So there is little other choice in this matter. He must be judged for his crimes, and if he still refuses to cooperate, then he must die."

Giovanni stepped forward, "If that is how this is going to play out, then we are running out of time and really need to get back. The problem is that the trip back to Rome will not be an easy one. It took us weeks just to get to Crete. Is there nothing you can do to help us?"

The two looked at each other for a moment to consider a plan. When they finally decided, Ariel took a step toward Giovanni, "I hope you know the task that lies ahead of you. It will not be easy to do what is being asked of you, and the price for succeeding may be more then you realize."

He nodded, "I've known that since I started on this adventure. My home was burned and the Church has been hot on our heels. I am prepared to do what must be done."

"Very well." Ariel said, not entirely convinced. "We will arrange for Charybdis to release you near Ostia."

A worried expression came over Adalyn's face, "Wouldn't that be breaking God's decree?"

"Perhaps," Ariel said casually, "but it is a minor infraction, given the current state of affairs, hopefully it will go unnoticed."

Adalyn nodded, "A calculated risk?"

"Yes," Roselyn replied, "but if it pays off, hopefully all of this will be undone."

"We appreciate that," Giovanni said humbly.

Ariel's eyes did not leave Adalyn as she spoke to Giovanni. Though she held onto hope that their plan to stop Michael would success, she still feared that this may be the last time she would ever see her sister, "Once you've returned to the mortal realm, you will not have as hard a time getting back to Ostia, however you must be prepared. Once you get to Rome, the road will only get more treacherous. I hope you understand what that means."

"He understands." Adalyn said with confidence. "He's cared for me since the very beginning. I would not be here now if it was not for him."

"For that, you have my unending gratitude." Roselyn said smiling, "It is good to see that there still really are good people in this world. I admit that I was beginning to lose faith, but seeing how you've cared for her bodes well for your kind. Good luck to the three of you. We hope to see you again soon."

Ariel glared into Giovanni's eyes, "Keep her safe, as you have been."

"I don't need you to tell me to do that." Giovanni replied.

The two angels nodded and vanished. Adalyn watched until the last semblance of them was gone, "Come, it is time to go."

VI

Charon was waiting for them at the dock. He saw the looks on their faces of exhaustion and mental injury. He turned to Adalyn, "Did you find what you came for?"

Adalyn nodded, "We did, now please get us out of here."

"Very well," Charon said as he pushed off the dock, "I will take you back to your ship."

The boat slowly pulled away from the shore as Charon pulled on his oar and rowed back across the river. Several times along the way, Giovanni felt like the small boat was about to tip over, but Charon held it steady.

Nicolas watched as the small island faded into the fog. A tear fell from his eye as his thoughts dwelled on Cyrillus, "Goodbye, my old friend."

It did not take long for the boat to reach the black pier. While Giovanni helped Nicolas off the boat, Charon spoke to Adalyn, "It was good to see you again, old friend. Take care of yourself... I hope never to have to ferry you to the Well of Souls."

Before getting off the boat, Adalyn gave him a hug, knowing that she may never see him again, "Thank you my friend, I will be careful."

Giovanni was waiting for her to finish talking to Charon. When she signaled that she was ready, he held out his hand to her. She took it and squeezed tight as they began to walk back the way they had come.

Not a word was said between the three as they walked. Adalyn could hear Nicolas' heavy breathing and was sure that he still had tears in his eyes. Giovanni's hand shook as they walked. He was trembling and seemed to be torn between confusion and some deep fear that he was obviously not in the mood to talk about.

They had achieved a great victory in the underworld, but it didn't feel like one. Despite getting the weapons they needed and putting an end to Lucifer's plans, there was no joy amongst them. They had been beaten, tormented, and one of them had met a horrific end. The tension in the air was so potent that it almost choked Adalyn.

It wasn't long before the group was back at the dock where Giovanni's ship was waiting. It bobbed up and down on the water though it was anxious to get going. It was a welcomed sight as they stepped onto the gangway.

Once they were onboard, Giovanni let Nicolas rest against the mast as he pulled up the ramp and got the ship ready to go. Adalyn grabbed the other half and pulled to help him get it onboard quickly. They then used planks to push the ship away from the dock.

A few seconds later, the ship began to turn and head back out into open water. Giovanni watched as the dock vanished from view before he turned to see how Nicolas holding up. The young revolutionary was barely conscious. He was still dealing with the injuries he'd received from seeing his sister, and Lucifer. Giovanni could plainly see that the worse injuries were the ones that were far deeper then skin.

Nicolas watched the ship creep slowly through the bog, "I cannot believe what happened. Cyrillus was one of our best men… to die in such a worthless way."

Adalyn stood off to the side as the bog went by. "I wish I'd never gotten all of you involved in this. What Giovanni said was true… Padre Antonelli and Cyrillus would still be alive if not for me."

"I do not agree." Nicolas retorted. "Cyrillus lost everything when his wife died. He joined our cause because was looking for a fight and an easy out, nothing more. That man held a grudge and wasn't about to give it up. He was

my friend, but he wanted to die. There was never any coming back for him."

Giovanni nodded, "And Padre Antonelli made his choices too. He had lived a long life of faith and discipline only to see everything he believed in get shredded by Michael. Rescuing you was his redemption. I don't think either one of them would blame you for what happened."

She nodded, "Thank you both, I hope you're right."

Nicolas had burn marks on his neck from when Lucifer grabbed him, but they were not as bad as they could have been. He was more stunned from the blow of hitting the ground and watching his friend die then he was from the neck injury.

Giovanni fetched a cloth, dipped it in a bucket of water near the cabin, and wrapped it around Nicolas' neck to make sure he was going to be okay, "This should help with those marks."

The ship continued to creak slowly past the bog, further then when they first arrived. It wasn't long before the broken trees disappeared and fog thickened. The group found themselves in the middle of nowhere and unable to see anything. Adalyn stood at the railing, waiting to for a sign of something come. Suddenly, she heard a low boom similar to the one that she had heard when they had sailed from Crete.

"Oh no…" She whispered.

She quickly turned and called to Giovanni, "Help, get me to the mast now!"

He looked at her weird, "What's going on?"

As though answering his question, the water in front of them hollowed out and a maelstrom appeared where the water used to be calm. The boat began to rock violently as they ran to the mast. The hull groaned under the intense pressure.

Giovanni reached for it and grabbed on. Adalyn held on to the rope which had been wrapped around the mast until Giovanni could get his arm around her. He held on to her as tight as they could.

Nicolas snapped out of his thoughts and ran for the tiller. Using all his strength, he tried to steer the ship into the current of the whirlpool, "Everyone hold on!"

The ship began to spin downward faster and faster until it reached the bottom of the funnel. Within moments, the group found themselves engulfed in darkness once again. This time, Giovanni could feel Adalyn there with him. He was not alone and to him, it was a comfort.

BOOK III

For the Glory of Rome

I

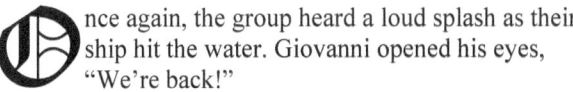nce again, the group heard a loud splash as their ship hit the water. Giovanni opened his eyes, "We're back!"

"But where are we?" Adalyn asked in an annoyed tone as she fluttered her soaked wings. "Ugh… I hate getting my feathers wet!"

Giovanni looked at the shoreline that was visible in the distance, "Your friends did say that they would ensure that we would appear near the harbor city, correct?"

She nodded, "Yes."

"Can we trust them?" Giovanni asked suspiciously.

"I trust them unquestionable," She replied sternly. "They were always sisters to me. I would trust them with my very existence."

Nicolas stood up slowly, "Then we should get underway."

Giovanni turned to him and shrugged, "In which direction? We have no idea where we are, all we know is that Ostia is nearby."

"We sail north." Adalyn said in a positive tone. "I can feel it."

They both looked at her oddly. Her eyes were covered by their bandages. There was no physical way that she could possibly know where they were.

"How can you possibly know that?" Giovanni asked.

"I can feel it pulling at me." She replied. "Travel north and we will definitely find Ostia… and Michael."

The two men looked at each other for a moment, shrugged, and moved along. Nicolas pulled the sail into position while Giovanni manned the tiller. The ship began to move forward as the wind caught the sail.

**

An hour went by with no sight of Ostia. The closer they got, the more Giovanni distanced himself from Adalyn. He knew that every moment drew them closer to Rome would be a moment closer to her returning to the Kingdom of Heaven. He didn't know how to handle it, so he kept his distance from her. It got to the point where she stood alone at the bow and he was standing at the stern watching the time pass.

Nicolas could sense the tension between them and knew something was wrong. He decided to confront Giovanni, "My friend, how long do you intend to avoid her?"

Giovanni didn't even turn to face him, "I don't know what you're talking about."

"Do not deny something so obvious." Nicolas shot back. "You have said little to nothing to her since our meeting with Ariel and Roselyn. What's the matter?"

"I'm going to lose her, Nicolas." Giovanni replied. "I fought so hard to bring her back and then protect her... I thought that if I fought hard enough, I would somehow be able to keep her at my side."

Nicolas leaned on the railing next to him, "I know you love her, but think about the reality here. Where would you keep her, cooped up in a small house somewhere? What kind of life would that be?"

"I would not subject her to that." Giovanni replied. "I would have built a new house away from the town; somewhere she could enjoy the world."

"Think clearly on this." Nicolas said, trying to be a voice of reason. "It would still be isolation. She's an angel and she belongs with her own kind."

Nicolas could see that Giovanni already came to this realization, so he came up with something that Giovanni may not have known, "When I was little, my mother used to tell me that angels always watched over us and kept us safe.

I'd like to think that's true, especially given the evidence lately. If you think about it that way, Adalyn will always be with you. She will be in a position to watch over you, and if we all survive the day, I'm sure she will never forget how you cared for her."

Giovanni twisted his lips thoughtfully, but still said nothing. Nicolas was about ready to give up, so he gave Giovanni his one last bit a wisdom, "Giovanni, when my sister, Antonia died, the last thing I said to her was extremely mean because she had made more work for me. I told her that she was a bad sister and I would trade her for a mule if I got the chance. The next time I saw her, she was being burned alive in our home. I never even got the chance to say goodbye. Not a day goes by where I would not give anything to go back in time and change the last words I spoke to her, but that will never happen, and it's something I have to live with forever."

Nicolas took a moment to word what he wanted to say next carefully, "You have been afforded a rare luxury. The knowledge that, survive or perish, by day's end, you will have to say goodbye to her. You have been given ample time to say goodbye. Is this how you want to spend your final hours? Do yourself a favor; don't make the same mistake I did. Talk to her, she needs you now more than ever."

Giovanni turned and stared at Nicolas for a moment. At first it looked like he was going to stay put, but finally nodded and walked up to the bow. He wasn't sure what he was going to do, but Nicolas was right, his time was limited.

Adalyn was leaning on the railing, looking off into the distance. Her wings were so low, that the outer feathers nearly touched the ground. He could clearly see that something was bothering her. He walked over and stood next to her, "Are you okay?"

She shook her head with tears falling down her cheeks, "No, no I'm not okay."

"What is it? What's wrong?" He asked.

She turned to him, "I was so happy about the prospect of returning to my kingdom, that I forgot about what I'd be giving up here. You have been so kind to me. Even when I was unreasonably mean to you, you opened your home to me and loved me. Now I here I am returning that care by jumping on their offer without even thinking. I could not have been more selfish."

Giovanni closed his eyes, knowing that he would be letting go of the one last glimmer of light in his life, "It may be better for you if you take the offer. If you stay here you would eventually die. You would live out your days being hunted down by the Church, and with your wings there is no chance of a normal life. Your place is with your friends, the other angels."

Adalyn put her hand on his shoulder, turned him so that he was face to face with her, and took him by the hand, "That's the you that won my heart. That's the selfless person who gives without even an inkling of want for a reward."

She smiled as she continued, "But I want to hear from the selfish you, the one that deserves to be heard for once. Tell me what you want of me Giovanni. Put personal honor aside and tell me what would make you happy. You saved my life by giving up yours so you have more than earned the right to ask this of me."

She pressed her body against his before speaking again, "Giovanni I... if you ask me to endure here with you, I will do it gladly and without hesitation. All you have to do is ask. Do you want me to stay here and live out a mortal life with you or do you really want me to return to the Kingdom? Tell me truthfully, what is in your heart."

Giovanni quivered as he sucked in one last deep breath, he quietly thanked God she could not see the tears in his eyes, "It is for the best."

"Very well," She said in an angry and hurt tone, "If that is what you desire, I will return to the Celestial realm when my task is complete."

He nodded, but neither one said another word.

**

Another hour went by, but the two did not say anything to each other as they went about tending to the ship. Nicolas was keeping his eyes on the coast, searching for the city. When it finally came into view, Nicolas called out, "There it is! I see the port near where I've been living."

Giovanni nodded, "Then that is where we are going. Let's head in to the same dock we tied up at last time. They don't seem to care about who docks there as long as they get paid."

Nicolas piloted the ship up to the dock as Adalyn went below deck to get herself into her disguise. The moment that the ship was close enough, they tied up the sail. Giovanni threw mooring lines over the side and then lowered the gangway. The two of them ran down the ramp, and quickly tied the ship to the post.

Giovanni stopped for a moment when he saw a small stain of blood still resting on the wood of the dock. It pulled at his heart and he wondered where the body had been taken. His moment was interrupted as the dock master came over to collect his fee.

The dock master recognized him and smiled, "Hello again sir, may I assume you aren't here right now?"

Giovanni smiled, "Hello again. You're correct, we're not. You did a good job on my ship last time. Here are six zecchinos, I want this ship cleaned and repaired with only the best you can get."

The dock master nodded. "Thank you very much my good man, it shall be done."

Adalyn appeared from the cabin as the dock master turned and left. Her wings were sufficiently hidden. She joined the group and stood next to Nicolas, on the side opposite of Giovanni as they headed for the town.

As they stepped off of the pier onto solid ground, three guards passed by them. The two groups exchanged glances, but neither said a word. They continued walking as another man passed in front of them. This man was hooded so that they could not see his face.

Giovanni got a bad feeling and beckoned everyone quietly to pick up their pace, but it was too late. Before they had a chance to react, the man pulled his cloak back, revealing the armor of a Papal knight. Behind them, they could hear a sword unsheathed and the hiss of a wick on an arquebus.

The group stopped in its tracks. Giovanni realized quickly that they had walked into a trap. *Shit... now what?*

As the man's cloak fell away, the group realized that they were standing in front of the commander of the Papal Knights, Captain Federico. The captain smiled, "You three are not easy to find. We've been chasing you for weeks, from here to Crete. Do you know how much stress you've caused his holiness?"

When they didn't respond, Federico smiled, "You should know that the Pope has ordered your arrest. You are to be brought before him. I would most likely guess that you will be declared heretics, and once you have been tried, he will most likely have all of you hanged, drawn, and quartered. I personally find such displays distasteful, but I may make an exception for you three."

He then noticed that they were missing one man, "There were four of you. Where is the other man?"

Divinity

Adalyn lowered her eyes, "Cyrillus didn't make it back. He died protecting me."

"I see…" Federico quickly crossed himself in reverence. "God rest his soul. The Pope demanded all four of you be brought in, but I'm sure he'll settle for three."

"Please sir." Adalyn spoke. "Hear us out. There is something going on you don't know about."

The knight thought for a moment. To the group, he looked like he was deep in thought, suspicious about something, "I have traveled long and hard to solve the riddle surrounding you Adalyn. What is it you think I don't know?"

She explained, "The Pope isn't acting alone here, he is being used… he has been blinded by his lust for power and doesn't even see it."

"That is enough!" Federico sneered. "I will hear no more of this heresy!"

Federico unsheathed his sword and pointed it right at Adalyn's throat. Adalyn remembered a similar scene from weeks earlier when another sword had been pointed at her in the same manner. It filled her with a sense of dread.

Suddenly, she realized who she was talking to, "I know you, I recognize your voice. You showed me kindness when you stopped the Pope from striking me even though doing so may have resulted in your own doom. You are not a bad man and I can sense that you will not harm us."

Federico looked deeply conflicted, "You assume too much. Please, drop your weapons."

Adalyn nodded, "Giovanni, Nicolas, do as he says trust me, we will not come to harm here."

The two of them hesitantly did as they were told. Captain Federico nodded and turned to his guards, "I will tend to this group of heretics personally. I've chased them across the sea for weeks. It will be my honor to bring them before his Eminence."

The guards looked at each other confused by their orders. They turned back to question the captain when they saw a stern look on his face. He glared at the three of them, "I am not a patient man. Follow my orders and do not make me repeat myself."

The three guards obediently saluted and quickly marched away single file. Federico sighed and lowered his sword, "Damn those temple guards, I say. Not a hint of honor or discipline about them. It is little wonder that you were able to escape Rome so easily."

Giovanni narrowed his eyes, "You have no intention of turning us over to the Pope, do you?"

Federico shook his head, "I am a knight, which means most people think I am little more than a mindless grunt. Well the Pope may not know it, but my knights often know certain happenings even before he does. Do you really think that I am so blind that I cannot see when things are amiss? I have served the Church and the Pope without question or hesitation for long enough to notice such things. Lately though, the Pope's orders have been questionable to say the least. Some of his actions have been downright hypocritical. If any king would have ordered us to do some of the things he has, that king would be excommunicated."

Adalyn stepped forward, "The Pope is being manipulated by Michael, one of my comrades."

Federico's face turned to shock, "Michael, as in the Archangel Michael? The leader of God's armies and…"

She nodded, "He is the Most High's steward during his slumber, but Michael's mind has turned to madness. Greed and power are all he cares about now."

"My God…" He gasped. "Can this be true? Michael is evil? I myself have prayed for his guidance. I knew that the pope was receiving help from the beyond, but I did not know it was coming from such a high-ranking individual. This is hard to believe."

"Believe it." Giovanni said harshly. "I've seen it myself. He cut down one of his fellow angels and tried to kill Adalyn. We need to stop him."

Federico shook his head, "This is unreal. I admit I'm having a hard time coming to terms with this story. Still, it would explain a lot, and I do have another angel in flesh and blood right here in front of me. The facts are hard to dispute, I will give you that."

He turned and looked in the direction of the Basilica, and then back at them, "What is your plan of action?"

"We need to get back into Rome," Adalyn said urgently, "Once in there, I will face Michael. If I can bring him down, the Pope will not be able to reach his goals, and hopefully the wars will begin to decrease."

"This is your plan?" Federico replied in shock, "Get into Rome and have a crippled angel face off against the might of the warrior archangel? This is foolishness."

"You have to trust me!" Adalyn pleaded. "I have to face him. I am the only one who can. I know this may seem like a long shot, but we don't have any other choice."

Federico fell silent. He didn't know what to think or do. Would it be easier to just take them to the Pope and be done with it?

Adalyn sensed his uneasiness, "Please…"

Her voice made up his mind, "I will make sure no Papal knight stops you, but I do not have command of Roman guards."

Nicolas smiled, "Leave them to me, I will go speak with the elders, we will come up with something to draw them away, don't worry about that."

Giovanni rolled his eyes, "No more powder bombs…"

"No," Nicolas chuckled, "This will be far blunter. Don't worry; we'll take care of everything, you have my word."

He turned to Captain Federico, "I will take my leave now, with your permission of course."

Federico nodded, "Go."

Nicolas nodded and turned to his friends, "I'll see you both later, you best not get yourselves killed. Do you hear me?"

Giovanni nodded, "And you as well, my friend."

Nicolas disappeared into the town. Federico looked back at Giovanni and Adalyn, "I will issue the orders to my men. They will move back in to Rome and will not stop you, so you shouldn't meet any resistance. Oh my honor, none of my men will harass you."

The two began to walk past him, but he spoke, "One last thing."

"What is it?" Adalyn asked.

"The Pope," Federico sighed, "he is the leader of the Church, and I am sworn to protect and serve him. In exchange for my help, I ask only that he not be harmed."

Giovanni narrowed his eyes, "After everything he has done?"

Adalyn nodded, "Giovanni, it's a reasonable request. Once Michael is defeated, his push to wage this war will vanish. He's just a willing puppet in this mess. We do not need to harm him."

Giovanni sighed, "I guess I have no choice. Very well, on my honor, the Pope will not be harmed as long as he stays out of the way."

"Very well." Federico nodded. "I accept your word... I'll go give the orders. By the way, take the horses tied up right at the western road. They will get you to Rome quicker than your feet will."

He was about run off when one last thought occurred to him, "Oh and this meeting never happened."

Without another word, the knight ran on ahead of them. He knew time was of the essence if they were to succeed. His mind still had many questions, but he decided he'd ask them later if they all survived.

Adalyn and Giovanni prepared their swords for the battle ahead. Giovanni removed the decaying snake's head from the sack and squeezed the fangs. They smeared the last bit of venom from the Eden Serpent on their blade and then cast the head into the sea. As before, the blades turned green momentarily as the venom coated the steel.

Giovanni looked over his sword, "This is the final showdown, are you ready for this?"

Adalyn smiled, "Don't worry about my safety, my strength has returned and Azrael taught me how to fight without the use of my eyes. He said in the end, the eyes were the most likely sense to trick you and that trusting in them was foolish."

Giovanni nodded, "It sounds like Azrael was a wise man."

"He was…" Adalyn replied. "He was the best of us. Even Michael had trouble beating him in sparring matches, and Michael is an archangel. I'm hoping that I will have a few surprises in store for him."

II

The Pope watched the city from his window in the Basilica of Santa Maria Maggiore. Rome was a peaceful city that day. They had finally cleaned up the mess that the revolutionaries had made on the outskirts. He considered it a very meaningful accomplishment, even though it had cost the Pope the ability to kill the angel from Venice that had caused him so much trouble.

One of the guards knocked on the large door to his chambers, breaking his concentration. The Pope sighed and stood up, "You may enter."

The guard rushed in out of breath, "Forgive me Eminence…"

The Pope walked over to the young man and placed a hand on his shoulder, "Take a moment and catch your breath."

The young man nodded as he breathed heavily. When his lungs finally stopped aching, he was able to speak, "Thank you Eminence, I come to report that there is a sizeable force coming together near Ostia. They are heading here."

The Pope's eyes widened, "What? How can that be?"

"I don't know sir," the nervous man said, "but they are coming! It appears that they have been hiding in many of the buildings in Ostia."

The Pope became frantic, "Where is Captain Federico? Have the Papal knights stand ready to defend Rome!"

The guard nodded, "I'll find him and give him your orders, Eminence."

As the young man left the room, a shadow appeared behind the Pope. He could sense it there, "I trust this army is being led by your enemies?"

The shadow took Michael's form, "No, but they approach as well. I sense that they are here for me. Very bold Adalyn…"

"Then you will go out to meet them." The Pope ordered. "This is your responsibility, I expect you to deal with it. We just finished repairing the damage from the last incursion. I don't want things getting messy around here again."

Michael turned and pointed his sword at the Pope's chest, "Don't you dare try to order me around. I could set your entire precious city ablaze with a single thought and make you watch. You are nothing but a tool to me, never forget that."

The Pope backed away slowly and nodded, "I am not giving you orders. I simply expect you to hold up your end of the bargain. I have done everything you asked."

"Just remember that next time you presume to give me orders." Michael hissed. "I will deal with Adalyn, but the army coming this way is your problem. You can deal with them as you see fit."

With that, Michael vanished. The Pope stood looking out the window, "What has yet to come?"

**

Giovanni and Adalyn made their way to Rome. To their relief, no guards were in view as they approached the outskirts. The two proceeded into the courtyard of the Basilica of Santa Maria Maggiore without incident. They noticed that the entire area was deserted.

At that moment, the silence was broken with the sound of every open door and window in Rome slamming shut. Adalyn turned to see the gates of the Basilica slam closed as well. It was obvious that someone knew that they were there.

Giovanni kept his sword in front of him as he surveyed the area. He spoke softly to Adalyn as he looked around, "It's too quiet here... This could be a trap."

Adalyn shook her head and stepped away from Giovanni, "Enough of this." She said before turning towards the basilica and shouting, "Michael!"

Her yelling was met with complete silence. She became angry and called again in a much more aggressive tone, "Michael!"

Adalyn focused her mind and tried to listen to the air around her. In her mind, she heard a distant sound approaching. She realized quickly that the sound was wings flapping.

Adalyn nodded, "Michael, it's about time."

Suddenly a dark figure appeared and charged at them. Adalyn screamed, "Giovanni, watch out!"

She tackled Giovanni to knock him out of the way. The dark figure missed its target, shot around to the other side of the courtyard. It then darted back and stopped less than a hundred feet from them.

The dark smog around the entity began to dissipate as it took human form. Michael appeared in its place. He was down on one knee with an angel's sword of flame in his hand, ready to strike.

Michael rose and spread his wings, "You must be her protector, Giovanni is it? I am honored to finally meet you. You should know that you have caused me much trouble. More than I ever thought possible from a human."

Giovanni pointed his sword at the angel, "I will not allow you to cause any more harm, not to Adalyn or the rest of my world!"

Michael scoffed, "So the fisherman is now a warrior for God? You have truly come far, boy. It is amazing that you've managed to stay alive this long. Who knows what

you might have accomplished had you not crossed my path."

Adalyn turned in the direction of the voices, "Michael, your fight is with me. It's always been with me. Leave him alone."

Michael turned away from Giovanni and faced Adalyn, "You are quite correct. Although I must admit when I heard you were going to the Netherworld, I never thought I would see you again. It is an incredible accomplishment for you to have come this far."

He nodded as he looked her over, "You've proven more resourceful then I had originally believed and you know, since Azrael is gone, you could join me and become my right hand. You were his best pupil. I think you would make a fine replacement, and with a word from me, I could get your expulsion overturned."

Michael placed a tender hand on her cheek, "Think of it, once you've returned, you could be my voice on the inside. Together, we could free our people from a life of servitude."

"What?" Adalyn demanded in a shocked tone as she slapped his hand away and stepped back.

"Think of it," Michael continued, "angels like you and I are giants amongst these pitiful creatures, yet we're the ones living the life of the servant. Lucifer wants to change that and allow us to use our gifts. What do you say?"

She scoffed at his offer, "Never, you betrayed the Most High, you sentenced me to exile here, and you killed Azrael. Your plans would lay ruin to the Celestial World. It does not matter what happens to me now, but you will answer for your sins."

"And who are you that would judge me?" Michael said, clenching his jaw, "Is that not a job restricted to the Most High?"

"Perhaps," She nodded, "but I will have to do."

He laughed, "So brash, very well!"

Michael's sword burned brighter than ever before. He stood for a second poised to strike, glaring at her, "Come on then, let us fight."

Michael smiled as he drove straight at her again. Dust kicked up in his wake, making him look like a shooting star. His speed was incredible.

Adalyn did a somersault over him with the aid of her wings. She quickly landed, whirled around, and slashed at her opponent. Her sword slammed against his with a loud hiss. Much to Michael's surprise, her sword did not break. Instead, the blade began to glow green. He stood there staring at it for a moment, "What cursed sword is this?"

Adalyn spoke through her teeth, "You underestimate me at every turn and it will be your downfall. Did you think me foolish enough to come into battle with a corporeal blade? This one has been cursed with the venom of the Eden Serpent."

Michael's grin turned to malice, "So you have fallen so far as to use black magic? At least now this will be interesting."

Giovanni came up behind Michael and attempted to stab him in the back, but Michael knew that the young fisherman was coming. The archangel reached behind him and clenched his fist, which stopped Giovanni in his tracks, "Fool, do you really think you can sneak up on me? I did not come here to swat at flies, be gone!"

Michael made a throwing gesture with his hand, Giovanni struggled against him, but it was no use. He went flying back against a nearby pylon. Giovanni's head struck the stone, and he hit the ground unconscious.

With Adalyn's help neutralized, Michael turned his attention back to his opponent, but she was gone. He paused for a second, smiled, and looked up to see her plunging down toward him. He quickly shot back with a quick flap of

his wings, "You do realize that this is a futile effort. I taught Azrael everything he taught you, including blind combat."

"Yes, I know that," she admitted, "but I believe you may yet underestimate me again."

He nodded and laughed, "Arrogant child, you do not stand a chance of winning here. Once I have finished with you, I shall await our new master, Lucifer. He has enough power to help me defeat the Most High! Then we shall build a new kingdom, one where angels rule on high in paradise and these flawed creatures serve us as they should. It is a shame that you will not be around to see it."

"That will never happen." She said proudly. "He is mortal now, trapped in hell."

Michael's smugness turned to a look of shock, "What?"

She smiled, "I have dealt with him, and you can expect no support from the Netherworld."

Michael did not believe what he was hearing. He closed his eyes briefly and reached out with his mind. A shocked look came over his face as his eyes reopened, "You speak the truth! Somehow, you defeated my master! Do you realize what you have done?"

"Yes I do." She replied, just slightly beaming. "I've halted your madness. Your plans would have brought everything, including you to an end."

Michael shook his head, "No…"

"You stand alone Michael." Adalyn said almost sympathetically. "Surrender while you can. I'm sure the Choirs will take your past deeds into account."

He scoffed at her and released an angry sigh, "You fool. This changes nothing! I will still lay waste to the Most High's beloved."

He swung his sword around and pointed it at her, "And I will send you to Hell to greet them!"

She spread her wings and rose up off the ground, "You'll die before you ever get the chance!"

Michael ran at her, jumped into the air, and spread his wings. He flew towards her, increasing speed as he did. As he approached, Adalyn twirled her sword in a figure eight pattern and waited.

Once Michael was close enough, she spun around, pulling herself off to the side. As Michael passed by her side, she brought her sword around. The ploy worked, and her sword connected with Michael's cheek. It was a move he didn't know that Azrael had taught her.

He fell to the ground, shocked by the pain such a small wound had caused, "What is happening... this scratch feels so strange. What have you done?"

Adalyn landed nearby, "It is over Michael. You are mortal now."

His eyes widened, "What?"

"Yes." She nodded and showed him the sword, "Have you forgotten? The venom of the Serpent of Eden is a very dangerous tool. The Most High knew what had to be done with his most beloved after eating from the Tree of Knowledge. The very same substance that corrupted the apple Eve ate now corrupts your existence. You are being stripped of your immortality just as I was when you exiled me!"

Michael's body began to tingle. He could feel his energy begin to drain. Suddenly, in front of him, emanating from his chest was a yellow sphere. It grew bigger and bigger until it finally exploded right before his eyes. He screamed out, realizing what had happened, "No!"

She pointed her sword at him, "Surrender, you can no longer return to the Celestial World anymore then I can!"

Michael looked down at the ground and then at his hands, "Maybe not..."

Divinity

His hands began to ball into fists, "But at least I can send you to Hell!"

With that, Michael ran at her screaming. He viciously began swinging at Adalyn over and over. She was completely on the defensive and just barely able to fend him off as the vicious assaults continued.

Giovanni regained consciousness when he felt an unusual pulsing under his tunic. He reached into his shirt and grabbed a small piece of metal that had been hidden there. It was Azrael's sword.

As Giovanni raised it to his face, the blade pulsed even faster and blade began to glow yellow. Giovanni looked out at his love trying desperately to hold on. Her blade connected with Michael's again, but this time, Michael knocked it from her hand, leaving her defenseless.

I hope this works... Giovanni thought as he drew his arm back and threw the pulsing blade into the air, "Adalyn, catch!"

She heard the wind breaking around the object flying towards her and quickly reached out her hand to grab it. When the hilt touched her hand, she realized what it was. Instantly, the sword illuminated in a burst of flame. She held it up in front of her and felt the heat from the blade on her face, "Azrael... thank you."

Seeing his friend's old blade, Michael stopped in his tracks, "How is it that you can now wield that sword?"

Adalyn smiled, "Azrael has intervened."

"So I'm facing both of you now, is that it?" Michael scoffed as he resumed his attack charge. "So be it!"

Adalyn twirled around, now fighting with an immortal blade. She was able to beat back his attacks with this new, more powerful blade. Michael's strikes were relentless, but she successfully held him off for a short time.

After a few minutes, Michael tackled her and drew a small knife. Even in mortal form, he was extremely agile.

Divinity

He slammed her into the ground and pinned her down smiling, "You die now!"

As he was about to plunge the knife into her throat, he heard the sound of metal cutting behind him. A sharp pain entered his side, causing him to stop in his tracks. He dropped the blade and looked to see what had happened.

Giovanni was standing behind Michael with his sword half submerged into the archangel's hip, "That's enough from you!"

Michael hissed, "You should have killed me."

"I would have," Giovanni replied, "but I didn't want to risk hitting Adalyn."

Michael shook his head, "And that concern is your most fatal flaw."

Adalyn was restrained, but she was still able to turn her wrist just enough so that she could ignite the sword into his side as he tackled her. It was a risky move, but she was able to angle her sword enough to stab him between the chest and back plates of his armor. She pushed the sword deeper into his side, "Go to hell Michael, Lucifer is waiting for you!"

Michael began to laugh hysterically as he felt his body give out. The laughing continued as his body dissolved into dust. His eyes became glassy and he watched the world turn black.

With his last ounce of strength, Michael reached up towards the heavens, "Father…"

His legs crumbled as he fell to the ground and his body turned completely to dust. Giovanni breathed deeply as he looked over at Adalyn. She turned to him and reached out her hand. Slowly, he moved to her side, took it, and held on tight.

Adalyn was exhausted as she held up Azrael's blade. She looked at it and smiled as it began to lose its luster, "Thank you…"

Divinity

The blade pulsed one more time and crumbled in her hand. Its job was done and its powers were exhausted. She watched it turn to dust just as Michael had when he died.

III

Giovanni helped Adalyn get up off the ground and held her in his arms. The two were about to kiss, but stopped inches away. Giovanni looked down, "Are you okay?"

Adalyn nodded, "Yes, it is done."

Her lips twisted. She couldn't hold it back anymore. There was something she'd wanted to tell him and now seemed like the perfect time, "Giovanni I lov..."

The sound of gates moving again interrupted her. Giovanni watched in horror as a large band of men entered the courtyard. They were heavily armed with stolen arquebuses and swords, but they weren't soldiers. They were more like an angry mob of farmers, fisherman, and townspeople. The massive army roared as they poured into the city and headed for the basilica.

Adalyn tugged on Giovanni's shoulder, "What is it, what's going on?"

"Lutheran Revolutionaries." Giovanni said softly. "I've never seen this many of them before. It looks like Nicolas kept his word; they are moving to take the basilica."

Adalyn gasped, "No Giovanni, they mustn't take down the Church! That will throw the world into chaos!"

Giovanni watched them enter, "With all the pain it's has caused, I don't see how that is possible. Perhaps it would be best to allow these people to take over and see what happens."

She grabbed Giovanni's shoulder, "It's not that simple. The Papacy, with all its flaws, is able to keep countries from chaos and through religious council has prevented them from bringing chaos on one another."

Giovanni looked at her sternly, "Yeah they do it by causing strife themselves!"

Divinity

"Perhaps, but they also create balance," Adalyn replied, "Losing that balance would tear the world apart. They have their hands in everything, so if the Church falls, the whole world will be thrown into another dark age and millions will be killed! This is what Lucifer wants! Like it or not, the only way to bring peace to the land is to keep Rome standing!"

Across the way, Captain Federico had been watching the fight and rejoiced when Michael fell, but his celebration was short-lived as the revolutionaries entered the courtyard, "My God, they've betrayed us! That Nicolas is leading an army against us!"

Federico ran out on to the court yard blowing a signal horn, "To arms, everyone, to arms!"

A large brigade of guards and knights alike emerged and lined up with guns and swords poised to strike. Federico had kept his word, but believed in being ready for anything. It was a philosophy that he thought might now save Rome.

The Pope also appeared on the scene and stood next to Federico, "Don't forget your oath, Captain. You must defend Rome and the Papacy with your life. These peasants must not drive us out."

Captain Federico gave the Pope an annoyed look, "You needn't remind me of my duties, eminence. I am well aware of the oath I took and you should not be out here."

Adalyn could not stand by and allow this to happen. She had felt too much suffering, too much pain, and had simply had enough. Without a second thought, she jumped from Giovanni's arms and ran out in front of the two armies as they readied for attack. She put her hands out going both ways and spread her wings as far as she could, "No, everyone stop! Please listen to me!"

Giovanni ran after her and tried to pull her back, but Adalyn would not budge. She was going to stand there until they either listened, or she was killed in the crossfire.

Giovanni, seeing no way out of this, stood with her. He would protect her any way he could.

Nicolas stood at the head of his ragtag army. He had been asked to lead the followers of Luther to victory being one of the few members who had previously entered the basilica under secret and lived to tell about it. He saw Adalyn trying to get everyone to listen with no luck. He thought about his next move for a second and shook his head. *If I don't do something, she's going to get herself killed!*

Nicolas stepped out in front of the men and extended his sword to the side, "Everyone, stop here… no one attacks until either I say so or they make a move!"

One of the other revolutionaries standing with Nicolas objected, "Sir, we outnumber them, delaying now will give them time to call reinforcements. If they bring in more men, we will lose our chance to take Rome! Forget those two fools, we should attack now and deal a crippling blow!"

Nicolas watched Adalyn as she refused to move. He then turned back to the revolutionary, "You would kill the servant of God in the process? Are you willing to risk your immortal soul and that of our people just to take the city?"

The man thought for a moment, but did not respond. He had not thought of that. Nicolas nodded and continued, "I travelled the world with them. It is because of their efforts that we are able to stand here today. If anyone has earned my loyalty and the right to be heard, it's them. Stand down for now. If any of you attempts to make a move, I promise it will be your last."

The revolutionaries fell silent, knowing Nicolas' reputation. Captain Federico saw Nicolas halt his advance. The Pope had seen it too, "That infernal angel did us a great service, now is your chance. They have lowered their swords. Attack Captain, kill them all!"

Adalyn turned to him, "Federico, please…"

The captain looked at the Pope, and then over at Nicolas who was holding his men back. Federico shook his head, "My oath is to protect, and I do not see any danger here."

He raised his sword in the air, turned it upside down and sheathed the blade, "All knights, stand down!"

"Are you insane?" The Pope protested, "Now is your chance!"

Federico was beginning to get very annoyed and signaled two of his guards, "Men, a battlefield is not the place for the Pope. Take him to safety."

The two soldiers did as they were ordered. Despite the Pope's protests, the two guards secured the Pope and took him safely out of the way. They brought him inside the basilica and closed the door.

Adalyn breathed a sigh of relief, "Thank you!"

She then turned back to the revolutionaries, "Everyone, for the sake of your own salvation, you must stop. Can you not see that this is wrong? This is exactly what the forces of evil want. You are playing into their hands! Who are any of you to judge what is right and wrong? Or how someone else should practice their faith? Can you not understand that all you need to do is believe? In the end, all that really matters is how you lived your lives."

She turned to the Papal army, "The Church you follow has much to answer for. Their leaders have corrupted its purpose, sending many non-believers and those whose views conflict with that of the Church to their deaths. They teach that people can buy their way into the Kingdom with pardons, and try to keep the poor masses ignorant of true knowledge. Humanity can never advance as long as this type of barbarism continues."

A few of the revolutionaries cheered at her words. When Adalyn heard it, she turned to them with a stern expression on her face. The icy expression quickly silenced their cheers.

She stood facing the group of revolutionaries for a moment, "Yours has no less blood on their hands. You believe that violence is the only way to solve your problems. How many of these houses of God have you desecrated? How many have you killed in favor of your beliefs? Do you believe that you are truly any better, or that your methods are admired in any way? How many have you killed in the name of God and what right do you claim to do such a thing? Has he asked you to do so? Has he physically appeared and asked you to kill innocent people?"

Many of them lowered their heads as she spoke, "Your leaders on both sides would have you believe that the only way to get into the Kingdom of Heaven is by the Church's good graces, or adhering to a strict set of rules that in the end eliminate all but a very small number. The Kingdom of the Most High is not within these walls, so you have no reason to invade it. Nor is it within the walls of the small chambers where you worship in secret. Anyone who tells you otherwise, speaks of something they do not know!"

Inside the basilica, Pope Leo X heard those words and took a step back. He knew what kind of damage these words could do to him and his Church. He could not sit by and listen to such heresy. With a sense of urgency, he quickly disappeared from view into one of the back rooms.

Adalyn continued to speak with passion as the tears welled up in her eyes, "Believe me... the Kingdom of Heaven is not within any single building. It is not a tangible place you can ever go in your lifetime."

She walked over to one of the knights and placed her hand on his chest. He looked at her as she smiled, "It is within you... all of you."

She continued talking as she walked back to the center of the line, "And it is outside of you and all around you! It is in the air that you breathe and the ground that you walk upon. All of the Most High's creation is a part of his kingdom, never doubt that. If you do this, if you continue to fight, all you do is weaken the Most High. Thus, you will be giving power to those who would abuse it. It matters not whether you are a believer or not, a king or a peasant, a Church-goer or a follower of Luther, when you hurt, he hurts, and when you die, he grieves for you. It does not matter what or who you are. Please lay down your swords and end this for the sake of all you hold dear, I beg of you. We must…"

She was about to continue when a sharp object pierced her chest from behind. It was a spear that had been thrown by the Pope. He had emerged from the basilica before any of his men could react, "No! Fallen one, you will not bring down my Church!"

Blood poured out both sides of the wound. Giovanni saw it and screamed, "No… Adalyn!"

She fell to her knees and her mouth dropped wide open as though to scream. Her arms extended to either side as she tried to balance herself. The pain shot through her body as though carried in the remaining blood that pumped through her.

Giovanni's heart was in his throat as he scrambled to her side, "No!"

Suddenly the blindfold, which had been protecting Adalyn's eyes, came undone and blew away in the breeze. She saw the bright blue sky and the warm sun as though it were her first time. Instead of the red and black eyes that Giovanni had first seen, her eyes were a beautiful sky blue that looked almost like they had thundering clouds running through them.

Everyone nearby would have sworn that her eyes were visibly glowing, even in the daylight. It was the most

beautiful thing Giovanni had ever seen. He caught her as she began to fall.

Nicolas and Federico ran over from their respective forces to help. Federico cut the spear so she could lie on her back. Giovanni rested her comfortably in his lap as he tried his best to keep her alive, "Adalyn no, please God, no… Adalyn… Adalyn!"

Giovanni shook her gently, trying to get her to respond. He succeeded in bringing her around for a brief moment. Her eyes were still as blue as the sky, but the light was fading fast.

Adalyn looked up at him with amazement, "Giovanni… I can see you."

She put her hand to his cheek, her eyes were pleased by what she had been waiting to see, "I recognize your face. It still feels familiar to me… so handsome…"I am glad that I was given the chance to see it before the end."

He smiled, "Meeting you was the best thing that ever happened to me. I would not trade it for anything. You are the glimmer of light in a room of shadows."

"I will truly miss you…" She said softly as the blood began to drip from the corner of her mouth.

"No, no you won't!" He said shaking frantically, "You are going to be okay. We'll get a healer over here. You… you just need to hold on!"

Adalyn winced in pain, "I want you to know, had I gone back... I would have put in to be your guardian… that way… I'd never leave you."

Giovanni nodded, "I know, I know, you still can!"

She shook her head, "No, Giovanni. A power greater than anything you could conjure calls to me…"

He turned to Federico, "Don't you have a healer in your group?"

The knight looked at her wounds and shook his head, "She's bleeding internally from her heart. There's too much damage, no healer can save her now."

"No." Giovanni said in desperation as he turned back to her as tears fell from his eyes. "This isn't right, I'm supposed to protect you and keep you safe, remember? Tell me what I have to do to keep you in this world... please!"

Adalyn smiled one more time, "Giovanni... you spared me torture and helped me save everything I love. I can rest easy now. Do you remember... not long ago you told me that you loved me, and I didn't say anything?"

Giovanni nodded as she continued, "I wanted to, but I was afraid something like this might happen and didn't want you to feel pain.... I see now, too late... it was so foolish. I have known for a while now that I love you... and before I join Azrael in the Well of Souls, I wanted you to know that... I love y..."

Adalyn's body fell limp as she released her final breath. Federico looked away and signed the cross. Nicolas' eyes welled up with tears while Giovanni pressed her closed, "No..."

Giovanni rested his head in her chest, but the absence of a heartbeat only made things worse, "Why... I tried so hard... It should have been me. Damn it... why couldn't it be me..."

Taking in a deep breath, Giovanni threw his head back and screamed, "Why?"

Nicolas wiped his eyes, stood up, and looked at Captain Federico. The captain returned his gaze and the two of them returned to their troops, neither one's eyes left the other. Nicolas stood in front of his men, removed the wick from his gun, dropped it on the ground, and knelt behind it. Federico nodded, unsheathed his sword, and drove it into the ground. He returned Nicolas' gesture and knelt behind the sword. Men on both sides watched their leaders and followed their actions.

Pope Leo X stood by looking on in shock at what was happening. He turned to Federico, "What are you doing? Now is your chance, attack them! Kill them all before they can destroy us!"

Federico did not look up, "Be silent, neither I, nor my men will take any further orders from the likes of you!"

The Pope saw the eyes of many people in the courtyard staring at him. He took a step back, nervously, "Such insolence… heretics, all of you! You will never reach the Kingdom of Heaven. I will see to it you are all excommunicated!"

Giovanni heard his voice, gently laid Adalyn's head on the ground, and grabbed a nearby sword. He stood up, with a look of sheer hatred on his face, "You depraved murderer! I'll kill you for this!"

He charged at the Pope, intent on killing him, but Federico stepped into his path and grabbed him before he could hit his mark, "Stop my friend, you mustn't kill him."

Giovanni fought to get free, but the battle-hardened knight was far stronger. Giovanni sneered, "Let me go you bastard! Why are you defending him?"

"Because Adalyn asked me to," he replied, "when she asked us to stop the killing, she meant all of it, even him."

The knight's words took the will to fight out of Giovanni's arms. Giovanni let out a deep sigh as the strength left his arms. He stopped struggling and returned to Adalyn's side as the Pope still bore the brunt of the angry stares.

The Pope slowly backed away from the crowd, "Captain… I suggest you dispose of that insolent peasant. Attempted murder is a capital crime."

Federico turned back to the Pope, fed up with his attitude, "Hear me now, Eminence. We will never take another order from you. However, I pledge on my life to you that my knights will keep you safe from harm until the day you die, but that comes with one condition."

"And what is that," The Pope asked.

"That Giovanni the fisherman be pardoned from all crimes against the Church, now and forever." He replied.

"Never," the Pope shouted, "I will not be strong armed this way!"

Federico shrugged, "Then good luck to you, Eminence. You should be just fine traveling without armed escort, right?"

Leo X contemplated Federico's words for a few moments before changing his mind, "Very well, the Church hath granted Giovanni clemency, now and forever. So it shall be entered at my earliest opportunity."

The Pope then slowly retreated back to his residence and locked the door behind him. Once he was alone, he dropped to his knees and prayed for protection. He didn't know whether his forces would hold off the revolutionaries or allow them to pass.

Giovanni remained at Adalyn's side, cradling her lifeless body as two spheres of light circled down from the heavens. They were slow and graceful and came to a stop on either side of Adalyn.

Giovanni grabbed her and tried to protect her body against them as they took the form of the two angels Giovanni had seen before in the Netherworld. The two stared at Giovanni for a moment before Ariel stepped forward, "Peace, my friend…"

Captain Federico's eyes widened as he looked at the Seraphs. Similar expressions came from the revolutionaries on the opposite side of the courtyard. Lt. Piangi came up next to Federico, "Have you ever seen the like?"

Federico shook his head, "N… no…"

Bright rays of sunlight illuminated their wings as they stepped forward. Ariel and Roselyn looked at their sister's body, but as they got closer, Giovanni pulled her away. He was unwilling to let them near her.

Ariel looked up at Giovanni with tears in her eyes and spoke, "Giovanni, you both have done well. The Most High has regained consciousness and he has been watching you. He saw your struggle with Michael. He heard Adalyn's passionate words and was moved by them. Your heroics have not gone unnoticed. You stood against all, even the Most High's own decree, and you emerged victorious."

Giovanni felt his face turn red and he began to yell, "You have been watching yet you did nothing to help and now she is dead! That is all you are good for, isn't it? You stand by and allow people to suffer while you live lavishly. How are you different than those who inhabit Rome? My only mission was to save her, the rest of the world could have burned for all I care. All I wanted was for her to be happy, but I failed and now all God can do is offer me congratulatory words? Your indifference is what killed her!"

Ariel stepped back with a hand over her mouth as Roselyn spoke up, "He grieves for you, but humanity will never grow if he constantly interferes in the lives of his people. I know Adalyn told you this. The toil of those who suffer, those who give and those who help will be rewarded in the end."

"It is not fair." Giovanni said in a low voice. "She has done nothing wrong, yet here she lays expelled, beaten, scarred, and murdered. Will you do nothing about this injustice?"

Roselyn fell silent for a moment. It was all Ariel needed to get her words in, "You are right, sir. It is not fair, and we bear plenty of the blame for it, but what is done is done. We can't undo the actions of another angel, right or wrong. However, the Most High asks you to give her body

to us, and I promise you, those responsible will pay for what they have done."

Giovanni cradled her one last time. He held on as though in some way, he could keep her alive. After a few painful moments, he hesitantly handed her body over to them, knowing that he'd never see her again. "Please, take care of her."

The two seraph angels nodded as they turned back into spheres of light. Roselyn spoke to him as they disappeared, "Don't worry, she is our sister. She will be well cared for, you have my word."

The angels merged together into one bright sphere as a beam of light shot down from the heavens. Everyone watched in awe at as the sphere disappeared and the light faded. Then, as quickly as they had appeared, they were gone again.

Giovanni stood alone in the courtyard. Realizing that he had nothing left, he collapsed in the dirt. Nicolas ran back over and got under his arm. Captain Federico did the same thing on his other side.

Nicolas turned to his men as he held Giovanni steady, "This battle is over, return to your homes."

Federico nodded and turned to his men, "All of you stand down, return to your posts."

As the two crowds began to clear, the newfound friends guided Giovanni out of Rome. It took some time, but they managed to get him back to Anselm's house where Padre Antonelli had led him during their first visit to Ostia. He said nothing during the entire trip.

Divinity

IV

Giovanni was placed on a sheep skin blanket, unwilling to move for days. He wouldn't respond to anyone or even eat. At times, he didn't even look like he was alive.

Eventually, Nicolas had to hold a sword to his throat just to get him to take down food before he became too weak. It pained him greatly to have to do it, but what other choice was there? Giovanni was going to wear away if he didn't eat.

After some time passed, Federico came by to visit. He stood outside the small house and knocked on the door with the hilt of his sword. Nicolas greeted him, "Hello Federico, it is good to see you again."

The Captain nodded, "And you as well sir, how is Giovanni?"

Nicolas shrugged, "We've gotten him to take food on his own now, which was not easy. He's also finally started to speak again, rather than just staring at the wall all day and night. His body has healed, but I fear his spirit may be permanently damaged."

Federico sighed, "It is truly cruel what he has been put through. To have gone to such great lengths and risked so much for the one he cared about, only to lose her when they were so close to victory."

"Agreed," Nicolas said solemnly, "but we have done all we can for him here. His wounds aren't anything a healer can attend to. I think he might be ready to stand on his own two feet. The only problem is that he has nowhere to go. His home was burned to the ground when all this started."

"I know." Federico replied. "I was there, and I gave that order, but you needn't worry about that. Arrangements have been made for him."

Nicolas looked towards Giovanni's room, "So you intend to take him back to Venice then?"

Divinity

Federico nodded, "Yes, on my orders, his old ship has been given a total overhaul. We'll take him back on that."

"We?" Nicolas asked.

"Yes, I'll be taking him personally." Federico replied. "In addition, his ship will be crewed by three of our best sailors."

"I wish I could come with you as well." Nicolas said sadly. "Unfortunately there has been another upheaval."

"Another rogue Lutheran sect?" Federico asked. "Your envoys appear to have failed this time."

Nicolas shrugged, "We're doing what we can. It's gotten easier since the Papal army has backed down, but the Church still has agents everywhere… it is a shame. Adalyn worked so hard to get this far. Yet her words seem to have fallen on deaf ears."

"She did not fail." Federico insisted. "She opened both our eyes, saved Rome, and exposed the leaders as the corrupt fools they are."

"I suppose." He agreed. "I just wish it had a greater impact, perhaps if she lived, these rabble rousers would have thought twice about stirring up more trouble."

"They may still realize their error," Federico replied, "Only time will tell."

Nicolas nodded and led him into the next room where Giovanni lay. He looked up as they entered the room, "Captain Federico…"

He smiled, "Hello Giovanni, how are you today?"

Giovanni shrugged, "As good as one would expect."

"That's good," He responded, "Because you've got a long trip ahead of you."

Giovanni sat up, "Where am I going?"

Nicolas chimed in, "You need to return to Venice. It's time you got your life back up and running."

Giovanni could not believe what he was hearing, "And live where? The Church burned my home to the ground."

Divinity

"I know." Federico said sadly. "I apologize for that, but we're taking care of it. We've made arrangements for you."

"Have you now?" Giovanni asked.

Nicolas agreed, "It's for the best Giovanni, we've done what we can for you here, but we all have matters to attend to. I myself am leaving for eastern France. There is another uprising there that the Church has been powerless to stop. Many will die if the revolt is allowed to go forward."

"Fine." Giovanni no longer cared about the cause or what happened to him. "When do we leave?"

Nicolas looked at Federico, who responded, "As soon as you are ready. I will be travelling with you along with a few of my knights. You can rest up and save your strength. We'll take care of the sailing."

Giovanni moved his legs and struggled to stand. It took him a moment to regain his balance, but he was able to hold himself up, "Okay, let's go."

Nicolas' eyes narrowed, "What, now?"

Giovanni nodded, "Yes, now, I won't be a burden on anyone any longer."

Nicolas frowned, "Giovanni that is not what I meant! If you wish to stay here longer, you are certainly welcome to. Considering everything that you've been through, I'd prefer it."

Giovanni shook his head, "No, I just want to get out of here."

"Okay, Giovanni," Federico shrugged, "as you wish, let's go."

Giovanni bid farewell to Nicolas and the others who had taken care of him as they went their separate ways. Nicolas smiled, "Farewell my friend. We'll see each other again."

"As you say." Giovanni replied.

Federico walked Giovanni to the dock and got him to his ship. As they approached the dock, Giovanni could not believe what had been done to his family's fishing vessel. It had been painted the colors of the Papal banner, lead plated windows had been installed in the aft cabin, the main mast had been rigged with a headsail and the main lateen had been replaced with a square rigged yardarm and sail. The aft sail had also been replaced with a brand new one, although it had not been altered at all.

The tiller had been replaced and new laps had been installed. He sighed; it no longer looked anything like the boat that he had fished on since he was a boy. It had definitely been turned into a luxury yacht.

Federico left his side for a brief moment and turned to the three men onboard, "Are we ready?"

The three men saluted, "Yes sir."

Federico nodded, "Okay then, let's get this ship moving. I'd love to be underway before nightfall."

The crew quickly pulled the sails down and released the mooring lines as Giovanni climbed onboard. Slowly, the ship began to move away from the dock as the sailors grabbed planks and pushed at the docks. The ship groaned under the pressure as it began to move.

Giovanni noticed this time that it didn't lurch forward and the mast wasn't making loud creaking noises. Instead, it glided gracefully over the water. The ship had brand new, bright red sails hanging from a yardarm, as well as new finish on the deck. The ship looked brand new.

Giovanni ignored everything that was going on around him and retreated down to his cabin. Without a second thought about the new fire pit or amenities that had been added to the cabin, Giovanni lay down on the cot. He slowly passed into a dreamless sleep.

**

Divinity

The weeklong voyage did not go by quickly for the young fisherman, but nothing really did for him anymore. He no longer saw the world in its splendor. The color had faded to shades of gray and had all but blurred to him. He spent much of his time in the cabin, not wanting to talk to anyone.

It was quite rare for any of the knights to see Giovanni on deck at all. However, four days into the trip, he finally came up on deck just to stand near the rail and watch the coastline go by. Federico walked over and stood next to him, "Rest well?"

Giovanni looked down into the water, "I don't sleep at all anymore. Every time I close my eyes, I see her in her last moment as the spear pierced her heart."

"I know," Federico said softly, "I've been in the heat of battle and seen people I consider close friends cut down like that. The dreams are really intense at first, but they do get easier to bear as time goes on."

"I can't get her out of my head." Giovanni cried out. "How am I supposed to go on living a normal life after everything that happened?"

Captain Federico shrugged, "That is not an easy question to answer, you saw more of the world in the span of a few weeks then most people do in a lifetime. That's not easy to walk away from."

"I saw more than that." He said softly. "I saw angels, I walked the paths of hell, I sailed with the boatman, and met Lucifer himself. Can any living person truly say they experienced all that?"

"I would guess not." Federico conceded. "I am truly envious of you Giovanni, to have travelled so far, faced unbelievable odds, and yet still come out victorious. You are as tough and brave as any knight I have ever commanded."

"No, I was not victorious." Giovanni said angrily. "My family is dead, my friends are dead, and she is dead... How

Divinity

does one go back to a monotonous life after that? Was I a fool to think that there could a future for us after all the chaos ended?"

Federico sighed, "Giovanni… I'm sure that she thought so, and you still have friends. For what it's worth, I don't think you were a fool. You fought for what you believed in. Remember, there is always hope as long as there is one person willing to fight for it. So it basically comes down to this; how do you want to live? Do you want to give up and die, or go on living life as full as you can in her memory?"

Giovanni thought about those words for a moment before responding, "I'm spent. I need rest…"

Federico nodded and stood out of the way, "Perhaps that's best."

The tired out fisherman returned to the cabin where he stayed for two more days. His dreams were a continuous nightmare of Adalyn being tortured. It was a reoccurring theme for him.

During the second night, Giovanni's dreams took him to an unsettling place. When he fell asleep, he found himself in the dark wooded creek they had proceeded through on the way to hell. This time, he followed the current of the black water straight to its source.

After a few minutes, he came to a large whirlpool, but unlike Charybdis, this whirlpool flowed upwards like a spire. Giovanni watched as the water spiraled upwards into dark clouds the rotated in the opposite direction. This was physically impossible and defied all laws of nature, yet here it was.

Giovanni watched as several small green auras flowed past. The decrepit faces of those who had not lived full lives appeared in the water. Suddenly, Giovanni heard a voice call to him, "Giovanni…"

Divinity

His eyes darted back and forth over the black water searching for the source of the voice. A few seconds later, he saw another spirit in the water. This one's aura was unusually brighter than the others. As it drew close to him, its face appeared. Giovanni gasped, "Adalyn!"

Adalyn's face was gray and her skin was decrepit. He could barely recognize her in the water, but he knew it was her. As Adalyn's specter came within a few feet of Giovanni, its eyes snapped open and it spoke again, "Giovanni..."

Giovanni's eyes shot open and he found himself back in his bed, "The Well of Souls, that's where she is!"

Giovanni jumped out of bed and ran up the stairs. The door to the cabin flew open as he ran out on deck, startling Captain Gonzaga. Giovanni was panting and his face was flushed as he spoke, "Come about, steer us a course south-south east, make for Crete."

The knight at the tiller looked at Federico confused. Federico shook his head, "Belay that."

Giovanni turned to Federico and grabbed the front of his tunic, "Captain, I know where she is! We can save her!"

"What are you talking about?" Federico asked confused. "Giovanni, she's gone. We saw her die."

Giovanni nodded, "I know that, I was there, but I know where angels go when they die. Her spirit flows in the Well of Souls."

Federico's eyes narrowed, "What are you talking about?"

Giovanni tried to explain, "North of Crete, there lies the whirlpool, Charybdis, which is an entry way to Hell. The path to Hell takes you through the Well of Souls where the indifferent go when they die."

Federico's eyes widened, "Giovanni... there is no way. We don't have the provisions or anything to make such a trip. Even if we did, how would you get her out of there?"

Giovanni shook his head, "Federico, I was there. You know I was! Please help me…"

Suddenly, Giovanni felt a blunt pain on the back of his skull and his eyes went black. Federico nodded to the soldier standing behind Giovanni with the back side of his sword against Giovanni's head, "Take him below."

"Yes sir." The knight replied.

As he nodded and helped Giovanni off the deck, Federico stood alone for a few more moments and slammed his fist down on the rail. "Poor boy." He said as he walked the length of the boat. *The moment I leave him to return to my duties, he'll most likely either drown or hang himself. All of my prestige, my honor, and power, and I can't even save one person. It's so common in this day and age, but if that is his fate, then at least I can bring him to rest in the land of his family. I know that at least I can do that much.*

Giovanni lay down on his old bunk. He slowly regained consciousness from the the hit he took to his head. He sprawled out feeling the new mattress and sheets. It took him a few minutes before he finally got comfortable and moved his arm to the edge of the bed.

When Giovanni put his hand down beside it, he felt something graze against him. He reached out and grasped the object quickly, bringing it up to his face. It was Adalyn's raggedy old clothes, still covered in her blood. As he cradled it close to his face, he could smell her sweat and other familiar odors from when he had carried her out of Rome that first night. He closed his eyes and for a moment, and it felt like she was still right there next to him. He felt his eyes begin to tear up as he fell asleep, "No…"

BOOK IV
A Fateful Decision

I

Above the clouds in the council chambers of the Choirs of Angels, Gabriel stood in Michael's place as the other angels filed in. The council was in full session and thousands of angels could be heard locked in their own individual conversations. The whole room sounded busy as everyone proceeded in.

The remaining archangels had requested the presence of the entire congregation due to the importance of the matter. Unfortunately the message fell on deaf ears in some cases. Many angels were unable to be there due to the amount of damage control and inquisition that had to be conducted to make sure that Michael had no other followers.

Of the remaining Six Archangels of God, only Gabriel, Uriel, and Jophiel were able to attend this emergency meeting. When Ariel and Roselyn appeared at the door with Adalyn's body, there were many gasps and angered voices. Some were shocked by the condition of her remains while others were outraged that she had been allowed to return, having not been briefed on her demise. Gabriel stood up and raised his hand to silence everyone in the room.

Once they were seated, Gabriel called attention to the floor so that he could speak, "This meeting has been called in response to an urgent request by two of our seraphim sisters."

Gabriel turned to the door and nodded, "The Choirs recognize Seraphs Ariel and Roselyn. Please step forward."

The two angels immediately walked through the chamber doors. Ariel was holding Adalyn's lifeless body in her arms as she approached the center of the room. The two angels stood before the Choirs and gently laid Adalyn's body on its side so that everyone could see her injuries. Their eyes never left the podium as their accusing stares pieced Uriel's heart.

Loud gasps and outraged yelling could be heard around the room. They finally saw the full extent of Michael's treachery. Adalyn's skin was horribly scarred from head to toe, she was filthy, and covered in blood.

Ariel stared up at the Council of Archangels as Uriel shot out of his seat, "What is the meaning of this?"

Ariel took a step forward, her eyes burning as she looked at the council, "The will of the council has been carried out, Adalyn is dead."

Angry cries filled the air as Gabriel attempted to reclaim order, "Everyone return to your seats. We shall come to order!"

Ariel and Uriel fought a war with their eyes while Gabriel called for order. As the chamber quieted down, Ariel continued speaking, "We have come before you today to protest this mishandling of justice."

Uriel rolled his eyes, "The decision regarding Adalyn has already been made. If you remember, Azrael made a similar request... and it was rejected..."

"And now Azrael is also dead," Ariel shot back, "murdered by the same person responsible for our sister's demise. The blood of two angels now stains this floor and..."

"That's enough!" Gabriel interrupted. "I hope you both understand that we have allowed this meeting because of your exemplary record of service to the Most High, as well as your standing rank amongst the other Choirs of Angels. Antics will not be tolerated and if we find that you have called us here lacking in reason, then you will be impaired of the right to call another meeting pending disciplinary action."

Ariel took a deep breath and released it in an attempt to calm down, "We do realize that, honorable ones. I apologize for the outburst, and thank you for hearing us on such short notice."

Divinity

Gabriel nodded as he sat down, "Very well then, plead your cases."

Ariel turned and looked around. Every single eye in the room focused on her, but as far as she was concerned, only three sets mattered. She was determined to make the Archangels see their error.

An ominous feeling came over Ariel's body as she took another deep breath and spoke, "Brothers and sisters of the Nine Choirs of Angels, we come before you today to protest a severe injustice and abuse of authority committed against one of our own."

In typical fashion, Roselyn stepped in and continued, "As all of you know, Adalyn, our beloved sister was wrongfully expelled from the Celestial World for having supposedly falsely accused a high-ranking angel of treason. We have, however, uncovered proof that she had been deceived."

"She was cast out by a very cruel being!" Ariel added. "A traitor to the Most High and… of all people, one of his most trusted generals."

Roselyn's eyes filled up with tears, "After Adalyn's exile from this world, she was cast into one of the oceans of Earth. Her uncontrolled descent into the mortal realm cost her the use of her eyes. She didn't even have a chance to survive on her own. Lucifer was not even treated so poorly!"

Her voice began to tremble as she fought to finish, "She was badly injured, tortured, mutilated, and violated by the Most High's children to the point of murder! Only one young man saw fit to help her! One mortal saw what almost every angel here failed to…"

Ariel nodded, "One who is now in turmoil and questioning his beliefs. One who is preparing to sacrifice his life to try to save her. So much damage has been done, enough to create a divide between the mortal and immortal

realms. We implore you, please, do the right thing and restore her. We realize that not all of the damage done can be repaired, but at least take a step in the right direction. She was removed for one reason and one alone; she followed orders. Restoring her to us will help begin the healing process."

Jophiel stood, "Honorable friends, is it not true that she accused the angel Azrael of misdoing? Did the evidence not later prove him to be innocent? Was he not also the same angel that sacrificed himself to save her and bring Michael's treachery to light?"

"She did accuse the wrong angel, this is true," Ariel admitted, feeling her face heat up, "but Azrael had been framed by Michael, who took his form in order to trick our sister."

"But would it not be a fair assessment then that we had fair reason not to trust her word?" Jophiel asked.

Finally, Ariel couldn't take it anymore and had to say what was on her mind. Clearly the archangels were trying to cover themselves and she would have none of it, "In any case, the point is irrelevant, she reported what she saw and it was the council's job to weed out the truth."

She stepped forward and thrust the index finger of her right hand directly at Jophiel, "A job, I might add that you failed to do, and that failure set into motion a series of atrocities culminating in her inevitable death!"

Roselyn gasped as she covered her mouth with her hand, "Ariel…"

The whole room erupted in anger. Angels could be seen shooting out of their chairs and pointing fingers in an accusing manner. Complete pandemonium erupted from the floor unlike any the council had ever seen.

Jophiel went pale as he fell back in his chair, completely blow away by Ariel's accusation. Ariel froze in place, knowing that she had just crossed the line. Gabriel

Divinity

quickly stood up and raised his hand, "Order, order, I said. We shall have order."

The room ignored his requests. Gabriel spoke up again in an angered tone, hoping to defuse the situation before a riot broke out, "Order, I will not say it again!"

Ariel lowered her head, feeling that her sudden outburst may have cost Adalyn her only chance. A tear fell from her left eye as Gabriel inhaled deeply and looked at the two seraph angels, "Ariel… I don't think harsher words of accusation against us have ever been uttered on this floor. Do you truly believe that we are guilty of her murder?"

Ariel was about to speak, but Roselyn cut her off knowing that Ariel needed to cool down, "No honorable ones, we don't mean to implicate you personally, but the fact remains that our sister is dead when the only crime she committed was following orders. For that, we all share some of the blame. This is something even the Most High could not deny."

Gabriel looked over at Uriel. Uriel had a nervous look on his face. For the first time in thousands of years, he didn't know how to respond. They exchanged glances until Uriel nodded. Gabriel sighed and turned back to the two seraphim angels, "That was very brash, you two… however, your point is acknowledged, and you now have our attention. What is it you seek to accomplish here?"

Roselyn walked closer to the stand where the Archangels sat, "Again we ask you to restore our sister to us. Give her back that which was wrongfully taken. It is within your power to do this for us. To allow what Michael did to stand would be a crime of immeasurable cruelty. We beg of you, undo the damage that has been done."

Uriel and Jophiel stood up as Gabriel turned to them. The three of them stood with their backs to the Choirs as though they had not even heard Roselyn's plea. They remained this way for what seemed like an eternity, arguing.

Ariel tried her best to see if she could read into what they were saying. Their expressions were that of anger, confusion, and frustration. She could not tell which way their decision would go. The entire chamber was silent, but not a soul could hear what they were saying. Finally, the three turned back to the council.

Gabriel spoke first, "We have discussed this matter fully."

Uriel spoke up next, "The council concedes that Adalyn's case was a grave mistake with tragic consequences."

Ariel frowned, "However?"

Jophiel sighed, "However... restoring her life is not a decision for us to make. The council does not have the authority to undo the actions of an archangel, or to give life. Only the Most High can make that determination. We have noted that Adalyn's actions in the service of the Most High, even after her betrayal and expulsion, were most impressive. Therefore we will take her case before him ourselves. Give us some time, we will return shortly with the answer. The council is adjourned until then."

The three angels spread their wings and shot straight upward into the sky. Once they were gone, other angels got up and began conversations, a few flew between the rows. Others kept their eyes on the floor where Adalyn's lifeless body lay.

Ariel sighed and dropped to her knees, "I can't believe I did that. I lost control. What is wrong with me...?"

"Your feelings have always been very close to the surface. I know you loved her very much." Roselyn said. "We all did, what happened to her was beyond cruel, and I think they realize that. Your emotions just bubbled to the surface. I don't think anyone here cared for her as much as you did..."

Ariel nodded, "Perhaps… I just hope that I didn't cost us our only hope. I would never be able to forgive myself."

**

The next hour seemed like an eternity for Ariel and Roselyn. The anticipation hung like a cloud over the entire hall. Ariel watched the sun dial at the entrance to the chamber as it ticked by. Everyone wanted to see if the Most High would agree to something this radical.

Finally, the hour ended and the three Archangels returned. They filed back to their seats as quickly as they could. Gabriel was the only one of the three not to sit down. Roselyn noticed that he had a rather pale look on his face and shuddered slightly as he finally began to speak, "Brothers and sisters, this is truly an unprecedented occasion. After conferring with the Most High, it has been decided that he needs to address the council on this matter personally."

Ariel and Roselyn went wide-eyed. Ariel quietly whispered to her sister, "The Most High… we're in for it now."

Uriel stood up, "All rise as his holiness, the Most High, cometh!"

Every angel in the room shot to his or her feet. They stood silently as a large orb lowered from the skylight in the ceiling and settled in the middle of the room. It resembled the most beautiful star anyone had ever seen. However, once it settled, a humanoid could be seen at its center.

There was a brief moment of silence and then to everyone's surprise, the star spoke. Its voice was deep, thundering, and seemed to echo throughout the room. The language was one that no one in the room had ever heard before, yet oddly everyone understood, "*Amen I say to you, the lord Most High hath heard your plea. This whole tragic situation is one that has sent ripples through both of our worlds. It must be corrected. Michael's own mandate is not*

Divinity

the same as my own order. Therefore, restoring your sister shall not be considered a reversal of my decree."

There was a brief silence as the star slowly began to vibrate. A sudden loud hum could be heard throughout the chamber as the vibration became more violent. It resonated throughout the chamber and shook the walls.

Ariel swore that she saw the energy flow from the star and spread out the window. *What is this…?*

The energy emanated like a slow-moving shockwave across the Celestial Plains. Down in the depths of the Netherworld, the hum reached the Well of Souls. It caused ripples in the water that spread out in every direction until they found the green entity that they were looking for. The entity suddenly opened its eyes and began to rise out of the water, through the fog, and into the sky.

The specter continued its ascension until it reached the Celestial Realm, and entered the Choirs' council chamber. It settled over Adalyn's body and slowly faded into it. At that moment, a loud gasp came from the floor.

Roselyn covered her mouth with her hands as Adalyn's arm began to move. The Most High spoke, "*Behold, your sister is restored to you.*"

Adalyn slowly turned to lie on her back. The two seraph angels knelt down next to her as she began to breathe and finally her eyes opened. A look of shock came over her face as her eyes slowly focused.

Roselyn kissed her cheek and whispered in her ear, "Adalyn… are you okay?"

Adalyn moved around a little and faintly groaned, "I think so. Where am I, what happened?"

Opening her eyes, Adalyn saw her friends looking down on her, "Roselyn… Ariel… what…"

Suddenly she saw the star above her. Her eyes widened and she quickly flipped over on her hands and knees, "The Most High!"

Divinity

The voice above her began to speak again, "*Behold, young Adalyn, you have been restored to your sisters because of your steadfast loyalty and your services even when faced with expulsion and betrayal. All of this has been taken into consideration, and you are to be commended. As a token of our appreciation, you are to be raised to the rank of seraph. There you will join your sisters amongst the highest of Choirs of Angels.*"

Adalyn began to feel her body rise off of the ground. She levitated a few feet in the air and began to notice the world change around her. Everything instantly seemed brighter and more beautiful than it had previously been. She could not explain the sensation running through her body, but it was an exhilarating feeling.

Suddenly, two more wings sprouted from Adalyn's back, her skin began to glow like light shining on gold, and the feathers on her wings turned from white to a fiery red. She gasped as her knees once again touched the ground.

The entire assembly burst out in cheers and applause. Ariel and Roselyn smiled. They were ecstatic for their sister, "Well done Adalyn." Ariel said happily, "I knew this day would come."

Ariel noticed small puddles on the ground in front of Adalyn. *Is she crying?* Ariel asked herself. *Something isn't right...*

The Most High spoke again, "*Arise young Adalyn, you prostrate yourself before no one anymore.*"

Adalyn slowly raised her head, revealing the tears streaming down her cheeks. Roselyn looked at her with a concerned expression, "Adalyn?"

The Most High paused at seeing her face and changed his tone, *"What troubles you my child, are you not pleased by my appointment?"*

Adalyn fought back the remaining tears as she spoke. Though she chose to speak in one of the languages of man, when the words left her lips, the audible sound was the language of the Most High. It was a shock at first, but she was determined to speak, *"Forgive me my lord Most High, I am indeed grateful, but I need to know..."*

The star dimmed slightly, *"Then ask, my child."*

Adalyn fluttered her new set of wings. She sniffed quietly as she spoke, *"What happened to Rome, are they safe? What about Giovanni, what is going to happen to him now?"*

The Most High's light dimmed a little more, *"Peace has fallen on Rome. Your words halted what would have been a terrible tragedy. Both the knights and the revolutionaries in Rome have benefitted from your words and are working for peace. Rome will never be decimated as it could have been that day. You saved it."*

Adalyn's heart clenched in her chest as the Most High hadn't answered the more important part of her question. She shook her head, *"Almighty, I fear you are holding back the part that I really want to hear."*

Ariel and Roselyn looked at her with worry in their eyes. It was not the normal place of an angel to question the Most High as she was. Even so, the Most High appeared to tolerate her questions, *"His future is uncertain."*

Adalyn lowered her eyes to the ground, *"Uncertain... you mean he is going to die, isn't he? Did I really do that much damage?"*

Ariel comforted her, "He loved you very much. There can be no deying that. To lose you after losing his family and a good friend... some people just aren't able to cope with that much grief."

"...I love him." Adalyn admitted as she lowered her eyes.

Quiet gasps filled the chamber as Ariel stepped back with a shocked expression, "You...?"

Divinity

Adalyn nodded, "I can't live a lie. Is love unforgivable for our kind, truly?"

Ariel and Roselyn fell silent knowing that what Adalyn was admitting to could possibly get her exiled again. The Most High watched quietly as Adalyn came to terms with everything. It took her a moment to muster up enough courage to speak her mind. She never dreamed in a million years that she would ask the Most High for something so radical, but how could she live with herself otherwise?

Once Adalyn found the strength, she looked up at the glowing sphere and spoke again. The words were in the foreign language, but the nervousness in her voice was unmistakable and translated to everyone in the room, *"My lord Most High, you granted me life and your rewards are greatly appreciated. My time amongst the clouds has been a dream...but I must decline this promotion."*

Every eye in the chamber focused on her and sounds of absolute shock echoed through the room. The Most High remained silent for a few moments. He knew what she was going to ask, but was still unprepared for it, *"Think carefully Adalyn, on what you are about to ask for. Your actions have granted you the right to claim the reward your heart desires, but such a decision would be permanent and cannot be undone. If you decide that this is what you truly want, you will not be able to return until your death. Even then, you may find your existence here different as a spirit. Are you absolutely certain that this is what your heart desires?"*

Adalyn looked around the room for a moment, seriously considering what her decision meant. Her answer could mean a lifetime without the people she considered family. It would be heartbreaking to say goodbye, but somewhere out there, someone who had given everything to protect her was now suffering. It was something she knew that she could not live with. Her instincts as an angel

Divinity

forbade her the luxury of ignoring suffering, even if she had wanted to.

Finally Adalyn nodded, *"I long for the one I love. If it is my choice, then I wish to give up my wings in exchange for a mortal heart."*

The sound of sobbing appeared from the direction of Adalyn's friends. Realizing whom she was about to hurt, Adalyn closed her eyes, *"May I have a moment with my sisters to say goodbye?"*

Again, the Most High did not respond, but his aura dimmed slightly, signaling that she could do so. Ariel and Roselyn rushed to Adalyn's side. Roselyn's chest ached as though a piece of her heart was about to be lost forever. She spoke frantically, "Adalyn, what are you doing? Why do you want to leave us?"

Adalyn put her hand to Roselyn's face, "We saved our home. At long last the Celestial Realm is safe from danger. All of the creatures of this realm can thrive once again. We can live in peace without the looming danger of war. It has all been saved... all of it... but for me, it will never be the same. The voice of the one I hold most dear cries out to me from beyond our realm. My heart breaks from being parted from him. My wings have become a heavy burden, and even the cloud of the seraphim can no longer hold me. I cannot escape the truth... I no longer belong here."

Ariel fought with every last ounce of strength she possessed to prevent the tears from falling from her eyes. She was almost blinded by their build up, "What are you saying? Are we not your family? Do you not love us, your sisters?"

A hurt look on appeared on Adalyn's face as she wiped the tears from her sister's eyes, "How could you even ask such a question? You know that no one could ever replace you in my heart. I have enjoyed the centuries we spent playing amongst the clouds... but someone else needs

me more than the Seraphim, someone who risked everything for me. Who would I be to do any less?"

Ariel looked away, "You're really doing this aren't you? You're really going to leave us and return to the mortal world?"

"Yes," she replied with a faint smile, "and I expect you two to visit me whenever you can!"

Ariel pinched Adalyn's chin and turned her face so that the two looked at each other eye to eye, "Adalyn, say it to me honestly and I'll believe you. Would this be your decision, even if he weren't dying? Are you sure you're doing this for the right reason?"

Adalyn nodded, "Yes it would be my decision, and I'm absolutely sure it is the right one. Please do not be sad for me. He loves me, I know he does. This is what I want. It is my choice, and my decision will bring happiness to more than one person. Think of it as my final duty as an angel; to be there for someone who needs me."

"Very well," Ariel smiled with tears in her eyes, "go find your friend."

Roselyn also fought through the tears and put on a smile for Adalyn. Adalyn raised her right hand and caressed Roselyn's cheek. Roselyn couldn't hold back her emotions any longer. She grabbed Adalyn and hugged her tightly as tears streamed from her eyes, "My sister… may you live a full and happy life."

Adalyn embraced them both, "I will always love you, never forget that."

The two angels squeezed Adalyn tightly, refusing to surrender the moment. It was too much for them to accept. Their sister was leaving, and there was nothing they could do to stop her.

Having no other choice, Roselyn and Ariel finally released Adalyn and hesitantly backed away as she turned back to face the Most High, *"I am ready, my lord."*

The Most High's orb rose high above the floor of the Choir hall and a huge bright light shot down, engulfing Adalyn. She was elevated off of the ground and into the light. She closed her eyes and held both hands by her side as she rose above the clouds. Her entire body tingled as she flew higher.

Suddenly the world began to fade into darkness. Giovanni's eyes opened and he found himself in a puddle of sweat. He was breathing heavily as he sat up, "Was it a dream? What just happened…?"

.

II

Giovanni got up, cleaned himself off and walked up on deck. He surveyed his surroundings before turning to Captain Federico. He had returned home to Venice and his ship was tied up at his private dock, but something was different. In the place of an old cottage sitting in ashes, a beautiful new house had been built. It was an ornately designed, wooden, two story home.

Giovanni's eyes widened when it came in to view. He saw several men wearing papal crosses rushing around to put the final touches on the house. Almost everything looked completely different. This house was fit for a minor nobleman.

Captain Federico walked up next to him and placed a hand on his arm, "Impressed?"

Giovanni turned as he spoke, "I don't believe it. What is the meaning of this?"

"It is a matter of honor." Federico answered. "The Papal Knights pay for what we wrongfully destroy. You saved Rome and possibly our mortal souls, this is the least we could do in return."

"I see." Giovanni said softly.

Federico looked at him with concern, "Are you going to be okay?"

Giovanni nodded, "Yes, I think I just need to get back to work, get back into my routine, you know?"

"I think that's for the best." Federico said in a relieved tone. "Get your mind off of things. You can not dwell on what happened. The only way you will survive is to accept it and try to move on. I think she would want that."

Giovanni off loaded what supplies he had brought with him, including his weapons. Federico helped as much as he could, and when they were finally done, the Captain

Divinity

called his men to attention. They quickly finished up their work and lined up in parade formation in front of the house.

One stepped forward, holding a folded paper with the seal of the Pope on it, "Sir, I have new orders for you from the main office."

Captain Federico took the paper and sighed, "It would appear that I have been recalled. They need my services elsewhere."

He refolded the paper and shrugged, "Such is a life of duty."

Federico turned to Giovanni, "Good luck my friend, and may God look after you. Remember, life may not always be what we hoped, but it is a gift, do not waste it."

Giovanni nodded and extended his hand to Federico. Pleasantly surprised by the gesture, Federico took it. Giovanni smiled as they shook hands, "And you as well, sir. If your journeys ever bring you back to Venice, know that no matter what, you have a place where you will always be welcomed as a friend."

Federico nodded, "You are too kind, and I'm certain we'll see each other again."

Having said all that needed to be spoken, Federico headed into town with the small group of Papal Knights. Giovanni watched them march until they were out of sight. He then opened the door and went in to inspect the house.

Inside, was a fully furnished house with food on the table and a warm fire going in the stone fireplace. Giovanni was happy to see that they had managed to salvage it from his old cottage. It would serve to remind him of the times his family spent sitting around it telling stories. The entire house was lined with dark wood and the interior was painted to match.

Giovanni quickly ate and went out to the shore. His old bench was still there, slightly charred, but still useable.

Divinity

The beach had not changed either. In fact, nothing in the area had.

How hollow life is going to be. Giovanni thought to himself. *Padre Antonelli is gone, I failed to protect her, and my family is gone too. I have no one left.*

Giovanni's breathing became more rapid, "No!" He shouted, "I won't let this be the end! I'll find her, even if I have to search for an eternity."

Giovanni ran back into the house. He packed up a small bag of supplies and grabbed one of the arquebuses that he had brought in from the ship. He worked diligently to get everything he needed for a long trip, but by the time he was ready to go, the sun had almost completely set on the horizon and visibility in the harbor was too low.

Giovanni sighed as he realized he wasn't going anywhere that day. *It's too dangerous to try to take the ship out at night with visibility like this. I'll need to wait until morning.*

A feeling of defeat filled the air as Giovanni sulked back to his house. He pushed open the door and proceeded inside. He had yet to explore the second level, but he didn't care. Instead he chose to rest on the cot in the small room next to the kitchen. As he entered the room, he wiped a tear from his eye. *Tomorrow then, I'll leave at dawn. I have to save her. There is nothing else for me now. If I don't try, then everything I fought so hard for has been for nothing!*

Giovanni lay down on his bed and closed his eyes, "For nothing Giovanni? Do you really believe that?"

Giovanni opened his eyes and sat up, "Papa?"

To his amazement, his father was sitting right next to him on the bed. The man smiled warmly as Giovanni sat up, "You saw the world over. You went further than I ever expected you to in your life time. You have seen great things and gone against all odds for what you knew was right. God has acknowledged your actions, you've earned

Divinity

the admiration and respect of all the angels and saints, and I am very proud of you. Is that not enough?"

"No, I lost Papa." He admitted sorrowfully. "I lost everything. Two of my friends died, she died, and everything I knew is gone. I swore that I'd protect her from harm, but I wasn't strong enough. I have to try to set things right."

Giovanni's father put his hand on his son's shoulder, "You did not lose. You took what I taught and you did what was right. You fought hard and helped prevent a disaster. Believe me when I say that great things will come of it my son. Don't throw your life away on a pointless quest to the Underworld. She would not want that."

"You would rather see me live a life of sorrow and loneliness?" Giovanni demanded with tears in his eyes.

"Of course not, Giovanni." His father replied. "I want you to live on. I was sent here to tell you not to leave tomorrow. Doing so won't bring her back; it will only result in more pain and death for you. Even if you make it to the Underworld, you will not find her in the Well."

Giovanni's eyes narrowed, "Should I not at least try? You always said never to never give up on what you believe is right."

"I did say that," the ghost admitted, "but the angel you saved gave up the remnants of her divinity to give you a second chance at life. Don't you think it would be selfish to throw that away?"

Giovanni shrugged, "You are absolutely sure that there is no way for me to rescue her Papa? No chance at all?"

"The Most High's decrees are absolute and unbreakable." His father replied. "There is no power on Earth that could bring her back to you."

Defeated, Giovanni lowered his eyes, "Very well, Papa, you win. I will stay here and live the life that was given back to me."

His father nodded and began to fade away, "Never forget how proud I am of you..."

Giovanni jolted himself awake, "Papa... another dream? What is happening to me? Am I going mad or is someone trying to tell me something?"

III

Giovanni fought the urge to take his ship back to Crete and instead spent the next few days repairing his fishing lines to prepare for his first trip since he got back. Part of him still wanted to attempt the trip to the Underworld, but doing so alone would be suicide. Though he did not care about his own life, he knew that the reason Adalyn was gone was because she had sacrificed her remaining power to save him. Wasting the precious gift she had given him so long ago would be selfish, but how he was going to fish on a boat that looked like it was designed as a wealthy man's private yacht was beyond him, it was something he would need to figure out later.

The following Saturday, Giovanni stopped his work and looked out to the stone reef where he first saw Adalyn. For hours, he just stared out at the exact rock where he first saw her. Finally he dropped the nets he was working on, went back into the house with tears in his eyes, and went to sleep.

**

The distant sound of bells woke him up the next morning. It was Sunday and time for Church. Though it was the last thing he wanted, he got up, dressed in some nice clothes that had been left in his closet, and headed out.

The road seemed a lot longer than usual. The Church seemed far away, but Giovanni was able to get there on time. He remembered how long it felt when he was still sick and pressed on.

Giovanni eventually entered the Church and sat down in one of the back pews. From there, he watched the new priest give his sermon. The unimpressive speech from this novice almost put Giovanni to sleep as it droned on for an hour.

During a brief intercession, he spoke to the priest, "Hello Padre."

The young priest looked at him, "Peace be with you my son."

Giovanni was about to ask the priest something, but this was not Padre Antonelli. The priest was wearing the same dark robe as Padre Antonelli, but he did not have the same inquisitive, kindly tone. This priest was a lot more nervous and quiet.

Giovanni found it very difficult to listen to anything the priest said. It was the same typical words of repentance and forgiveness with no real creative twist. After twenty minutes, he could not take it anymore. The young fisherman got up and walked out of the church.

Giovanni walked home at a steady yet aggressive pace. His face was flushed because of how angry he was. Nothing in this town was different, at least not in a positive way.

When he got home, Giovanni slammed the door and tore off his good clothing, trading them for his regular shirt and trousers. He looked out the window, "It's not fair, damn it! Why did they have to die, what for? He gave up his life to save her and she died anyway. They should both be here now!"

Giovanni walked outside, sat down, and began working on the netting again. As he sat by the water, he began to hum his old tune. He repeated the same line over and over until he got sick of it.

She really did like that song. He thought to himself as the hours slowly passed.

As the sun began to draw closer to the horizon, Giovanni began singing it out loud. He paused at the end of the first line for a moment until he finally mustered up the strength to continue.

"Sing loud,

Let your soul run free,
Horizons calling,
Adventure lies ahead,
Danger in the distance,
It won't touch you,
Don't be afraid,
Release the fear in your eyes,
It will pass you by,
And all will be all right,

--

How could it be,
That our time has come,
As the winds change their course,
On invisible wings,
My sails will fly,
To take you away…"

The second verse hit him like the sting of a wasp. He stopped to wipe away the tear in his eye. He tied another stitch in the net as two more tears fell from his face. *Damn it,* he thought to himself, *you need to finish your work. Just try to put it all out of your head for now or you'll never get the net done!*

The sound of the nearby waves crashing on the shore was soothing as Giovanni worked. He sewed in stitch after stitch and tugged after each one to make sure they would hold. He repeated this a couple more times until suddenly he heard something over one of the waves, "Giovanni…"

He dropped the net and shot up, knocking the bench over, "Huh, what was that?"

Giovanni felt a chill run down his spine. He felt a similar sensation both times Adalyn's friends appeared to him. He was sure that something that was going on and turned to his doorway. Sitting behind the door was a loaded arquebus. Giovanni was glad that he had managed to hang on to it after returning to Venice. He quickly lit the wick and walked down to the shore line, keeping his eyes trained on the horizon, "Not letting another of these cursed demons get the jump on me!"

Divinity

Was someone there whispering at Giovanni, or had he truly gone mad? When nothing came into view, he shrugged, "I must be hearing things."

Giovanni pulled the wick off of the gun and turned to get back to his work. He was about to sit down when another wave crashed on the shore and the low whisper appeared again, "Giovanni…"

"Good lord!" Giovanni yelled. "Be silent, I can't stand this anymore."

Without thinking, Giovanni ran back inside his house and grabbed the golden crucifix off of his wall. He squeezed it tightly in his hand, "Why?"

Another sound came from the waves, "Giovanni."

Enraged, Giovanni ran back outside and threw the crucifix into the water, "Damn you!"

As the tears returned to his eyes, Giovanni breathed in deeply, "Stay your senses, man; you are starting to lose it!"

Giovanni walked back to his bench and resumed working on the net. As he tied up another line, he began to sing again.

> "Sing loud,
> Let your soul run free,
> Horizons calling,
> Adventure lies ahead,
> Danger in the distance,
> It won't touch you,
> Don't be afraid,
> Release the fear in your eyes,
> It will pass you by,
> And all will be all right,
>
> --
>
> How could it be,
> That our time has come,
> As the winds change their course,
> On invisible wings,
> My sails will fly,
> To take you away…

Divinity

--
In the dark,
Calm turns to fear,
In the cold of night,
Trembling with tears,
Sleep now,
Nothing will harm you,
Hear the sounds,
Let peace surround you,
Safe and sound,
Sleeping in my arms..."

He was about to start over again when he heard a faint voice, singing back to him.

"In time, all things pass,
Night will fade away,
And darkness will vanish,
As it has before..."

Giovanni looked out on to the ocean, somewhat spooked by what he had heard. Mentally, after everything he had been through, he felt that he was prepared for anything, or so he thought. He held on tight to the gun in his hand and waited for whatever was taunting him to reveal itself.

Suddenly, a figure appeared on the waves out in the distance. There was no way to tell who or what it was from where Giovanni was standing. The creature approached his house, floating closer and closer to him.

At first Giovanni was nervous. He didn't know what to make of it. Was it a demon, another angel, or something else altogether?

Giovanni stood up with his heart in his throat and raised the arquebus, ready to fire. The figure began to take the shape of a woman. Her features slowly began to form in a magnificent flash of bright light.

Giovanni dropped the arquebus and raised his hands to his eyes, almost blinded by the brightness. If whatever this creature was attacked him now, he would be

Divinity

defenseless, but he did not care. He was prepared to die as he had nothing left to lose.

After a few moments, Giovanni could hear a low hum and the bright aura disappeared. Adalyn was left standing in its place. She had her hands slightly raised at her sides as though presenting herself to him. Giovanni watched as the waves carried her ashore. She was wearing a white gown that shimmered in the sun as she approached. In her hand, was the golden crucifix that he had just tossed into the ocean, "I think you lost this."

Giovanni was certain that he was dreaming, but after rubbing his eyes several times, he finally came to the conclusion that what he was seeing was really there. Without another thought, he dashed down the beach, ran into the surf, and grabbed her.

Part of Giovanni was expecting to pass right through her and land in the waves, but when her body pressed against his, he knew that she was there. His skin tingled as he felt the warmth of hers. There was no doubt in his mind that he was not dreaming.

Giovanni nearly knocked Adalyn off of her feet when he grabbed her. He hugged her tight, afraid to let her go. The touch of her warm skin felt too good to be true. All the scars that she had received during their adventures had disappeared and her skin was smooth and silky like that of a newborn baby. It had not yet been toughened by the harshness of the world.

Giovanni slowly brought his lips to her ear. He had seen and felt her, now he needed to hear her to be sure that he wasn't going mad, "Are you real?"

Adalyn closed her eyes as he pressed her tight, "I… I hope so."

There were so many questions racing through Giovanni's head, but he held his tongue in order to savor the moment. She was in no rush to release him either. Giovanni

Divinity

pressed her closer and could feel her body against his. Their hearts beat in sync with one another as they stood in the surf. His breathing became labored and the air seemed to get stuck in his throat as though he had forgotten how to release it.

Adalyn smiled as she felt the emotion emanating from him like rays from the warm sun, "I've missed you..."

The young fisherman stepped back slightly, placed a finger on her chin, and brought her eyes to level with his. Shockingly, he saw the same beautiful fiery blue sky that had been there before. Her eyes glowed brighter than ever as she smiled at him. Their brightness was almost mystical.

Giovanni spoke the moment that he was able to get air to his lungs, "I've missed you too, more then you could know."

Giovanni pressed her against his chest again, "You are as beautiful as ever. Your eyes are unbelievably bright. I've never seen anything like them before."

"They are the mark of divinity." Adalyn replied. "The Most High allowed me to keep them."

Suddenly, Giovanni noticed that something else was out of place. His hand was on her back, but he wasn't feeling feathers. Now he was kicking himself for not noticing something so obvious sooner, "Adalyn, your wings..."

She chuckled as her back arched against his hand, "Isn't it obvious? I'm not an angel anymore Giovanni. I'm human, just like you."

"How?" He asked.

"A gift from the Most High," she said happily, "for you... for both of us. He gave me something that no angel has ever been granted before."

Giovanni looked at her quizzically, "A life of your own?"

Divinity

"A choice," she replied, "to stay amongst my brothers and sisters as a seraph, or live a mortal life here with you."

Giovanni's eyes widened in disbelief, "You gave up eternity for me?"

Adalyn raised his chin and kissed him, "Eternity was no longer mine to claim. I could never forget what you did for me. You cared for me, loved me, and protected me when you could have just as easily turned me over to the Church. If not for you, my soul would have been lost. You saved it, and now it has returned to you, rightfully."

She slowly placed her lips on his ear, "I wanted to tell you all along… I love you. Infinity holds nothing on a lifetime here with you."

"I feel the same way." Giovanni whispered. "I'd forgotten how to live when you died. After everywhere we went, everything we did, the rest of my life paled in comparison. I did not know how I would be able to go on after that."

As Adalyn looked into Giovanni's eyes, she noticed that he had a nervous look on his face, "What is it, what's wrong?"

It looked like he was struggling to force the question out "Adalyn, I need to know…"

"Yes?" She asked with a worried look in her eyes.

He kept his eyes locked on hers, almost fearing the question he wanted to ask, "How long do we have…?"

Adalyn narrowed her eyes, "Are you asking me how long I'll live?"

Giovanni nodded nervously. She thought back to what the Most High had told her for a second and then looked back at him, "I honestly don't know. I wasn't told much about the conditions of my life, but I was told that you must keep me in your heart for me to be here."

"What does that mean?" He asked in a shaken tone.

Adalyn looked out at the ocean with a hand on her racing heart, knowing that it beat in sync with Giovanni's, "Our hearts are joined, Giovanni. Mine races when yours does, mine will break if you turn away from me, and mine stops when yours does. I can't be killed by illness or harm, but I don't know how long I really have. So you need to treasure me, my love, live every minute as if we don't have another and I will do the same for you."

Giovanni nodded, "I will, always."

Adalyn smiled and threw her arms around Giovanni as the surf passed over their feet. An hour went by as they stood in the sand. Only a few words passed between them as the sun began to set.

**

Once the sky darkened, Adalyn beckoned Giovanni to follow her out to the end of the dock. She stepped onto his boat and stood at the bow, looking out at the sea for a moment, "I never thought that this would be my destiny."

Giovanni walked up behind Adalyn and placed his hands on her shoulders. She looked at her fingers as she raised her right hand to her face, "One last drop of divinity."

Adalyn turned to face him, smiled, and snapped her fingers softly. Glitter flew from her fingertips as they clicked. Behind her, huge colorful explosions went off in the sky. The explosions were accompanied by loud thundering noises that could be heard for miles.

On the back of the boat, Giovanni noticed a faint flicker of light. He turned and was shocked to see a small group of people standing at the other end of the boat, "Adalyn, look."

Adalyn turned and saw that they appeared as though they were glowing and she swore she could almost see through them. Giovanni recognized the first one he saw, it was Padre Antonelli. The old priest smiled and nodded to his old friend. A bright look of happiness could be seen in

his eyes as he had long waiting for this day to come. Also amongst them was Cyrillus, standing with his wife Menia. Both of them smiled and waved to the new couple.

Adalyn recognized the last two on the side. It was her friends Ariel and Roselyn. Ariel was trying to be the strong one even though she already missed her sister deeply, while Roselyn wept tears of joy. Adalyn couldn't help but have tears form in her own eyes as she looked at them.

As the group slowly began to fade, the two angels flapped their wings and shot upwards into the night sky. There, two bright stars appeared over Giovanni's house.

Adalyn smiled, "Thank you both."

Giovanni looked at her oddly, "What's going on."

"You'd better be good to me, Giovanni." Adalyn said with a grin. "That's my sisters' way of letting us know that they're always watching over us."

As the colorful lights of the explosions illuminated the night sky, people in the town and the nearby houses ran out to see what was going on. Everyone stood in awe as they watched the spectacular view.

Adalyn nodded, "That was the last of it. No more divinity, no more immortality, no more flying, and no more adventures. It's all gone now."

Giovanni smiled, "Life is an adventure, as long as we make it one. There is a bright horizon calling us, and together, there is nothing we can't do."

"A bright horizon…" She repeated happily. "I like the sound of that."

She kissed him and smiled, "So this is forever then?"

"No," Giovanni replied. "Forever isn't nearly long enough."

Epilogue

Three years passed since Giovanni pulled Adalyn from the harbor. Pope Leo X's health eventually failed him and he passed away of pneumonia in December of 1521. He was replaced by Pope Adrian VI.

Nicolas abandoned his violent ways and returned to Athens to live out his years in peace. Giovanni only saw him once or twice more. However he received many letters from his old friend and discovered that Nicolas had taken up fishing.

Captain Federico soon inherited his father's rule as Marques of Mantua. After his time spent with Adalyn and Giovanni, he became a man of peace, and worked to prevent putting his people in harm's way. He abandoned the wayward ways of the soldier and accepted his new responsibilities. The Patrisi house still saw frequent visits from Federico whenever the marquess could get away. One of his first visits was to give Adalyn away at their wedding.

*

One morning, as the sun began to peak over the horizon, Giovanni was roused by the gentle sound of waves breaking on the shore. He sat up and noticed that the front door was open and Adalyn was nowhere to be found. He quickly got out of bed, put a shirt on, and walked towards the front door, stopping only for a moment to straighten the golden crucifix above his doorway. He then walked outside to find his wife.

Adalyn stood by the water, barely a silhouette in front of an orange sky as the sun came up. She stood perfectly still as the sun caressed her skin. Her eyes were closed and she had a look of content on her face.

As Giovanni approached, she opened her eyes and turned to see him. She smiled and turned closer, revealing a

Divinity

small bulge in her stomach. She looked down and placed her hands over it with a joyful smile spread across her cheeks.

Giovanni walked up behind her, ran his arms under hers and placed his hand on her stomach. She closed her eyes, leaned back into his shoulder, and clasped her hand around his. A deep sigh escaped her lips as she relaxed her muscles.

It was a familiar scene that sent Giovanni back to the first time he had taken her hand there so long ago. He breathed in deeply as the warm sun continued to rise. The two stood at the shore in silence, watching the sky change color signaling the dawn of a new day, and the beginning of a new adventure.

JAMES HARRINGTON:

James Harrington was born and raised in Boston, Massachusetts. He holds a Bachelor's in History, but also studied religion and how it related to his chosen subject matter. It was from those studies that Divinity was born.

James has written several essays and short stories, but had never gotten a full-length novel published until his big breakthrough with *Magnifica, The Last Enchanter*. Following its success, two more titles were added to the *Magnifica* series.

James currently lives in Massachusetts with his wife and son.

For more info on James and his books, please visit his facebook page:
The Creative Works of James Harrington.
https://www.facebook.com/JamesHarringtonsMagnifica
Or his Blog page:
http://jamesharringtoncreativeworks.wordpress.com/

Other Novels By James:
Magnifica: The Last Enchanter
Magnifica: Tears of the Fallen
Magnifica: Gravestalker

Divinity

www.ingramcontent.com/pod-product-compliance
Lightning Source LLC
Chambersburg PA
CBHW051537250626
47157CB00001B/88